Different Strong
Chosen Different Book Two

By Nat Kozinn

Recap

One year ago Gavin Stillman graduated from Section 26. Upon certification that he had control over his abilities, Gavin went to work as a human food tester, using his extraordinary control and awareness of his body to test recipe changes and artificial food additives. Dissatisfied with his job, Gavin began spending his naturally sleepless nights roaming the streets and delivering vigilante justice to criminals in the lawless slums of the Los Angeles Metro Area. Gavin's activities eventually lead him to a trail of dead bodies, the handiwork of The Beast, a dangerous and powerful Different the world believed dead. At great physical and emotional cost, Gavin was able to defeat The Beast. Despite saving hundreds, Gavin was arrested for violating the anti-vigilantism provisions of the Different Acts of 1996. Gavin's friend Nita, a powerful 13-year-old girl who helped him defeat The Beast, proved unable or unwilling to provide him aid. Gavin was released from prison on the condition he remains on parole.

1

Mark my words; the OEC Field Office Program is a terrible idea that is destined to fail. The law cannot sway back and forth depending on which way the wind blows. Differents acting as law enforcement agents was a bad idea before The Beast and it is a bad idea after the creature attacked the Metro Area. I will stand alone on this island even if it is swallowed back into the sea. The Field Office Program is a time bomb waiting to explode.

"An Unpopular Opinion" by Roberta Clemens, Los Angeles Times

My muscles are screaming for more oxygen. I don't have any to give. I'm breathing as deeply as I can, but it's no use. I've been running too long. I am going to have to stop and catch my breath. I put my hand on an old, useless electric pole and take deep, slow, methodical breaths. I flood red blood cells to my lungs, gathering oxygen that I send all over my body. While I'm at it, I use my lymphatic system to clear out the lactic acid building in my leg muscles.

Within a few seconds I feel ready to start running again, but before I can, I hear someone else behind me. It's someone who's moving faster than any human can, faster than I can. My partner, Victor Campos.

"What are you doing?" Victor demands.

"I had to stop and rest," I answer.

"I thought you're supposed to have the perfect human body. You've been running for six or seven miles. There are a lot of humans who can run farther than that."

What does he know about what the human body is capable of? He doesn't have a human body. He has something much better than that. He's Physically Enhanced, Athlete Type. He has super dense muscles that make him stronger and faster than any person should be. He was five miles behind when we started running, and he still caught up to me with ease even though he's six foot five and built like an extra-thick brick wall.

"Humans can't run that long at full sprint. What's the point anyway? The kid is long gone. He moves so fast he makes you look like a snail," I respond.

"Speedsters don't have much endurance. They need to stop and rest for an hour after a few minutes of sprinting. They make you look like an ultra-marathon runner."

"How do we know if we're still on his trail?"

"Speedsters always run in a straight line, especially in the Metro Area. It's hard to round a corner at two hundred miles an hour. Look down at the street, do you notice anything?" Victor asks and points.

The sidewalk is covered in debris, a mix of dirt, concrete, cardboard, and even old clothes. It looks like a landfill. There's a path cut right through the filth.

"Running at two hundred miles an hour generates a lot of wind. I'm going to the roofs and see if I can spot where he went. You keep after him down here."

With that, Victor takes a running start and leaps two stories up onto the roof of a half-collapsed building. I turn and break back into a sprint, a bit slower than before. I don't want to hear it from Victor if I have to stop and rest again.

Victor is moving above me. Even though he has to jump from rooftop to rooftop, he's covering more ground than I am running on the street. The way he moves reminds me of The Beast. Power mixed with grace. I push The Beast out of my mind. He doesn't deserve my consideration. I put my head down and keep following the path the Speedster left in his wake. Victor seemed confident that we will catch up to him, but I'm skeptical. He was moving so damn fast.

It's no wonder the cops couldn't catch him and had to call us. He's a bolt of lightning. I thought this was going to be easy when we found him hiding in that corner of the kitchen, covered in spices. It would have been funny if it wasn't so tragic. As soon as we talked to him, he stood up and shot out of the building like he came out of a cannon.

It was only Arnold Chapman's first week out of Section 26 and he just started his job as a delivery boy. I don't think he's keeping that job. I'm not sure if he took some drugs or had some sort of psychotic breakdown, and frankly, it doesn't matter. It's my job to catch him.

I finally have the job I always wanted. The job I told everyone, including myself, I was perfect for. I'm an agent for the Office of Exceptional Cases. My duty is to apprehend dangerous Differents. Now I have to put my money where my mouth is and do the job. It's extra motivation that my own partner doesn't think I am qualified. And it just so happens, if I fail at the job-- I go back to prison.

Victor drops down onto the sidewalk and waits for me to catch up. I make sure to focus and time my breathing so I don't appear to be winded.

"Why did we stop?" I ask.

"I saw the trail come to an end. He's in a half-collapsed building up ahead. It looks like it was a school before the Plagues. It's big; it's a good place to hide."

"What should we do?"

"What do you think we should do? You're supposed to have the ideal human mind too," Victor says sarcastically.

"I guess we should split up; each take half of the school and search for him."

"Wrong. Well, half wrong. What if you find him? You aren't fast enough to catch him, or strong enough. It takes big muscles to move that fast. Besides, a building this size is going to have a half a dozen different exits. You were right about splitting up though. And you should go try to find him. I'll stay on the roof and pounce down on him when he runs out."

"What should I do when I find him? We're out of range of think.Net out here. I knew we should have brought Linda."

"We don't need think.Net and we don't need Linda. How was a fifty-year-old Telepath supposed to keep up anyway? That kid is going to run by you so fast you won't have time to do anything. If you do get lucky and somehow manage to sneak up on him, yell so I know he's coming. You're just scaring him out. I'm apprehending him. Don't try anything stupid. Are we clear?" He says with a look that tells me "yes" is my only option.

"Clear."

We go our separate ways. He climbs onto the roof of a building overlooking the school, and I head inside the school, or what's left of it anyway. The entrance I walk through is missing a key feature of entrances, the doors. Inside is a war zone, there isn't an intact piece of wall in sight. Many of them have been demolished on purpose, the work of salvagers.

The walls are made of concrete. Concrete means rebar, which means steel. Steel is rare and valuable thanks to the Plagues. Cabot's bacteria could and did eat rebar, but the concrete often protected the metal from the little buggers. The remaining steel rods can be salvaged, but they need to be removed from their concrete casing. It is a difficult job that requires painstakingly smashing through the concrete with a sledgehammer. Ten hours of labor will earn about ten dollar's worth of metal, but there is no shortage of desperate people willing to work on these terms.

The missing walls make it easy to search through the barren rooms. Dozens of looters have been through this school over the years. They picked it clean of anything of value. All that's left are papers, broken desks, and broken chairs. Whatever metal held them together was salvaged long ago. There's a time worn children's drawing still hanging from one wall, A Dog Named Lucky, by Brian age 8. Not bad for a kid that age, good sense of perspective.

My hunt goes quickly. I clear all of the classrooms in short order and the gym and lunchroom are big piles of rubble, leaving only the auditorium. I step into the large room while stretching out my perception of time. To me, it will seem like I'm moving slowly and carefully almost in slow motion, but I'll really be moving at normal speed. Great for making sure I can move quickly while still taking silent steps. I search through what's left of the rows of seats that used to fill the auditorium. The metal was eaten away by Cabot's bacteria, leaving behind piles of wood, which my Speedster could be resting behind. I get to the middle of the room and look back over my shoulder. Someone stands up and stretches. There he is! He's covered in dirt and blood and shaking with fear. We lock eyes.

"I'm sorry, I didn't mean to do it. I had to get them off my skin," the Speedster pleads. His arms are scratched to shreds, the product of his own fingernails tearing red ribbons in his flesh.

"It's okay. Come with me, and we'll figure it out," I say in a soft friendly tone.

His eyes are jitter bugging out of his head, and the pupils are fully dilated black pits. His carotid artery is pulsing so violently in his neck; his heart might jump right out onto the floor. He's breathing short desperate breaths through a mouth covered in drool. That's a weird mix of conditions for his body to display. I wonder what drugs he's on? It looks like uppers, downers, and everything in between.

"This isn't fun. The drink is poison," the desperate kid pleads.

"Sure it is. Come with me and will make sure you don't have to drink anymore," I say with my hands up.

I watch his deranged eyes move from me to a doorway that has an exit sign. I'm about ten times closer to the door than he is, but that still may not be close enough. He starts running like a bolt of lightning. I slow down my perception of time as far as I can and make a full speed charge to intercept him. I move at top speed, which is like a sloth compared to the Speedster. He's almost at the door. I'm close enough to stop him if I stick out my left arm.

The radius and ulna bones in my left arm shatter into a thousand different pieces. Those pieces burst through my skin like shards of glass, tearing my arm open from the inside out. I'm thrown backwards into the wall, causing massive bruising to my left shoulder. Arnold goes flying too. He hits the wall headfirst and goes down. I run over to him and roll him over with my good arm. He's unconscious, bleeding from the head, and his left leg is bent like a pretzel, but there's a pulse. We have to get him help.

"Victor! I'm in the auditorium; I need your help!" I yell as loud as I can.

It takes Victor fifteen seconds to make his way to the auditorium. He sees my broken left arm hanging limply at my side and our suspect, bleeding from the head.

"This counts as stupid," he says.

#

"I don't care if you thought he was going to get away. I told you to be careful and let me handle him. I did not tell you to clothesline him like a professional wrestler. You could have killed that boy. You're lucky it was just a concussion and a broken leg. He's seventeen. Does he deserve the death penalty because he's a stupid teenager who took the wrong drugs and freaked out in public?" Victor yells at me.

He's been saying the same things for the past two hours. He said them as he carried the Speedster back to the Slug line, the whole ride to the hospital, when we were filing the report with the detective, while we rode our P-Train back to the office, and now, he's saying them in front of our boss, Captain Murphy. He's right. I was stupid. I let my desire to succeed overwhelm my good judgment. I told Victor that the first time he gave me the speech. It hasn't slowed him down.

While I listen, I direct my immune system to attack bacteria that entered my arm through the holes in my flesh caused by my own broken bones. It's an infection smorgasbord in there.

"That's right, Gavin. I know the whole 'Beast Slayer' thing has gone to your head, but we don't need that vigilante stuff here. We are officers of the law. Your job is to apprehend criminals so the justice system can deal with them," Captain Murphy piles on.

"And how long is your stupid stunt going to put you out of commission?" Victor asks.

"It is a bad break. The bones in my forearm are shattered. I basically have to regrow them from scratch. Still, it should only take me four or five days. And I won't be out of commission. I'll get a cast, and then I'll be good to go," I answer.

"I guess that's not so bad. Especially considering you basically stepped in front of speeding Slug-car," Captain Murphy says with a laugh.

Victor shoots him a dirty look.

"Are we going to get a toxicology report on Arnold? He seemed pretty messed up in the head. I couldn't identify what drugs he had taken," I ask.

"Oh yeah, we'll get forensics on this, cordon off the whole area, canvass for witnesses," Captain Murphy says with a smirk. "It'll be a misdemeanor vandalism charge or disturbing the peace. He'll probably have to sweep some sidewalks. You don't worry about him, you worry about doing your job, which means the next time Victor gives you an order, you follow it. We have a chain of command here, and it is not optional. Don't let that happen again. Now go see Linda. She can make you a cast while you file your report."

I head out of Captain Murphy's office, picking fragments of bone out of my open wounds. I've lowered the blood pressure in my arm to a slow trickle. This will keep it from becoming inflamed and/or bleeding everywhere. I'm annoyed about Captain Murphy's attitude but it was pointless to argue. The captain had to make a big show about respecting the chain of command, because he's deluding himself into believing he runs this OEC Precinct Office, not Victor.

After The Beast terrorized the Los Angeles Metro Area, people were up in arms. They wanted to know how the government could allow one Different to kill hundreds of people. There were protests in the streets calling for more laws to control Differents. The government response was to expand the Office of Exceptional Cases, the OEC. The OEC is a branch of the Defense Department and the sole organization legally authorized to employ Differents as officers of the law. It was designed to apprehend Differents who were too powerful for the normal police, or even the army, to handle.

Before The Beast, the OEC rarely deployed agents in the Metro Areas. Differents here are all tested, catalogued, and tracked by Section 26, which keeps everyone under control. The OEC mostly operated in the Non-Assisted Areas, where powerful Differents were born outside Section 26's clutches. There hadn't been much reason to keep agents close to the Metro Areas until The Beast went on his rampage. It took the OEC several hours to scramble a response and send an agent to the Los Angeles Metro Area. By the time they arrived I had already stopped The Beast, but not before he killed hundreds of people. Victor was the agent they sent.

In the wake of the rampage, the government promised to station OEC agents in all of the Metro Areas so there could be an immediate response to another Different like The Beast. This meant Field Offices had to be created quickly, which meant that middle-aged police department bureaucrats, like Captain Murphy, were appointed as heads of the offices even though they have no real training or expertise in dealing with Differents. Every time Captain Murphy has to make a decision, his face turns red and he looks like he's about to have a heart attack. Usually Captain Murphy defers to Victor, who has been an OEC field agent for six years and is highly regarded within the OEC. Victor makes all the important decisions, and the captain couldn't be happier about it.

I knock on the door of Linda's office.

"Come on in. I'm already mixing the plaster for your cast," Linda says through the door.

I open the door to see Linda's smiling face. She's always smiling at me. Apparently I remind her of her son, which is good for me because it means home-cooked treats. Linda works as the Telepath for our office. She used to work for Ultracorps as part of think.Net, but younger and more powerful Telepaths rendered her obsolete. Now she works for the OEC. She provides a secure connection to interact with the government Librarians, and she can help if we need to apprehend a fellow Telepath. She's also a trained nurse.

"My God, that arm looks awful. What did you do to yourself?" she asks her voice full of concern.

I open my mouth to answer, but she cuts me off.

"Don't bother. I'll see it all when we make your report. Sit down. Put your arm on that table and try to keep it still. I'll have to wrap it in gauze before I put the plaster on."

She works swiftly and silently, wrapping my arm then applying the plaster. This isn't the first time she's done this in the four months

I've been with the OEC. Training with Victor can get a little rough. Soon, she's covered my whole forearm and made the cast.

"You know how this works. Keep the arm still for twenty minutes so the cast can set. While we're waiting you can file your report. Open wide."

She doesn't mean my mouth, she means my mind. Filing a report is a relic from another age; we should come up with another term for it. It's from back before the Plagues, when everything had to be done on paper. Information was written down and stored in folders, which were stored in cabinets. Entire buildings were constructed to house all the files the government kept. It's a much simpler process now. Of course, the government being the bureaucratic wasteful entity it is, hardcopies still need to be made and stored in some waste-of-tax-money office somewhere. I used to have to file papers like that in my old job. I don't miss it.

Linda taps into my mind. I can feel her creeping in, searching, scanning. She wants my memories of the altercation with the Speedster. I offer them up by remembering the experience myself. I recall cornering the Speedster in the restaurant's kitchen in the Metro Center, then him screaming crazy gibberish and running through the plaster wall, Victor and I chasing the kid down, and finally me tackling the Speedster in the school.

Linda will then interface with the government Librarian and share the memory with him or her. The Librarian is capable of storing and recalling millions of memories like those. If OEC higher-ups want to see what happened, they will log into the government Librarian through their own Telepath, who will share the experience with them. They'll remember what I remember. Linda also makes a synopsis for those who want to avoid having a memory implanted in their brain. People who grew up before think.Net tend to find the process disturbing.

"All right, I got your report. Detailed, as always," Linda says and stands up.

"I couldn't tell what narcotics he was on," I say. "It was a weird mix of symptoms. His blood pressure was through the roof and he was shaking like he was on uppers, but his pupils were dilated and he was detached from reality which would indicate hallucinogenic and he was drooling…"

"There's always some crazy new thing. Trust me, if you ever have a kid, the news will terrify you with the latest horrible drug every week," she says cutting me off.

"I don't see why anyone would take a drug that induced that mix of effects."

"Because kids are stupid," she says and points to my cast. "Speaking of stupid kids, I'm meeting my son for dinner. He's got a job interview at the LA news desk, which could mean he's moving back to town! You know the drill with the cast; don't get it wet, yada yada. I'd tell you to come back in a week and have me check on it, but I know you'll take the cast off whenever you decide you're healed. I left you some stew in the Cooler chamber," Linda says and heads out the door.

"Wish Martin luck!" I yell after her.

I wish I could go out to dinner, but I don't have that right. In order to get out of jail after fighting The Beast, I had to sign a plea deal where I promised to work for the OEC and agreed to go on parole indefinitely. One of the terms of my parole is that I cannot leave the OEC office unless it's for official business, especially at night. It's to make sure I don't fall back into my old vigilante habits. It also makes sure I can't have a social life. I pretend that it's the government's fault, and I'd be swimming in dates and dinner invitations if they'd let me out.

It's not a very believable piece of self-deception. I've spoken to exactly five women since Becky and I broke up. It turns out that getting a woman badly injured and her father killed is bad for relationships. Who knew? Becky said I was just a kid and it was bound to end anyway, but I don't know. It felt like something that would have lasted. But after everything that happened, she couldn't even look me in the eye when she came to see me in jail and told me we were through. When I got out, she wouldn't accept my think.Net call. I think the last straw for her was my deal with the government to work for the OEC. After losing her father, the thought of me continuing to risk my life was too much for her. She'd rather pretend she never knew me. It would have been better for her if that were true.

The worst part is there's no chance for it to start up again with her, even if she could somehow forgive me. After The Beast's attack, the press focused on the fact that he was a Cabotist. Anti-Cabotist fever hit the Metro Area like an epidemic. The Cabotist church was burnt down and Pastor Newman was killed. The Cabotists all disappeared, Becky included. She didn't even say goodbye. We had already broken up, but I still think a goodbye would have been appropriate.

I should stop thinking about this. It's going to be a long night here in the OEC office, and I don't need to start going down the long depressing road of Becky again. There are some nights I wish my body could still sleep. Luckily, I have the cure: there are still a few episodes of Happy Days on think.Net that I haven't watched. It's impossible to be depressed when watching a Pre-Plague TV show. They are magical places where everything always works out in the end. I go on think.Net and queue up the next episode. It's the perfect way to waste another evening. And besides, I have bones to rebuild and infections to fight in my shattered arm.

#

I hate coming here. I ate this garbage they call food for almost a year, thousands of pounds of the stuff in fact, and they paid me. I can't believe that I actually have to buy an Oasis Burger now, and I'm wasting the little bit of freedom I get to boot. They let me out for lunch, mostly so they can avoid having to pay to feed me.

At least choking down the meal today has an upside, because today I'll meet up with Ben. Other Thursdays I eat here alone so no one gets suspicious that I'm here for lunch only to meet with him. He eats here every three days; I eat here on Thursdays. We have our meetings when our two lunches meet up. It's insanely paranoid, but Ben doesn't think it's crazy enough.

We've been meeting every three weeks for the last four months. I don't know why; nothing has come of these powwows. Ben isn't any closer to figuring out what Nita is up to, although I'm sure he has some new theories. Still, I owe him. If it hadn't been for his help and his Maceo Steel knife, The Beast would have killed me. Meeting him every now and then so he can rant for a few minutes seems like a fair repayment. Besides, I still want to know what Nita is up to myself, and I want to make sure The Beast is really dead. Ben has managed to instill some fear that The Beast survived, even though I know he's only saying that in order to manipulate me. If The Beast is alive, Ben might be the one person who can find him.

Ben used to work as an Ultracorps Librarian, the Head Librarian in fact. He directed all of the think.Net traffic onto the hundreds of other Big Brain Differents for processing. All of the think.net calls, entertainment programming, data analysis, record storage, everything that happens on think.Net went through him in some convoluted way I don't really understand. That was until five years ago when a then eight, now thirteen year-old girl named Nita Martinez, with a bigger brain than Ben, took his job. Shortly after, Ben learned that Nita had grand plots and schemes. He tried to raise the alarm at Ultracorps but no one believed him. He ended up going on the run and being named a fugitive because the government, Ultracorps, and Nita are all scared of him.

Of course, this is all according to Ben himself. I can tell if people are lying, and Ben certainly believes that story, but there's always the possibility that he's insane and hallucinated it all. I'm reasonably sure that isn't the case. He's demonstrated knowledge that only an Ultracorps insider could possess so at least some of it is true. In that case, I'm meeting with a wanted man, which I'd imagine violates the terms of my parole agreement.

At least I should be hard to identify thanks to all the extra fluids I sent to my face. I got mobbed by a crowd asking for pictures and autographs the first time I came in here. With the extra water in my face, I look like some poor heavyset slob who eats too much Oasis Burger, not The Beast Slayer.

I walk to the counter and order an Oasis Burger, fries, and a soda.

A number 2, the most popular menu item. I need to be as forgettable as possible. I wait for my food before heading to a booth in the southwest corner of the restaurant. It's a cramped crummy seat, so it's always empty. It does serve a purpose though, as the acoustics are perfect. The shape of the walls around the booth dampens the ambient noise from most of the restaurant, everywhere but the northwest corner where Ben sits. That way, I can turn up my hearing sensitivity without going deaf from all the people talking. Ben has some sort of homemade hearing aid that lets him do the same thing. Then we both whisper but can still hear each other from across the room. To anyone looking, we seem like two separate people murmuring to ourselves in their respective corners. It's pretty ingenious. I wish I had thought of it. Genius is Ben's forte though.

I sit down and start picking at my fries. Ben will be in place soon, unless he stands me up again. He gets delayed because he has to turn around every time he sees a Walter. Another paranoid act, but this one might be worthwhile. The mindless clones of Walter Reynolds are only supposed to be smart enough to handle simple repetitive tasks, but during the incident with The Beast, we figured out that Nita might actually be able to see through their eyes utilizing the think.Net network. What's the point of his silly disguises if he still has to spend so much time making sure he isn't seen? Lucky for me he shows up on time and sits, he's in his favorite disguise, a Slug conductor uniform. He starts talking immediately.

"Hey Gavin, any new developments? Were you able to access the government file on the New Mexico thing?" he asks. He's talking louder than he's supposed to. He does that a lot when he's excited. It hurts my ears.

"Oh, hi Ben, it's nice to see you. How are you? Me? I'm fine, thanks for asking. No need to worry about the cast on my arm, it's nothing. And you're being too loud again," I whisper back.

"Sorry. You know I get like that when I'm too excited."

"I don't know why you are so excited. There aren't any new developments as usual. I looked up Santa Fe on the government Librarian. It was another dead end; the government file didn't say anything that the news articles missed. A dangerous Different, a Strong-Man, was identified in the Non-Assisted Area near Santa Fe. An OEC agent, my partner Victor, moved in with military support and the Strong-Man was incapacitated. They tried to sedate him with Tranq, but ended up overdosing him. It was a sad story and didn't include any information on secret prisons where powerful Differents like The Beast might be held."

Ben takes a moment to think about what I said, then whispers back.

"You probably don't have access to the classified file. The OEC helped Ultracorps recover that Different, I'm sure of it. You need to try to ask your partner about it, but subtly. Anyway, have you heard from Nita?"

"That would qualify as a new development, so no, I haven't heard from Nita. I haven't spoken to her at all since she told me I was going to be arrested after I killed The Beast. She hasn't called me, and I don't have any way to call her."

"I'm starting to worry she might never call. Your getting hired by the OEC ruined you for her plans. Nita likes to have control of her pawns. She has influence at the OEC, but no real power. You're of no use to her if you're going to answer to someone else, especially the federal government. What about those friends who helped you out after The Beast gutted you? Wasn't there some Strong-Man? Have you talked to him? You should try to see what he knows about Nita," Ben probes.

"It's a little awkward with Gary. He came to see me when I got out of jail. I accused him of working for Nita and lying to me about Becky being dead. He got angry and stormed out. I don't think he knows anything."

"He has to. He was covering. You should see him again and try a gentler approach. You get more flies with honey and all that. What about that teacher of yours, Larry Rosen? I remember his file, it was full of redactions, he has a nose for trouble. He must know something"

"I can't get him to return my calls. And enough about what I should do, what about you? I have a day job, and I'm on parole. Have you figured out anything new?"

"I've got a line on something big, but I'm not ready to share yet. But trust me, if it pans out, it's a doozy. Could be the big one, could be you-know-who."

"You always talk about The Beast because you know it's the one thing that keeps me coming here. I'm done with my burger. I'll see you on the twenty-seventh," I whisper.

I get up and dump my half-eaten tray of food in the garbage on my way out the door. Ben hasn't given me any useful information since my fight with The Beast. These meetings are becoming a waste of time, but I should see Gary anyway. I owe the big guy an apology.

2

What can be said about William Jefferson that has not already been said? The young man is a supremely gifted athlete with as superb a work ethic as I've ever seen in a nineteen-year-old. His physical gifts alone are enough for him to succeed in the league. So is his dogged determination to constantly improve his game. The combination makes for the finest basketball prospect I've ever seen. If that isn't enough, William majored in Mechanical Engineering before leaving the University of Minnesota early after declaring for the draft. The professors I spoke to expressed little doubt that William could have excelled in that field had he so desired. William Jefferson is an incredible basketball player and just as fine a young man. He deserves to be the first overall pick in this year's, or any previous year's draft. If he does not become a star, I have no business working as a professional scout.

"William Jefferson NBA Scouting Report" by Skip Pisel

June 6th

Sit-ups: 836
Pushups: 1,075
Pull-ups: 287
Running: 17.34 miles, 96 minutes total, 5:31 average mile time
Diet: 2,575 calories, 193 grams protein, 290 gram carbohydrates, 72 grams fat
Sleep: 8:37
Funds: $165.35
Ammo Count: 5 rounds 7N1, 24 rounds 9mm, 2 Stun Grenades, 1 Smoke Grenade, 2 Standard Grenades.
Activities: Eliminated Target 16: Male Gamma Enhanced Senses. Administered Cocktail Revision 3 to Test Subject Male Gamma Speedster

Target Notes: Target followed established path back home from work, passing the alley at Clyde and Forest at 8:55PM. Took position in the shadows and proceeded with a single stab from a six-inch blade. Death verified, otherwise uneventful. Location well within the operating boundaries.

Money Man Plan Attempt 3 Notes: Administered Money Man's cocktail to Speedster. Results were disappointing. Subject lost control of his faculties but more fear than violence. Money Man will no doubt have changes to recipe. He remains transfixed on this ill-conceived plan, convinced that the only way to win hearts and minds is by exposing The Beast Slayer as a failure. Not worth the time. There is one way garner support and it is a simple method. Win.

Personal Notes: Dehydrated beans and whey additive have brought the protein in diet to acceptable levels. Carbohydrates still too high. Need to increase percentage of fresh fruits and vegetables in my diet, but the cost remains prohibitive. Will investigate viability of growing my own.

Mental State: Accidentally looked Target 16 in the eyes during stabbing. Must avoid doing that. Task difficult enough already. Cannot think of them as people. They are walking atom bombs.

3

I understand the concerns, but the incident with The Beast proved that our police officers, brave though they may be, are simply not equipped to counteract the range of threats posed by Different individuals. It is only by some miracle that criminals like The Beast don't strike more often. The citizens of this Metro Area have a right to expect their Government to protect them. The Office of Exceptional Cases Field Office Program will ensure that this Metro Area has access to law enforcement personnel with the ability and training to neutralize Different threats.

"Why We Need the OEC" by Forest Brown, think.Net News LA

"That's easy for you to say. You're like a super soldier. You're too strong," I say to Victor.

I hate these training sessions, and Victor's making me do extra work because of the week I missed due to my broken arm. I'm making up for lost time now that my cast is gone. I prefer learning off of think.Net. It has hundreds of articles and tutorials. All I need to do is see the lesson once, and I learn it for life. I've already mastered several forms of jujitsu, kung-fu, judo, and other martial arts whose names I can't pronounce correctly. That doesn't satisfy Victor though. He's not big on studying; he thinks I need time in the gym. I think he likes having another opportunity to bust my chops.

"Yes, I'm stronger than you, but I'm holding back. I know how to pretend to have the strength of a normal man. I'm not beating you because of my muscles; I'm beating you because you start the fight thinking you're going to lose. You spend your time thinking of excuses for why you lost, not strategies on how to defeat me. Step one to doing anything is believing you can do it. First think you can hit me, and then do it," Victor says.

"Thanks for the after school special message."

"Wisdom is wisdom because it's true. Do you think Billy the Kid dominated the league just because he was the fastest and the strongest? He believed he would win every game he played, and then he did whatever it took to achieve that. That's what all the greats did. Did you complain about The Beast being stronger than you when you fought him? We're supposed to take out guys like him, and they aren't all going to take it easy on you because they're religious nuts."

It's a low blow about The Beast even if he's right.

"Is that what you learned while you were pretending to be an athlete?" I say. Victor's previous job was baseball player, until he was outed as a Different, arrested, and humiliated. It's a nice bit of ammunition I can fire whenever I want to achieve a petty victory on him.

"Get up," Victor says, ignoring my counter verbal low blow.

I pick myself up off the ground and put my hands back up. Victor does the same with his hands. He wasn't wrong about The Beast. The Beast only wanted to kill me during the last of our three fights. I beat him because he was already riddled with bullets, and I had the help of friends. Thinking about this isn't helping me. I need to focus on taking down Victor.

I move in on him. You know what they say, fifth time's a charm. Then I make myself believe it's true. I imagine myself knocking his smug face to the ground. I slow down my perception of time as much as I can. Victor still moves a lot faster than I do, but at least I have a moment to think about what painfully slow move I can try to pull off. I decide to throw the first punch this time, a right cross. Victor's always telling me to seize the initiative. He knocks away my punch with a swipe of his arm. I knew he'd do that, so my real move was a kick to his left shin, which lands beautifully. He lets out an exhale of pain and drops his hands, leaving his chin open.

I try to catch him with a left uppercut, I send signals to all the right muscles to contract and expand in perfect timing, crafting a beautiful punch, but he's so damned fast he dodges it like I'm moving in slow motion. Whenever I almost score some points he likes to put me in my place, so now he'll come at me hard. He's going to lead with his left; he always does even though he's a righty. Instead of waiting for it and being too slow to react, I lunge at his left side. Sure enough, he throws a quick left jab, but since I'm already moving towards his fist, the punch doesn't have any force behind it and glances off my shoulder. The missed punch leaves me an opening, which I exploit with an open palm strike to Victor's nose, stunning him, and follow it up with a leg sweep, knocking him to the ground with a thud.

That's the upside to these training exercises. When I do get lucky and manage to land a blow, I get to hit with full strength. Victor is tough enough to take it. It helps work out some of my frustration. Victor picks himself up off the floor. He gives me a big grin, trying to show it's all in good fun, but I can tell he's in a little pain. Poker faces don't work on experts in human anatomy.

"Nice work, Gavin. See what believing does for you? It could be time to up my exertion level. You might be ready for ten percent strength," Victor says to steal my thunder. "Now don't you see why this training is worth it? You need experience that think.Net articles and old kung-fu movies can't give you."

He's right. I am learning from these actual fights. I can learn the moves and proper form on think.Net, but I can't learn how to read my opponent. I can't learn how to adapt to unexpected situations. I know how to throw a beautiful left hook; I just don't know when to throw it. I don't want admit that to Victor, though. Good thing I have the perfect excuse for changing the subject.

"Do you mind if I ask you something? I was looking through old OEC records, you know because I don't have much to do at night. Anyway, I read about this case outside of old Santa Fe. You took down a really powerful Strong-Man who had been causing havoc in the Non-Assisted area," I say.

"Yeah, I remember. What's the question?"

"I guess I was wondering how you took him down. The file said he was in the upper echelons of strength, maybe top twenty all time, which, no offense, is much stronger than you. So how did you do it?"

"I started with believing I could win. Then I came up with a plan and executed. He was stronger than me, but he wasn't faster. I moved in and hit him, then retreated before he could grab me. It took a long time, hours in fact, but I was patient and picked my spots. Eventually, I wore him down. It's a good lesson for you. You're not all that quick or powerful, but you're smart and you can use that extra time thing you do to formulate a proper strategy. Devise a path to victory, and then do whatever it takes to stay on the path," Victor says shaking his finger to emphasize his point.

"I'll try to remember that. What ended up happening to the Strong-Man?"

"He died. The Army moved in and tried to sedate him, but they ended up overdoing it. Turns out determining the proper Tranq dosage for a two thousand pound man is pretty complicated. I'd love to say I was broken up about it, but the guy was scum. He did some horrible things in Santa Fe," Victor says. I watch him for signs that he's lying, but there's nothing. He maintains eye contact and his heart rate remains stable.

"Are you sure that's what happened? Did you actually see him die?" I ask.

"I saw the body. Why are you asking me this? What do you think happened?" Victor asks while giving me a cross eyed look.

I'm spared from having to come up with a lie because Captain Murphy walks into the training area.

"Time to hop to it boys. We've got a call, and it's a big one. Linda wasn't able to get much information, but there's a killer Different on the loose. Victim was murdered on Vermont and Melrose. Metro Area police are already there waiting for you. Here's our chance to show what we can do," Captain Murphy tells us excitedly.

#

We walk down the dark street in anxious silence. Victor and I have barely said a word to each other since Captain Murphy told us about the call. We changed into our blue/grey army-style uniforms, fueled up the P-Train, rode it to the closest point, engaged the lever to remove the train from the rails and attach it to a support column, climbed down and started walking, all without saying a word about what we are going to do. Victor is just as nervous as I am even though he's got a lot more experience. He may have taken down killers before, but none since he's been stationed in Los Angeles. We've only gone after petty thieves and drugs dealers, which barely count as criminals in the Metro Area these days. Now we've finally got the chance to show our stuff.

The destination comes into view. Three cops in uniform stand in front of a fenced-off alley. I can tell something is wrong right away, I mean besides the dead body. The cops seem calm. I can see a pretty young Hispanic police officer, and she's standing with a relaxed posture. If there's a killer Different on the loose, I would expect the cops to be freaking out. There should be more of them here too.

"I'm sure I don't have to tell you to keep your mouth shut and let me do the talking," Victor says under his breath.

"I know. The cops hate me," I reply.

I might be a hero to the people of Los Angeles for stopping The Beast, but the cops remember me as the punk who broke the law and got away with it. I had to hit a few of them back when I was being a vigilante, in self defense of course. I don't think I caused any serious injuries; I tried to be careful. But even still, people who assault cops don't usually get hailed as heroes.

We walk up to the female officer. She is beautiful, especially for a beat cop, with almond eyes and pink cheeks. She is also shockingly small. She must be incredibly tough to deal with scum at her weight class.

"We're here to see Detective Rose," Victor says.

The cop doesn't say anything. She points her thumb down the alley. We follow the thumb, and right in the center of the alley we get to the body. It's covered by a sheet. A heavyset man in an overcoat and a fedora is resting on the wall beside the corpse. He's in a think.Net stare. We've met him before. He was at the hospital to officially arrest the Speedster after I almost killed the kid.

"Excuse me? Detective Rose?" Victor asks.

Detective Rose holds up his hand signaling he needs another

minute. He doesn't seem stressed. He's leaning casually on the side of the building. Something is definitely not right. No one is acting how they should be if there is a Different murderer on the loose.

I take a quick stock of the alley. It's a good place for a killing. The buildings on either side are of uneven height so there are lots of shadows to stay hidden. It would also make it hard for any witness to get a good look. Detective Rose finishes his think.Net call wearing a giant grin. His eyes regain their focus and take stock of Victor and me. His smile turns upside down and there's a flash of what looks like panic in his eyes.

"You two again? What do you want? What are you doing here?" Detective Rose demands.

"We received a call about a victim killed by a Different," Victor says.

The detective stops and takes a deep calming breath before he answers. When he speaks, the panic has disappeared from his face. "Beep! Wrong!" Rose says, like this is a quiz show. "It was a Different killed. Not a Different killer. Regular old stabbing, as in not your job. Somebody messed up downtown."

"A Different killed? Who was he?" I ask. Despite Victor's best effort, his evil eye stare can't hurt me.

"A nobody," Detective Rose answers dismissively.

"How was he killed? Were there any witnesses?" I ask.

"I know you can't wait to grab some more headlines, Beast Slayer, but this isn't your job. It's mine. Now you and the guy who ruined baseball can go take a walk," Detective Rose says and points his finger out of the alley.

That'll show Victor for thinking he's more popular than I am. People don't like cop assaulters, but they also don't like guys who cheat at their favorite pastime. Ruining baseball is not a path to popularity in America.

Victor and I look at each other. He shrugs.

"False alarm, I guess. Let's head back to base. I'll call Captain Murphy on the way and let him know. At least we'll still have time to finish our training session when we get back," Victor says. He's trying to play it cool, but I can tell he's disappointed. He is ready for some real action. We both are.

"He was pleasant," I say to Victor as we head out of the alley.

"A real peach."

As we get to the perimeter of the crime scene, we pass the gorgeous female officer. She gives us a *pssst*.

"Yes ma'am?" Victor responds.

The officer gestures with her hands that we should keep our voices down. I focus in on her name badge. M. Vazquez.

"This isn't the first one," she whispers.

"What do you mean?" Victor asks.

"This isn't the first dead Different. There have been a lot of Differents killed in this precinct. I found another body a week ago, and it's the same story for a lot of cops on the beat around here. It's never anyone important, so nobody is taking it seriously. I think someone is targeting Differents," she replies.

"Like a serial killer?" I ask.

"I don't know because the murders never get investigated. My own captain said I was being crazy."

"It does sound a little crazy. You'd need some big cojones to target Differents as victims," I say.

"And imagine the balls it takes to want to hunt that killer," she replies, deadpan.

"Why are you telling us this?" Victor asks.

"I thought you might care, being as you have something in common with all the victims. And maybe you can do something about the fact that my department is ignoring these cases."

"Do you have any leads?" I ask.

"Thank you for bringing this to our attention," Victor says, cutting off the officer before she can answer. "I will be sure to raise the issue with my superiors. Have a nice day Officer Vazquez."

Then he nods at me to leave and we walk away. I want to stay and ask her more questions, but Victor is not having it. It occurs to me that I was recently reminded to follow orders.

"Maria," Officer Vazquez says before we get too far away.

We turn around, and Victor asks, "Excuse me?"

"My name is Maria," Maria says, and she's looking right at me.

#

I haven't been back to Ultracorps employee housing since before my fight with The Beast. While I was in jail, they took everything I owned in my apartment at the Barracks and put it in storage. It wasn't much, a few clothes and some knick-knacks from my childhood. They brought it all to my new apartment/jail cell at the OEC office.

Of course, they forgot my father's pocket watch. At least, that's what I told Captain Murphy. I've seen him fingering a watch of his own that he keeps at his desk. I figured it would be the right heartstring to pull for permission to go to the housing complex early in the morning. I have to get there before 9AM while Gary's still working the elevator

My lie worked even better than I hoped. Captain Murphy's eyes teared up and put his hand on my shoulder and told me to look as hard as I could for the watch. Then he said if I needed the whole day, he'd look the other way. There's no doubt that I should be feeling shame for that. I'm lucky I don't have to feel emotions I don't want to experience. I can't say I'm proud of the lie, though.

I head into the main lobby of the complex. The same unpleasant woman who worked the desk when I lived here is still on the job, Theresa. Captain Murphy bought my story, but he might not be the only one keeping track of me. It's best I maintain the lie as well as I can. I approach and see she's in the think.Net stare. She was always on think.Net every time I walked by.

"Excuse me," I say.

She comes out of her think.Net stare and looks at me. She doesn't say anything. She goes into the more traditional stare right at me.

"My name is Gavin Stillman. I used to live in Tower 3..."

"It's you!" she says excitedly. She's got a look on her face like she finally realized something. "You're The Beast Slayer!"

"Yeah that's me. Like I said, I used to live here..."

"I can't believe you're here. No one is going to believe me.

Wait!" she shrieks.

She picks up a small mirror from her desk and runs to stand next to me.

"Do you mind if I snap a think.Net Memory so I have proof you were actually here?" she asks excitedly.

"Sure, go nuts,"

She spends some time getting her mirror in the right position, and then she goes into the think.Net stare. The Telepaths of think.Net will record the last visual image her brain received. Now all her friends will be able to log on think.Net and see a picture taken with her eyes. If she wants to spend twenty times as much, she can have a short video. She comes out of the stare.

"Thank you! Thank you!" she yells and runs back behind her desk. "Now, how can I help you?"

"As I said, I used to live in Tower 3, and I've lost my father's pocket watch."

"I can't believe you're really here. It's so brave what you did, saving all those people, going up against that monster. I'm so glad they let you out of jail."

"Thanks for the kind words," I reply with a smile. I'm lucky I always have to choose to smile. Otherwise my smile might seem forced. Or, maybe that means my smile always seems forced?

"I'm sorry. I'm sure you're sick of people fawning all over you. I've never met anyone famous before."

"That's all right. I was asking about my father's pocket watch. It may have been left it my old apartment. Do you have some sort of lost and found?"

"No, we don't. But I'm glad you found me anyway," she says back with a smile.

I think she's flirting with me. It hasn't happened to me much, so I can't be sure. If she is, she's only doing it because I'm a famous hero… which I guess isn't such a bad reason. But I don't have time to worry about this now. I'm here for a specific purpose, not to boost my ego.

"Do you mind if I go up to my old apartment and check?" I say flatly, ignoring her flirt.

"Sure, go right ahead. You just have to tell me if you're free on Friday night?"

"Sorry. I'm flattered, but I'm also still on parole. I'm allowed here because I talked them into letting me look for my father's watch. Maybe once I'm a free man," I say. Now that is one good excuse.

"A shame," she says and goes back into her think.Net stare.

I walk by her desk and out the exit that leads to the rest of the employee housing complex. I have to remind myself that it's people like her who saved me. I was rotting away in jail, waiting for a trial where I was going to be found guilty, because I completely was. Lucky for me, some of the citizens I saved from The Beast spoke up in my defense. The press picked up the story and soon I was being called "The Beast Slayer." There were rallies, protests, and letter writing campaigns, all urging for me to be pardoned.

It worked. Soon the governor joined my side, he needed a popular issue to cover the fact that he was in charge when The Beast slaughtered hundreds. He pressured the federal government to offer me the parole deal. I even get paid enough to cover my Cost of Living Obligations from Section 26, barely.

There are seven towers in the Barracks, all surrounded by luscious green landscaping and even a pool. I never really appreciated how nice this place was. I resented being forced to live here. Now, I have some perspective on how bad living arrangements can get. It sure beats being locked in an office.

I make my way to Tower 3 and its forty oval-shaped stories, arranged to maximize the number of balconies. I miss having a balcony. My office/jail hardly gets any sunlight at all. I have to spend twenty minutes every morning pressed up against the window in the bathroom so I can get enough sunlight to produce the Vitamin D my body needs.

I check the time on think.Net 8:52AM. Perfect, Gary should be finishing up his shift operating the elevator. I head into my old building and onto the elevator. I hit the button for the fortieth floor. I bet that gets Gary thinking. There's no way my old roommate Nick is out and about this early. He goes back to sleep right after he does his wakeup call to the city. No one besides Nick and I have ever lived on the fortieth floor. Gary starts pulling me up.

The elevator gets to the fortieth floor and the doors open up. I don't get off though. Instead, I yell up.

"Gary! It's me, Gavin. Can we talk?" I ask.

Suddenly, the doors close and the elevator drops like a stone. I am going way too fast. Did he drop me? I slow down time to try to come up with a plan, but before I can think of one the elevator comes to an abrupt halt. I'm jolted into the air so hard I almost hit the ceiling. If I was a normal human, I would have lost my lunch. I might have deserved that.

The elevator comes back to the first floor and stops. I hit the button for the fortieth floor, but nothing happens. Looks like Gary wants me to take the stairs as further punishment. I do just that. Even with regulating my blood's oxygen absorption and breathing, I'm still a bit winded when I get to the top floor.

I head to the maintenance room. I try the door, but it doesn't budge. It isn't locked. Gary must be holding it closed. I'll be able to force it open as soon as I become stronger than a freight train.

"Gary, please! I just want to talk!" I yell, but I get no response.

He's furious and he has a right to be. I was beyond a jerk to him. That wasn't a great way to thank him for helping after The Beast gutted me.

"Okay Gary, you don't want to talk. That's fine, but I hope you'll listen to me. I want to say that I am sorry. I was wrong for what I said to you. I was angry that I was in jail, and I wanted to blame everyone but myself. You were never anything but a friend to me, and I repaid your friendship with malice. I am truly sorry," I say and make sure my voice trembles a bit so Gary knows it is hard for me to say.

Even if I didn't believe what I said, Gary wouldn't know the difference. Unfortunately for my ego, it was all true.

After a few seconds, Gary opens the door. He looks like he can barely fit through the doorway. You'd think they would have made it bigger. Anyone strong enough to lift an elevator is going to be huge. All Strong-Men are large. I should probably say something.

"Hey Gary, you should make yourself a bigger door," I finally say.

"I busted open a bigger hole the first week I worked here. I got chewed out by the Head of Facilities because it violated some fire code or something. They took the cost of fixing it out of my pay," he tells me.

"They should really update the fire code to account for thousand-pound men like you."

"Whatever you say. What do you want Gavin? My elevator shift is about to end. I've got deliveries to make," Gary says coldly.

"Are you heading to the lab? Maybe you can check out Sarah for me. Let me know if she still looks fantastic," I say and wait for Gary to smile. He doesn't. "I told you Gary, I came here to apologize. I'm ashamed of what I said to you."

"Ashamed? Can you even feel shame? What does an apology even mean from you? Did you decide enough time had passed and a normal person would come apologize now?"

"I probably deserve that. But believe it or not, I am capable of realizing when I've made a mistake. I'm sorry, Gary. It was unfair of me to accuse you of those things."

"I can't even believe what you accused me of. You thought I became friends with you because Nita ordered me to? You thought I lied to you about Becky being dead on purpose? We all thought she was dead. Aside from you, The Beast had never left anyone alive," Gary says.

"When I hear you say it now, I know how crazy it all sounds. But when I was rotting away in a cell, my mind went to some dark places. I wanted someone to blame for what happened. I wanted to believe that I was in jail as part of some conspiracy, not because I broke the law and deserved to be imprisoned," I say. "Then Becky broke up with me, and I had a fantasy that if I had known she was alive, I wouldn't have gone after The Beast, and we'd still be together. Now I've accepted that it was all my fault. Not Nita's, not Larry's, and definitely not yours. I'm sorry it took me this long to apologize."

I watch my words sink into Gary. I can see them affect him; it was a good spiel. Maybe I was so convincing because I kind of believe it myself. I don't want to admit it, but I know I might be wrong about Nita. I don't really have any hard evidence that she was manipulating me and The Beast. I've got what Ben has told me and my gut. I need to pay attention, Gary's about to say something.

"You know what? I'm sorry too. Yeah, you accused me of some horrible and crazy stuff, but I should have let it go. I can only imagine what you've been through. I'm sure if I had spent a few months fighting The Beast, thinking my girlfriend was dead then finding out she wasn't, and sitting in a jail cell, I might think some wacko ideas too. I forgive you."

"Thanks, Gary. You don't know what that means to me," I say with a big smile.

Gary wears his own grin. Then he closes in and hugs me, his arms big enough to wrap entirely around me.

"I have to forgive you. Who doesn't want a famous friend? 'The Beast Slayer,' hah, we've got to go out some night. Everybody's going to want to buy you a drink," Gary says with excitement.

"Sounds great, but I can't. I'm still on parole. I had to lie to get here."

"Risking a parole violation just to see me, how can I still be mad at that? Still, even if you can't enjoy all the perks of being famous, it must feel pretty good to be the big hero."

"It's not bad," I say with sly smile. "I'm going to a gala the Governor's throwing at the Natural History Museum next week."

"Look at you, Mr. Fancy Pants. That's some rough parole they got you on," Gary says while he heads over to the crank that powers the elevator. He starts reeling the elevator up like it's a jack-in-the-box.

"The Governor likes to parade me around to show how serious he is about securing the Metro Area against other dangerous Differents.

These things are always boring, but at least it means I get out of the OEC office for a night. Usually I'm trapped there."

"That part does sounds crappy at least," he says as he finishes turning the crank. "Hey, I've really got to get going. You heading back to the Slug? Mind if we walk?"

"Sure," I say and head out of the maintenance room. "I've always wondered how you get the elevator down while you're on it."

"I don't. I've got to take the stairs, so lead the way."

We start heading down the stairs. It suddenly occurs to me that I didn't come here just to apologize to Gary. I promised Ben that I'd ask about Nita.

"So what is it Ultracorps has you delivering today?" I ask.

"There's some construction project by the train yards that I've been running deliveries to all week. I think I'm moving ForteSilk today. Shouldn't take more than a few hours." It's a little hard to hear him over his deafening footsteps. That's what happens when you weigh a thousand pounds.

"Is that how you knew Nita? From making deliveries?"

"Yeah, she really does everything with that super brain of hers, including handling my delivery scheduling sometimes. She's not helping the unemployment rate," Gary says with a laugh.

"That is hard to believe. I guess she's got her finger in every pot. What kind of stuff does she have you deliver?"

"Manna and construction materials, mostly."

"That's all? Nothing juicy?"

"She had me deliver a huge cage full of rabbits to a lab once. I'm man enough to admit those things were adorable. I don't like thinking about what happened to them," Gary says with a shudder.

"Ouch, that's brutal," I say. I have to keep prying. "Is that all? She never sent you to a secret lab where they perform alien autopsies?"

I hear Gary's footsteps come to a dead stop behind me. I turn around at look at him. He does not look happy. I never give him enough credit; he's smarter than he seems. Being strong doesn't make you an idiot.

"You know what, Gavin? Maybe you need to find an excuse to stick around here and wait for the Slug behind mine. Nice seeing you, old friend," Gary says flatly. Then he pushes me aside with his shoulder and continues down the stairs.

I'm left standing there, wondering why I let myself listen to a lunatic like Ben. He just cost me a friendship and I don't have many of those to spare.

4

Log of Notable Nita/Ultracorps Activity Week 207

Large Walter deployment in West Covina, near the Slug yards. Deliveries of Maceo Steel, Styro, and ForteSilk without corresponding construction orders.

Theories: Ultracorps has been assured of new construction project even though Metro subcommittee has not approved contract. Possibly an attempt to repair relationship after Governor Hayes overturned water contract. Will continue to follow.

Colorful wax paper wrappers litter the floor of the dark, dingy basement, the result of many late nights filled with fast-food eating and many mornings with cleaning avoided. Ben sleeps on a bare, tattered mattress with a torn quilt coiled around him like a snake suffocating its prey. Beads of sweat adorn his face as he tosses and turns, fighting his vice-gripped blanket physically and his dreamed demons mentally. After a few moments of slumbered suffering, Ben sits up from his bed with a shout.

It was the fire dream again, and Ben knows who's responsible for the inferno. His unconscious mind creates the fire as ill-fitting metaphor; it's control Nita desires, not destruction. It'd be more apt if the tortured souls in his dreams were riddled with puppet strings instead of flames, but Ben does not control his slumbering mind. Though he is surprised his unconscious brain isn't a little more accurate.

Ben reaches down for a large Pho-Plastic jug of water and takes several deep swigs. He's determined to extinguish the flames, though they existed only within his mind. His stomach fills, and he has to stop drinking before the water level can climb to his head. His thirst abated if not satisfied, Ben takes stock of the room around him.

He knows he should clean the jumbled mass of filth. Not out of any misunderstandings of which qualities are closest to godliness, but because of the unstoppable, furry juggernaut known as the common street rat. Ben worked diligently to turn this old concrete basement into a fortress, sealing any cracks in the old concrete with B-Crete and installing an impenetrable Maceo steel door at the entrance. Still, he has no illusions concerning his buttressing prowess. He may have made the place nigh-impregnable to any human enemies, but no matter his intellect, or how diligently he worked to secure the space, the rats will inevitably find a way in as they have with every previous safe house. If rats ever unified and turned violent against mankind, the human race wouldn't stand a chance. The one thing worse than bowing to a thirteen-year-old little girl would be bowing to a rat overlord. At least Nita wouldn't demand to be fed garbage as tribute.

Ben begins the herculean task of picking up his room. He gathers merely a few drops of the garbage ocean before he stops in his tracks and lets the small amount of refuse he picked up trickle out of his hands. A thought has struck him, and it is infinitely more valuable than vermin prevention.

Just a few inches from his bed there is a large slab of B-Crete balanced precariously on a pile of old bricks. This ramshackle piece of furniture is Ben's desk, and it has been the location of many feats of ingenuity. Today's stroke of genius revolves around a hearing amplifier he makes frequent use of. He's had an idea to rework the circuits of the device, which should lower the electrical power required, allowing for a smaller battery and an overall decrease in the size of the gadget. An important breakthrough considering that the hearing aid is often employed in situations where discretion is prudent.

Ben grabs a pen and a water-stained old paper notebook and begins furiously mapping the new circuit design. He draws resistors and transistors and calculates ohms and amps. He performs what some would consider complex arithmetic seamlessly, moving without pause. His hand is slowing his mind down, not vice-versa.

Despite the loss in speed, Ben learned long ago that his ideas needed to be transferred from the mental world to the physical one. It's not that Ben needs a way to remember the circuit; his brain never forgets a single thought. No, the notes are needed to force Ben to remember the very act of the thought occurring in the first place. Moments of inspiration overtake Ben frequently, and it's quite easy to move on to the next brilliant notion, completely losing track of the previous profound revelation.

Ben finishes his circuit map and tears out the piece of paper. He places it squarely in the middle of the desk, one of the few areas not already covered in previous notes of fevered insight. Shrinking the hearing aid must be recalled later because Ben does not have time to implement his changes at the moment. It is the third Thursday of the month, the day of his scheduled meeting with Gavin. That hearing aid serves an invaluable function. It will ensure that Ben can have his conversation with the boy without being overheard by any of Nita's lackeys.

Gavin should have news on Santa Fe, and when Ben remembers that fact he gets so giddy he stomps his feet like a little boy. Ben is sure Gavin found something. It has been way too long since he had any good luck following Nita's trail; regression to dumb luck predicts better results eventually. Sure she's smart, but she she's also a child crippled by the arrogance accompanying her age. She left a track somewhere. Ben just needs to find the right thread, pull it, and the whole web will unravel. Then everyone will see the folly of giving Nita all that power. She's too young; it doesn't matter if she's the smartest human on the planet, experience and maturity mean something. They'll all see how crazy it was to give her Ben's old job.

Ben is feeling a tad encumbered by the weight of the lies he told Gavin about The Beast being held in Santa Fe, but really, he was talking theories more than lies. If The Beast somehow survived an almost certainly fatal three-hundred-story drop, and Nita was able to miraculously remove The Beast from the Metro Area without being discovered, and there is, in fact, a secret Ultracorps facility near

Santa Fe, then The Beast could conceivably be held there. Even with all those suppositions, Ben still doubts it.

Nita is too smart to keep such a dangerous weapon around even under those improbable conditions. The Beast is a toy she can't play with any more. If someone spotted the creature, the government would be exposed for lying about The Beast being dead for the second time. The government would deny it, and it would not take long for the government investigators to turn their eye towards Ultracorps. Ben hopes it is true, because if the public found out, it might actually mean the end of Ultracorps. Secretly keeping a mass-murderer alive is something that cannot be undone through public relations and campaign donations.

Ben needs to hurry up and get moving. There are only three hours until his lunch meeting with Gavin. He goes over to his basement "bathroom," which consists of a bucket in the corner for his business and a cracked mirror on the wall. He turns the knob of his WormLight, releasing the Manna to feed the bacteria which produce the light that illuminates Ben's face. He opens up a rectangular makeup case, revealing a smorgasbord of colors. He picks up his brush and begins applying a smattering of greys and beiges, mixing tones, hues, and shades to craft the perfect disguise. Soon his face is covered in pockmarks. His healthy, if not overly attractive, face now looks like it was scarred by one of Cabot's Plagues. That Plague was designed to mark the "Forgotten Sons" and remind them of the Lord's disappointment with them. It turned out that most people who had chicken pox were immune, so a small percentage of the United States population actually received the scars, which makes for the perfect disguise. The scars aren't uncommon enough to draw excessive attention, but they are unique enough that anyone giving a description of Ben would focus on their existence.

His face obscured, Ben heads over to a pile of clothes in the corner and starts digging. As he searches, he performs mathematical permutations in his head to determine a new combination of clothes that he has not previously worn; he wore the Slug conductor uniform last time, so it's out. The calculations lead him to a red t-shirt, grey pants, and grey boots.

Properly disguised, Ben takes one last look at himself in the cracked mirror, turns and climbs the ladder out of his basement abode. He opens the Maceo Steel door that leads to the ruins of the house that this basement was once a part of. The non-subterranean parts of the structure collapsed long ago. Cabot's Plagues ate the metal pipes inside the building, spilling water everywhere, weakening the structure, leading to its eventual collapse. This left the basement with a vacancy Ben filled some thirty years later.

Ben walks down the cracked and crumbled sidewalk that surrounds his neighborhood. He's heading towards the C 26 Slug line. There's an E 22 stop that is much closer, but he used that station last week, which means Nita could have found the route. The extra bit of walking is more than worthwhile if it keeps Nita off his trail.

After twenty-five minutes of traipsing through depressingly dilapidated streets, Ben is foiled just before he reaches the train stop. A Walter stands in front of the entrance, mindlessly and dutifully sweeping trash off the streets. Ben's heart nearly leaps out of his chest and he decides this is the end: Nita has finally found him. The cops will soon surround him and arrest him. Probably not even that. Nita wouldn't want Ben in jail asking all manner of inconvenient questions. She'll probably eliminate him. Ben frantically scans the rooftops around the station, expecting to catch a glimpse of the sniper who will finish him off. But there are no snipers, and the only real person he can see is an elderly man slowly making his way up the staircase to the Slug station. The old man is about twenty years past retirement age, so it's unlikely he's a secret Ultracorps operative.

Ben exhales as he realizes he may have jumped to a faulty conclusion. This might in fact be a Walter performing its assigned cleaning task, not the current eyes and ears of Nita. Still, prudence would be wise. There is always the possibility that Nita is watching through its eyes and biding her time before swinging the axe down on Ben's neck.

There isn't any way past the clone janitor, so Ben will have to go to plan B, another long walk. This time to the F 17 line. He'll have to move quickly. He can't afford to be late again. Gavin was extremely upset the last time Ben was tardy, and Ben is already balancing on thin ice with the boy.

5

Gavin Stillman is a criminal in the technical sense. There's no denying that. But is he a criminal in the moral sense? This young man was willing to risk life, limb, and freedom in order to help people he had never met. That sounds like the description of a hero, not a criminal. If there was ever an individual who deserved leniency, who deserved compassion from our legal system, Gavin Stillman is that man. That is why I'm lending my voice to the already raucous crowd calling on the Governor to push federal prosecutors into granting clemency to "The Beast Slayer."

"Now is the Time for Forgiveness" by Forest Brown, think.Net News
LA

Those old James Bond movies were ridiculous. Who in God's name would who want to get into a gunfight while wearing a tuxedo? I can barely move my shoulders, and this bowtie feels like it is strangling me. The last thing I want to do right now is battle Dr. No's henchmen. Why would anyone ever choose to wear something so uncomfortable and restrictive?

I shouldn't complain; anything that gets me out of the OEC offices at night is a good thing. Besides, I don't have a choice. This gala is black-tie and I'm not about to disrespect the man who invited me, Governor Hayes. He kept me out of jail, now it's time to repay him by letting him parade me around like a show dog. He even bought me the tux.

I have to admit it has been a good trade so far. Not only am I not locked up in Great Basin Prison, the food at these events is always fantastic. I still fantasize about the mushroom-cheese puff pastry I had at a fundraiser on a yacht a couple months ago.

Tonight's event is at the newly remodeled Los Angeles Natural History Museum. It is an absolute zoo out in front of the building.

There are giant WormLights set up so the think.Net reporters can get a good view of all the important people as they make their entrance on the red carpet. The guests are dressed as impeccably and expensively as they always are at these events. I've never see so many diamond necklaces, gold watches, and silk-blended fabrics.

I make my way to the start of the red carpet with my head down. I don't make it more than three feet before someone spots and me yells, "It's The Beast Slayer!" and I feel the spotlight turn on me, literally and figuratively as the WormLights all turn. The lights are so large I can actually see the strands of bio-luminescent bacteria inside. Every reporter yells at once to get my attention so they can get a good shot of me for the tabloids.

I do my best to oblige each request and keep a big grin plastered on my face. I'd love to be able to tell myself that I hate all this attention and I'd rather be left alone. Unfortunately, self-deception is not one of my strengths. I want them to love and admire me, and why not? I risked my life to save a bunch of strangers; I've got a better right to be famous than most celebrities.

After several minutes of posing, the reporters' interest in me finally starts to wane, as new exciting guests make their entrance. I take the hint and continue on down the red carpet. I make it to the grand stone staircase that leads to the museum and start heading up. A voice stops me, one I've heard before.

"Pretty popular, aren't you?" she asks. I remember that voice; it belongs to Officer Maria Vasquez, the cute officer with the Different serial killer theory.

I turn around and face Maria. I watch her eyes scan me up and down. The look on her face answers the question of why a man would ever wear an uncomfortable tuxedo. She looks fantastic herself, though she's wearing the same clothes as before, a blue police officer's uniform.

"You think I'm popular, wait till Bobby Singer comes in, then you'll see everyone really go nuts. Movie star outranks hero any day," I say and then immediately regret calling myself a hero.

"Don't whine to me, I'm a cop. I know all about being

underappreciated," she shoots back.

"You're right. Besides, I've got no right to complain. I get to go inside. I don't think they're going to let you in. That uniform doesn't count as black-tie."

"I'm not special enough to be allowed inside. Instead, I get to stand out here all night and make sure no one tries to murder all you super important people," she says with a smile.

Before I can deliver a witty retort, I feel a blow hit my back. It's a slap, not hard enough to cause me any real damage, but it would hurt if I could feel pain. The slapper meant it to hurt. It's Detective Rose, the detective who gave us a hard time when we got the false alarm about the Different killer.

"Hey there Beast Slayer, don't you look nice. Not bad life you got for a parolee," he says with a wide smile and eyes full of hate.

"Not a bad life for a detective either, although isn't guard duty a little below your rank?" I shoot back.

"Somebody has gotta make sure no important daughters get snatched," Rose says.

"Ouch, a little too soon for that joke, don't you think? Governor Hayes' people wouldn't be too pleased if they heard you say that," Maria says.

"I don't give a crap what that Different loving son of a-" Detective Rose stats to say but is cut off by Roger, the Governor's young, perpetually panic stricken assistant.

"Gavin! There you are. The Governor has some esteemed supporters he'd like you to greet. Please come along," Roger orders me.

Roger almost never leaves the Governor's side. I must really be wanted if he's strayed this far. He starts leading me off by the arm.

"Sorry, duty calls. Take care," I manage to say as I'm shuffled off.

"Bye sweetie," Rose says and blows a kiss.

Maria rolls her eyes.

Roger leads me up the stone stairs and into the main hall of the museum. It is breathtaking. Large tapestries hang from the ceiling, embroidered with messages commemorating the event and thanking the Gambert family, the renovation's financiers. The banners are interspersed with Double helix-shaped artwork made of B-Crete that crisscrosses overhead, making it feel like we're walking inside a piece of DNA. In the center of the hall is a large fountain and two fifteen-foot-tall spires made of Motion Sculpture. They look like they're spinning in place, which is more or less true, at least as far as I understand quantum physics.

I don't have long to take in the sight, because Roger is pulling me by the arm. Luckily, I can slow down my perception of time to soak it all in. The main hall truly looks spectacular.

I came to the museum on a class trip when I was eight. It looked nothing like this before the renovation. There were exposed beams and chunks of the wall missing, scars left on the building by the Plagues. The exhibits were cool, I remember really liking the stuffed lions and tigers. But even as a kid, I could tell the place needed repairs. Now, it finally got a huge cash infusion.

Roger leads me over to a large group of old wealthy people, who are getting positioned to have their picture taken.

"Here he is," Roger says and leads me to my position right in-between Governor Hayes and the Lieutenant Governor, Lewis Khan.

Governor Hayes looks like he came from a mold that produces politicians. He's tall, fit, and handsome, with just a touch of grey in his blonde hair. He's wearing an incredibly expensive tuxedo and a smile that looks simultaneously genuine and phony. Most of his support comes from the fact that he's what people think a governor should look like. That and his daughter was kidnapped during his campaign, garnering all the sympathy votes.

Lieutenant Governor Khan is the Governor in a funhouse mirror. He's short, rotund, and balding. I'm sure his tuxedo was expensive too, but it fits him so poorly I can hardly tell. He's sweating profusely even though it's a lovely sixty-seven degrees here.

The two make the ideal political duo. The handsome, empty-headed baby-kisser and the conniving little behind-the-scenes puppet-master. It's the kind of pairing the public always complains about but routinely elects anyway.

"There you are. I'm not used to waiting, my boy. Isn't being on time a hell of a lot easier than fighting The Beast?" the Governor says to me under his breath. Somehow, his smile doesn't move at all. I'm not sure I can do that, and I have inhuman control over my body.

"Sorry sir, it's a zoo out there. There are so many reporters," I say back. I'm not late, Roger told me to be here five minutes from now, but I don't think the Governor wants to hear my excuses.

Finally, everyone is placed perfectly, and they are ready for the photos. We are surrounded by think.Net reporters. They snap Memories and upload them to think.Net for viewing. The reporters clap their hands to let us know when they are snapping a Memory, so we know who to look at. After a few minutes the pictures end, and we break up into conversation. I turn to the Lieutenant Governor and extend my hand to shake.

"Nice to see you again, sir," I say.

"If you say so," he replies, ignoring my hand. "I have to be going now." He turns and walks away, his entourage in tow. He looks like he's leaving the event all together. I guess he was just here for the photo op, or he really doesn't like me. He is always rude to me.

I turn to Governor Hayes, who's talking to an elderly couple. Even in this elegant crowd, they stand out as wealthy. She's wearing a lengthy fur coat and half the queen's jewels, and he's wearing a gold watch that's big enough to pay the national debt.

"Governor Hayes! I wanted to talk to you about the Metro Area's Water system. I know you voided the Ultracorps takeover, and I applaud the decision. Have you had a chance to consider your other options? My company..." the elderly man says.

"Have you met The Beast Slayer?" the Governor interrupts and pulls me close. "Mr. and Mrs. Gambert, I'd like to introduce you to Gavin Stillman. Gavin, these are the individuals who made this all possible. It was their generous donation that paid for the museum's renovation."

Mr. Gambert extends his arm for a handshake, which I oblige. Mrs. Gambert puts her hand out with her palm facing the floor. What is she doing? I slow down time for a second so I can think… I'm supposed to kiss her hand! I grab her hand, kneel down, and plant a small kiss. God I hope that's what I am supposed to do. Her smile tells me I did the right thing or close enough. I'm still new to being a socialite.

"Mr. and Mrs. Gambert, this is all so incredible. I came to the museum when I was kid and it looked nothing like this. It is an amazing transformation," I say with sincerity.

"Is it true you remember it perfectly?" Mrs. Gambert asks.

"Edna!" Mr. Gambert scolds.

"What? The news said he had a perfect memory. I just want to know if that's true," Mrs. Gambert says innocently.

"It's fine, sir. I do have a perfect memory, but only for things that happened to me since I Differentiated. My childhood memories are like yours." I have better access to them than she does, but I don't think she wants me to get technical.

"See? He doesn't mind," Mrs. Gambert says.

"I'm glad you like what we've done to the museum. We've been blessed, and we are lucky to get to give some back. Some of us are too old to go fighting monsters on rooftops, so we do what we are able," Mr. Gambert says.

"It is a wonderful gift you gave the Metro Area."

"The news said you don't feel fear. That's how you could fight The Beast. Was that true?" Mrs. Gambert asks from out of nowhere. I might have a groupie.

"Not exactly. It is hard to describe. I know when I should be afraid. I know when my body's telling me to run away. But it's just a message, I can choose to ignore it or even tell it to shut up."

"That sounds like courage to me. I should know, I had to find some myself back in Korea, even with BlueHawk on our side. The Metro Area is lucky to have you watch over us," Mr. Gambert says.

"Show me something! Show me something special you can do," Mrs. Gambert demands.

"Edna, please, you've already gone too far," Mr. Gambert pleads.

"He said he doesn't mind. You don't mind do you?" she asks.

I don't mind, per se, but I have no idea what I should do to show her my abilities. If she wants to wait ten or fifteen minutes I should be able to grow an inch more hair. I'm sure that would impress. Oh, I know.

"I don't mind. This is what I used to do hide my identity back when I was the Vigilante."

I start loosening various muscles all over my face. The point is to make my face look flabby and wrinkled, like a much older person. It is not an attractive process.

Mrs. Gambert's face quickly moves from intrigue to horror. She lets out a small shrill scream. Every eye in the area is focuses straight on me. Suddenly, this doesn't seem like a good idea. I stop half-way and start turning my face back to normal. Governor Hayes shoots me a dirty look. Tough room.

#

It's a nice night, but my bar is low. Averaging 30 minutes a day outside has changed my standard. I had enough of being asked rude and prodding questions by grey-haired elites. There's something about getting older that makes you think you have the right to ask any question you want. It's nice to have some peace out here in front of the museum.

Someone's coming up behind me, soft steps. Officer Vasquez. I act like I don't hear her so she comes up and taps me on the shoulder. What can I say, it's been a long time since a woman besides Linda has touched me, and she only does that to treat my injuries. I whirl around with a smile on my face.

"Did you tell your captain about the dead Different in the alley?" she asks with a stone-face. I stow my smile.

"I'm not sure. Maybe my partner Victor did. I don't think it matters. Captain Murphy doesn't have much pull with anyone. He's just the human bureaucrat who talks to the higher-ups. Victor and I pretty much run the show."

"Your Captain isn't a Different?"

"No, the government wanted to say a human was in charge to make everybody feel safer about having the OEC in the Metro Area.

Why does it matter?"

"A guy on my squad told me about another dead Different they found yesterday. I think he was a Cooler or something. Anyway, my Sergeant couldn't care less about all the dead Differents we've been finding. I tried to talk to my captain about it, and he was somehow even less interested. Detective Rose is handling all of the cases and he doesn't see a pattern either. I thought maybe your captain would do something, you know, if he was a Different."

"Because he might care about his own kind?"

"Yeah, that's what I was thinking," she says.

"You're right, he might care if he was a Different, but even if he was, it wouldn't matter. Like I said, no one cares what he has to say, and our mission is to go after criminal Differents, not help Different victims. That's the law. Unless you find some proof that a Different is the killer, we can't get involved."

"There's no proof of anything because no one is looking for evidence. They all blame it on gangs or muggings gone wrong, and then tell me they don't have the resources to cover every murder in the Metro Area. Nobody besides me seems to care."

"I care. I care a lot, but I'm on house arrest. I'm only let out of the office if there's a criminal Different on the loose, or if the Governor needs me to dance for him. There's no way I can help you."

"Looks like I'm on my own. That's fine. I'm going to track that killer down," Officer Vasquez vows and walks off. She really meant that. She isn't going to let this rest. I wish I could help her. Maybe there's a way I can.

"Officer Vasquez, wait!" I yell, but she doesn't stop.

I chase after her. "Maria, please, I thought of a way I can help," I plead.

She stops in her tracks and turns to give me a cold stare.

"I thought you couldn't help unless I find proof a Different is doing the killings."

"Do you think it's possible the killer is a fellow Different?" I ask.

"It's hard to say. Some of the Differents that have been killed were Betas, hard to believe a normal person could do that. But then again, they've all been killed with knives or guns. No laser beams or crushed skulls."

"Who were these Betas, what could they do?"

"What's with all the questions? You said you could help, so tell me, how?" she demands. She's a severe person.

"This. This is how I can help."

"By checking over my police work? I've been doing this longer than you have. I don't need lessons or second guessing," she says her eyes full of fire.

"It's not like that. It's not that I'm a better cop than you. I'm struggling to find a way to say this without sounding like a total jerk," I say and slow down time to give myself a chance to choose my words carefully. "It's not that I'm better at being a detective, it's that my Differentiation gives me certain mental advantages. I think faster than normal people because I can slow down my sense of time. I can recall every piece of information my brain has absorbed since I first got my abilities. Every sight, every sound, every smell. That's how I tracked The Beast; I used my mind to identify his bite-marks on multiple victims, my memories were like pictures of the crime scene. I can be like a human crime-lab, if you share what you learn with me I might be able to put it all together."

She thinks about what I said for a second, and her body-language turns just a bit less hostile.

"You did sound like an arrogant jerk, but you also managed to convince me you might be useful. So what do you want to know?" she asks.

"Not here. I've got to get back inside to do more performing for the Governor. Accept my knowledge request?" I ask and log onto think.Net and think about sending her the request.

She receives and accepts the request. I got her info. I have to stifle my body's natural desire to smile from ear to ear.

"What's that?" Maria asks and turns her head back towards the museum entrance.

"I don't know," I answer earnestly. My attention is a laser beam pointed right at her. I have to force myself to tune my awareness to a wider band.

When I do, I hear running, screaming, and general panic. Fancifully dressed patrons are streaming out of the museum, stricken by fear. They stumble and yell as they make their way down the stone steps.

They are screaming about fire, and some madman burning the place down. Maria and I look at each other and without a word, turn and run towards the throng of people. We have to fight the river of human panic to get back inside the museum. We're pushing against dozens of people all intent on moving in the opposite direction. I start out with a few ginger "excuse me's," before I give up and lower my shoulder. Despite my size and strength, it is still a hell of a fight to push through the horde.

Maria quickly pulls ahead of me. Her uniform and commands to "clear the way" prove much more effective than my polite asks and shoving. When I finally make my way to a clear spot on the stairway landing, Maria is waiting and smiling.

"They forgot you were a celebrity," Maria says deadpan.

"What do you mean? That was all about getting my autograph," I say with a smile. "Looks like a fire." I point at the entrance doorway. Up above the stream of fleeing gala-goers there is cloud of thick black floating out of the doorway along with the people.

"Maybe," she says slowly, but I can see her mind is whirling.

Thankfully, people are sheep, especially scared people. While there is a continuous flow out the two main doors, the smaller doors to the side are all but clear. I step forward, pull the door open, and perform the after you arm gesture. Maria rolls her eyes.

The second we step through the door, we're hit by a wall of heat. Flames flicker in the far corner of the main hall, sending plumes of smoke that fill the grand chamber. People cough and hack as they scramble to make it out of the building. Some of Maria's fellow uniformed officers are helping herd people out the doors. I don't see Detective Rose anywhere, that guy is useless.

There's a group of people trapped in the corner. They're all screaming and scrambling to move backwards, but the fire isn't that close to them and there are big gaps in the flames, why don't they run out?

I feel an alert in my head, a think.Net call from Victor. Why would Victor be calling me? I ignore the call and continue trying to assess the scene. It looks like there's a man screaming at the group in the corner. Is he naked?

Victor calls again. He wouldn't call twice for no reason.

"My partner is calling me, I'll just be a second," I say to Maria and take the call. I know I'm being strange and rude, but Victor calling once is odd, twice means there is a problem.

>>>*I'll be there in four minutes.*

<<<*You're coming to the museum? Why?*

>>>*What do you mean why? Aren't you there?*

>>>*Yes, there's a fire. Since when are you a fireman?*

<<<*Are you kidding? The fire was started by the building's Heater, Stephen Grange and he's still on the scene. How do you not know this? Murphy told me and he heard it through the police.*

>>>*The naked guy! Okay, I think I see him.*

<<<*Good. Three minutes and forty-five seconds. You have to keep him from burning the place to the ground before I get there.*

Victor ends the call.

"We're not just dealing with a fire, the building's Heater started it, and he's still here," I say and point to the naked man.

He's pacing back and forth, moving into and out of the flames as if they mean nothing. His body must be immune to the heat. He's screaming at the group of three dozen or so people huddled in the corner. They all push and shove to dig deeper into the corner, trying to stay as far away as they can from the ranting mad man. The Governor is in the group. Several of his aides stand between him and the lunatic.

The Heater is really worked up. There's too much other noise to make out what he's saying, but I can tell he's impassioned. Maybe it's a political thing?

He takes a 90 degree turn to the right and keeps ranting and raving. Now he's shaking his fist and pointing, he's getting truly riled up. Only he's screaming at a stuffed crocodile.

"He's bonkers," Maria says.

"Looks like," I say. "That changes the plan. I should try to talk him down. Maybe we can end this without anyone getting hurt. While I distract him, you get those people out of here." I break into a speed-walk towards Stephen the Heater. I move quickly but calmly. Calm is the name of the game right now. If I'm calm, it will help the Heater be calm.

"Who put you in charge!?" Maria yells as she runs after me.

I gesture for her to be quiet. "We need to be calm. We're going after a Different which makes this an OEC matter."

"Fine," she says with a swallow. I wouldn't like it if I was her either.

Stephen is walking again, muttering gibberish to himself as he paces. His feet melt the floor as he walks, leaving smoldering footprints in the tile floor. He's made his body so hot, it already ignited all the combustible material in his vicinity. A half-dozen cocktail-height tables have been turned into mini bonfires. I have to stop him soon, or the fires will spread and the whole building will be gone.

The strategy for dealing with a deranged person is to try to engage with them warmly and calmly. They are not thinking rationally so you have to focus on their emotional needs instead of trying to reason with them. If they feel safe, they may start to relax.

I come to a stop about fifteen feet away from Stephen. I can feel the heat pouring off him, his body is a few hundred degrees warmer than the fires that surround us. Stephen has stopped pacing and is engaged in a raucous debate with himself. I can't really understand the argument but it has something to do with snakes crawling all over his body and who put them there.

I plaster my face with the biggest grin I can generate. When normal people pretend to smile, they activate different muscles in the face than are activated during a genuine smile. Fake smiles don't look like real smiles and studies have shown that people can tell the difference. I can control all my muscles, my smile always looks like the real thing. Hopefully it's the little touch that will help win the Heater over.

"Hey Stephen, how's it going?" I ask loudly, but with a low pitched and even tone.

Stephen's eyes dart right to me, or at least they look at me. His pupils are dilated and his eyes are unfocused. His mind is a million miles away. There are streams of drool trickling out of the sides of his mouth and he takes short panicked breaths. He has scratched his own arms to bloody shreds. He reminds me of that Speedster kid who broke my arm a few weeks back.

"It's you!" Stephen says in a deranged voice.

"That's right; it's me, The Beast Slayer. I'd love to come shake your hand Stephen, but I'd wind up a little overcooked. Do you think you could turn down the heat a bit?"

"I can't," he says. "If I don't burn them, they'll eat me."

"Okay, that makes sense. I want to help you out, what can I do?" I reply in my calming tone. There's no point in arguing, I won't win and it'll upset him. But I do need to keep him talking. I put my arm behind my back and signal to Maria save the people huddled in the corner.

"Nothing can stop the snakes! Only fire can keeps them away and I can't keep burning forever," he says. It's amazing how much conviction the human brain can generate when believing complete insanity.

"Maybe you can turn it down a bit, that way we can get a doctor or a snake handler in here and they can help you." I take a sideways glance and see Maria has started leading the people out of the corner.

"They won't stop it! They want it to happen!" Stephen screams. We're heading in the wrong direction here.

"Hey now, you know me. I'm The Beast Slayer. I'm one of the good guys. I want to help you. You seem like a good guy yourself."

"There aren't any good guys!" Stephen screams and suddenly his eyes come into focus. "You're a liar. You're taking them." He points at the escaping party-goers.

"We have to get those people out of here. We don't want the snakes to get them do we?" I say. This situation is coming off the rails. I take a deep breath and flood my blood with oxygen. I have a feeling it's about to get too hot to breathe.

"You! You did this!" the Heater points at me and screams.

He clenches his jaw so hard it looks like he's trying to grind his teeth to dust. Then his whole body turns a deep shade of red and starts to violently shake. The heat hits me like someone turned on the broiler. Pho-Plastic lamp shades that had been smoldering before burst into flames. Stephen slowly stalks towards me, his body pouring out heat like the sun.

It's time for a Plan B. Step one: Keep him from burning myself or anyone else alive for three minutes. Step two: Hope Victor shows up with a Step three. I turn and break into a jog making sure to lead Stephen away from the still fleeing gala-attendees.

While I run, I filter the water out of my bloodstream and direct it to my bladder. With no water, my skin quickly dries out, which should help me keep cooler and alive an extra half-second if Stephen gets too close. It isn't ideal considering my body is already overheated and I need sweat to cool myself, but that's a longer term problem. Stephen's body must have a way of coping with the heat. His blood should be boiling and he's burning any oxygen around him before he can breathe it. I wonder what's different about the cells in his body.

Now isn't the time to be thinking about this. Stephen is hot on my heels, in every sense. As Stephen runs, a trail of flames follows in his wake. He glides past a display of stuffed lions taking down a stuffed gazelle and the whole stuffed Serengeti scene erupts in flames. It looks like a demon from Hell is after me.

I turn back from watching Stephen just in time to catch a glimpse of a tiny step leading up into the next section of the museum. Even with time slowed, I can't stop my foot from catching on the edge of the step, which sends me splaying forward onto the floor.

I land with a thud and roll over to see Stephen closing in on me, I can already feel myself start to burn. I always hated those tiny little unnecessary single steps you only see in places like museums. I would constantly trip on them when I was a kid. In fact, I remember tripping and falling in this very museum when I was here on that class trip, everyone laughed at me. Is this my past flashing before my eyes?

I am about to die, Stephen doesn't have to do anything but keep walking towards me. I try to scramble to my feet, but my muscles fail from lack of water and oxygen. I end up tripping again and cutting my chin open on the tile floor.

There's a loud boom and a flash from behind Stephen, then another. Stephen stops in his tracks and turns around. Maria fires another shot from her sidearm. I watch her squeeze the trigger, but the bullet never makes it to Stephen. His body is so hot, the metal ignites and melts before it can reach his flesh.

The gunshots were enough to draw Stephen's attention and he stalks off after Maria, spreading more flames as he goes. Plan B is looking like more of a failure and it wasn't much of a plan in the first place. Victor will be here in 2 minutes and 30 seconds, but by then Stephen will have started a fire that's too big to put out. The main hall of the museum looks clear, but there are countless other rooms where people may have run, not to mention maintenance workers and other staff. If this building goes up, people will die. I need to get Stephen out of the building and into the open.

"Lead him to the front!" I yell to Maria, who nods and fires another useless shot to make sure Stephen stays after her.

While he is distracted, I run around him and towards one of the 50 foot long tapestries hanging from the ceiling at the far end of the main hall. Thankfully, the flames have not spread here yet. I take a running start, leap, and grab onto the heavy felt fabric, using my body weight to pull it down from the rafters.

I drag the tapestry over to the nearby fountain and dunk it. The heavy fabric drinks up the water like a sponge. The tapestry is so water-logged it feels like it weighs a ton. I strain my right shoulder's rotator cuff pulling the fabric out of the water.

I bunch up the fabric in my hands, and hold it out in front of me like a towel I'm going to use to get a child out of the bathtub.

"Watch out!" I warn Maria as I take a running start towards Stephen.

Stephen turns around right as I leap into the air, tackling him, while simultaneously wrapping the water soaked tapestry around him. As soon as the fabric hits his skin, scalding hot steam shoots out in all directions. I ignore the painful, yet relatively minor burns. I was going to have to regrow my top layer of skin anyway. I quickly wrap as much fabric as I can around Stephen and then pick him up in a bear hug.

Corralling him takes a herculean effort. Stephen isn't a large man, he weighs about 150 pounds, but it's 150 pounds that is punching and kicking as hard as it can from behind the soaked tapestry. Add another 100 or so pounds from the tapestry and I'm carrying 250 pounds of scalding, ungainly weight. To make it worse, my muscles are already weakened from a general lack of water and oxygen in my system. It's an absolute miracle that I manage to tackle Stephen through one of the glass doors at the entrance to the museum.

Razor sharp shards of glass rip open cuts in my already singed flesh, but that's merely the start of my injuries. Our momentum carries Stephen and I through the door and out onto the stairs. My tackle turns into a rag-doll like tumble as I bounce and slide down the stone steps.

My descent takes an eternity as each moment causes a new injury. I sprain my left shoulder in the first bounce, roll onto my front and crack two ribs. I do another end-over-end spin and land on my back, which miraculously only causes severe soft tissue injuries. I try to plant my left foot and stop myself, but my leg catches under me. I hear the bone snap, right as my nerves send me pain signals that let me know my tibia cracked. There are four more bruising and battering bounces before I finally come to a merciful stop at the base of the stairs.

A purple fabric bundle lands five feet to the right of me. Steam is still shooting out from the sides, but I'm hoping the fall took Stephen out and he's just going to take a while to cool down. The steam comes to an abrupt stop and within a few milliseconds the tapestry straight jacket erupts in flames that instantly spread to the red carpet that recently welcomed us all. Stephen rises up from the flames like a phoenix that's suffered a head injury. He pushes himself up to his knees, slowly.

I scream "Run!" to the crowd of gala attendees around us, but that was a waste of breath, the tuxedos and sequin dresses are already fleeing in terror for the second time in a few minutes.

I push myself up onto my feet, keeping 95% of my weight on my right leg. Stephen finishes just a second behind me in the race to stand up. He's close enough to me that he's cooking me where I stand.

"I'm sorry. I didn't want to do that. Cool yourself down and we can figure out how to help you," I say.

Stephen doesn't even look at me; he mutters to himself and scrapes at his arms. I turn to limp away before I'm cooked in my shoes. Stephen notices me moving.

"You have to help me get them off!" Stephen says then he starts to stumble after me.

We're quite the pair running through the street. He's battered and deranged and I'm burnt and crippled. Partygoers flee in front of us like we're parting the red sea. I don't have an endgame here.

Right then, step two of plan B ends up coming through with a flourish.

"Bring him over here!" Victor yells. He's standing in front of a fire hydrant a couple hundred yards up the street. Thank God they have lots of fire hydrants in the fancy Metro Center.

I limp over as fast as I can with Stephen following close behind me. Right before I get Stephen into position, I trip over a crack in the asphalt and collapse to the ground. I try to push myself up, but the muscles in my right thigh cramp up. I flood extra blood to the area, but I'm out of time.

Stephen is nearly on top of me. He's got his hands out in front of himself, pleading desperately for my help. I won't be able to help him because he's about to burn me alive. Do I want time to move slowly or quickly while I die?

I hear a hiss of water spray. It's Victor opening the hydrant, if only I could have gotten Stephen thirty feet further. Instead, this is how I die.

But I don't. A human blur saves me. I have to slow down my perception of time to see him move. In less than a second, Victor leaps behind Stephen and shoves the Heater in the back. He pushes hard enough to send the deranged man flying thirty feet through the air and into the water streaming out of the hydrant.

As soon as Stephen hits the water, the entire area becomes one giant steam room. The steam is hot enough to scald, but compared to the temperatures I had been experiencing, it feels like a cool breeze. The steam is obscuring my vision. I can hear though, and what I hear is Victor screaming in agony. I can only imagine the burns he suffered from touching Stephen without protection.

As the steam starts to clear, a figure emerges. Stephen somehow managed to stand back up. Getting thrown thirty feet through the air took its toll though, and he's struggling to stand. I have to make my move now, before he heats back up.

I focus and raise myself to my feet. I lower my shoulder and pick up as much speed as I can, moving in a one legged hop. Stephen sees me coming.

"Why won't they leave me alone?" he asks.

I answer him with a perfectly delivered right uppercut that lands square on his chin. His neck snaps back, and he falls to the ground, out cold.

"The Beast Slayer did it!" someone yells from behind us. I turn around and see a crowd of fabulously dressed onlookers cheering and clapping. The Governor is among them. I'm going to be on the news tonight.

6

Though William unanimously won Rookie of the Year, he did not seem overly enthusiastic to receive the award. When reached for comment, he had this to say, "While I appreciate the honor and the esteem of the voters, I would not say I was happy with being selected as Rookie of the Year. The goal of every basketball season is to win the championship. Our team failed to do that this year. I do not play for awards or individual achievement. I play to win. Nothing else matters."

"William 'Billy the Kid' Jefferson Wins rookie of the year" by Roger Burns Minneapolis StarTribune

July 6th

Sit-ups: 639
Pushups: 867
Pull-ups: 191
Running: 11.21 miles, 61.7 minutes total, 5:26 average mile time
Diet: 2,445 Calories, 180 grams protein, 290 gram carbohydrates, 65 grams fat
Sleep: 8:11
Funds: $617.19
Ammo Count: 5 rounds 7N1, 24 rounds 9mm, 2 Stun Grenades, 1 Smoke Grenade, 2 Standard Grenades.
Activities: Followed Target 18: Male Beta Heat Absorber. Identified Target 19: Female Gamma Energy Producer. Administered Cocktail Revision 4 to test subject Male Beta Energy Producer.

Target Notes: Target 18 exited the Slug Line 37 Colfax Avenue stop at 7:55PM, which is within his established 7:40-8:05 window. He entered Culver Gym as he has every Monday, Wednesday, and Friday, for the past two weeks. His pattern is established. I will eliminate the Target in two days. Also identified a possible Target

19: Female Gamma Energy Producer. Likely works in the area. Will continue to monitor.

Money Man Plan Attempt 4 Notes: Friend on the Force administered cocktail to the Heater. Aggression was at proper level, but the loss of mental acuity in the test subject diminished threat potential. Subject lacked the ability to combat OEC agents. Remain skeptical that the proper combination of drugs can be found. Media results were the opposite of desired. Mostly positive press for the OEC and The Beast Slayer specifically. Money Man remains determined. Even said something about having to get this batch from ancillary source involving Friend on the Force. Do not want to know more.

Personal Notes: Met with Money Man. Provided $1,000, but half of that was meant for Friend on the Force. Will deliver the money. Argued with Money Man that the increased risk of exposure and low probability of success made the drug plan a mistake, but would not listen. Endured another rant about the "Devil Spawn" and divine duty to expose evil. Continue to question his ability to stay rational on the subject of Differents, but there is no other source of funds. Wish I hadn't given everything away to charity.

Mental State: Went by the diner yesterday. Previous plan to avoid proved futile. We ate there in that beginning time when we couldn't be apart. Had a game in Los Angeles and she came too. Rest of the team made fun of me for being whipped so young, but I didn't care. Memories got me depressed, lowered my productivity for the day. That's why I avoid the place. Will redouble my efforts.

7

Log of Notable Nita/Ultracorps Activity Week 210

Intercepted HAM radio communications that referenced reports of earthquakes near old St. Louis. Odd because there are few fault lines in the area and few quakes historically. Location is quite close to a large series of Ultracorps-owned copper mines.

Theory: The Ultracorps mines are actually an underground facility designed to house dangerous off-the-grid Differents. Need to investigate mine output reports to be sure.

Ben smiles the massive grin of self-satisfaction as he approaches the Ultracorps-owned office building. His toothy joy is spurred on by his latest in a running series of epic disguises. He added chin putty to his usual complexion-based facial obfuscation, which could not have worked any better. Ben's normally round chin is transformed into one with a steep bone-based peak, making him look like an entirely different person of Anglo-Saxon descent.

Ben's genius disguise is not limited to his face; his entire ensemble sells his new identity as an Ultracorps-employed exterminator. He donned the stereotypical grey coverall this morning, sporting the red embroidered letters "Richard." That flair was added by Ben over two frustrating and expletive-filled hours with many needle stabs. Along with the uniform, Ben wears gloves, a tattered Lakers hat, and work boots. He carries a metal canister on his back that looks like it is full of vermin poison.

Ben has the *pièce de résistance* on his hand, his fake Mark of Differentiation. He hand-altered his original tattoo with a tiny paintbrush with such incredible precision, one would need a microscope to spot the difference between it and a real machine-made tattoo. To all the world Ben is now Richard Gladstone,

GAMMA, Enhanced Senses.

The disguise should work perfectly to get Ben into the building. That is, assuming the fake work order he created on think.Net went through as planned. Ben tries to avoid using think.Net whenever possible. He's excellent at manipulating the imaginary mental world generated by a series of Telepaths and Big Brains. He should be; he used to be the administrator of the whole network. The problem is that while Ben is excellent, Nita, the new administrator, is near perfect. Any time he goes on think.Net he could be walking into a trap, but sometimes great risk is needed to net a high reward. He made thousands of dummy accounts before he had to go on the run. There's no way she has found all of them. The work order went through, Ben is completely certain... pretty completely certain.

Ben needs to check some records that lie within this office building. Ultracorps is up to something new, near old St. Louis. He obtained this information from an ancient source, a HAM radio. The radio network comprised of nerds is much smaller than it was Pre-Plague, but there are still enough enthusiasts to cobble together a dorky underground news network comprised of curmudgeons too stubborn to use the much more easily accessible and affordable think.Net. The advantage is that some of these enthusiasts live in the Non-Assisted Area, the sparsely populated swaths of the nation that exist outside the eight Metro Areas. One of those individuals, CardinalFan4Life, lives outside one of a handful of small towns constructed near the ruins of old St. Louis. He reported a slew of unusual earthquakes that hit the area a few days ago. Ultracorps operates a series of copper mines in the area. It could be some new mining technique, but maybe it's something else. Maybe they aren't copper mines, but rather experimental research labs full of dangerous and unreported Differents.

Ben has long suspected Ultracorps of keeping Differents outside the Metro Areas and using them for their own devices without the legally required testing and training from Section 26. The mines would make the perfect cover for a combined secret prison and research lab. There is the slight possibility that Ben is wrong about his conclusion, and in case he is, he'd rather not schlep all the way out to St. Louis for no good reason.

Ultracorps records could help prove or disprove Ben's theory. Of course, the records aren't going to be labeled "secret research lab," but accounting records can be telling to the informed eye. It's too dangerous to try to access those files on think.Net, but the government requires hard copies of every document in case think.Net has a critical failure. Many of those files are held in the clean and pristine building Ben walks into.

A mousy young secretary sits at a desk lost in the think.Net stare. Ben approaches, but before he can perform the customary fake cough to get her attention, the secretary speaks.

"Can I help you?" the secretary asks without ever looking at Ben. Awareness of the real world while on think.Net is a rare feat.

"Umm," Ben stammers, thrown off by her stare. "Maintenance got a call about a roach infestation. I'm here to sniff 'em out and get rid of 'em. I swear there are more of them bugs now than before the Plagues."

"I'm sorry," the secretary says, finally signing off think.Net and looking at Ben. "You must have the wrong office. I don't remember seeing any work orders on the docket. Haven't seen any roaches either. Sorry to disappoint."

"Not again," Ben moans. "Dispatch is always screwing up. Still, do you mind checking to see if one of the floors called it in? This thing weighs a ton. I don't want to haul it back to base to get told to haul back here."

The secretary disappears back into the think.Net stare. "Wait. You're right. It came through from the night guard late last night."

"Yep, that's when the little bastards come out. Don't worry. I'll take care of 'em," Ben says and starts heading down the hallway, towards the elevator.

"Tenth floor. You're lucky the Strong-Man just came in," she yells after him.

Ben hits the call button, which lights up an LED that tells the Strong-Man to lower the Maceo Steel room by way of a ForteSilk cable. The doors open and Ben steps inside the elevator, hits the button, and waits for the person on the top of the shaft to turn the crank, which requires thousands of pounds of force, and lift the elevator.

On the tenth floor, Ben walks past a few horrified employees. No one likes seeing an exterminator in their office. The funny thing is that they're scared of the usually harmless vermin instead of the consistently dangerous fellow human being, especially one walking around with a backpack full of poison. As Ben walks, he lifts up his nose and sniffs deeply, acting as if he's following a scent like a bloodhound on the trail. His olfactory bulbs supposedly lead him directly towards a room that just so happens to be labeled "Records." What a coincidence. The room is full of nearly a dozen men and women transferring pieces of paper from one folder into another folder inside Pho-Plastic filing cabinets.

"Attention, employees!" Ben yells, "There was a report of a cockroach infestation in this room. My nose is telling me that there are thousands of the little buggers living in the walls in here. I'm going to need you all to clear the room and stay out while I gas it. This is for your own safety."

Some of the men and women let out shudders and groans of horror, but despite their disgust and obvious desire to get out of the soon to be roach-motel office, they carefully close whatever files they have open before filing out of the room. As soon as the last employee leaves, Ben goes to work. He's a man on a mission, hunting through the rows of filing cabinets. They are arranged by industry, and Ben lets out a little excited gasp when he spots Copper. He opens the filing cabinet and rifles through the various mines around the nation until he gets to the records of the mines near old St. Louis.

There are a half-dozen mines operating in that area. Each of them was producing between one and two tons of copper a month. That is a substantial haul in this day and age. Cabot's Plague that destroyed copper was one of his most effective. The bacteria he created spread easily and were able to survive in virtually any condition. They propagated in rain water around the globe, and when they met with any exposed copper, the bacteria consumed the metal and left behind useless copper compounds. Only the most deeply buried copper deposits were spared.

Ben goes through the records. There are hundreds of pages of daily output records, but Ben needs merely one second to look at each sheet and memorize every number. There isn't any evidence to support his theory about a secret lab, the mines are in fact producing copper, but there is another interesting anomaly. A few weeks ago, the most productive of the five mines simply stopped producing any ore at all. There was no slowdown, no gradual decrease like one would expect from a mine where the supply had run dry. One day it was producing as normal, and the next day it gave nothing and hasn't produced a speck of copper since.

Jumping to conclusions can be one of his weaknesses, and Ben knows it. He needs to consider all possibilities, including the not all that unlikely chance of a Plague outbreak. That area had been clean for years, but Cabot's little bugs are nothing if not resilient. To eliminate that possibility, Ben runs over to a different filing cabinet, labeled Containment. In the event of a Plague outbreak a team is sent out, including a Heater Different who fries the bacteria and sterilizes the area. Ben searches for the dates in question, but finds nothing. No teams were anywhere near the area at the time.

Ben's theory on the mine being a lab is shot, but something else is going on there. Before he can postulate a full range of theories, he hears the door open and sees a large man in security uniform step into the file room. Ben ducks behind a cabinet before he's spotted. The guard starts looking through the room, and his eyes hone in on the open cabinet drawers.

"Hey, exterminator! You in here?" the guard yells.

Ben considers his options for a moment, before deciding his best plan of action is to bluff through whatever is going on here.

"Hey! You shouldn't be in here, man. I've already started gassing the room. It's dangerous," Ben says waving his arms as he steps out from behind the cabinet.

"That's funny. I don't smell anything," the guard says.

"The poison is odorless to you. You need my enhanced sense of smell to detect it."

"You don't say. Then how come you're in here breathing fine? Something else is funny. They said that I was the one who called in the infestation report last night. Now I've been pulling double shifts all week so I might be a little tired, but I'm pretty sure I'd remember doing that. And what about all these open files? Everyone who works here knows leaving your files open gets you fired, gas or no gas."

Ben opens his mouth to spin more yarns, but then decides the jig is up. He hits a release on the top of his "poison" tank and thick, harmless white fog spews out and fills the room almost instantaneously. The milky cloud blocks Ben from the guard's view, giving Ben the opportunity to escape. He can't see any better than the guard, but his memory of the room is perfect. He steps around cabinets he can't see and through an invisible doorway.

The hallway is filling with smoke, but Ben's tank is running out of juice. It's creating more of a smoke haze than a blanket. Another large guard at the end of the hall spots Ben through the mist and charges towards him.

"Hey! Stop!" the guard yells.

Ignoring the guard, Ben drops the tank off his back and takes off running down the hall, away from the guard and the elevator down to freedom. He tries to follow an exit sign to a stairwell, but another guard steps out from behind that door, cutting off another escape route. Chased from both directions, Ben's one option is to step into an uninhabited office. He slams the door behind him and locks it.

The guards pound on the door and scream threats, but Ben is confident the door will hold for at least a minute. His confidence is shattered by the jingle of keys. He reaches into his pocket for a save from a piece of technology, a plastic door stop. He wedges it under the door, which should buy him a few more seconds.

Luckily for Ben, the employee who works out of this office is a successful one who earned himself or herself a room with a window.

Unfortunately, the window is old-fashioned plate glass. Ben's best efforts to smash through it with a chair prove embarrassingly fruitless.

But Ben is a strict adherent to the Boy Scout motto to always be prepared. He reaches into a pocket and pulls out a small electronic device. The impressiveness is diminished by the fact that Ben built it out of an old Pre-Plague Walkman. He holds the recycled device to the window and pushes a button. The device starts to vibrate, emitting a high-frequency sound wave that rattles Ben's teeth. It picks up steam until the glass explodes in a hail of shards.

Ben retrieves the device and looks out the window. He spots a rooftop a few stories down that should be the perfect landing spot. He pulls down the flaps he sewed into his uniform, under his arms and between his legs, revealing strips of extra fabric. Thankful that he's wearing work gloves, Ben clears the glass from the bottom of the window frame and then lifts himself up, balancing on the edge. The door behind him smashes into splinters and the guards charge in, but before they can grab Ben, he jumps. As he leaps, he spreads his arms and legs and the billows of fabric fill with air, giving him the appearance of a flying squirrel. The makeshift glider slows him down just enough so that he lands on the roof with a painful thud instead of a deadly splat. He stands up and dusts himself off. He needs to figure out what's going on with that mine, and he's going to need Gavin's help to do it. Good thing the boy will be at the Governor's press conference tomorrow.

8

The position of Governor was given the power of the veto for precisely this situation. The Metro Area council made a grievous mistake. At a time when unemployment continues to plague the Metro Area and hard working families are struggling to survive, the subcommittee decided to award yet another contract to Ultracorps. While Ultracorps can and does do great things for the Metro Area, they unfortunately employ few individuals in pursuit of these functions. We need thousands of jobs, not the tens that Ultracorps would create. The contract to manage this Metro Area's water system should be awarded to a company that will be able to give back to this Metro Area through employment opportunities.

Los Angeles Metro Area Governor Robert Hayes' statement upon
Vetoing Metro Council Bill 24678

"He's going to be on the shelf for two months they tell me," Captain Murphy says.

We're standing over Victor, who is laying in a hospital bed under a medically induced coma. He looks terrible. His skin is peeling off in sheets, and his eyebrows and hair are completely singed off. Two months sounds like it might be optimistic.

"Burns are a tough injury. Heal-Blood doesn't help much. They're going to have to scrape off his dead skin every day so healthy skin can grow. It's an excruciating process," I explain.

"How about you? You look a little overcooked there yourself. How long you going to be on the disabled list?" Captain Murphy asks with concern that seems more about my ability to perform my job than my health.

"I should be fine in a few days. They set the bone in my leg so I'll have that healed up soon and they gave me a brace to keep me on my feet until then. I know my skin looks bad, but my burns weren't as bad as Victor's. The pain is the worst part, which is why they're keeping him in a coma. I don't have to deal with that. Infection is another big issue, but my mastery over my immune system helps me cope with that too. I can also accelerate the healing process, because I don't need anyone to pull the dead skin cells off of me. I can direct my body to absorb—"

"A few days," he interrupts, "That's great news. Focus on healing your face first. We're getting bombarded with interview requests for you. You guys did it. We finally got a big one. That should shut up all the Aldermen who want to close down the Field Office Program."

"Any word on the Heater? Are we going to find out what drugs he was on? When I was a food tester, I was taught to identify potential harmful additives, which included most narcotics. If I could get some of his blood I could figure out what drugs he had taken," I say.

"That isn't how it works Gavin. You injecting his blood or whatever you're suggesting isn't going give us evidence that is admissible in court. Besides you don't even know if it was drugs, maybe he had a mental breakdown," Captain Murphy says and waves his hand dismissively.

"I don't care about evidence for court. He reminded me of that Speedster we took out a couple weeks ago. Same look in the eyes, same physiological symptoms. Maybe there's some new drug that has a weird effect on Differents' systems. What about that Speedster, can you get a copy of his arrest record from the police? They should have done a toxicology test."

"There isn't any arrest report Gavin. The police let him go."

"They let Arnold go? Are you kidding me?" I say opening my mouth wide to indicate my shock.

"I thought you'd be happy they gave him a break. He was a kid who took the wrong drugs and freaked out. When a stupid human kid does that and get's arrested, he's allowed out in the morning with a stern warning. Shouldn't a stupid Different kid be treated equally?" Captain Murphy says with a smile. He's proud of what he deems to be his progressive attitude.

"The wrong drugs? Who would even want to try a drug that makes you violent, paranoid, and delusional?"

"A stupid kid. He told the cops someone gave him a bunch of pills and he took them even though he didn't know what they were. You know who takes mystery drugs? Stupid kids. I know you'd rather think the bad guy is some monster you can fight, but there isn't any bad guy, there's just stupid. Now why don't you go back to the office, have a beer, and give yourself a pat on the back for saving lives. This was a good day," Captain Murphy says and pats me on the back.

"I'm not allowed to consume alcohol, it's one of the terms of my parole. There's no point anyway, my body can process the alcohol without becoming inebriated."

"Whatever you're allowed to do to relax then. I've got to get going, the press is waiting downstairs. They're going to have to settle for me, even though you're the one they really want see, Mr. Hero," Captain Murphy says and walks out of the room.

I stare at Victor for a few minutes. He saved my life, and I didn't get a chance to thank him. When he recovers, he's going to have something new to resent me for. The press seems to be giving me all of the credit for taking down the Heater. I've already read a few articles that don't even mention Victor. Nobody wants to think that a guy who tainted a couple of World Series could change and become a hero. Severe burns and none of the credit is not a good reward for saving the day and my life.

I can repay him by figuring out what happened to the Heater. Something's not adding up. Captain Murphy might not believe it, but there's something deeper going on here. Maybe the Speedster was young and dumb enough to take a random drug, but Stephen the Heater is at least thirty, why would he be stupid enough to do that? I have to find out what was wrong with Stephen, which means I have to find him.

He's got to be in the hospital somewhere. He didn't suffer any burns, I'm not even sure he can be burnt, but between the tumble down the stairs, Victor's epic shove, and my killer right uppercut, he's got plenty of other injuries that need treating. I'm assuming they would stabilize him before moving him to a secure facility to await trial. If I find where he is, maybe I can sneak a little peek at his blood toxicology report.

I head into the hallway and start searching. I lock eyes with a nurse, who eyeballs me like she's looking at a ghost. Since I've been ignoring my pain signals, I forgot that I look like a roasted turkey leg.

"Sir, you need to go back to your room. You're badly burnt," the nurse says with concern.

"Actually, it's not as bad as it looks," I tell her and flash my "D" tattoo, "I'm with the OEC. My abilities help me deal with the burns."

"Wait… It's you, The Beast Slayer. It's really you! I just assumed you were one of the victims from this afternoon. I'm sorry I didn't recognize you because…" she says with a look that says she doesn't know how to tell me I look half-dead.

"Because my face is covered in horrible burns? You really don't have to worry about it. I don't feel any pain, and I'm a quick healer. I'm not going to have any scars or anything."

"Wow, that's amazing. You're the one who took out the Heater, and you're still on your feet. People who got within fifty feet of him are in worse shape than you are. You really are a hero," she says genuinely.

"My partner did the hard part, but thanks for saying that. Speaking of the Heater, is he still in the hospital? Do you know where he's being kept?"

"Technically I'm not supposed to tell anyone this, but I suppose you're with the OEC, so you're on the need to know list. We have a Maceo Steel room in the basement where we're keeping him. He had some bad internal bleeding and a nasty concussion. It'll be a while before we can get him stable enough to move. He's being kept under heavy Tranq sedation."

"Thank you," I say as I walk away.

When I get to the basement, it's obvious which room Stephen is being kept in. It's the one with two police officers standing in front of it. And it is a mismatched pair. There's my one friend on the force, the beautiful and lovely Maria Vasquez, and then, the horrible Detective Rose.

"Hey, if it isn't everybody's hero. Are you sure you won the fight, kid? You're looking worse than the guy in the hospital bed," Rose says with a sneer.

"My partner's the hero, I'm just the guy who is still standing. And I'm not as bad off as I look," I say to Rose before I look at Maria, "Hi." She gives me the tiniest nod.

"Can we help you?" she asks like she's never met me before. That'll bruise the ego.

"I was wondering if they did a toxicology test on Stephen. When I was fighting him, he seemed like he might have been on drugs or something like that," I ask.

"Yeah, the reports came back and the results said they're none of your business because it isn't your job," Rose say.

"I'm not trying to step on anyone's toes. I'm trying to understand what happened. If you let me in I could test his blood," I reply and hold up my hands to show I mean peace.

"Sure. You want to arrest and prosecute him too? I told you your job is done. Now, the only way you're getting through that door is over my dead body. You did your job monkey, go back to your cage," Rose says and puts his hand in his overcoat. He wants me to know he's fingering his gun.

The image of knocking him out and taking his gun flashes through my mind.

"Listen, this was a good day, you're the big hero," Maria chimes in, somehow reading my thoughts with her normal human mind. "Now it's time to let other people do their job. Go home and heal up," Maria tells me.

I take the hint and turn to walk back up the stairs. I don't know what I'm more disappointed in, that nobody seems to care what made that Heater go crazy, or that Maria acted like she didn't know me. That's not really true, it's Maria. It makes me feel bad that my mind puts more importance on a woman I'm interested in than figuring out what's making Differents go ballistic in the Metro Area.

If I want to figure out who drugged the Differents, I need to find the Speedster and ask him some questions. That's going to be impossible on my thirty minute lunch breaks. I have to devise another way out of the office.

#

I hate wearing this goofy uniform. It looks like army camouflage gear had an illegitimate child with a blue police uniform. I'm not sure what it's supposed to help me blend into, blue vomit? It's really harsh fabric too. I can feel it causing minor injuries to my still-burnt flesh.

This appearance is for a public thank you from the Governor. My guess is that it's because he's been taking a lot of heat from the Different community and its allies over his refusal to sign off on the Ultracorps management takeover of the municipal water system. He wants to show that he's a friend to Differents by congratulating me. Of course, he originally voided that Ultracorps contract because of the outcry from people in the anti-Different community who didn't want to put more power and jobs in the hands of Differents in the wake of The Beast. Such is the life a politician; you're forced to talk out of both sides of your mouth. Different-friends have more money and Different-foes have more votes and a politician needs both.

I'm lucky I was able to heal the burns on my face in time. I spent all of last night carefully directing the process of removing dead skin cells, fighting off infection, and growing new healthy skin. I didn't think I would make it. Now I'm ready to address the crowd, assuming the Governor calls me up to speak. I'm going to thank everyone for the honor, but I'm going to be sure to give the credit to Victor. That'll elicit a torrent of boos from any baseball fans in the audience, but me thanking him is the least Victor deserves.

I'm standing up on a stage with a few of the Los Angeles Metro Area's Aldermen and the Lt. Governor. Governor Hayes finally walks out onto the stage and addresses the crowd of supporters and reporters. He looks like hell. He's wearing makeup to cover the massive bags under his eyes and to give color to his pale cheeks. He looks like he hasn't slept in days. Has he had to work that hard to deal with fallout from the fire?

He starts addressing the crowd. He speaks loudly so everyone can hear him, but it doesn't sound like he's yelling. I don't think I could pull that off with my voice; he's got a lot of experience at this.

"Thank you all for coming here today. As you know, we had an incident involving a disturbed Different individual. For reasons unknown, this individual threatened the lives of myself, and many of this Metro Area's best and brightest. We do not know what motivated this person, but we do know this press conference could have been morbid. I could be standing here telling you all about a great tragedy that befell our great Metro Area. I could be listing lives lost and reporting on entire swaths of Metro Area burnt to the ground. Or perhaps I would not be standing here at all. But that is not what happened. Instead, there was only a few thousand dollars in property damage. Instead, there were only a few dozen injuries with everyone expected to make a full recovery!" the Governor says, then pauses while the crowd applauds.

"There is one man to thank for this, and we all know who it is. It is not the first time that he has come to the aid of our Metro Area, although this time he had the legal authority to do so. Let's all give a big round of applause for OEC Agent, The Beast Slayer, and the LA Metro Area's own, Gavin Stillman," he says and indicates for me to step forward.

I'm greeted by an uproarious round of applause. I'd be lying if I said it didn't feel pretty good. I'd also be lying if I said I didn't feel guilty about the fact that I'm getting all the congratulations while Victor, the true hero, is still sitting in a hospital bed months away from recovering. The public doesn't want the truth. They want a hero, and they already consider me one. I tell myself I have no choice in the matter. I'll fix things when I get a chance at the microphone. The Governor addresses the crowd again, but instead of calling me over, he starts his own speech back up.

"Gavin, you have accrued a debt this Metro Area can never repay. You have also showcased the great adaptability of this Metro Area. After the actions of the terrorist Different The Beast, we all said never again. We said it was time to get the Office of Exceptional Cases on call in the Metro Area so that we could be protected from dangerous Different individuals. Gavin has proven we succeeded. The OEC is here, and they can protect this Metro Area. We adapted. Los Angeles has always adapted. When the city of Los Angeles needed water, we found it. When the nation needed Los Angeles to be more than a city, we transformed ourselves into a Metro Area. Adapting is what we do," the Governor pauses for another clapping break.

"It is because I know this Metro Area can adapt that I can take some measure of solace, before making an announcement that breaks my heart. Unfortunately, certain issues have come up in my private life that render me unable to perform the duties required of me as Governor of this Metro Area. That is why, effective immediately; I must resign as Governor of the Los Angeles Metro Area. I leave you in the immensely capable hands of my Lieutenant Governor, Lewis Khan. It has been my most esteemed honor to serve you all as your Governor. I cannot thank you enough for giving me this opportunity.

"Unfortunately, I will not be taking questions. I hope you can all understand my desire for privacy on this matter. I now yield the microphone, and the Governorship of this great Metro Area, to Lewis Khan."

Well, that was unexpected. Governor Khan steps up and is immediately bombarded by questions from all sides. The former Governor quickly makes his way off the stage, ignoring the barrage of questions. The Aldermen on the stage start filing off and I take the cue to follow them. It's time to give the new Governor the floor. I was worried about all the questions I was going to get after this press conference. I don't have to worry about that anymore. All of the reporters forgot I existed the moment Governor Hayes made his announcement. I start making my way through the crowd to meet up with Linda and Captain Murphy, so we can head back to the OEC office.

As I push through the crowd, I feel a tapping on my shoulder. I turn around, and I'm greeted by the sight of Ben, wearing a baseball cap and a fake beard to hide his identity.

"That was a surprise, huh?" Ben says with a smirk.

"What are you doing here? Aren't you a wanted fugitive? I can't be seen here with you. There are cops everywhere," I respond.

"Look around Gavin, does it seem like anyone's paying attention to us? I could be dressed like a clown and no one would notice me."

"Okay, fine. What do you want? Why are you here? Do you have any more friendships you want me to ruin?" I demand.

"I'm guessing it didn't go so well with your friend the giant?"

"No it did not go well. I managed to repair then immediately destroy my relationship with Gary thanks to the crazy ideas you put in my head. There's no big conspiracy. He doesn't know anything about Santa Fe or Nita trying to have The Beast kill me, or if The Beast is still alive. You were wrong about Gary. He wasn't my friend because Nita ordered him to be, he was my friend because he liked me. At least he used to like me before you convinced me to accuse him of being part of some sort of massive conspiracy whose purpose you don't know and whose existence you have no evidence of," I whisper as loudly as I can to show my anger.

"Okay, we'll call that one a dead end," Ben says with no reaction to my angry rant. "But that's not why I came here to see you. Aren't you surprised the Governor resigned? Popular politicians don't usually leave office by choice. He was probably going to win reelection next year, then who knows? Governors have always made for good Presidential candidates, especially successful ones."

"You heard him. It's a personal matter. Do you know anything more about it?"

"Not exactly, but I do know it Nita is involved. The Governor shut down the Ultracorps takeover of the municipal water system. Nita is not going to take that lying down. She sent The Beast out to protect that contract before. She showed she's willing to do whatever it takes to get that contract."

"How could Nita get the Governor to resign?" I say somehow finding myself sucked in.

"I'm still trying to figure that one out. Lately, I've been consumed with trying to find out what happened to a copper mine located outside old St. Louis; for some reason I feel like they are related. It was a highly productive mine, then about a month ago out of the blue it shut down in a single day."

"You feel like they are related? Aren't you supposed to be a genius? That doesn't sound very scientific."

"Because I'm a genius I know the value of my intuition," Ben says with a smug grin I can see behind his fake beard.

"It was probably a Plague outbreak; you know how Cabot's bacteria love to eat copper."

"I may or may not have committed some trespassing recently and looked at the records for Plague containment teams, but none were sent to St. Louis recently. It wasn't easy to get those records, let me tell you, I pretended to be an exterminator there to kill some roaches..."

"I don't care about a copper mine. What could that possible have to do with the governor? More importantly, even if I believed you that this matters—which, let's be clear, I don't—why are you telling me this? I don't know anything about mines or St. Louis."

"Because there are some records relating to Manna deliveries in the St. Louis area that have been redacted. Lots of Manna, maybe enough to feed The Beast. Maybe Hayes found out about it, and that's why Nita had to get rid of him. I need a way to look at the paper files to know for sure. Ultracorps keeps a lot of records in the lab facility you used to work in. I need you to go back to the lab, find a way into the archives, and look at the hardcopies of the files to see if that mine has really been shut down."

"Sure, I'll violate my parole by leaving the OEC office without permission, trespass on Ultracorps property, and then steal official documents. All because you think a mine shutting down two thousand miles away was a little suspicious. Why don't you just have me try to beat an explanation out of the former Governor? That would actually involve breaking fewer laws. Do you think I'm stupid? I know you're talking about The Beast again to manipulate me. He's dead. He fell from a three hundred-story tower. He's not in some mine in St. Louis."

"There is one way to find out for sure," Ben says suggestively.

"I don't have any way to get into the lab, and even if I did, I don't see why any of this matters. Mines shut down. Not everything is a conspiracy, Ben. I think you might need help," I say sincerely.

Ben sees something behind me and his face goes white. "Good idea. I'll make an appointment," he says hurriedly. "Ultracorps is going to get that water contract. You'll see." Then he abruptly turns around and hustles away from me.

I turn around to see what scared him off. It is Officer Maria Vasquez and she's headed right for me. My mind immediately recalls yesterday when she acted like she didn't know me in the hospital. I push it out of my head. I don't want it to affect my attitude. I need her help even if my ego is bruised, no matter how black and blue.

"Hey Gavin," she says with a smile that shows no awareness of how rude she was last time. "A shout out from the Governor. Quite the honor, even if he did resign afterwards."

"Oh, I didn't know you remembered my name," I say. I'm doing a great job of keeping the last time out of my mind.

"I'm sorry about that. Rose is no fan of Differents and he's got a lot of sway at my precinct. If I cross him I could wind up working transport. That would mean I couldn't look at the Heater's blood test results."

"You saw the results? What was he on?" I ask finally letting my purpose overcome my hurt feelings.

"Here," she says and hands me a scrap of paper with a long list of chemicals on it. It's a mixture of both prescription medication and street drugs. "It was hard to get. Rose was outside the room most of the night, but I managed to talk to the Lab tech in her office when I said I had to go to the bathroom."

"All of this was inside him? It doesn't make any sense. Who would mix all these drugs? Are you sure you haven't heard of anyone else taking these drugs?"

"Nope, and I'd hear if it was happening in other precincts. That mix is a recipe for some wild stories, Different or human," she says with a smile.

"Why would two Differents be the only ones taking these drugs, and why weeks apart? I need to talk to that Speedster."

"That's not all. The street drugs on the list, a whole stash of those drugs went missing from our evidence room a couple of days ago. Now, this isn't exactly a freak occurrence, my captain is yelling about something new that went missing from evidence every week but still…"

"It's quite the coincidence," I say.

"That might be all it is. Coincidences happen."

"Like all the dead Differents in your precinct?"

"Touché. Just don't let your crazy investigation get in the way of my crazy investigation," she says with a smile.

"There is enough crazy to go around."

9

My Forgotten Sons may ask themselves where this leaves them. My first children have their strengths. Even in the harsh world I create, it is doubtless they will continue to live on for some time. I give my Chosen Sons salvation. To you, my Forgotten Sons, I give damnation.

Chosen Sons: 46

The Beast cannot take it anymore. He has been locked in this room for what seems like an eternity. He healed from his fall weeks ago. It has been nearly that long since the voice on the loudspeaker spoke to him. The voice that was so concerned not long ago has gone silent.

When he first awoke in this room, he actually thought it was some kind of purgatory. The bare metal room and nothing but the pain of the injuries he received from the fall felt like a punishment, but then the voice on the loudspeaker promised him that he was alive.

The Beast used to think it was the voice God, or at least one of His servants. After all, it must have been divine intervention that saved him when he fell from the top of the Shimmering Tower. The Beast is strong, but even he is not strong enough to survive such a fall without the help of the Almighty. He has vague memories of one of his Chosen Son brothers carrying him into the cage. He thought it was God sending an angel of salvation.

Then someone else came into the cage, a human. The Beast could smell the man even under a layer of FerteSilk body armor. The man fed The Beast for those first few days. The Beast was fed through a straw since he had so many broken bones. Someone went to the trouble of making a meat milkshake. In a few days, thanks to the food, The Beast was able to heal enough to crawl around his tiny room. Then the man stopped coming, but the food did not. A slot in the side of the room opened, and meat arrived. The Beast can still taste the bounty of different animals that came from that slot.

One day the voice on the loudspeaker asked, "Are you back to your old self?"

"I am, praise the Lord," The Beast replied.

That was the last time The Beast heard the voice. That day, instead of meat, food made of Manna came through the slot. Manna which came from a Chosen Son slave. No one should be allowed to eat that slop, least of all a Chosen Son whom God speaks to directly. That was when he first started to question why the Lord sent him to this place. The Beast refused to eat the Manna for two days until his hunger finally overwhelmed him.

When the Manna came through the slot, The Beast realized where he was being held, Great Basin Prison. A fortress built into the side of the mountain, designed to hold Chosen Sons. This is where the most "dangerous" Chosen Sons are kept, those who refuse to live by rules forced on them by lesser creatures, those whose blessings from God were so great the humans are too afraid to let them live to their potential. So instead, they throw them into cells made of Maceo Steel and forget about them. Locking away the humans' fear and guilt over Differents in a jail cell.

Why would God save The Beast just to let him be imprisoned by weak, worthless humans? Is it a punishment for The Beast's many sins? Did God decide that death was too good for The Beast? Does he want him to suffer the humiliation of being subject to the whims of the Forgotten Sons?

Maybe that is not why. God told him his purpose back in the Los Angeles Metro Area. The Beast was made for death. God made him in order to hasten the demise of the Forgotten Sons. That means The Beast was brought to this prison by God in order to enact that purpose. God led him to this place so he could kill the humans imprisoning the Chosen Sons and free his powerful brothers who are being held here. The Beast is meant to lead a new army, an army powerful enough to free the entire race of Chosen Sons. This revelation makes The Beast giddy with excitement. God is not angry with him. He simply requires The Beast to execute the task he was made to perform: killing.

He is going to need to find a way out of this cage. It will be no small feat. The cage is made of one of God's miracles, Maceo Steel. An unbreakable substance made by a fellow Chosen Son. The humans worked him to death, and, as an added insult, Maceo's miracle is now used to cage his brethren. As strong as God made The Beast, he is not strong enough to break out of this jail cell. He needs to think of another way out.

There are three openings to the cage: a large door that has remained closed since his nurse stopped coming in, a small air vent covered by a Maceo Steel grate which, even if The Beast could pull the grate off, is too small to climb through, and a sliding door that opens to drop in the Manna food, which is too small to climb up as well. That door is the key. When the door closes, it does so with great force. The Beast does not know why the humans are keeping him here, but whatever the purpose, they obviously want him alive and healthy. The door could change that.

He spends hours waiting for the door to open; he cannot be sure how long, as he has no way to keep time. He cannot see the sun, and the WormLight that brightens his room shines constantly. Eventually, he watches the door open and a Pho-Plastic container full of Manna food drops down, usually a faux-meat flavored abomination. The Beast asks the Lord for protection, then places his arm inside the open slot.

The door slams shut. The Beast howls in pain.

The bone in The Beast's left forearm shatters. The sliding door pulverized it, sending out shards of bone that cut through his arm like razor blades. The door closed with the force of a speeding train. He knows that he should be thankful his arm did not get cut off. The blinding agony in his arm makes gratitude difficult. He lets out a continuous stream of pain-induced howls, his voice cracking because his vocal cords have not been used in months.

"Are you injured? What happened?" the voice on the loudspeaker asks.

"My arm, it's caught in the food door. Please, hurry," The Beast says.

"How did you get your arm stuck in the door?"

"It was on accident. Help me, please."

"It did not look like an accident."

"I was curious. What do you want from me? I got nothing to do down here. Are you going to send help? I'm dying here."

"Hold please," the voice answers.

The Beast had not realized they could see him. There must be a video monitor somewhere in the cage. That complicates things. He is going to have to wait to free himself, which means enduring more agony from his trapped arm. The Beast prays he is strong enough to do what must be done when the door to his cell opens.

After what feels like an eternity, the speaker turns on. "We are sending assistance. Be advised, the team we are sending is armed and will not hesitate to use deadly force if this is a trap."

"I'm the one who's trapped. I'm in agony. I won't do nothing. I swear it."

Luckily for The Beast, lying to a Forgotten Son is no sin at all. It is the same as lying to a dog.

He hears men coming down the hall, at least five of them. He can smell the gunpowder and oil from their weapons. The voice was not bluffing about using force. They want to keep The Beast alive, but they are not going to risk their own lives for it.

He waits until he hears the key in the door. Then he shoves his right hand into the gap in the trap door where his left arm is pinned. He pushes with all his might, stripping the automatic door's gears and extracting his busted arm.

"Wait, stop!" the voice on the loudspeaker yells.

It is too late. As soon as a guard opens the door to The Beast's cell the tiniest crack, The Beast rips it open the rest of the way. He is greeted by five men covered head to toe in ForteSilk body armor. They are carrying high-caliber machine guns. The Beast charges into the group of guards, knocking them down like human bowling pins.

The Beast picks up one of the armored men and slams him into the hallway wall with bone-crushing force. The armor might protect the man from The Beast's claws, but it does little to absorb the massive impact. The man's insides shatter and burst. The Beast reaches out and grabs another guard by his body armor, throwing the man fifty feet down the hallway where he hits a wall like a ton of bricks.

One of the three remaining guards scrambles to his feet and attempts to stick The Beast with a syringe. The Beast catches the man's arm in mid-stab and picks him up by the wrist. The Beast swings the man like baseball bat into one of the other guards, who is struggling to get to his feet. The Beast feels bones break inside of both bodies.

The fifth guard opens fire with his machine gun. He is terrified and firing wildly, but some of his panicked shots manage to hit The Beast. The creature leans into the line of fire with his already crippled left arm, taking several bullets to his shoulder and bicep. The bullets cut deep. The guard has a powerful gun, but none of the shots hit anything vital on The Beast.

The guard's machine gun clicks empty. The Beast grins and knocks the man down, then jumps up and down on top of him, pulverizing the man's bones. He does the same to all the other guards. Now The Beast stands alone in the empty hallway. He considers tearing open one of the guards' body armor to eat the meat inside, but that will take time. Besides, these guards had the audacity to attack a Chosen Son. Their sin should not be rewarded with a trip to heaven.

The Beast heads down the hallway, looking for fellow Chosen Sons he can free. To his surprise, the other rooms on the level are not prison cells. They have hospital beds inside them, or rows of desks covered with test tubes. He even finds a room full of cleaning supplies. He does not know what to make of his findings. They do not seem right for a prison, but perhaps he was being kept in a separate part of the complex. The gifts God gave him are especially great. The Beast is going to have to make his way through the rest of the prison if he wants to free his brothers.

His searching leads him to a stairwell. The only way to go is up.

He stops, takes a deep breath, and listens, letting his senses inform him. He smells many odors coming from upstairs, including an abundance of gun oil and gunpowder. He can identify many different people, all of them human. He does not catch a whiff a single Chosen Son. The Beast finds this perplexing, if this is truly Great Basin prison, he should be overwhelmed by the scent of his brothers.

He is going to need to get some answers from the Forgotten Sons. Unfortunately, he already killed the humans down on his level. He can hear more of them up the stairs. They are barking orders at each other and moving furniture to mount a defense. They know The Beast is coming. He does not plan to keep them waiting long.

10

The question we should be asking ourselves is not if we need the Field Office Program, it should be why don't we change the law and let the OEC take on a larger crime fighting role? Thieves, murderers, and rapists abound in the Metro Area. Our brave police officers do all they can to help, but I don't think I'm being controversial when I say that they are overstretched. There are simply too many people in the Metro Area to police with a conventional force. Differents could change that. Speedsters could chase down the most evasive criminal. Strong-Men could enforce the law without fear of reprisal in even the most dangerous corners of the Metro Area. Telepaths could discern the guilty from the innocent. We have the people we need to make Los Angeles safe again. We just need the courage to use them.

"We Must Not Be Timid" by Forest Brown, think.Net News LA

"In one of his first acts since taking office, newly appointed Governor Lewis Khan reversed a decision made by former Governor Hayes, which voided a contract the Metro Area council had awarded to Ultracorps for the management and expansion of the Metro Area's Water system. Governor Khan emphasized that the Metro Area cannot allow itself to make decisions based purely on panic and claimed Governor Hayes exceeded the scope of his office when he vetoed the Metro Council action. Governor Khan went on to laud the actions of Gavin Stillman and the newly created OEC Field Offices. He pointed to the OEC as proof that the best policy is management of Different labor, not the abandonment of it. Now, on to sports..." The radio keeps squawking, but I stop paying attention. I can hear Captain Murphy on his way in.

"Hey Gavin, I just got off think.Net with a Doctor Wright. Why did you give him my info? You used to work for him in the Oasis Burger labs right? He was going on and on about some sort of problem with the water in something. Anyway, he said he needed to see you. He wants you to check over some data, said it couldn't be done over think.Net. He wanted my permission to let you out. We don't have anything going on here, so why don't you go ahead and see if you can help him out. Take the P-Train, that way you'll be ready if something comes up," Captain Murphy says.

I slow down time so I can consider my response. I never worked for a Dr. Wright, but according to the news, Ben was right about Ultracorps getting that water contract. Something tells me he's the one behind this. The question is, should I go? I had convinced myself that Ben was crazy, but maybe I was wrong. He was right about the water, who knows what else he's right about.

The problem is that I don't get to leave the office much during the day and I have another investigation that needs my attention. I need to figure out who's been drugging the Differents. This is my chance to talk to that Speedster. Maybe he can tell me something about the man who gave him the drugs. That investigation needs to be the priority. Maybe I can make it to Ultracorps employee housing and to the lab? How long has it been since he talked? I should have responded by now.

"Always nice to be needed," I finally say.

Captain Murphy gives me a strange look, but I don't think he's suspicious, just weirded out by my being a weirdo. I get up and start to walk away, but Captain Murphy stops me by putting his hand on my shoulder. My heart sinks in my chest.

"One more thing and it's a bit of a tough one. That Heater you guys caught, Stephen something. I got a note from the District Attorney. Stephen had some sort of medical complication. He didn't make it."

"He's dead?"

"I'm sure it had nothing to do with what you guys did. Something went wrong while keeping him under sedation. They were preparing him to be moved to Great Basin Prison. Don't beat yourself up about it. It doesn't take away from anything that you did. These things happen. If Stephen didn't want to die, he shouldn't have gone on a rampage. Anyway, thought you should know. Give me a heads up when you're on your way back from the lab."

I head out of the OEC building and walk two blocks to the raised garage that houses our P-Train. We have our own little slice of tracks, which leads into the main system. I climb a ladder to a Maceo Steel door, which I unlock. I haven't gotten to drive the train since my initial training. Victor usually does the driving. Six-year-old me would have had his mind blown at the thought that I get to drive my own train.

I step into the train and head to the controls. P-Trains are designed to be simple. There's one lever, which I push forward to accelerate and pull back on to decelerate or reverse. There's also an emergency brake. I check my fuel gage, and there are still plenty of Slugs in the tank. I pull the crank to spark the engine. Soon the bits of dried carbon chains excreted by bacteria, or Slugs as everyone calls them, are burning hot enough to evaporate the water that powers the P-Train's steam engine. I release the brake and push forward on the velocity. It turns out that twenty-year-old me still thinks this is pretty cool.

#

I can hear shuffling behind the door. Someone's home and it's taking them a long time to answer my knock. Arnold is still injured like I knew he'd be. Counter-intuitively, Speedsters, like Strong-Men, heal slowly. They have complex and dense, muscles, cartilage, nerves, and bone, all of which take longer to regenerate than normal human cells. That's one of the reasons The Beast was so unique. He was fast, and strong, and he could heal like a low-level Regenerator. I see a shadow pass in front of the light coming through the peephole.

"Go away! He told me I wouldn't ever have to see you again!" Arnold yells from behind the door.

"Arnold? I just want to talk. It will only take a minute," I say in a calm measured voice.

"No way! I know my rights, I don't have to talk to you! Please go. I want to forget the whole thing ever happened," Arnold says, his voice moving from outrage to pathetic pleading over the course of his yell.

"I'd like it all to go away too. That's why you should invite me in and answer my questions and I'll leave quickly. Of course, I could stay out here screaming so all your neighbors can hear us air dirty laundry! Will that help it go away!" I yell in a booming voice that echoes in the hallway of the Ultracorps Employee housing apartment building.

"Okay, Okay," Arnold says and pulls the door open.

He doesn't look great, he's skinny as a rail and the cast on his leg is filthy.

"Are you okay? Is your leg going to heal?" I ask.

"Maybe in a couple more weeks… Don't pretend you care about me; tell me why you're here."

"I want to know what happened a few weeks ago. I want to know why you went crazy in that restaurant."

"Uh, it's like I told the detective, some guy I know who likes to party, he handed me a bunch of pills and I, uh, took em," Arnold says, but he's stumbling over his words. His face has gone ghost white.

"A man handed you mysterious pills and you took them?"

"Yeah, uh, yeah. I know stupid right? Who does something like that? I guess I was bored with my job. I mean all day everyday it's pick up food from here go there, now go there. It's a real drag," Arnold says while looking down at his feet. He hasn't made eye contact in several seconds, I can see his carotid artery pulse in his neck indicating an elevated heart rate, and he's rambling. All symptoms the human body displays in order to cope with the stress of concealing the truth.

"Arnold, you're lying and you aren't very good at it."

Arnold puts his face in his hands. "He said if I stuck to the story there wouldn't be any more trouble."

"Who told you there wouldn't be any trouble?" I ask.

Arnold doesn't answer.

"Who?" I demand and get in his face.

"I don't have to talk to you. I know the law." Arnold tightens his jaw and looks away.

"Don't you know I'm the Vigilante? I don't care about the law," I say and pick myself up to my full impressive height.

I feel terrible about intimidating this poor guy, but I have a ticking clock. I need answers and I need them now.

Arnold picks up on my implications and let's out an exasperated sigh.

"Fine. He lied to me anyway. He told me there wouldn't be any problems, but Ultracorps had a new job assignment for me after I got out of the hospital. Waste Picker. If I do ever heal, I get to use my speed to pick through tons of garbage every day."

I give him a dirty look that says I don't care about his problems. That does sound terrible though. I can only imagine the horrors one finds at the other end of the Hoover tube.

"I don't remember his name but it was the detective I saw in the hospital. He said as long as I stuck with the story, I'd be on my way and I could stay out of jail. If I didn't tell the story, he'd make sure I went away for a long time."

"What's the real story?"

"The real story is that I don't know what happened to me. I don't know why I went crazy," Arnold says and he looks me right in the eyes.

"There wasn't a man who gave you drugs?"

"No. The last thing I remember was eating my lunch, then I woke up in jail and everyone told me I had freaked out," Arnold says and he believes every word he's saying.

"Why did the detective want you to say a man gave you the drugs?"

"I don't know that either. But I didn't have any other explanations for the freak-out and he threatened to charge me with a whole list of crimes. I figured the lie wasn't going to hurt anybody. Maybe the detective didn't want to do the paperwork?" Arnold suggests.

Or he didn't want an arrest report and the accompanying toxicology scan. Could Rose really be the one drugging the Differents? He was at the gala where the Heater freaked out and he could have stolen the narcotics from the evidence room at the police station, but what's his motive? What does he have to gain by making Differents go berserk?

"Uhh, that's all I know man. Is there something else you need?" Arnold asks and I realize I've been standing there and thinking for ten seconds.

"If anyone but me asks, stick to your story." I say and head out of the apartment.

That conversation didn't take long. I still have time to do what Ben asked and check the Manna delivery records of those mines in St. Louis. I wasn't sure I wanted to risk it, but after this bit of success, I'm feeling lucky. Maybe I can make some headway in my second insane theory investigation of the day.

#

Nobody stops me when I walk into the lab. I pass by the receptionist, who gives me the barest minimum of a wave as I walk by. That's what she used to do when I came to work every day. Security isn't much of a concern in a lab that mostly focuses on food additives and crash test systems for trains. Even less people would have interest in hardcopy files of Manna product deliveries, but that's just what I'm here for.

I make my way through the building, keeping my head down so I don't get spotted and have to answer some awkward questions. Still, I can't help but pick my eyes up for a second as I pass by my old lab. I spot Dr. Cole and Dr. Wilson hard at work. They're hunched over a Bunsen burner, and they both looked annoyed. I bet they miss me, or at least I'd like to imagine they do.

I continue past my old haunts and proceed towards the filing area. Just as I'm about to make it, something I never thought I'd be unhappy about happens. I run into my old friend/crush Sarah, or Crash Test Dummy as we called her. She rides in trains that are crashed on purpose in the lab in order to see what injuries she sustains. One of the possible career opportunities available to Regenerators. Luckily for me, she also moonlights as an organ donor. Back when The Beast gutted me, I needed new kidneys, and she was there to provide them. She walks out of the kitchen and at first continues right by me, but then she stops in her tracks.

"Well, if it isn't The Beast Slayer. What are you doing here? I thought you were still on parole?" she asks.

"One of my old bosses asked me to come down and help him with something," I reply. Please no follow-up questions, please no follow-up questions.

"I saw you take out that Looney Toons Heater on think.Net. Impressive work. You keep adding to that hero resume of yours."

"Only if I have friends to keep me alive. My partner is the one who should really get the credit for beating the Heater. He saved my life. Getting saved is a pattern I follow. Thankfully I didn't need any organs this time," I say, trying to sound grateful for her saving my life after The Beast gutted me.

"Remember what I said, any time you need a kidney, consider it yours. You keep getting into fights with maniac Differents and you might need to take me up on the offer."

"All part of working for the OEC."

"Sounds like it beats being a lab rat, in the excitement category at least. Enjoy getting to live your old boring life for one more day. Have some Palm Fries to relive your glory days. I'll see you around," she says and walks away.

That was a relief. It could have gone much worse. I have no idea how much she knows about me accusing Gary of being part of some conspiracy with Nita. I never mentioned her, but it was implied she and my teacher Larry were a part of it. Either she never heard about my accusations, or she's a hell of an actress.

I head into the room stuffed with cabinets, stuffed with folders, stuffed with papers. According to Ben, that Ultracorps copper mine shut down too quickly for any normal explanation. He thinks the mine is still being used, just for something else, like holding dangerous Differents, maybe even The Beast.

According to the police, The Beast's corpse was sucked down the ruptured Hoover main. They claim he was torn to shreds by the debris in the pipe, and that's why no trace of him was ever found.

But what if a body was never found because he didn't really die? What if Ultracorps, what if Nita, is keeping him hidden from the government? The Beast thought he was talking to God when it looked like he was accessing think.Net. If Nita truly was impersonating the Lord, maybe she has more holy missions for him.

I know that I can't be objective when it comes to The Beast. I know I have a whole host of unprocessed trauma and emotions surrounding my first confrontation with that monster, and all of the people he killed before I stopped him. Maybe I am connecting dots that aren't really there because I desperately want a chance to make up for my past failures. But just because I'm biased doesn't mean I'm wrong. Ben is insane when it comes to his theories about Nita, but he was right about the water contract.

No matter what that mine has become, as long as people are working there that facility will need food, which means Manna product deliveries. Ben said he was locked out of the think.Net files, so the hardcopies are our only hope.

The search does not go quickly. These files are kept as a formality in case of some sort of catastrophic failure of the record keeping Librarian. Nobody has ever bothered organizing the files in an accessible way. I know I didn't give it much thought back when part of my job was filing.

It takes me more than an hour of digging to find the files related to the mine. It was receiving regular Manna product shipments for awhile, five hundred pounds of various foodstuffs a week, which sounds about right for a mine and its workers. Those deliveries suddenly stop about a month ago. I can see an order to halt shipments, but there's no sign of continued deliveries. I suppose that's not surprising; even if Ultracorps is hiding something, they aren't going to leave it out to find in the files so easily.

I start digging through the records of other nearby mines. Ultracorps owns four other productive mines around old St. Louis. As I look through the records, something strikes me about the mine closest to the one that was shut down. On the same week that the deliveries were halted to my mine, the mine next door had a fifty pound weekly increase in their own Manna product delivery. Now maybe some of the workers were moved from the closed down mine to the one next door, but maybe not. Maybe those fifty pounds are going somewhere else.

That's enough to feed The Beast, but not by much. I don't know how Nita would have been able to get The Beast all the way out to St. Louis, or why, but maybe that was the only Ultracorps facility they were confident would hold him. Or maybe they've been moving him around so no one finds out they are keeping him alive. Or maybe I'm giving in to paranoid delusions because I'm still angry that fighting The Beast put me in jail and ended my relationship with Becky. I replace the files I was looking at, but not before making sure I've memorized every word and number. Then I turn off the WormLight and head out of the room.

I feel the ground beneath my feet start to shake. Either there's an earthquake, or Gary is here making his deliveries. I follow my ears to the source of the tremors, and I indeed see Gary. He's carrying a box larger than I am on each arm. It doesn't look like it's straining him in the slightest. I lock eyes with him, and I watch his face run through a wide spectrum of emotion in less than a second. First he's confused, then I see the beginnings of a smile. He shakes off the smile, there's a flash of anger in his eyes, and then he turns stone-faced. He keeps walking towards me.

"Hey Gary, long time no see. How're your deliveries going?" I ask.

Gary keeps coming at me without reacting to my words at all. I have to quickly step out of his way to avoid being trampled. I guess he's still mad at me. He should be. I'm mad at myself for letting Ben talk me into questioning him. I should have demanded more evidence if I was going to believe Ben's theories. Maria isn't the genius Ben is, and neither am I, yet we were able to find evidence for our wacko theory about the serial killer. Why couldn't Ben give me more? I suddenly feel foolish for coming here. I'm risking my freedom and my reputation for some guy who's at best a little nutty, and at worst a complete psychopath who is angry that he lost his job as Head Librarian to a little girl named Nita. I've even convinced myself that some asinine changes in food delivery schedules are meaningful intel.

I've let Ben turn me into an ass yet again.

#

"We got another call," Captain Murphy says. "Don't worry, it's not an emergency, there's no perp on the scene. It's a dead body. They think a Different might have done the killing. I talked to the officer who took the call, Maria something. She confirmed that it wasn't a mistake this time. It's on the corner of Vermont and Pico. It's your first solo call, be careful. If you need anything, Linda and I will be here." I can't tell if he's being supportive or condescending.

"Good luck, Gavin. I'm sure you'll do great. And make sure you hurry back. Martin got the job at WWOR, which means he's moving back in the Metro Area. I'm cooking tonight in celebration, my world famous Meat Sauce. I sprang for the real stuff. If I'm feeling generous, there might be some extra," Linda adds with a wink.

"That's fantastic news! Congratulations. Now you know I'll be quick," I say and walk out.

I feel a like fugitive as I step out of the OEC office and it feels good. I know this isn't a real call. I know that the victim is a Different, not the perpetrator. I know that Maria made this call so I can help her, and it was no mistake. That means I'm violating my parole. I'm fine with lying to Captain Murphy; it's Linda I feel a little bad about. At least she had a good day with her son moving back to town.

It doesn't take long to get to the Vermont Ave and Pico Blvd intersection. When I get close I stop the P-train and activate a unique feature available in law enforcement trains. I flip a switch, activating a mechanism that lifts the train off of the top of the tracks and attaches itself to a support beam holding up the tracks. That way, my train stays where I need it while other trains can flow by freely. Regular P-Trains have to stop at the designated stops.

I drop the ForteSilk ladder, lock the door, and climb down. It's a couple of blocks to where the victim is located. I get there and see

Maria waving me into a taped-off alley. Waving was not necessary, as the crimson river of blood flowing out of the alley and into the gutter is a big clue as to where the body is.

In the alley I see a young woman lying face down in a massive pool of blood. If she didn't die from another injury, then she drowned in her own blood.

"We have to be quick. I waited as long as I could to call it in to my captain, but I had to check in. Detective You-Know-Who is on his way with some more beat cops. We've got five minutes tops. It looks like another stabbing," Maria says diving right in.

"Just like the first time I met you. Were there any witnesses? How long ago did this happen?"

"Not very long ago. No one saw the attack. A nice old man saw her collapse into the alley, and she was dead in a minute. All she said was, 'What happened, what happened?' before she died. I took the old man's information and told him we would contact him later. I didn't want him to see you here."

"Who was the victim?"

"She was some kind of human magnet or something. According to her records, she was used by Ultracorps to find leftover metal in the Non-Assisted Area. She wasn't anyone important; she barely made enough to cover her Cost Of Living Obligations. No prior arrests, never been suspected of anything. She's been out of Section 26 for just a few months. It's hard to believe she made any enemies that quickly."

I lean down and stick my finger in a pool of the blood, then I put my finger in my mouth.

"That's disgusting; what are you doing?" Maria asks in horror.

"I'm being a human crime-lab. I can tell if there are any drugs or other toxins in her system, at least the ones I'm familiar with. I used to do this for a living. I was a fast-food tester for Oasis Burger. I would tell them how new artificial additives would affect the product. Palm Fries tasted a tiny bit better."

"What's the nauseating verdict?"

"It takes me a minute. I have to wait until the blood hits my digestive track. I can move things through my system more quickly than normal people, but it still takes time."

"You really know how to talk to a woman, don't you?"

"I don't get to see many locked in the OEC office all night. So what do you say? Should we turn her over? See what killed her?"

"It's all you," she says and throws her hands up. "I've already broken enough department rules by contacting you and waiting to call in to my captain. I don't need to add tainting a crime scene to my list of accomplishments. Besides, can't you make your fingerprints fall off or something, in case they actually check for prints this time?"

"I can do something like that."

I cut off the blood flow from the tips of my fingers and draw out water from the cells there. It should be enough to obfuscate my finger prints. While I'm in my internal world, I also start analyzing the chemicals in the dead woman's blood. I tried to describe the process once to my old boss at the Oasis Burger Labs. I told him it's like how you know that a pin is sticking in your arm, or that a hair is tickling your throat. I can tell these compounds are inside my body, and if I have enough experience with them, I can identify the particular substances. As part of my training as a food tester, I was exposed to a wide variety of toxins and poisons so I would know how to spot them if they made their way into the recipes.

"Nothing strange in her blood. No poisons or narcotics, at least any of the ones I'm familiar with," I say as I lean down and flip the young woman over.

As soon as I turn her over, we can see what killed her. She has a single large stab wound in her chest. It's placed perfectly. The attacker, found a spot right between the ribs, plunged through one of her lungs, and cut into her heart. This could have happened inside a hospital and she still would have died.

"Looks like her aorta was severed. She bled to death in less than a minute. I don't see any other wounds besides the one to the chest, do you?" I ask.

"No. That's a lucky stab for a mugger, or unlucky I guess,"

Maria answers.

"Very lucky. And not only that, whoever did it knew they hit their mark. Otherwise, they would have kept stabbing," I say.

"You're right. Every stabbing I've ever seen had defensive wounds on the hands. Nobody gets stabbed once."

"So we either have an incredibly skillful mugger who targeted a Different because he likes a challenge, or someone did this on purpose, someone wanted to kill her. Your serial killer theory is looking more and more likely."

"They were waiting for the victim. Look at that pile of old concrete in the corner, the dust on the top is all spread around. Someone was sitting there," Maria says. I follow her eyes to the pile, and she's absolutely correct.

"Wow, good eyes. You don't even need me."

"I'm glad you're impressed. I wonder if it's because I've got years of experience on you, or the professional training and preparation," she says dryly. "I told you, I don't need you. It's just nice to have someone else to work with. I've been looking into these killings alone for a long time."

I slow down time to come up with a smart-aleck answer, but I'm stopped by the sound of footsteps approaching. Several men loaded down with equipment that jingles as they walk. Police officers and they are headed this way. They are already close. I wasn't paying enough attention to my ears.

"Your buddies are almost here," I say to Maria.

"You have to get out of here now. They can't know I called you. That'd be the end of me on the force, or at least the end of us working together to try to solve these murders," she says with panic in her voice.

"It's too late. If I walk out of the alley they'll see me."

"You have to do something!"

I slow down time while I scan my surroundings. The other end of the alley is blocked by large chunks of old concrete. It would be difficult to climb over the rubble, and impossible to do it without making a whole lot of noise. I look up at the buildings on either side of the alley. The one on my right is five stories, half-collapsed, and clearly abandoned. I trace a climbing path up the building; I think I can make it to the roof.

"I'm going up," I say.

Before she can respond and talk me out of it, I take a running start and leap up onto the building. I'm able to make it up to a windowsill on the second story. I shimmy over to some decorative molding that runs up the height of the decomposing building. Using my fingertips, I climb the molding up to the 5th floor, where a chunk of the molding crumbles under my hand.

I hear the piece of molding that broke off crash onto the street below. I stop and listen. The officers are close now, too close. I have to stop climbing. I can't risk making any more noise and getting spotted. I freeze where I am, holding on to molding with suspect structural integrity. Before the other cops round the corner, I make eye contact with Maria. She's not a happy camper. They'll be able to spot me if they look, but hopefully no one will look up. The group of officers arrives, lead by Detective Rose.

"There she is. What's a nice lady like you doing with a dead lady like her?" Detective Rose asks.

"You know how hard it is to make friends as a cop. I was hoping we could go get our nails painted or put streaks in our hair," Maria answers. She's got a dark sense of humor. I suppose it's fitting for a cop.

"Looks like we got another Different out walking in the wrong side of town," Detective Rose says loudly.

"Could be, Detective," Maria says. "Although it looks as though she died from a single stab wound to the chest. Quite the shot for some junky mugger. Not to mention the fact that nobody touched her pockets, you know, like a mugger would."

"Leave the detective work to the professionals. Any witnesses?" Rose asks.

"Nope," Maria says with a stone face. She's a good liar. She's also really committed to this cause. Not only did she call me in, she lied to a superior officer.

"Okay, now setup a perimeter. You'll have to find someone else to get your nails painted with," Rose says condescendingly.

"You sure you don't want me to stick around? Canvass the area and see if I can find any witnesses?" Maria asks, she's really pushing it.

"Is this about your freakin' Different serial killer theory? Get it through your head; lots of people hate Differents, but that doesn't mean they are crazy enough to do anything about it. You can't go talking about wild conspiracy theories with no proof. You're going to have to figure that out if you ever want to make detective. You want me to think you can make detective don't you?" Detective Rose says like he's talking to a child.

"I do," Maria says her gaze pointed at the ground.

"Alright then go do the job you're trained for, tape off a perimeter."

Maria slinks off. She's fortunate; I'm going to be stuck up here for a while.

"What do you think she could do? Make her breasts bigger?" one of the officers with Detective Rose asks as he inspects the dead woman.

I turn off my hearing before anyone answers. It's not something I want to hear.

I go on think.Net and start a call to Linda. It's time to start making up some excuses. I don't know how long I'm going to be trapped up here.

The muscles in my right hand are starting to get tired, so I shift my weight slightly, which has the unfortunate side effect of ripping the piece of molding I'm holding off the building. I try to find a grip for my left hand, but I pull off another chunk. I'm going down.

I land with a thud that bruises all of the soft tissue along my spine. Then a whole bunch of police sidearms appear in my face. I turn my hearing back on.

"The Beast Slayer? What the hell are you doing here?" Rose exclaims.

11

For a large corporation, becoming hated by the public is a sign of success. It happened to Ford Motors. It happened to the Union Pacific Railroad, Standard Oil, and General Electric. I could go on and on. Success breeds jealousy and hurt feelings. This has always been the case. Now, I'm not saying Ultracorps has been perfect, or that all of their business practices are always above board. But in the grand scheme of things, we all know we are lucky to have Ultracorps. It feeds, clothes, and houses us. If Ultracorps has expanded too rapidly, or taken over too many industries, it is only because we needed it to. Any ire directed at Ultracorps should instead be levied on the politicians who have failed us for so long.

"Look in the Mirror Before Hating Ultracorps" by Forest Brown, think.Net News LA

"This is not complicated. The hostage taker is a Different, which makes this OEC jurisdiction. What the hell do you think they made the Field Offices for?" Captain Murphy yells at my old friend Detective Rose.

"We are not going to be intimidated by some freak. Shooters are taking position around the building. You do whatever you want with your agents till then. But if my snipers get a shot at that lunatic, they are going to take it," Detective Rose replies and shoots me a dirty look. He still hasn't made any trouble for me after catching me at his crime scene. What is he waiting for?

Rose turns his back and starts talking to a group of a half-dozen officers, each of who is carrying a massive rifle. This is not going to end well.

"Can you believe that guy?" Captain Murphy asks.

"I thought cops only fought about jurisdiction in the movies," I reply.

"You heard him, you're going to have to take the Acid-Flinger out before Captain Cowboy gets everybody killed. Are you ready for this?" Captain Murphy says. I'm a little disheartened by how genuinely he asked that question.

"I took out The Beast. I think I can handle the guy who makes Sparkle Clean."

Of course, what I don't mention is that when I fought The Beast I was crazy because I thought he killed my girlfriend and didn't really care if I died. Even then I only won because Ben helped me and The Beast wanted to convert me, not kill me. You know what, I'll go ahead and push those thoughts out of my mind. It's like Victor taught me: I have to think I'm going to win, then do whatever it takes to make that happen.

"He's up on the third floor. They think he's got twenty to thirty hostages. He melted the stairs, so there's no easy way up. He's keeping the hostages in a room in the center of the building away from all the windows. He ordered everyone to stay out or else he'd start melting people," Captain Murphy tells me.

"Give me your gun. I'm going in," I tell Captain Murphy who considers protesting for a second, then shrugs and gives me his .38 special. Not much of a gun, but it should be enough if I need it.

I haven't used a gun since I tried to kill The Beast with my .44 Magnum. We're allowed to carry guns, but Victor refuses to, and until now I always followed his lead. I don't want to shoot anyone, but even less, I don't want to get melted alive. I hope I'm not faced with a choice between the two. I start heading to the front of the police perimeter.

As I walk by, Detective Rose shouts, "Watch yourself, freak! We normal humans can be a little mistake-prone. You wouldn't want to get caught in the crossfire."

"Thanks for the heads up. I'll be sure to be careful risking my life inside the building while you and your buddies stay nice and safe out here behind your perimeter," I reply. I don't like being called a freak.

I get in front of the police tape and start making my way to the front door of the building. I keep my eyes trained on the windows, in case the Acid-Flinger appears and reigns down chemical death. Before I go in the front door, I take a look at one of the smoldering craters. The acid has burnt a hole at least twenty feet through the old asphalt and into the soil, and seems to be making its way through some bedrock now. I don't want to imagine what it would do to my skin.

I head into the main entrance of the building, through the lobby, and to the stairs. Captain Murphy was right; Robert really let this staircase have it. There's a smoldering pit of acid at the bottom of the steps that looks like it's burning a path straight to hell. There's barely anything left of the stairs. Even the walls are being slowly eaten away.

I see a path to climb up, but I have to be careful. If I make too much noise, he could hear me and start killing the hostages, or try to melt me. I also have to be sure that I don't put my hands in a pile of acid while I climb. I start inching my way up the wall. As I go, I get an alert in my head, a think.Net call. No I.D. There's only one person I know who can hide their I.D.—Nita. Why in God's name would she be calling me now? It's not exactly a good time, but I'm far too curious to ignore the call.

<<<*Hello, Nita.*

>>>*Gavin, I am glad you took the call. I was concerned that you would not want to speak with me.*

<<<*Not want to speak with you? Why would you think that? Because you helped me defeat The Beast, and then left me hanging as soon as I was arrested for fighting him? Or maybe I might not want to speak with you because you lied and told me my girlfriend was dead so I'd go pick that fight and most likely die?*

>>>*It pains me that you would think me capable of such acts. I know that arguing with you will likely be fruitless, but I feel compelled to try for the sake of the friendship we once had. Gavin, I am truly sorry that I misled you about Becky, but that was not my intent. Perhaps you've heard the axiom "Never attribute to malice that which is adequately explained by stupidity?" This may be hard to believe considering my intelligence, but I do make mistakes, many*

more than I would like to. I simply misunderstood the information I received from the hospital concerning Becky's condition. It saddens me greatly to think of the pain I must have caused you. My carelessness with an issue as vital as life and death is inexcusable.

<<<Don't you know I don't feel pain? I can control my emotions.

>>>I know that is not true, Gavin. Perhaps you can choose not to experience emotions, but there is no doubt you felt an immense sense of loss when you believed Becky to be dead. I know that I was the genesis of that pain.

<<<Let's say I believe you about Becky. Why'd you leave me rotting after I was arrested? Why haven't you called me until now?

>>>Shame, primarily. I was ashamed of the hurt I caused you, and the fact that I could not do more to assist you after being an accomplice to your crimes. I did advocate on your behalf with the District Attorney's office, but my arguments fell on deaf ears. I also used my position at Ultracorps to promote many positive news stories about your confrontation with The Beast. Those stories helped sway the public into demanding your release.

<<<So what happened? Did you get over your guilt? Why are we talking now?

>>>I still have not overcome my shame. However, the current situation necessitates me putting aside my emotions. I want to work with you to help resolve the situation with Robert White as peacefully as possible.

<<<How do you know about Robert, and how did you know I'd... Never mind, you know everything. Well, except when you're wrong. So, how do you propose to help me?

>>>Robert White is a gifted Different, but physically he is no match for you. If you can safely avoid his acid, you should be able to incapacitate him with ease.

<<<How am I supposed to avoid his acid?

>>>That is where I can assist you. I have established communication with a human Ultracorps employee named Betsy Auger. She is a former Lieutenant in the Army. She knows Robert well. She wants to help, and she is prepared to offer aid should the

opportunity arise. When you need a distraction, she will provide one.
   <<<Thanks. I guess.
   >>>You are welcome, but I do not feel the thank you is deserved. Although it brings me further shame to admit this, I am not helping you out of altruism, or even concern for your safety, at least not primarily. Sparkle Clean is a successful product bringing in over two hundred million dollars in revenue annually for Ultracorps. Robert's acid is a key component in the product. I am hopeful that Robert can overcome whatever mental illness has caused this break from reality and return to being a productive member of society. I trust that you will attempt to end this situation without killing Robert. I am dubious that the Los Angeles Metro Police would do the same. That is why I refrained from contacting them. I will keep our line open, but other issues are calling my attention. Think about me if you need help.

That seemed honest. I want to stop and think about what just happened. I want to go back and analyze the entire conversation to see if she gave some hint of her true motivations. I want to ask her if The Beast is alive and being held in a mine outside St. Louis, but there's no point. If Nita has him she'd lie about it, and if she doesn't, I'll destroy whatever little trust still exists. There's too much to consider and not enough time. I have to push those concerns out of my mind and focus on the task at hand.

It takes me another few minutes to make my way up the wall and onto the third story. Right as I get to the top, I accidentally pull off a chunk of the B-Crete that used to hold up the stairs. It scuffles its way down the wall and lands in the pit of acid at the base of the stairs. I watch it melt like ice on a hot water pipe. I try not to imagine what I would look like if I fell in that pit. I pull myself up onto the third floor and wait to see if Robert heard me coming. I hear screaming.

"Bobby, please! Why are you doing this? Whatever is wrong we can find some way to help you. Talk to me," a female voice pleads. Her voice is calm and assertive. She has experience with dangerous situations. I bet that's my Army Lieutenant.

"You don't understand. No one does. We breathe their lies. Don't you see? I have to make them listen!" An unstable male voice yells in answer, Robert. Something in his voice reminds me of that Heater I stopped a few weeks ago and the Speedster kid who went nuts in the restaurant.

It seems likely the Lieutenant is already distracting him. I slowly make my way down the hallway, towards the door where I heard the voices. A scream stops me in my tracks.

"I hear you! You can't fool me! Stop right there or everybody dies!" Robert yells.

There's a crash on the wall next to me followed by a hissing noise. It's acid eating through the wall. A massive hole appears right next to my head and keeps growing bigger.

<<<*Nita, I'm going in. Tell Betsy to make her move.*

Nita doesn't say anything, but I hear a woman yell, "Bobby, stop it." Then she cries out in pain. I stand up, pull out my gun from my waistband and charge through the door.

"Freeze!" I scream. I'm ready to shoot before I get melted alive.

Robert doesn't even notice me. He's huddled over Betsy who is screaming in pain.

"Betsy, oh my God, Betsy! How did this happen? Stay calm. I can help," Robert says with concern.

"Freeze!" I scream again, but he still ignores me.

I wind up to pistol whip him before he can do any more damage to the poor woman, but then I realize what he's doing. He's using his hands to dig the acid out of her shoulder. His skin must be immune to the acid's effects. I keep my gun pointed at the back of his head while he works. It takes him about ten seconds to get rid of all the acid. Meanwhile, Betsy has passed out from the pain, but it does look like she'll survive.

"I'm so sorry, I'm so sorry," Robert says over and over again while he works.

When the acid is gone, he stays kneeling. He looks like a defeated man.

"Stand up! Slowly!" I yell to him.

It seems like he's finally heard me. He gets to his feet.

"Put your hands over your head!" I demand. I'm flying blind here. Victor usually handles the arrests. I'm trying to remember what cops usually say on think.Net shows.

Robert complies and puts his hands over his head. "I'm so sorry, I thought I was stopping the bad men," he says.

"We're going to the window so I can give the police the all clear. Now turn around, and walk in front of me. Any sudden moves, and it's the end of you."

"I never wanted to hurt anyone. I just wanted them to off me," is his response, but he seems to understand, and complies with my orders.

I stand next to him with my gun in his back as we make our way towards the front windows. I open up one of the windows to yell down.

Before I can open my mouth, there's a boom loud enough to damage the microscopic hairs in my inner ear. I feel a warm liquid hit my forehead. I look over at Robert. He doesn't have a face anymore. He has a gaping bleeding hole where his face should be. His body crumples to the floor in a heap. It takes me a few seconds to process what happened. Those bastards shot him!

My brain goes ballistic with rage. I don't even try to suppress the emotion. Without taking any time to think about what I'm doing, I jump out the window onto the ground below. The three-story fall bursts blood vessels all over my feet and causes damage to my right Achilles tendon, but I couldn't care less.

Police officers are already streaming out of the perimeter and towards the building. It's a sea of blue coming at me. I pick out one young scared-looking officer who is on his way past me. I grab him by the collar.

"Who gave the order to shoot?" I demand even though I know the answer.

He doesn't answer, but he points his trembling figure back behind the perimeter, right at a grinning Detective Rose. I make a beeline for the pig. He looks amused as I charge towards him.

"Looks like your lucky day. Pauly isn't always such a good..." Detective Rose starts to say.

He can't finish his sentence because my fist gets in the way of his tongue. I feel his jaw crack from my punch and watch as three of his teeth spill out to the ground. He follows them down to the asphalt. I jump on top of his chest and continue my assault. The skin on my knuckles tears and my bones chip, but that doesn't stop me from hitting him. What does finally stop me is two officers tackling me to the ground.

I don't give up though. I break free from the two cops holding me down. Three more join in, but still I won't stop, I writhe and kick as hard as I can. Finally, I feel a friendly hand on my shoulder, snapping me out of my bloodlust. I look up and see Maria.

"Calm down," she says, and I finally do.

The five officers who were pinning me down lift me to my feet, but they keep hold of my arms. Captain Murphy emerges from the crowd of officers that has gathered around us. Detective Rose is helped to his feet.

"You're done. You hear me? Done," Rose spits out through his busted jaw. He'll be able to speak for a few more minutes before the swelling makes it impossible to move his mouth "No protests or letters are going to save you this time. Cuff him."

"Whoa, whoa, everybody relax!" Captain Murphy decides it is finally time to speak up.

"Relax? Your little pet freak is out of control. First I catch him sneaking around my crime scene and now this? It's time for him to go back in a cage," Rose says.

"Sneaking around your crime scene?" Captain Murphy asks and looks to me. I shrug and try to form as innocent a smile as I can muster. "In any case, let's not let this situation get blown out of proportion."

"Out of proportion? He's a murderer. I already had the situation under control. The sniper shot Robert in cold blood, and it was on his orders," I say.

"He was still a threat. I warned you we would shoot if we got the chance."

"So if you say the word threat you can kill any prisoner under my control?" I fire back.

"Enough. Obviously, there was confusion on both sides. Now we all know there are going to be a lot of questions from the press as it is. There are going to be even more questions if the Metro Area's hero ends up arrested as a result of all this. Why don't we chalk this up to two law enforcement agencies still learning how to work together, and go our separate ways? Right now, we're all heroes who saved the day. Once accusations start flying and grand juries get convened, nobody is going to end up looking good," Captain Murphy says. I've never heard him sound so competent.

Detective Rose glares at Captain Murphy for a moment, then it looks like a thought strikes him. He gives the officers holding me a nod and they let go, roughly.

"See, not so hard. Why don't you two fellow law enforcement agents shake hands?" Captain Murphy says. When he catches the look in my eye he adds, "That's an order for you, Gavin."

Detective Rose and I walk towards each other. He has to lean on another officer for support while he walks. Is it wrong to feel good about that?

We meet and shake hands. He makes sure to squeeze my bloody knuckles, but I just smile. The joys of being able to turn off your pain response. I tell myself I'm enduring this humiliation so I can stay out of a jail cell. That way I can find some way to make sure justice is served to Detective Rose. Whatever it takes to win.

We release hands, and Detective Rose says something under his breath I cannot understand due to his broken jaw and missing teeth. I decide discretion is the better part of valor, and I let him get away with whatever smartass comment he made.

"Way to be the bigger man," Captain Murphy says and puts his hand on my shoulder. "You might want to clean your face. You've got a mess all over you."

I touch my face and realize it is covered in blood. But it is not my blood, or Detective Rose's. It is Robert White's blood. I can taste it in my mouth; it tastes like a chemical fruit salad.

12

Jefferson came back to start Game 7 only five days after doctors found a crack in his fibula that caused him to miss Game 6, evoking images of Willis Reed in the 1970 finals. Unlike Reed, whose contribution to his team was largely emotional, Jefferson provided meaningful minutes to this Timberwolves squad. Visibly limping and grimacing with each step, Billy the Kid still managed to score 18 points on 6-12 shooting, including the game-winning shot with 12 seconds left.
"Timberwolves Win Championship on the Back of Hobbled Jefferson"
by Roger Burns, Minneapolis StarTribune

August 25th

Sit-ups: 861
Pushups: 1022
Pull-ups: 311
Running: 16.29 miles, 93.66 minutes total, 5:46 Average Mile time
Diet: 2,630 Calories, 197 grams protein, 296 gram carbohydrates, 73 grams fat.
Sleep: 8:17
Funds: $9,101.85
Ammo Count: 167 rounds 7N1, 324 rounds 9mm, 12 Stun Grenades, 12 Smoke Grenades, 12 Standard Grenades. Love that resupply!
Activities: Eliminated Target 21. Tattoo confirmed Male Gamma Cognitively Enhanced. Administered Cocktail Revision 5 to Male Beta Substance Producer.

Target Notes: Passed by Target 21 on way home from meeting with Money Man. Tattoo indicated Gamma, not a major threat. Ran ahead and took position in an abandoned apartment. Fired single shot, killing target. Increase in ammo supply allows for use of Dragunov. Easier to act with less preparation. Expecting an increase in kills.

Money Man Plan Attempt 5 Notes: Administered cocktail to Acid-Flinger. Closer but still far from the cigar. Still too irrational to present a realistic threat.

Personal Notes: Met with Money Man. He provided $20,000 in cash. I demanded end of drugging. Surprisingly, Money Man agreed. Said he is developing a new strategy but would not share details. Does not trust me any more than I trust him.

Mental State: Feeling strong. Resupply helped eliminate pent up anxiety. Funds and supplies are adequate to continue activities for some time even if relationship with the Money Man deteriorates. I'm going to show them what one man can do. Imagine what would be possible if the whole human race stood up.

13

With our police department too afraid to move in, this Metro Area's hero, Gavin Stillman, once again risked life and limb to save the lives of complete strangers. With his partner unavailable due to injury, "The Beast Slayer" was forced to act alone in order to save the hostages taken by the criminal Different Robert White. As has become his habit, Gavin saved the day, with the only casualty being the criminal himself, who police were forced to shoot after he continued to resist despite being apprehended by Mr. Stillman. We do not know what has caused this seeming increase in violent outbursts by Different individuals, but we do know this, the Metro Area is fortunate that "The Beast Slayer" is fighting for us all.

"Another Win for the OEC" by Forest Brown, think.Net News LA

""You don't think it's a little suspicious that Rose didn't mention me following him until now?" I say to Captain Murphy and Victor, the latter of whom is sitting up in his hospital bed. He's finally looking better.

"You're unbelievable Gavin," Captain Murphy says and shakes his head. "You get caught lying to me, violating the terms of your parole, and interfering with a police investigation and somehow that's proof that someone else is up to no good? You have it in for Detective Rose, but so far all he's done is be a nice guy. He was happy to keep quiet about you sneaking around until you went and broke his jaw and he gave that Speedster kid a break, letting him off with a warning. Now suddenly he's killing Differents on purpose?"

"Rose didn't give the Speedster a break out of the kindness of his heart. He did it to cover his own ass. I talked to the Arnold. He didn't take the drugs on purpose. He doesn't know what happened. Rose made up that story so he could let Arnold go without an arrest report or blood toxicology test.

"Really? When did you have a chance to talk to Arnold? I don't remember authorizing that. Is that what this is all about, your crazy Different drugging theory? That's why you were at Rose's crime scene?" Murphy demands.

"No, I was there for something else," I say and pause. He isn't going to like this. "I was helping a police officer who thinks there's a serial killer targeting Differents."

"Jesus Christ!" Captain Murphy yells. Then he puts his face in his hands and rubs his eyes in exasperation.

"It's true. Victor was there the first time I talked to her. She says Differents have been getting killed all over her precinct but the higher ups don't care. She says…"

"I'm going to walk out of this room and pretend I don't know all the things I've learned about you in the last few hours. I'm not going to report you to my higher-ups because they might send you back to jail for violating your parole. I'm giving you a break Gavin. I hope that doesn't get me added to your list of suspects," Captain Murphy says and heads to the door before adding. "This is your one pass. If you violate your parole again, I'm reporting you for everything. See if you can talk some sense into him," he says to Victor, then walks out of the room.

I stand next to Victor hospital bed, paralyzed by awkward silence for what feels like an eternity. I know Victor is waiting for me to talk first so I give in and get it out of the way.

"This probably wasn't the best place for Murphy to give me a grilling. You need to be resting," I say.

"The *captain* knows you won't listen to him. He's hoping I can stop you from destroying our relationship with the police department, which will mean they don't call us in, which will mean the end of the OEC and you going back to jail. Is that what you want?" Victor asks.

"So the police can get away with whatever they want because we can't risk making them angry? I want to be a good guy, not someone who looks the other way when I see the wrong thing happen."

Victor doesn't say anything for a moment. When he does speak, his voice betrays more emotion than I've ever heard from him.

"I was out on my third call ever for the OEC. It was in the Houston Metro Area. A Different who could generate electricity had shocked a police officer. The officer was alive but in critical condition. The assailant was on the run in the swamps outside Houston. We knew it was a race against time. The Houston Police didn't care if it was our jurisdiction. The Different had almost killed one of their officers, and they were not going to stop hunting him. We had to get to him first. It took me and my Telepath partner a few days to track the offender down.

"He was hiding inside an old shack. My partner could tell he was in there, but couldn't read his thoughts for some reason. We finally got him to come out. He couldn't have been more than fourteen or fifteen. He was dressed in tattered rags and he was filthy. I yelled to him, 'Stay where you are! Lay down on the ground!' But he didn't listen. He was screaming, but I couldn't understand him. He had his hands up though, and he was walking towards us. Suddenly, I heard a boom from behind me, and the kid went down. A Houston police officer had shown up on the scene, saw the kid ignoring our commands, and opened fire.

"The bullet hit him square in the chest. I knew there was no chance he was going to make it. I could tell by the look in his eyes that he knew he wasn't going to make it either. He kept repeating '*Dios me perdone, dios me perdone.*' Then I realized why he was ignoring our commands; he couldn't understand them. He didn't speak English. We killed a kid for the crime of not speaking English. I still see his face some nights when I'm trying to fall asleep. He wasn't a criminal. He didn't deserve to die, and he spent his last moment on this earth asking God for forgiveness for what *he* had done," Victor says and closes his eyes.

"You didn't kill him. The Houston Police officer did," I reply.

"Tell that to my conscience. Maybe if I had been faster, maybe if I hadn't been afraid, I would have been able to save that kid. What I'm saying is I know how it feels."

"I don't feel guilty. I feel angry. Rose is getting away with murder and who knows what other crimes."

"Gavin, do you know how I made peace with letting that boy die in the Houston swamps? I had to accept the limits of my own power. I'm strong Gavin, stronger than you, stronger than most Differents out there, but I'm not strong enough to right all of the wrongs in the world. I had to accept the fact that despite the gifts God gave me, there is still going to be evil in this world, more than I can possibly fight on my own. I'm not strong enough to fix everything and, newsflash Gavin, neither are you. There are 25 million people in the Los Angeles Metro Area, which means more murder, corruption, and greed then anyone can fight. What takes true bravery is accepting that you only control a small piece of this world and doing your best to do the right thing in that part you do control. If you keep after Rose, you're going to end up back in jail and you won't be able to help anyone."

"What about imagining you can win, then doing whatever it takes to accomplish that goal?" I reply.

"Life is more complicated than one motto. Let your girlfriend on the police force worry about corruption in her department. That's her job. You focus on doing your job, which is protecting the Metro Area from Differents."

#

I walk down the hospital hall, away from Victor's room, but his words stay with me. Am I imagining plots against Differents to feed into egomaniacal fantasies about my own capabilities? Maybe there is no grand conspiracy. Maybe Differents are dying and going nuts because we live in a dangerous, destructive world where terrible things happen all the time, and there's nothing I can do about it.

I pass by a janitor mopping the floor. That's weird, he isn't a Walter. Is that a fake moustache... It's Ben. I turn around and face him.

"I told you I'm good at disguises. You've got an enhanced memory and still almost went right by me," Ben says.

"That's because janitors are usually Walters. You might have been spotted if anyone gave janitors much thought. You're lucky," I say.

"I am, but janitors aren't. Did you go to the lab? Did my little ruse work? I was right about the water, wasn't I? Wasn't I?" Ben asks rapid fire.

"You were right about the water contract, so I did check out the files. The food deliveries stopped at the same time the mine was shut down."

"No, that can't be right. Ultracorps is up to something with that mine, and whatever it is, they'll have to feed people."

I consider letting that be the end of it. It would be nice not to have to deal with this lunatic any more. But there is the ever-so-tiny chance that all of his crazy theories are right. Maybe The Beast is alive, and maybe Ben knows how to find him. I'll tell the truth; it's never wrong to tell the truth, right?

"I did find something strange. On the same day the Manna deliveries were halted to the mine in question, another mine about thirty miles away got a big uptick in weekly deliveries. Fifty pounds of various Manna products to be exact."

"See, I knew it. That's enough to keep The Beast fed, isn't it?"

"Barely, but maybe they moved some workers from the closed mine to that one, and they needed more food. Do you have access to Ultracorps personnel records?" I ask.

"Personnel records? Don't be an idiot. Fifty pounds of Manna a week is enough to feed ten people, or one Beast. Do you think if there was room for ten more workers in the mine they wouldn't have already been there? Have you seen the price of copper? I'm sure Ultracorps was like, 'Of course we could have more workers and produce more copper, but we don't want more money.' All of those mines were already operating at capacity. That's why it was so strange for one to get shut down."

"What do we do now? Go to St. Louis so we can kill The Beast?"

"Whoa there with the bloodlust. Aren't you supposed to have inhuman control of your emotions? He didn't even kill your girlfriend, remember?"

"Yeah, he just horribly maimed her, left her for dead, and killed her father."

"Touché, but this is bigger than The Beast. If Ultracorps is really hiding him, it proves they think they're above the law. If we handle this right, there could be grand juries and a hearing in front of the Senate. Maybe Ultracorps will get shut down. At the very least, some people at the top will have to resign, maybe even Nita," Ben says with a wide grin.

"What's the plan? What's handling it "right" mean to you? How do we get to St. Louis?"

"We don't. I do. I've been a fugitive for five years. I know how to move around being without being caught. You're on parole and a celebrity; you would never make it. Besides, I'm sure Nita is still watching you like a hawk. But this bird is free to fly."

And with that, he drops his mop and runs to the stairs. There goes his disguise.

#

Right as the Fonze is about to do his signature move and fix the jukebox, I hear a blood-curdling scream. It didn't come from this episode of Happy Days. I log off of think.Net and hear more wailing. It's Linda.

I run into her office and see Linda collapsed on the floor. She's in the fetal position, and it seems like she's struggling to breathe. Could she be under some type of Telepathic attack?

"Captain Murphy, help!" I yell, then turn my attention to Linda. I lean down and put my hands on her shoulders, and give her a gentle shake. "Linda, are you okay? What's wrong?"

"They killed him. They killed him," she whispers.

"They killed who, Linda? They killed who?"

"Martin. They killed Martin. Oh my God, they killed my little boy," Linda says then goes back to wailing like it took every ounce of her strength just to say those words.

#

Linda is walking at an exceedingly slow pace. It's like she wants to relish the last moments she has before she knows for sure her son is dead. Until we get there and see the body, it could all be a mistake. Maybe it's someone who looks like Martin, or maybe he was hurt, not killed. I can't imagine being a mother whose only hope is that her son is badly injured.

We get to the crime scene and are greeted by a sight I've seen way too many times lately: a bunch of cops surrounding the corpse of a Different. I spot a familiar face in the crowd, but not the one I wanted to see, Detective Rose. He's got a black eye and his jaw looks like its wired shut. I'm surprised he's back working already. I assumed he'd milk his injuries for as long as he could. The detective spots the three of us coming and steps forward to intercept. My instinct is to beat the crap out of him again, and arrest him for murder and drugging those Differents, but if I try that, I'm the one who'll end up in handcuffs.

"No! No one called you. Leave!" Detective Rose says through his wired-shut teeth. He emphatically points us away from his crime scene. He is not going to let us through.

I want to make a smart-aleck comment about his jaw, or what he thinks would happen if we go at it again, but now is not the time. This is not about me. This is about Linda and her dead son.

"Relax, we aren't looking for any trouble. Somebody from your precinct called because he might be this lady's son. She's needed to identify that body," Captain Murphy says and points at the sheet.

Detective Rose is stunned. That was not one of the possibilities he expected to hear. He's experiencing some other emotion I'm having trouble understanding. Is it fear, or maybe guilt? It's hard to read his expressions with his jaw wired shut. He finally stammers a response.

"I'm sorry," Rose says to Linda and it sounds like he actually means it. "Her. Not you two," he says and indicates she can come through.

"You're kidding, right!?" Captain Murphy yells, his face turning beet red. That happened quickly.

Another cop in a trench coat walks up.

"What's going on here?" the cop asks.

"Nothing, Sergeant. Protecting the crime scene," Detective Rose says.

"We have reason to believe the victim is the son of this lady here on my right. She is an OEC agent, our Telepath," Captain Murphy says.

"Ma'am, I am sorry for your loss. Please, come this way. All of you," the sergeant says immediately changing his tone.

"But Sarge, I know this guy, he's going to want to poke around," Detective Rose says and points at me.

"So what? Let him. What's the harm? You said it yourself we don't have any leads. Have a heart, Detective. This lady's kid just died. You might not like the OEC, but they are officers of the law. We're all on the same side. I'd want them to let me through if it was my son lying under the sheet at their crime scene," the sergeant says.

We're lucky the sergeant is here. Besides orders from a higher ranking officer, the only way Rose was letting us through was if I broke his jaw again. Rose slowly steps aside.

We walk past the crowd of police officers towards the body which is covered by a sheet. Linda pulls it down and reveals his face, or what's left of it anyway, most of it was ripped off by the bullet. I get visions of Robert White's head being blown off right next to me. There's still enough face to tell who the victim is. It's Martin. I recognize him from pictures Linda showed me on think.net. Linda recognizes him too. She lets out a horrific noise no one should ever have to hear, let alone be forced to emit.

Everybody turns away to give her a moment with her son. I tune what she's saying out of my hearing. She deserves that. Captain Murphy approaches one of the nearby officers.

"Is there anything to go on? Do we know what happened?" Captain Murphy asks.

"Not much. We're guessing robbery gone wrong," the young officer replies.

"A robbery gone wrong? Are you nuts? Did you see his face? No handgun did that. That was large caliber bullet, not some junky's peashooter," I say.

The officer shrugs. "That's for the detectives to worry about, not me."

I wish Maria were here, not this useless excuse for a human

being. Maybe she can still help though. I need the assistance of someone who knows how to analyze crime scenes and cares enough to do it. I log on think.Net and think about talking to her.

>>>*Maria, I need your help. I'm at the body of another dead Different. Your fellow officers think it was a robbery gone wrong, but this guy's head was nearly blown clean off. I think our killer has upgraded from a knife to a gun. What evidence should I be looking for?*

<<< *Another body? This guy is a machine. What does the blood spray look like? Is there just blood around the wound, or is it spread further out?*

>>>*It's everywhere. It looks like a Jackson Pollack painting here.*

<<<*We'll have to hold off on the art walk for a little while. Large caliber bullet and wide blood splatter is indicative of a long range shot from a rifle. If someone is shot from in close, even with a high caliber hand gun, there isn't much blood spray because the bullet doesn't have time to accelerate. This sounds like an assassination, not a robbery. Do you see the bullet slug? That would help us identify the caliber of bullet that was shot.*

As tactfully as I can, I walk around the body. If he was shot with a rifle, the assassin probably shot from above, up on one of the nearby roofs. That means the bullet would have continued on a downward trajectory after passing through Martin's head.

"We should look for the bullet slug in the ground," I instruct Captain Murphy. He starts doing as he's told. I do the same.

It doesn't take long for Captain Murphy to say, "I found something."

I head over to where he's standing and look at a divot in the old asphalt. It's the right size and shape for a bullet. But something's missing, the slug. It looks like someone dug it out of the ground. There are scrapes around the hole. This killer really is a pro. I feel a presence over my shoulder. I turn around and see Detective Rose.

"We found where the bullet went. But there's no slug. Do you think a junky-mugger had the foresight to cover his tracks like that?"

Detective Rose leans over and inspects the hole in the ground, or at least acts like that's what he's doing. He furrows his brow in the way people do when they're pretending to think.

"Sorry Beast Slayer, maybe you should stick to fist fights with your fellow freaks and leave the detective work to the detectives. This is no bullet hole. The shape's all wrong. Just one of many potholes in our crumbling streets. We could use one of your kind to fill 'em in. Do you have any friends that crap out asphalt?"

It seems like he's purposefully trying to goad me. He can't be insane enough to want another fist fight with me. Maybe it's something else. Maybe he's trying to make me focus on my anger towards him, not my investigation. It's not going to work. If I decide not to get angry, I won't.

"If you say so," I tell him. I walk away and go back to my think.Net call.

>>> *I found where the bullet slug was, but somebody dug it out of the ground.*

<<<*This guy knows what he's doing. Okay, well if they were taking this investigation seriously, the next order of business would be trying to recreate the trajectory of the bullet by drawing a line from where the bullet went through the victim's head, to where the bullet landed. Then we'd follow that line to possible shooting locales.*

>>>*I might be able to do an amateur's version of that job.*

I look at Martin's body. He's almost six feet tall. If I assume he was standing upright when he was shot, I can imagine the trajectory based on where he was standing and where the bullet hit the ground. It's a rough estimate, but it points to a roof across the street.

<<< *I found the building the shot came from.*

>>>*Go try to find some more clues then, detective.*

Without a word to anyone, I walk through the crowd of police to the building in question. It's in bad shape, and there's a condemned sign in the window. Before I head in, I turn back and see Detective Rose watching me. He averts his eyes when I turn around. I ignore him and head into the building.

The stairs are crumbling. I step slowly and carefully in case they collapse under me. My fear was warranted; one of the steps gives out as I walk. I catch myself on the handrail. I keep going and step over a stair that has already fallen loose. I look at the handrail next to that step. The dust has been touched. Someone else caught themselves on this handrail recently.

I make it to the top of the steps and open the door to the roof. I go over to the ledge where the assassin would have fired from, but I don't see anything. The debris up here looks like it hasn't been touched in years. I smell for gunpowder, but don't detect any. Maybe I was wrong.

"What are you doing up there?" Detective Rose yells up. "If you do find anything, don't touch it. This is my crime scene. I can't have you tampering with evidence."

He seems awfully concerned I'm going to find something, considering how certain he was that I was dead wrong just a second ago. I know he's involved in the druggings, is he involved in these murders too?

"Just a theory. Looks like you were right. There's nothing up here!" I yell down.

I turn to walk back down stairs, when it occurs to me that I've never tried to draw a trajectory in my mind before. Perhaps I wasn't quite as accurate as I'd like to think. Maybe the shot didn't come from the roof. Maybe it came from one of the lower floors.

I make my way down to the top floor. There are three apartments facing the alley. One of them has its door closed. The other two looked like they were looted and left open long ago.

I try the door, and it's locked. Strange, but lots of doors in Los Angles lock automatically. It was not a safe place even back before the Plagues. With a little effort, the door gives way. The rotten wood makes it easy. As soon as I step inside the apartment, I know I'm in the right place. The unmistakable stench of gunpowder fills my nose.

I walk over to the corner of the apartment and spot an area where the dust has been recently been disturbed. It is right next to a broken-out window. I'll have to thank Maria for teaching me to look for that sign. I'd love to think I'd have thought of it on my own, but attention to detail is about experience as much as focus.

I search the area where the sniper was sitting. I spot a shiny piece of metal. It's a shell casing, definitely from a rifle bullet. What kind of pro goes through the trouble of digging out a slug from the ground but doesn't bother picking up a shell casing? I put the casing in my pocket. I'll be keeping that piece of evidence from Detective Rose.

>>>*Maria, I found a shell casing. I'm going to send you the image on think.Net. We finally have a real clue.*

14

Log of Notable Nita/Ultracorps Activity Week 213

Gavin provided information that extra-Manna products are being rerouted to supposedly closed copper mine.

Theories: Mine is being used to house dangerous Differents Ultracorps wishes to keep hidden, possibly The Beast, but not likely. Going to St. Louis to figure it out.

Ben stands on a desolate street corner looking up at an elevated rail track. He's carrying a length of ForteSilk rope with a hook on the end. He is outside the bounds of the Metro Area in the ruins of old Los Angeles, an area formerly known as West Covina. The buildings here have all collapsed and surrendered to the encroaching prairie. Deep in thought, Ben mutters calculations of complex equations involving velocity, vectors, and angles of approach. He's even accounting for wind resistance. The arithmetic is paused by the sound of a train approaching. Its deafening boom is the result of a vessel moving at incredible speeds. Ben twirls the grappling hook in his hands to build up his own speed, does a few final mental calculations, and lets the grappling hook fly at the precisely determined moment needed to hit the speeding train.

Despite his calculations, his throw is not even close. This was not the matter of a few decimals off or a one he forgot to carry. He missed by many factors of many magnitudes. Unless he can learn to throw the rope at five hundred miles an hour, it simply isn't going to happen.

A new approach is required, perhaps one that spares Ben's ego.

He needs a way to get out to St. Louis, and the transcontinental train is his only viable option. These trains are separate from the Slug; they allow for travel between the Metro Areas. The system consists of a single raised Maceo Steel rail. The rail is covered in Move-Oil, a Different-made lubricant that is the most effective ever created. The train is powered by what is essentially a giant wind-up motor. A Strong-Man turns a dial to twist a ForteSilk coil, which unravels and accelerates the train to a top speed of eight hundred miles an hour, a little faster than most wind-up toys.

The lubricant allows the train to maintain much of its top speed for some time, but air resistance does eventually slow it down. That's why there are boosting stations between the Metro Areas where a Strong-Man winds the train back up. The location of these "boosting stations" is kept secret from the public, but Ben had access to the map when he worked for Ultracorps, and he memorized the locations like he memorizes everything else.

Since the grappling hook plan failed in spectacular fashion, Ben is forced to institute Plan B, making his way out to the closest boosting station, which is about a week away on foot. There the trains will be stopped, which should make it much easier to hitch a ride. A zero for speed is an easy variable to account for. He could buy a ticket like a normal person, but he needs to make a stop that's not on the official route. A passenger disappearing from a train would be cause for concern, one that Nita might eventually investigate. Ben wants to find out what's going on in that mine, and he doesn't want Nita to know he knows, or even suspects anything.

Whatever is happening in that mine must be important. It was producing almost a hundred thousand dollars worth of copper a day. Ultracorps isn't going to shut down a profit center like that willy-nilly. Ben told Gavin that The Beast might be held there just to keep the boy interested, but after the information Gavin found out about the Manna deliveries, it's actually an outside possibility that The Beast is there. Whatever is going on, Nita doesn't want people to know about it, which means Ben has to know, which means a long walk to the middle of nowhere.

#

It's time. Ben hits a button on his chest to deploy a parachute from his backpack. He's violently ripped from his perch atop the speeding train and lifted into the air, exposing his body to such extreme g-forces his lips are forced open and more than a few bugs are shoved down his throat. The force knocks the wind out of him, leaving him gasping to get a breath large enough to spit out the bugs. While he's still in the air, he sees a maze of smaller train lines that service the copper mines in the area. He solves the maze and spots the mine he's looking for, the one furthest out from the rest. The perfect place to keep *somethings*, or someones, hidden.

Ben lands with a thud, but he's still smiling, even with trouble breathing and the unexpected insect snack. He's going to find out something Nita doesn't want him to know, and that will be worth enduring many more hardships. He pulls a small blanket from his pack and picks out a comfortable-looking pile of dirt. As excited as he is, he needs rest to be ready for the challenges he'll soon face. It turns out that it is difficult to sleep while fighting hundreds of miles an hour winds atop a train car. He takes out a Manna Bar from his pack and scarfs it down. Then he sets the alarm on his wristwatch, a watch he's quite proud of. It's powered by his body's own movement, a design he invented. He then closes his eyes and begins the near-impossible task of falling asleep while still giddy about the coming day. Ben might be a Different, but even he has limits on mental miracles.

#

The outside of the mine looks like a set from one of those Pre-Plague Westerns. There's equipment scattered everywhere. Mine carts, pick axes, drill-looking things, and several other machines Ben can't identify. Whatever happened here happened fast; there's still copper ore in one of the mine carts. That isn't something that would be left behind lightly. If that ore were refined, it would be worth several thousand dollars. Ben spends a moment considering the logistics of taking the ore with him before deciding the risk isn't worth the reward. Plus, he really doesn't have the proper equipment for smelting.

He turns his attention to the task at hand. With his recently improved and shrunken hearing amplifier in his ear, he steps into the dank, dark tunnel of rock. He listens as he gradually turns the amplification level up. There isn't any drilling or hauling or pick axing, the mine is definitely shut down, but at the maximum amplification level, he can make out a few muffled voices coming from deep down. Someone is still here. Ben intends to find out who.

The mine is pitch black, but Ben's always prepared and pulls out a pair of home-made night vision goggles. The device amplifies the tiny bit of ambient light that exists even deep within the mine. His hearing and vision properly enhanced, he begins his descent into the bowels of the mine. He does not move quickly; equipment was left strewn about, creating many hazards and obstacles to avoid while he tries to silently move through the near-dark tunnel. Slowly but steadily, he closes in on the murmuring voices.

Ben turns a corner and is blinded by what looks like the sun. When he takes off his goggles, he sees it's just a small WormLight lamp. The lamp illuminates two men sitting at a table, a chess board between them. Each of the men has a handgun on their hip.

Ben stops, rests his hand on a disgustingly slimy wall, and listens.

"No, I don't want to play again. I'm going to blow my brains out if I have to play another game of chess with you. I swear, I'm going on strike if they don't get us some think.Net access down here," the younger of the two men says.

"We're hundreds of miles from the closest Metro Area and a half mile underground. I hope I don't need to explain to you why that isn't going to happen. But go ahead and strike, you think you'll be hard to replace? Sitting on your butt all day babysitting is a sweet gig. I bet the guys who used to work in this mine would trade you their sore back and cut-up hands in a second. Maybe the guy they replace you with will be better at chess. Trust me, even guard duty gets a lot worse than this," the older man answers.

"We're aren't guards. We're protectors, Petey."

"I don't know why they even need us, that girl isn't going anywhere. I'm sure after living in the Non-Assisted Area she's just happy to get three square meals a day and a book to read. She reminds me of my youngest. If she had a book, World War III could have started, and it wouldn't have bothered her at all. Let's say no one was surprised when she became a librarian, the old-school kind. There still are a few of them," Petey says.

The hearing amplifier in Ben's ear picks up the sound of someone breathing from a door behind the two "protectors." Ben needs to find out the identity of the girl being guarded.

He doubles back towards a fork in the mine and follows a different shaft until he reaches the end. Once there, he pulls out the vibration-generating device he used to break the plate glass in the Ultracorps office. He fiddles with the knobs, changing the frequency and setting a timer, then drops the device and hustles back towards the chess-playing guards, nearly slipping and breaking his neck on the damp rock floor several times. He scrambles and hides in a nook, pulling himself in just before his vibration device begins emitting low, deep thumps.

"What the hell is that?" the young guard asks, instinctively putting his hand on the gun on his hip.

"Relax, junior. It's not an angry mob coming for the kid. It's coming from somewhere in the mine, something must've been left on and finally broke down," the older guard answers.

"What's that noise?" a high-pitched female voice calls from behind the door the men guard.

"It's nothing, sweetheart. A problem with some of the equipment. We'll go take care of it," the older guard says, then the pair head towards Ben's device.

Once they are far enough away, Ben walks past their chess board and opens the door they were guarding, revealing a small, sparsely furnished room. There's a young girl with blonde hair who could not be more than fifteen or sixteen. She's laying on a mattress on the floor, a book open in front of her. She lets out a little shriek at the sight of Ben.

"Who are you? What do you want?" she asks, her voice trembling with fear.

"Sorry to scare you. I'm the new guy. Petey told me to watch you while they went to go check on that racket," Ben says, in a calm, reassuring voice.

"Okay. I hope they turn it off soon. It's hard to read with all that noise," she says while she buries her face back in her book.

"What are you reading?"

"My favorite book, *Alice's Adventures in Wonderland* by Lewis Carroll," the girl says, holding up the cover to prove she's telling the truth.

"A lover of the classics, how fantastic. This mine is a little like a rabbit hole," Ben says with a laugh.

"I haven't seen a Cheshire cat, or giant caterpillar yet, just old machines and cold, dirty walls," the girl replies.

"Yeah, it's not too homey down here I guess, though it beats the Queen trying to chop your head off."

"That's the one part that sounds like my life, except it was a whole town, not one fat queen."

"Is that right?" Ben says in a dismissive tone. He assumes she's being a dramatic teenager.

"Everyone I knew wanted me dead," the girl says as tears start to well in her eyes. "I can't even blame them. I almost destroyed the whole town."

"Now how could a little girl like you do something like that? I don't believe it," Ben says in his best reassuring voice, which isn't all that good.

"You should believe it. I'm a Different, one of the dangerous ones. I can make the ground shake, and I'm not very good at controlling it. That's why I couldn't stay in Los Angeles. At least out here I only destroyed some wood huts. If I had been in the Metro Area I would have knocked down tall buildings and hurt a lot of people," the girl says, stifling back the tears.

"You used to live in the Los Angeles Metro Area?"

"Yeah, before they knew how dangerous I was. Once they did the test, they knew I couldn't stay. My father sent me to live in De Sota. It's not as nice as Los Angeles or any of the Metro Areas, but at least everyone was safe. Or I thought they were."

"Who is your father?" Ben asks.

"I'm not supposed to say," the girl says looking down at the ground and shaking her head.

Ben thinks for a moment, then wipes the flesh-covered make up off his right hand, revealing his Mark of Differentiation.

"See I'm a Different like you. You don't have to be afraid," Ben says, still holding up his hand as if the tattoo means he couldn't possibly be a liar.

"You're like me? Can you help me control it?" the girl says, her eyes wide, ecstatic at the thought.

"Maybe, but I have to understand who you are and what you're doing here."

"My name is Jessica Hayes," Jessica says, slowly enunciating like she barely remembers how to say it.

"You're Jessica Hayes?" Ben asks. Now *his* eyes widen. "And your father is former governor Robert Hayes?"

"He's not the governor anymore?"

"No, and I think I might be figuring out why," Ben says with a grin that is wildly inappropriate given Jessica's despair.

15

Let us be clear Mr. Stillman, this offer should not be mistaken as vindication for your crimes. You have benefited from a unique combination of circumstances. Highly respected individuals have endorsed the notion of your release in order for you to serve the public good. These people have put their reputations on the line. If you fall back into your old habits, if you continue to believe you are above the law, they will not speak in your defense again. You have been granted a second chance that few in your position are fortunate enough to receive. Do not squander the opportunity.

Assistant District Attorney Laura Vance Plea Agreement with Gavin Stillman

>>>*I spent a long time searching on think.Net Gavin, trust me. It was a 7.62x54mmR shell. From what I could learn on think.Net, the shooter was probably using a Dragunov sniper rifle, a Cold War-era piece of hardware.*

<<<*What's a psychopath doing with a Soviet-made rifle?*

>>>*Maybe he doesn't know the Cold War is over and Mother Russia is mostly a nuclear wasteland. Or maybe he's not simply a psychopath, he's a psychopath who has enough money to afford expensive toys. Or he has a wealthy sponsor.*

<<<*Where do you even get a weapon like that?*

>>>*That's what I'm trying to figure out. I've got a list of the gun shops that might carry such heavy-duty weaponry, but it's going to be hard to get them to talk. That's not the kind of weapon anybody is going to be in a hurry to admit to selling. Nobody buys a sniper rifle for self-defense.*

<<<*Maybe you should ask around as Maria the private citizen, not Maria the cop. Maria the citizen is beautiful and charming. I'm sure she could get whatever information she needs.*

>>>*Good advice, and nice line. I'll see what I can do as regular*

old Maria. It's probably for the best. I think the captain has heard enough of my theories. There was a reason I wasn't out at that last call. It was in my precinct, and I was on duty. I should have been working the perimeter but nobody called me out there.

<<<It might be something deeper than that they're sick of you. I think Detective Rose is covering for the killer.

>>>I thought he was covering for whoever is drugged those Differents?

<<<Maybe they're related. You didn't see Rose at that crime scene; he did not want us poking around.

>>>I don't like Rose either Gavin but you've got a big hole in your investigation. Motive. What does Rose have to gain from drugging random Differents and covering up for a killer?

<<<I can't believe I'm saying this, but I've got to go. My captain came in and he wants to see me.

>>>A chat with the captain. My favorite. Good luck.

I end the call. Captain Murphy looks annoyed.

"Sorry about that. It was a personal call," I say.

"Who were you talking to? Considering your parents aren't around, you're a convicted felon, and you're locked up in here all night, I would think it's hard to make friends," he pauses. "Don't answer me. I find it unsettling that I can't tell you're lying even when I know for a fact you are. It makes me question how good a cop I am or ever was."

"Okay, I won't answer."

"Did you know that Differents' think.Net call logs are not subjected to 4th Amendment protections? Not that yours would be anyway, considering you're on parole. That means I can see all of your calls, Gavin. I know you've been spending a lot of time talking to a female L.A.P.D. officer. And since I also know you personally, I'm going to go ahead and assume she isn't your girlfriend."

"Is it necessary to insult me?"

"No, but it's damn satisfying after I find out you've been lying to me. Didn't we go over this? You were supposed to fall in line," Captain Murphy says and sticks his finger in my face.

"It's not against the terms of my parole to have a friend who is a police officer."

"You know I told you to drop it, and your friend isn't just any police officer, she's the resident conspiracy theorist. She's already been reprimanded several times for conducting rogue investigations of her own ridiculous theories."

"It isn't a ridiculous theory. She's on to something. There have been Differents showing up dead all..."

"Stop! I don't want to hear it. We've already got enough trouble getting along with the L.A.P.D., thanks to your love of pounding on their officers. If they find out you've been helping one of their troublemakers, they're going to stop what little cooperation they already offer. If we aren't getting any calls, this office is going to get shut down and the entire OEC Field Office Program won't be far behind. Is that what you want, Gavin? Do you want to go back to being a lab rat? Don't forget, that's after you finish out your prison sentence."

"What if she's helping me find who killed Linda's son?"

"What do you mean? And keep your voice down, she's in the other room," Captain Murphy says. That hit close enough to home that it gave him pause.

"That's what I was going to tell you. There's a serial killer out there and he's targeting Differents. I'm pretty sure that's who killed Martin. It makes a lot more sense than a mugger who uses a sniper rifle for a weapon."

"First someone was drugging Differents now someone is killing them? Let me guess who's the suspect at the top of your list, Detective Rose, the overweight assassin. There's no point in arguing with you Gavin, so let me just be clear, you aren't 'The Vigilante' anymore, you aren't 'The Beast Slayer.' You are Gavin Stillman, OEC agent and parolee. If you aren't willing to follow orders like Gavin the OEC agent, then Gavin the parolee is going to become Gavin the prison inmate. Is that clear?"

There are a thousand things I want to say right now. I want to tell Captain Murphy what a joke he is. I want to tell him that he's a figurehead who exists to make people feel safe while we agents actually run the show. I want to tell him he hasn't done anything resembling real police work in ten years, and now he's another useless bureaucrat. But I don't. Having complete control over myself comes through once again. I give him the answer he wants to hear.

"Yes, sir."

"See, that wasn't so hard. Now why don't you hit the gym, and do some of that training Victor is always riding you about."

"Yes, sir," I say again and head towards the gym.

I feel a voice in my head, but I didn't accept a think.Net call. Curiosity overruns my natural paranoia and I let the thoughts into my head. Did Nita find a new way to contact me?

>>>*Did you mean it? Do you think your serial killer murdered my Martin?*

<<<*Linda? How are we talking? I didn't get a think.Net call.*

>>>*I'm a Telepath, I don't need think.Net to talk to you. I'm my own mini think.Net. Now answer my question. Do you really think the serial killer did it, or were you saying that to appease the captain?*

<<<*I really think it, Linda. A serial killer has been targeting Differents, and Martin was one of the victims.*

>>>*Are you close to catching him? Do you have any leads?*

<<<*A few, but it's hard for me to conduct an investigation when I'm locked up for twenty-three-and-a-half hours a day. I don't think my friend on the force is going to get away with any more "mistake" calls, and anyway, Victor is going to be back soon so I won't get to go out on my own.*

>>>*That might be something I can help with. I'm the one who locks up the place at night and checks to make sure you didn't leave when I come in the morning. I can also access your think.Net files with your location data and the list of calls you made. I can alter those records.*

<<<*You can?*

>>>*This old dog still knows a few tricks. I was part of think.Net before you were a glimmer in your Daddy's eye. I remember enough*

to fool those young whippersnapper Telepaths they've got working today. I'll wait a few days for Captain Murphy to cool off. Then I'll start leaving the doors open at night.

<<<I don't know what to say.

>>>Say you promise to catch the son of a bitch.

<<<I promise.

#

I breathe deep and my lungs fill with air that tastes of freedom. I haven't been out at night in weeks, ever since the new Governor took over and stopped inviting me to parties. I've missed walking the streets of the Los Angeles Metro Area at night. I might be the first person to ever have that thought. The streets out here smell like garbage, maybe because they are covered in it. It doesn't matter to me. I can ignore those odor molecules. I'm happy to have the chance to do that.

I hope my new disguise keeps working. It kept everyone off my back during my Oasis Burger lunches with Ben. My previous old-man look is famous now, so unfortunately it wouldn't keep me hidden. It feels a little weird to be keeping all this water in my face, but I definitely don't look like myself. I look like a fat guy who lost a lot of weight but it hasn't hit my face yet.

I look down at my glove-covered hands, the second part of my crime. Covering my Mark of Differentiation is specifically outlawed in the Different Acts of 1986. But I figure, what the hey? In for a penny, in for a pound. It'll just be more years added to my sentence. A real possibility considering I'm breaking my parole to stalk a police officer.

I've been watching Detective Rose for over an hour. Maria told me where to find him. He was on call for a murder. Is it weird that I'm relieved the call isn't about another dead Different, just a normal twenty-year-old dead man? I tell myself that it's as big a tragedy that he died, but I don't believe it. I know I care more about my own kind, and I don't like that.

Detective Rose doesn't seem to care very much about the dead kid either. He doesn't spend any time investigating at all. I hear him say, "Another junky getting what he deserved." It makes me question what I believe about Detective Rose. Maybe he hasn't been holding up the investigations because he's part of conspiracy. Maybe it is just good, old-fashioned, incompetence and indifference.

I watch him stand around for another forty-five minutes, cracking inappropriate jokes and acting like an all-around ass. His still wired-shut jaw isn't stopping him from gabbing. Finally, the Strong-Woman comes and carries off the body.

He tells the officers around him, "I'm going to walk the beat. I'm on think.Net if you find anything. Don't forget, if there's another call tonight it's Santiago's, unless it's a big one."

I'm assuming a big one means another dead Different. I watch Detective Rose go out and walk the beat. Apparently, that means walking five blocks to a local café and sitting down to eat. It must be a criminal hotspot. I find an alley where I have a view through a window, and I watch Rose while I hide in the shadows.

He orders, and the waitress comes back a few minutes later with a plate of fried Manna and a cup of coffee. He starts shoving the thin strands of fried carbohydrates into his mouth. He has to suck each tube into his mouth individually because he can only open his jaw slightly. He's making a mess all over himself. And I thought I already disliked him. I have to tell myself I'm doing this for a good cause, otherwise I'm not sure how much someone would have to pay me to watch this.

After he's polished off his plate of greasiness, he goes into the think.Net stare. Either he's one of the few people who can talk on think.Net without moving their lips, or he's doing something other than call into the precinct house. Considering it took me weeks to teach myself how not talk when I'm communicating on think.Net, and that's taking into account that I have control over my entire body, I'm going to go ahead and eliminate that possibility.

After watching him spend more than two hours in the think.Net stare, I can say with certainty that he is not doing anything related to his job. Given the chuckles he lets out every few seconds, I'm guessing he's watching a think.Net show, or maybe even a movie.

My tax dollars hard at work. He finally comes out of the stare, gets up, and walks out of the café, yelling his goodbye to the waitress. Maybe he paid his check on think.Net, but he seems more like the abuse his police power type.

I follow him as he walks a few more blocks. I stay out of the illumination provided by the occasional WormLight on the street. Rose doesn't seem like he's worried about being followed. He doesn't seem like he's worried about anything at all. He walks past a group of teenage boys.

"Shouldn't you kids be in bed by now?" Detective Rose asks.

"What's it to you, metal mouth?"

He pulls out his badge. "Do you kids need a lesson on respecting your elders?"

"No, sir."

"Good, now get your asses to bed."

The kids listen and start to scatter. Detective Rose stops one of them. The kid has a cigarette in his mouth. Rose grabs the cigarette. "Don't you know smoking is a bad for your health?" Then he puts it in his own mouth and takes a big drag. An impressive feat considering his wired-shut jaw. He's quite the role model. He shoos the kid away and hooks his badge to the outside of his trench coat, where it can easily be seen. I guess he doesn't want to have to fish it out to get respect again.

He continues his "patrol" until we get to a block full of scantily clad women. They aren't exactly being discreet about what they're here for. They're plying the oldest profession in the world. One would expect these ladies of the night to shy away from a man with a badge on his coat, but they do the opposite: they all flock around him.

"Hi Detective Rose, how's my poor, hurt baby? You looking for a date tonight? I can make you feel all better," the leader of the pack of prostitutes asks.

"Not yet. Sorry to disappoint you all, ladies. Few more weeks and I'll be all fixed up."

He spends a few more minutes flirting with the women and

saying offensive things to all of them. It seems like he believes the women are genuinely interested in him, not because he's a potential payday, and a cop to boot.

After he's had his fill of committing sexual harassment, he moves on from the women, waving and winking back at them as he walks away. I have to stay hidden in an alley so he doesn't see me when he turns around. It was probably unnecessary. I don't think he was paying attention to anything but the women.

He continues on his way without incident back to the precinct house. I go into a café across the street from the police station, order a cup of coffee, and wait. After a few hours, he steps back out of the station, waving goodbye to someone inside.

I pay my check with cash and follow him to the nearby Slug station. I make sure to get on a different train car than him, and we ride five stops to Balboa Station. This is a fancy part of town; can he afford an apartment here? He walks a few blocks before turning into a building marked "Genoa Retirement Community."

I can't follow him into the building. I don't trust my fat face disguise enough to gamble on Rose not recognizing me if he sees me up close. So I take position in the shadows across the street and watch through the windows. Rose climbs a beautiful white tiled staircase and exits on the third floor. This facility looks lavishly expensive. Rose must be meeting with the person paying for the cover-ups. The mastermind.

I wait about an hour before Rose walks out of the Retirement Community. He wipes his eyes on his sleeve. Was he crying? He walks off back towards the Slug station. I wait to make sure he is safely out of sight before walking into the building.

I'm right; whoever Rose met with is loaded. This place looks like the lobby of the Ritz, not an old folks home. Everything is tile, marble, and wood. The WormLights are shaped like delicate glass flowers instead of the normal cylindrical design. I feel too poor to be let inside the door, but since I'm here I walk up to the attractive middle-aged woman manning the grand wooden reception desk.

"How may I help you?" she asks cheerily.

"Hello, I'm here to see my grandmother," I say confidently.

"Sir, it's the middle of the night. If you'd like to come back tomorrow morning, visiting hours start at 9AM."

"But I saw another guy walk out of here."

"Patients in hospice care have different rules for obvious reasons. Your grandmother isn't in hospice is she?"

"Yeah, she is."

"May I ask you her name sir?"

"Uhh Smith," I answer. My confidence melting away.

"Her first name, sir?" she asks on a tone that indicates she doubts me though her smile betrays nothing.

I'm halfway up the stairway before I even realize I already made my decision to run past check-in. I fly up the tiled stairs two at a time. I can hear the receptionist screaming for help below me.

Whoever Rose was visiting is on the 3rd floor, hospice. I guess some rich dying old man's wish was to kill Differents or drug them or both. I need to find out who he was seeing, and fast. I make it to the third floor in less than five seconds. I'm confident that I'm moving too fast for security. The trouble makers they're used to chasing are of the low-speed geriatric variety.

The entire third floor is hospice care. There are a lot of dying wealthy old people. I rush through the hallway passing by dozens of private rooms. I make sure I get a good look at each door. They have the names of the patients written on them. Later on, I can go back through my memories and research the names on think.Net to see if I can draw any connections to the Different druggings or killings.

One of the name cards stops me dead in my tracks. Eleanor Eden Rose. Inside the room is a frail withered shell of a person not long for this world. Even though she's as skinny as a rail, she still looks a lot like her son.

"He went that way!" I hear a male voice yell from the hallway.

#

"They tried to chase me for a block or so after I made it out on the fire escape, but they gave up quickly. Nobody saw who I was," I say and sip my mug.

This is my fourth cup of coffee in the last hour. The liquid is coursing through me and filling my bladder. I'm trying to absorb as much of it as I can, but it's a losing battle. I'd have peed all over myself already if I was a normal person. I should excuse myself, but I don't want to lose any time with Maria.

"Seems like a big chance to take. If you get caught, you go back to prison, right?"

"But it was worth it. We knew Rose wasn't investigating the murders and we suspected that he was drugging those Differents or at least covering it up. Now we have a motive for why he's doing it, to pay for the nursing home for his mom. You said we needed a motive right?"

"I guess. It's a little weak though. If we want to get a warrant we're going to need more."

"Did you always want to be a cop?" I say. Slyly turning the conversation to more personal matters.

"Me? No," she says shaking her head. "I was raised as a girly girl. Pink dresses, ribbons, tea parties all that jazz. My father was old-school… Detective Rose mentioned he had brothers, maybe they're helping pay for the room."

"You didn't see this place. Unless one of those brothers won the lottery, they can't afford it. It was a Pre-Plague money kind of place. What changed that made you want to become a cop?" I ask, undeterred in my efforts to derail the conversation from our stated goal.

"An accident to my brother Esteban. The train went off the tracks and crashed into the ground, a fifty foot drop at thirty miles per hour. Over two hundred fifty people on the train, and five survived. Esteban was not one of them. At least it was quick. If I was a year older, I would have been in middle school too and died with him," Maria says.

"That's terrible," I say. "I'm so sorry. I thought that wasn't supposed to happen; they always talk about how safe the Slug is. The rail is made of Maceo Steel, so how does a train get derailed from an unbreakable track?" I ask. I'm not sure if that was the right response to the story, but this might be one of those situations where there really isn't a right thing to say. At least I got her talking about something personal, that's a good way to form an emotional connection… I shouldn't think thoughts like that.

"The rail can't break, but the supports holding up the tracks used to be wood."

"It's amazing how many people have died through history trying to get from point A to point B," I say. There might not be a right thing to say, but I assume from the look on her face that was the wrong thing to say.

"Yeah… Anyway, after Esteban died, my dad's whole attitude changed. Tea parties got replaced with trips to the shooting range and basketball games. I wanted to be the female Billy the Kid, and my dad practiced with me every day. He taught me to work as hard as Billy. It wasn't that he was trying to replace the son he lost, although I'm sure that was part of it. The accident made him realize how fragile life is and how little he can actually do to protect it. He decided it was more important to have a daughter who could take care of herself than make a good housewife. It didn't take long for me to want to follow in his footsteps and become a cop. He didn't mind. My mother on the other hand almost had a heart attack when she heard I was joining the force. Hard to blame her since she only has one kid left."

"Is your father still an officer?"

"No, he died three years ago. Pancreatic cancer. It wasn't pretty. At least he got to see me join the force before he died. He made it a month past my first day. I'll always remember the look on his face when he saw me in my uniform for the first time, the pride was radiating off him."

"I'm glad you got to make your father proud. I'm sorry to hear he passed."

"Yeah, but enough of my sob stories. What about you? What are your parents up to?"

"That's not really going to put an end to the sob stories. Short version is mother ran off when she found out I was a Different.

Father died on a fishing boat when I was in Section 26."

"That sucks," Maria says. It's comforting to hear that normal humans aren't any better at knowing what to say than I am.

"How about your mom, is she still around? Did she get over you joining the force?" I ask, turning the attention back to her.

"Oh yeah, my mom's great. I'd say she's gotten used to me being on the force. I can see the pride in her eyes when she sees me in uniform, and I can tell it reminds her of my dad. She's happy to know his legacy lives on. That being said, she still makes me call her after every shift so she knows I'm all right. I was talking to her when you called me."

She got off the phone with her mother to talk to me. That's a good sign. Or maybe it just means she's really invested in tracking this serial killer down. Maybe she only agreed to have coffee so our partnership doesn't fall apart.

"Sounds like she got over it, but that doesn't mean she stopped being a mother," I say.

"That's right, and I'm the only one she's got now. I can't imagine what she'd do if she didn't have me to take care of her. Fifty-five-year-olds who spent most of their lives as housewives don't have many career options. She knits a mean pair of mittens, but I don't think she can go national with that."

"Yeah, wool is still too expensive thanks to the Plagues killing most of the sheep." God, am I a weirdo or what?

"Anyway, I should get going. I told my mom I'd be a little late, but if I'm not home soon, she's going to call my captain again. You can imagine how awkward it is at work the day after one of those calls."

"I'll walk you," I say, then to the waitress who is walking by, "Can we settle up?" It occurs to me that I probably shouldn't be the one to pay. I don't have any cash. I spent the few cash dollars I had at the first café. Paying on think.Net will leave a record of the transaction. Maybe Linda can scrub this transaction from my record, but maybe not. "I know it's not very gentlemanly, but do you mind paying, Maria? I spent all my cash already."

"Oh sure," She says and goes into the think.Net stare, thinks about the café, and authorizes the transaction request. She signs off think.Net and says, "We're good."

We step back outside into the night air. It got much colder while we were in the cafe. I increase my heart rate to raise my internal temperature as we walk.

"You know, you don't have to walk me home. I'm not one of your typical dates, unless you usually go out with women who are carrying a 9 millimeter. It's just a couple blocks."

"I don't go out on any dates. I'm a parolee, remember? This is the first time I've been out at night and free since I was Gavin Stillman the Vigilante. I was dating a woman before, but then The Beast…" I stop myself. I've got to slow down time and start thinking about what I'm saying more. No one wants to hear about ex-girlfriends.

"Oh my God, The Beast didn't kill her, did he?"

"No. Well, almost. He attacked her, but she survived, barely. Didn't do wonders for our relationship though." Seems like the no ex talk rule goes out the window if it also involves serial killer monster talk.

"I would guess not. Did she recover? Is she okay?"

"She recovered, but she didn't stick around long after. She was a Cabotist, or her father was anyway. You probably remember what happened in the Cabotist neighborhood after The Beast's attack. I can't blame her for wanting out of the Metro Area."

"That is rough. It's awful what they did to that pastor. I don't care what you believe, nobody deserves that."

"I guess so," I say. Maybe no one deserves to be strung up and torn limb from limb, but if anyone deserved it, Pastor Newman would have been on the short list. She doesn't want to hear that.

"How about you? Any jealous ex-boyfriends going to come after me? They could be cops. I should probably be worried."

"Hah, maybe a few, but why would they come after you?"

I don't have anything to say to that so we walk on for another half block in silence. Finally, she stops in front of a three-story apartment building. It's nothing great, but it puts Becky's house in the slums to shame.

"This is me," she says and turns to me.

I look into her beautiful brown eyes and get ready to make my move. Seems like a goodnight kiss might be appropriate. She senses my intentions and turns away.

"Gavin, I'm sorry. I don't think this is going to work," she says.

The words ring in my mind. I feel my brain's desire to experience an entire cocktail of negative emotions. Anger, embarrassment, sorrow, disappointment, and self-pity would all like to hit me like a freight train. I turn those signals off. If I don't, I might run away.

"Oh really? I thought we had a pretty good time," I say like it's no big deal.

"We did, and I like you, Gavin. I really do. You're a sweet, smart as a whip, and not too bad-looking, at least when you have your normal face on."

"What's wrong then?"

"We're doing something important here, Gavin. A dozen Differents murdered, drugs, crooked cops, and we're the only ones trying to stop all that. We have to be able to stay objective. If we get distracted, people could die."

"I didn't think about that. I suppose you're right, we are doing something important. I didn't mean to make you uncomfortable. I feel bad for bringing it up."

"No, it's fine. It's my fault too, I might have been leading you on a little bit. Like I said I like you, but the timing isn't right. Besides, you're locked up all day unless you've got some maniac Different to go fight. And you may have found some way to get out of lockup at night, but you've got to spend all that new free time following you new boyfriend, Detective Rose. I don't see any time for a girlfriend in that schedule ."

"There you are, right again. Look at all that evidence for why we shouldn't date. You will make a great detective," I say before I realize how nasty it sounds.

"It's for right now," she says, her police officer poker face unaffected by my barbs. "Who knows what the future holds. Maybe a Different like you can afford to have divided focus while chasing a serial killer, but as a normal human that's more than I can handle." She's straining to walk the line between being nice and being firm.

"Fair enough. Consider it forgotten. I won't let it affect us working together. Trust me, I'm good at pushing my emotions aside. Superhuman in fact."

"Good to hear… Well, goodbye," she says.

I extend my arm for a handshake, she goes in for a hug, and then we switch before finally settling on a weird high-five/half hug. I turn off the part of me that wants to die from embarrassment.

16

It is a dark day for baseball, ladies and gentleman. Instead of celebrating a thrilling game seven victory by the New York Yankees, we are left questioning the results of this series and every World Series in recent memory. When Victor Campos threw out George Burns at home from the base of the centerfield wall, a throw no human being could make, we all knew we were watching a farce. Victor stole not just the game, a result which will eventually be overturned, he stole our trust in the sport. From here on out instead of cheering for baseball's superstars, we will be forced to wonder if their performance is due to natural skill and athletic ability or if their dominance stems from the fact that there are Differents somehow hiding from the tests designed to find them.

"1919 All Over Again" by Gregory Winfield, LA Times

I hit the deck hard. I hear metal ricocheting around me. The bullets are coming incredibly fast, ten rounds a second. The Regenerator looks like she doesn't weigh more than a hundred and twenty pounds. Despite that, she's handling the gun like a pro. The machine gun fires so fast she's a human whirlwind of destruction.

Her magazine clicks empty. The police open fire again. I hear hundreds of shots being fired from all around the square. The bullets riddle her body while she struggles to put a new clip in her gun. The shots tear her apart, but she doesn't go down. I watch the wounds seal up almost as quickly as they form. The cops miss a lot, too. One bullet sinks into the back of a hostage lying on the ground behind the Regenerator.

"Hold your fire. The OEC is handling this. Stand down!" Victor yells.

It's only his third day back. I remember when we used to hope for some real action. We're both feeling pretty stupid about that now.

A hulking officer makes a run at the Regenerator while she's still struggling with the machine gun. She spots him coming, pulls out a small handgun, and drops the would-be hero in his tracks.

"I told you all to stand down!" Victor yells.

She puts the handgun away, finishes putting the magazine back in her machine gun, and goes back to laying down suppressing fire at the police officers all around her. They scramble to get behind cover.

She picked the perfect spot for this attack. She's standing right in the center of Beckett's Square. It's a three hundred yard diameter circle of flat concrete with nothing for cover. Standing in the center, she can whirl around and gun anyone down before they can get close enough to tackle her. Victor, all of the police, and I are basically pinned behind barricades. She's armed to the teeth with at least two handguns to compliment her machine gun, and she's surrounded by cases of ammunition. She has about twenty hostages lying on their bellies in a circle around her. I can hear them cry.

This is a different situation than the Heater and the Acid-Shooter we took down. Those two were dangerous, but they were also mentally unstable because of psychoactive drugs. Drugs don't work on Regenerators, at least not any that I know of. Besides, she is not acting like a drugged-up lunatic. She's cold and calculated. I wish I could see her face so I could look her up on think.Net, but she's wearing a scarf that's covering most of her head.

Whoever she is, she's one hell of a quick healer. I've seen three bullets go through her head, and the wounds healed up before she could even hit the ground. She's been popping Manna Bars to keep up with her healing body's insane energy demands. She's got enough supplies to keep this up for hours.

"Okay, OEC. You want to handle the freak? She's all yours," an officer yells over the din of bullets.

"Don't you try anything, or these hostages are getting their brains splattered," the Regenerator yells in response.

I go on think.Net and think about talking to Victor. He accepts the call.

<<<*What's the plan Victor?*

>>>*Don't have one. If I could get close enough, I could pin her*

down easily. The problem is getting that close.

<<<I'd say we can wait until she runs out of ammo, or calories for healing, but she seems well supplied enough to keep this up indefinitely.

>>>We might not be able to get her to run out of ammo completely, but it takes her a while to reload that machine gun.

<<<She's got those pistols.

>>>I'll have to get her to shoot all those bullets too. I'm going to try to draw her fire.

<<< I know you're fast, but can you really dodge bullets?

>>>No, but I can make myself hard to aim at. Is your gun loaded Gavin? I might need you to lay down cover if things go south.

<<<It's loaded, but I'm feeling a little overmatched. My five-shot pea-shooter doesn't exactly stack up. And what about you? Maybe you should try to borrow some ForteSilk body armor from the police.

>>>It's not worth the loss in mobility. I'm going to make my move. Be ready.

Victor lets out a high-pitched yell, then leaps into the center of the square. The Regenerator whirls around to face him, but she hesitates for a moment before she squeezes the trigger of her machine gun. What's with the hesitation?

Victor breaks into a gymnastic routine that would embarrass every Gold Medal Olympian that has ever competed. He is a blur of back flips, handstands, summersaults, cartwheels, and moves I can't even name. He is graceful and magnificent. I'm captivated by his skill, and jealous too. I can never hope to move like that. Human muscles cannot do that no matter how much they've been improved. Bullets splatter all around him, but he doesn't stay in one place long enough for the Regenerator to get a bead on him. This might actually work.

As soon as that thought occurs to me, it seems to occur to the Regenerator too. She lets go of her machine gun, which stays attached to her by a shoulder strap. Then she digs in her pocket, pulls out a small round object, picks something off of it, and rolls it towards Victor.

I yell, "Grenade!" at the top of my lungs.

Victor wasn't really paying attention to the Regenerator. His routine was more about him moving as quickly as possible, not reacting to her. It takes him a second to realize the bullets have stopped. When he hears me yell, he turns around and leaps as high as he can into the air.

The grenade detonates below him, but the shockwave knocks him out of the air. He lands with a thud. The Regenerator grabs her machine gun and prepares to fire. I've got to act.

I jump over the barricade and charge forward. I aim my .38 special at her machine gun and squeeze the trigger. The bullet pangs off the metal and knocks the gun out of her hands. I follow up with another shot that goes into her back. She pulls out one of her handguns and whirls around to face me.

I put a bullet right between her eyes. She staggers back but doesn't go down, so I shoot the pistol out of her hand. Not to be too full of myself, but I'm a hell of a shot. I learned how to shoot once and now it's in my muscle memory forever.

"Enough! It's over, time to give up!" I yell.

My shot to the head didn't slow her down, but it splattered blood all over the scarf wrapped around her head, obscuring her vision. She pulls off the scarf and throws it to the ground. She's in her mid-thirties and pretty. There are tears streaming down her face. Not your typical terrorist.

"I can't stop. You don't understand," she pleads.

As she says that she pulls out her other pistol. I try to shoot that one out of her hands too, but she throws her shoulder in front of my bullet. Now I'm empty.

"I'm sorry!" she yells.

Then she points her pistol at me and squeezes the trigger.

I drop to the ground, and the bullet whizzes by me. I look to Victor, who's struggling to get back to his feet. He isn't going to save me. I break into my best approximation of Victor's gymnastics routine. A summersault and a bullet hits the ground where I was lying, a cartwheel and a bullet hits to my left, jump in the air and a bullet lands at my feet, another cartwheel, and a bullet tears through my thigh leaving a gaping hole in my muscle. I fall back and barely avoid a bullet destined for my head. I scramble back to my feet in time to take a bullet in the shoulder.

I cover my head to protect from a headshot that never comes. Her pistol clicks empty. She ejects the cartridge from the bottom of the gun and pulls another from a bandolier on her chest. I'm not going to be able dodge anything with two gunshot wounds. I have to go for broke.

I charge at her the best I can considering the bullet lodged in my thigh. The damage to the muscle is slowing me down. Pain might not matter to me, but I can't direct muscle tissue that is torn to shreds. I'm closing in though, fifty yards away. She finishes reloading her handgun and turns to aim. I throw my revolver and hit her square in the face, but she barely flinches. She takes pain as well as I do.

There's nothing I can do but keep charging. I should only take three or four bullets before I get to her. Let's hope her accuracy fails and she misses everything vital. Right as she's about to put another bullet in me, Victor yells.

"Stacey?! My God, what the hell are you doing?" He recognizes her?

Stacey turns and faces Victor, but she keeps her gun pointed at me.

"Victor, I'm sorry. You don't understand. I have to do this," she says with tears in her eyes.

Victor has a steady stream of blood flowing down his forehead. He landed hard when that grenade blast hit him. I inch forward towards Stacey while Victor has her occupied.

"So tell me. Make me understand," Victor begs.

"I can't. They have my family. If I stop, they'll kill them. They're watching," she says and waves her arms towards the crowd of police, onlookers, and reporters.

When she turns to wave her arm, she spots me inching towards her. I get ready for the bullet, but something else happens.

"Save my little girl," Stacey pleads. Then she pulls a small object out of her pocket and pushes the red button on top.

The explosion rips Stacey to shreds. I push all of the air out of my lungs and signal my abdominal and diaphragm muscles to relax. The shockwave blows me twenty feet through the air. I land and bounce, tearing a chunk of flesh off of what was my good shoulder. I'm lucky that's the worst of my injuries. If I hadn't pushed the air out of my lungs, the shockwave would have made them burst.

I look to the center of the square, it's become a flaming crater. Victor managed to jump out of the blast radius too, but Stacey is gone, and she took the twenty hostages with her. What did she mean she had no choice? Who has her family?

Victor helps me to my feet. Medical personnel move towards the crater, but there's no use. We failed. Everyone is dead.

"You okay?" Victor asks.

"If you mean 'will I survive,' then yes. I'm far from okay though. What do you think she meant telling us to save her little girl?"

"I'm going to go find out," Victor says. He then turns and breaks into a run.

"Where are you going? What's going on?"

"Her name was Stacey Rothschild. Look her up, you'll figure it out!" he yells back.

#

"I really don't know what to say. I'm guessing you're already beating yourselves up about this. All I can tell you is that we'll get them next time," Captain Murphy says. "This is the nature of our jobs, sometimes we are going to fail, and nobody bats a thousand. Now some losses are worse than others, and this is a particularly bad loss. There are going to be lots of questions from the press, but that's what I'm here to handle. You two button your lips if anyone asks you anything. There's nothing to gain by trying to explain yourself. They've already decided how they're going to handle this story, and it's going to focus on the failure of the OEC. Nobody is saying that's fair, but that's how it is," Captain Murphy finishes. He got a little winded giving that speech. It was a long one.

"I suppose no one is going to talk about Stacey's missing

family?" Victor asks.

"I've been told the police are still working to verify that fact, and I am not supposed to mention it until they have more information."

"More information? The apartment was ransacked and I haven't been able to raise her husband, Charlie, on think.Net. What else is there to know?"

"I know that Stacy was a friend of yours, Victor, so I can appreciate your desire to figure this all out. But have you considered the possibility that you're too close to this issue and not thinking clearly? The police are investigating the kidnapping as one possible explanation, but there are other explanations. Maybe the two of them had a horrible fight and Charlie left the house with the kid and Stacey couldn't take it and snapped. Or maybe she was already acting strange, and Charlie took the kid so they'd be safe. Maybe he's not answering your think.Net calls because he's not ready to talk about all this. And I hate to say it, but maybe they were the first victims of her rampage."

"Maybe," Victor says flatly.

"That's why we'll have to wait and see. I've got to go down to the front of the building and feed the vultures. Victor, you should head on home; you need some rest. That's an order. And leave through the roof. Otherwise you'll have to face the horde. Gavin, how's the healing coming?"

"I'm all right. I'll be a little slow for a few days, but nothing that'll keep me from doing my job," I answer. My thigh is almost bursting from all the blood I rushed to the gunshot wound, which should help the tissue heal more quickly but Captain Murphy never wants the details.

"Right back up on the horse, that's the way to do it. You're a trooper, Gavin. Chin up. Like I said, this is all part of the job. I'm sure you'll be racking your brain trying to think of what else you could have done, and maybe there was something, but maybe not."

"Thanks," I say for some reason. That had to be one of the worst motivational speeches of all time.

"I'm going to head home after the unpleasantness with the press.

I'll see you to tomorrow," Captain Murphy says and walks out the door.

Victor and I sit silently until the captain is safely out of ear-shot. The silence is killing me. I want to talk first to break the tension, but this is Victor's tragedy. After a few more pain-staking seconds, he speaks.

"This wasn't some lover's quarrel gone wrong. I know Stacey, and that is not how she would react to anything. She would never hurt innocent people unless she felt like she had no other choice," Victor says with authority.

"She used to be part of the OEC?"I ask.

"Yeah, she quit a couple of years ago to have a family. Got a new job working to make better vaccines or something. She wanted a safer job. That didn't quite work out," Victor says and shakes his head.

"I was thinking about this. There are maybe five Regenerators in the Los Angeles Metro Area that can heal as quickly as Stacey could. Whoever targeted her either got lucky, or they purposefully picked the only one of those five who could dish out bullets just as well as she could take them."

"Her time in the OEC is classified. It's not information that's easy to come by. Even the people she worked with at Ultracorps didn't know what she did before. Hell, her husband Charlie barely knew."

"Would a detective have access to the file?"

"I don't know, maybe," he says with a shrug. "You're thinking about that detective aren't you?"

"Detective Rose. He's the one who's been drugging Differents all over the Metro Area. But that plan didn't work, so he switched strategies and found a way to make a Different go berserk without also making them insane, by threatening their family."

"Why would Rose do all that? Why would he want Differents to kill random civilians?"

"Because he's being paid off. I know for a fact he spends more money than a police officer could possibly make. I just haven't figured out who is writing the checks."

"I'm not going to ask about how you know about Rose's finances. If we all end up arrested, at least I can have plausible deniability about who has been helping you get out at night. Keep it up. If you find anything, you let me know. I'm going to follow orders and head home."

17

The Timberwolves' lead was never in danger. Nevertheless, Billy the Kid kept his foot on the gas, ultimately scoring 55 points in the 105-78 victory over the Lakers. When asked if he will take any time to enjoy the championship victory, Jefferson had this to say: "Sure I will, I have a whole month planned where it will be nothing but my wife and baby. After that, I'll be hitting the gym. My footwork in the post still isn't quite where it needs to be." It seems that despite winning his second championship and his second MVP award, Jefferson still seeks improvements to his game. A scary thought for the rest of the league.

"Timberwolves Win 2nd Championship in a Sweep" by Roger Burns,
Minneapolis StarTribune

October 3rd

Sit-ups: 871
Pushups: 1129
Pull-ups: 321
Running: 15.47 miles, 88.34 minutes total, 5:42 Average Mile time
Diet: 2,700 Calories, 203 grams protein, 303 gram carbohydrates, 75 grams fat.
Sleep: 7:55
Funds: $8,216.45
Ammo Count: 161 rounds 7N1, 281 rounds 9mm, 12 Stun Grenades, 12 Smoke Grenades, 12 Standard Grenades. Nice to have enough ammo to get some target practice in.
Activities: Planning.

Target Notes: Preparing for three possible targets. 25 Male Beta Physically Enhanced, 26 Male Gamma Anthropomorphic Control and a Male Police Detective, Human.
Test Subject Notes: Experiment Suspended.

Personal Notes: Regenerator did her job perfectly. Money Man hoped she would kill OEC agents, but they serve the cause better as failures than martyrs. Spoke with Friend on the Force. Concerned he won't live up to his end of the deal. Will follow tomorrow and confirm, otherwise will need to eliminate.

Friend on force provided intel concerning "The Beast Slayer" tracking me. Nearly time to make a move against the OEC. Victor is primary target. Met him at a charity event back in my playing days. He was quiet and intense. He is the man to beat. "The Beast Slayer" tracking me presents an intriguing opportunity. Developing a plan to neutralize the OEC while also utilizing Money Man's latest acquisitions.

Mental State: Hoping there's no need to eliminate Friend on the Force. Don't like killing normal humans, but can be justified as collateral damage in the war for survival. Worried about the rabbit hole that line of reasoning can lead down.

18

The tragic events in Beckett's Square should serve as a sobering reminder of the pitfalls of relying on Differents to combat crime. We outlawed Differents from law enforcement for good reason. Perhaps everyone else has forgotten what happened in the Chicago Metro Area in 1996, but I have not. Captain Freedom had the best of intentions when he attempted to stop the Bruno crime family, just like the OEC agents had good intentions. Good intentions didn't keep hundreds of thousands of people from dying as a result of Captain Freedom's actions; good intention didn't save those people in Beckett's Square. We need to stop this failed Field Office experiment before the next mistake results in a more costly disaster.

"A Wake Up Call for the Metro Area" by Roberta Clemens, Los Angeles Times

Something has changed. Detective Rose doesn't usually leave the precinct house so full of purpose. I've never seen him move so quickly. He's heading towards the nearby Slug station. Is there a problem in another precinct? Maybe there was another big call, but there hasn't been any breaking news on think.Net. I go on and call Maria as I follow Rose.

<<<*Maria, Rose stormed out of the precinct house like a bat out of hell. Did he get a call?*

>>>*Not anything I saw. I'm working the front desk and it's been slow. I was catching a little sleep so I have the energy to investigate more gun shops tomorrow.*

<<<*How's that going?*

>>>*Slow. There are about only about three hundred gun shops that might carry the kind of hardware we've been going up against. From the owners I've talked to already, that Dragunov sniper rifle is going to run at least twenty grand. I've been taking extra showers to clean off the filth from talking to those scumbags.*

<<<Whoever bought that sniper rifle might have bought the m-60 that the Regenerator was shooting earlier today. She had at least ten thousand rounds on her.

>>>That should help narrow down the list a bit more. Not many shops have that many total bullets, let alone just one type.

<<<Good luck. I've got to go; Rose is about to get on the train. The Slug, not a P-Train. Whatever this is, it doesn't look like official police business.

>>>Good luck yourself.

Rose gets on the Slug. I enter the car behind him and stand at the door so I can see when he exits. I watch him through the windows in the doors between the train cars. He sits down and starts staring at the floor. His eyes stay fixated on the floor almost the entire trip. He takes an occasional break from floor staring to put his face in his hands, rub his eyes, and mutter to himself. He is not a happy man.

I speed up time while the train moves. We ride all the way to the last stop on the line. What in God's name is he doing out here? Rose gets off the Slug. I wait a few seconds to give him a head start, and then follow.

He knows right where he's going. He's walking quickly and purposefully, his grey overcoat splaying out behind him. I'm having a bit of a hard time keeping up because of the bullet wound in my thigh. I walk with a limp to prevent more damage to the muscle.

I keep after him for a few blocks before he turns around suddenly and spots me. There's no alley or shadows to hide in. All I can do is let him look me over. I'm wearing tattered jeans and a t-shirt not my normal OEC blue/grey vomit. I've rushed a ton of water to my face to give me the fat-headed disguise I rely on. I'm a normal Joe on his way home from the late shift. The limp turns out to be a nice touch. Rose stares at me for a few seconds, then shrugs and continues on his way.

Soon we're outside the official Metro Area boundaries. There are no lights in the windows out here. Most of the buildings are abandoned, and those that aren't are full of people who can't afford the Manna cubes needed to feed WormLights. The moon provides the only source of illumination, which works to my advantage. I dilate my pupils fully to allow as much light in as possible while increasing the number of rods in my eyes and decreasing the cones. Now my night vision is as sharp as a human's can possibly be. Rose is older, which means his eyesight is failing, especially at night. I give him a two-block lead, which should be enough to keep my eyes on him while I stay hidden in the shadows. He turns around a few times as we walk, but doesn't indicate he sees me. He's being paranoid, but in this neighborhood, who could blame him?

After four miles of walking, he turns into a non-descript house on some block where the street sign has been missing for three decades. I try to go on think.Net to give Maria an update, but we are out of range. Interesting.

I watch Rose through the holes where the windows used to be. He pulls out a handheld WormLight and starts moving from room to room. What is he doing? I'm suddenly hit by an overpowering odor, one I've only smelled a handful of times before. That's gasoline. Why would Detective Rose... he's going to burn the house down. My God, what if Stacey's husband and kid are inside? I have to try to save them. I suddenly wish I had brought my gun. I wanted to make sure I took Rose alive so I could find out who's been paying him. I'm regretting that decision.

I can tell from the WormLight that Rose is in a room on the far side of the house and hasn't moved for a good thirty seconds. I head through the front door, stepping as lightly as I possibly can. I slowly walk through the house, keeping watch to see if the light moves, but Rose is staying still. Completely still. He put the WormLight down! I hear a click of a gun's trigger hammer behind my head, and then cool metal presses into the back of my skull.

"You picked the wrong guy to rob, buddy. Put your hands up slowly," Detective Rose orders.

I start to raise my hands over my head while I simultaneously contract all of the muscles in my calves, making me drop to the ground. A bullet whizzes by my head, missing by a few inches. When I hit the ground, I kick backwards with my right leg, knocking

Rose to the floor. He fires off three more panicked shots before I manage to pin his arm down. I squeeze on a nerve cluster in the middle of his forearm, which causes his fingers to relax. He drops the gun. I give him a nice left cross so he knows I mean business. The wires holding his jaw closed tear through my glove and rip up my hand. I deserve that. I already won the fight; that punch wasn't necessary.

I lift Detective Rose up off the ground and hold him in the air by his collar. It causes some new damage to the shoulder that's still injured from the fight with the Regenerator, but the re-injury is worth it for the increase in my intimidation factor.

"Where is Stacey Rothschild's family?" I demand.

"How do you know about that? Who are you?" Rose stammers through his busted jaw. He's healed enough for me to understand at least.

I pull the fluids away from the cells of my face, turning back into my usual handsome look.

"The Beast Slayer? Are you kidding me? Take your hands off me right now, or you're doing time," Rose says trying bluff.

"Are you going to call backup? How? We're out of think.Net range. It's just you and me out here. Now answer my question," I say and let go of his collar.

"I'm not telling you anything. You want to interrogate me, then arrest me. I'm not saying a word until I speak to a lawyer." He's going to try every possible strategy to avoid his fate.

I jam my finger into his kidney and he screams out in agony. Good.

"I'm already breaking my parole and the law by following you here. Do you think I care about your Miranda rights? You're going to tell me what I want to know, or you're going to experience pain like you've never felt before. I am an expert on human anatomy. I know how to hurt you so you stay conscious to feel it all. Tell me where the Rothschilds are," I growl.

"They're alive! I swear, they're alive. I was supposed to kill them, but I didn't. I might not like you freaks, but that doesn't mean

I'm going to kill a little girl and the one parent she has left," Detective Rose says.

"Aren't you a saint? Where are they!?"

"I gave them some money and told them to lay low in the Non-Assisted Area for awhile. The father, Charlie, said they'd go down to old San Diego for a few months, his brother or somebody lives down there. You have to understand, if he found out they were alive, he'd kill them and then me. This was the only way. You've got to believe me," Detective Rose pleads.

I do believe him. His heart rate is high, but that's because he's scared, not because he's lying. He isn't averting his eyes. In fact, it seems like he wants to tell me the truth. He's not just afraid of the pain I'll inflict on him, he wants to unburden his soul. Good, that means I'm finally going to get some answers.

"Who was going to kill you all if he found out the Rothschilds were alive?"

"You aren't going to believe me if I tell you," Rose says while shaking his head.

"Like I said, I'm an expert in human anatomy. That means I can tell if you're lying. As long as you tell the truth we shouldn't have any more problems, and you should remain relatively pain free."

"It's William Jefferson... Billy the Kid."

"The basketball player?"

"Yes."

I stare into Detective Rose's eyes. He isn't lying, or at least he thinks he isn't.

"Billy the Kid is dead. He took his own life because his family died in the Danny Libdo Tragedy. Everyone knows that."

"But they never found the body. He really went off to Eastern Europe. He joined some group that hunts Differents over there; they taught him how to kill. He's as good at killing freaks as he was at basketball, better maybe."

"So you're telling me a former basketball player is the one who has been murdering all those Differents?"

"It's the truth, I swear it," Rose says and he means it.

"And you were helping cover up for those murders."

"Yes," Rose says and hangs his head.

"Why?"

"Why? Because my mom's dying, and it's because of you freaks. She has cancer all over her body. They say it's because of all the toxins in her body from the Plagues. I remember in the refugee camps, she always gave us the fresh stuff. She ate the garbage like a rat, so that we kids could have enough. She deserves to die in peace. I have to give her that at least," Rose says without much volume in his voice.

"I told you I'd know if you're lying. Your heart wasn't in your little speech."

"It was when I first took the cash. But mom, the hell she's going through, silk sheets don't make a damn bit of difference. And the things I've done. So many bodies. But I can't stop. They'll never let me," he says, the weight of the admission bending his neck towards the ground.

"Did you kill Stephen Grange?" I ask and he nods yes. "And is that why you gave the sniper the order to shoot Robert White?" He nods again. "Did you give them the drugs?

"Billy and I both did it, we put it in their food. Billy didn't want to do it either. He thought it was a waste of time. Whoever's writing the checks, he's the one who wanted it done. Billy only cares about killing Differents."

"Who is writing the checks?"

"I don't know."

I jab my finger into his ribs.

"Tell me!" I say, then I realize I know he's telling the truth. So why did I hurt him?

"I don't know, I swear."

"Why don't you go to the police if you're so afraid? Your story is nuts, but I'm sure you have enough friends on the force that someone is bound to believe you."

"It's not just Billy, with how much money this guy has, for all I know half the force is paid off. I tell my captain, I end up face down in the dump. The Gambino family will put a hit on a cop for less than I'm getting paid." He does seem scared to talk about this. His hands are shaking.

"What were you doing here? Why were you going to burn this building down?"

"This is where I was keeping the Rothschilds. William ordered me to dispose of the bodies. I figured if I burned the whole building down, he'd never know that they weren't really dead in here."

"You know I'm going to have to bring you back to the OEC office, and you're going to have to repeat this story to our Telepath so she can corroborate that you're telling the truth. Then you're going to have to pay for your crimes."

"I know. It's what I deserve. I'm sorry for what I've done. I'm sorry for everything," Detective Rose says.

Tears start streaming down his face, and he pulls away to hide his shame. I don't think I have to worry about him anymore but to be safe, I bend over and pick up his gun. It's still got one bullet in the chamber.

I give Detective Rose a few moments to pull himself together. Finally, he stops crying and straightens out his overcoat.

"I'm ready to go face the music now," he says.

"Lead the way," I say and point the gun towards the door.

He steps out onto the stoop of the building, and I follow close behind him.

There's a deafening boom. Rose's body goes limp.

It takes me a split-second to realize it was a rifle shot. I dive off of the stoop just in time to hear another boom and a bullet whizz by my head. I don't need to look back to know Rose is dead.

I roll when I hit the ground, and another bullet lands next to me, kicking up a chunk of asphalt that lodges itself into my side. I see a shadowy figure move in the alley. He's climbing what's left of an old fire escape to get away. He already hit his target. He doesn't need to chance a fight with me.

I carefully take aim with the one remaining bullet in Rose's gun and squeeze the trigger. I see it hit the side of the building right next to his head. He moved at the last second. He keeps climbing to the top of the fire escape and takes a last look down on me. The moonlight gives me a view of his face. There's no doubt who it is, William "Billy the Kid" Jefferson, former point guard for the Minneapolis Metro Area Timberwolves, two-time NBA champion, and apparently, psychopathic serial killer. I have to get back into think.Net range and call Maria.

#

I make it my Slug stop and get off the train. The platform is already starting to fill up with people on their way to work, even though it's only 7:30AM. Good thing I've never seen Captain Murphy in the office before 9:00, and that's still a rarity. Even at the speed I'm moving I'll make it back with time to spare. I really did a number on my already-injured thigh with all that running around and need some time to focus on healing, and most importantly, some time when I'm not using my leg.

I could use some time to process what I've learned too. My brain just absorbed some shocking information and I haven't had the chance to think through all the implications. I need to think of a better way to explain what I know. Maria trusts me and it still took twenty minutes on think.Net to convince her I wasn't crazy.

I start limping through the small crowd when I feel a tap on my shoulder. I've felt that tap before: it's Ben. He's got a knack for bad timing.

"Hey Gavin, you up for another chat while you're injured? Feels like old times, don't it?"

"Ben, not the best time... Wait! Tell me, did you go to St. Louis? Was The Beast there?"

"Now you're the one who needs to work on their social graces. My trip was fine. St. Louis is lovely this time of year. I especially enjoyed the miles and miles full of nothing. Did you know the Arch is still standing? Ten feet of it anyway."

My brain wants to experience anger. I let the emotion flow. I've had enough of this lunatic and his antics. I grab him by the shirt collar.

"Tell me. Is he alive?"

"It wasn't him. He's not in St. Louis. Now take your hands off me, or this is going to get ugly. You might think I'm just a brainiac, but trust me Gavin, you don't want a piece of this," Ben says confidently.

I have to admit that threat makes me curious about what he can really do, but a crowded train platform while I'm riddled with bullet holes isn't the best time or place to get in a fight. I let go of his shirt.

"Great, so I risked my parole breaking into the Ultracorps records all for nothing. Did you enjoy checking out an empty mine?" I say mockingly.

"I didn't say it was all for nothing, and I didn't say the mine was empty. I said The Beast wasn't being kept there. Believe me, this information was worth risking your parole for."

"Okay, lay it on me."

"Like I said, The Beast wasn't being held there, but another Different was. Jessica Hayes," Ben says. He knows I don't know who that is and he wants me to ask.

"Who is Jessica Hayes?"

"You've got follow politics a little closer, Gavy. Jessica Hayes is Robert Hayes' daughter, as in ex-governor Robert Hayes, as in the daughter whose supposed disappearance helped spur Hayes into his first-term victory five years ago. It turns out she wasn't kidnapped in a heart-breaking tragedy. Instead, her ten year GIS screener test came back positive as a Different, and no politician with a Different kid could ever get elected. So she got shipped off to live in some town in the Non-Assisted Area."

"How did she end up in an Ultracorps-owned mine?"

"She's an Energy Producer. Her body is able to generate vibrations strong enough to create localized earthquakes. Problem is she's not all that good at controlling them. She destroyed the town she was living in before they ran her off. She was wandering in the woods, lost and confused, when some Ultracorps miner on a lunch break spotted her. Eventually, somebody up the chain—*cough*, Nita, *cough*—figured out who she was," Ben says with a smug grin.

"They're keeping Jessica prisoner?"

"Kinda. She doesn't think that she's locked up. She thinks she's keeping everyone else safe by staying there."

"So why are they holding her?" Getting to the point is not one of Ben's strengths.

"As a kindness to former Governor Hayes. Ultracorps in its benevolence decided to provide safe housing and also kept the whole issue out of the press, which made Governor Hayes so full of joy he resigned his position as Governor so someone who was not against the Ultracorps takeover of the municipal water system could take his place."

"If it's blackmail, why not make him reverse his decision on the contract? Why make him resign?"

"Hayes could have reversed his decision, but that would have been reversing a reversal. The public doesn't expect much from its politicians, but wishy-washiness is one thing that is unacceptable. If Hayes did that he wouldn't have stood a chance of winning reelection. Who knows who would have won the next election? Maybe it would be someone Nita couldn't control, like how she couldn't control Hayes before she found his daughter," Ben says. Still taking his time to get to his final point.

"Are you saying Nita controls the new Governor-- Khan?"

"He sure seemed like he was in a hurry to approve that Ultracorps water contract. It was the first thing he did when he took office. Only Nita and Ultracorps stock holders had that as a top priority for the Metro Area."

"Do you think she kidnapped his kids too?"

"He doesn't have any. It might be good old fashioned bribery. There are a few irregularities with his banking records, but I still haven't figured out what he's doing with the money. Anyway, Nita can trust a man who's motivated by money. No one can pay more than Ultracorps."

"This is all pretty nuts. Good job Ben. I just don't get what you want to do about all this. What's your endgame here?"

"I want Ultracorps bankrupted so Differents are free to work wherever they desire. I want Nita deposed from power so whatever insane plan she's hatching never comes to fruition. I want to expose her."

"How? By talking to the press? Even if you had hard proof, which I'm guessing is lacking, Hayes is who comes out looking like the villain here. Sending his kid to go live in the Non-Assisted area for political gain is awful, but he's already resigned. Maybe you could make Khan resign too, but he'll just get replaced with another politician who might be willing to take a bribe. Sure, Ultracorps will take a PR hit, but they're already the most hated company in America, and that hasn't slowed them down yet," I say. It's sad but true.

"I'm not done connecting the dots yet. For all we know, Nita is doing the same thing in every Metro Area. If you help me, we could find more evidence…"

"I'm going to have to stop you right there, Ben. As disturbing as all of this is, large corporations and politicians acting corrupt in the name of profit is not exactly shocking news. What is shocking is that there is a serial-killing former NBA player who faked his own death on the loose, and I'm the only one who knows about him. Right now, that is my primary concern. I can go back to trying to fix all of the vague evils in the world after I've stopped the actual and acute problem of Differents being murdered, drugged, and blackmailed."

"It can't just be about making money. She has a bigger plan. Nita is pulling all the strings in this Metro Area, and soon it might be the whole country," Ben pleads. He's obsessed with her. He doesn't even care that I just told him a former NBA player is killing people. You'd think that might bring on a few questions.

"I know you can't wait to stymie her as revenge for taking your job, but it's going to take more than you and me to stop all that. I got some advice on being a hero the other day I think you could use: part of heroism is accepting that you can't fix everything and having the courage to do the right thing when you actually can make a difference. That's what I'm going to do now. If you want to help, you can try to find out who was paying for the crimes I'm investigating. I'm going to be busy trying to hunt down a killer," I say and walk away.

"I'll do it," I hear Ben yell, but I'll believe it when I see it.

19

Log of Notable Nita/Ultracorps Activity Week 219

Investigating the anomalies of Ultracorps' increased food deliveries to Eat-N-Go led to discovering a series of anomalies in both companies' records. Eat-N-Go chain is owned by Governor Khan.

Theories: Obvious money laundering scheme to cover bribe money paid by Nita to Governor Khan for his support. However, cannot locate where Khan is ultimately depositing money. Tens of thousands unaccounted for. If I can discover location, may be able to draw a trail to Nita. Will also check Khan-owned medical clinic.

Ben stands in the shadows between two abandoned, half-collapsed warehouses. It's been dark for hours, but the street is lit up by WormLights, and he doesn't want to be seen. Ben watches a Strong-Man carry a massive barrel; the giant container is the same size as the gigantic man. The mountain of muscle hauls the barrel up the ramp and through a cargo door that belongs to an Eat-N-Go grocery store. The man disappears from Ben's sight, but soon there's a loud thud, the Strong-Man dropping the barrel into place. The giant man re-emerges flanked by a tattoo-less human worker.

"See you Friday, Freddy. We got two more barrels coming in," the human worker laughs.

"Two more? Christ, are you trying to kill me? I don't know if my back can take it. You guys bathing in this stuff or something?" the Strong-Man asks and shakes his head.

"Beats me. Not my job to know what we're doing with it. I'm just here to make sure all the deliveries come through."

"That and spending the rest of the time watching old movies on think.Net."

"We've all got our jobs to do," the human worker says while

folding his arms to show his mock offense.

"At least I get to hear your recommendations. You were right about that Rocky movie. Hell of a picture. I've had that theme song stuck in my head all week. Helps get me pumped up when I'm feeling gassed. The sequel any good?" the Strong-Man asks while throwing a few shadow boxing jabs.

"I'll tell you Friday. That's what I'm watching tonight. See you, Freddy," the human worker says and closes the cargo bay door.

Freddy the Strong-Man heads down the street, his heavy steps rattling the dilapidated street's cracked pavement. Ben steps out from the shadows as Freddy approaches.

"It's a little slower than the first one, but it gets going at the end and pretty soon you're right back into it," Ben says.

"Excuse me?" Freddy asks, confused.

"Rocky II. I couldn't help but overhear you asking about it. It's not quite as good as the first one, but still worth watching."

"Oh yeah? Thanks for the review from the alley. Have a good night buddy," Freddy says while hitting Ben with a cross-eyed look.

"You too. Say, you look a little peckish. You want a Manna Bar?" Ben asks while extending a small package.

"Seriously? Yeah, I really could use one. It's been a long day, and I already ran through my supply. Thanks a lot," Freddy says as he takes the bar. He quickly tears open the package and devours the eight-inch, incredibly dense stick in a single bite.

"No worries. We've got to look out for our own," Ben says and holds up his arm into the streetlight, revealing his tattoo.

"Right on. So what's your classification? It's too dark out to read your Mark," Freddy says licking his lips to capture every calorie and drop of flavor from his snack.

"Big Brain. I'm on my way to my think.Net node. Shift starts in twenty minutes. How about you?"

"Strong-Man, but I guess you probably can tell that from looking at me. I do deliveries mostly, just finished my last one for the night."

"Yeah? What kind of stuff do you deliver?" Ben asks while pretending to look at something on his arm, giving the impression that it's an idle question.

"Whatever needs hauling. I was dropping off some Sodium Benz-o-stuff at an Eat-N-Go.

"Sodium Benzoate?" Ben says, his eyes wide with shock.

"Yeah that's the one. You're a Big Brain, you must know what it's for."

"It's a preservative. You can put it on meat or produce to keep it from going bad. It can also be a component in an explosive."

"Well that Eat-N-Go must have lost their Cooler or something. I dropped off four hundred pounds of the stuff, and I'm supposed to do more later this week. They've been getting deliveries of it all month."

"You don't say," Ben replies.

#

"How many pounds of apples did you say you have available, Mr. Crowell?" the balding, sweating, red-faced Eat-N-Go store manager asks.

Ben has crafted another combination of transformative and identity obfuscating clothes and makeup. He dyed his hair grey and drew fake wrinkles of wisdom to become a sixty-year-old man. His mock personification of a Southern business man is aided by his white and blue striped seersucker suit and bolo tie, relics from Ben's days of having extra spending money.

Ben the Southerner and the Eat-N-Go store manager walk around the storage area of a grocery store. They're surrounded by ceiling-grazing towers of Soy Snacks, Millet-Cakes, Rice-Bites, and dozens of other pre-packaged nourishment. There are even bins of fresh produce. Bananas and corn, a rare sight.

"I was hoping we could start with a delivery of six hundred pounds," Ben says, doing his best Foghorn Leghorn impression. The old cartoons were one of the few inspirations for his over-the-top Southern drawl. "That'd be a trial run you see. That all goes off without a hitch, and then the sky's the limit. We've developed our own brand of fertilizer. I tell you what, it'd put chest hair on a supermodel. Best of all, it lets us grow apples all the year round."

"Is it true you don't use any Different labor to grow or harvest your produce?" the manager asks with disbelief.

"That's right. It is the genuine human article, like in your front yard growing up, or mine at least. I'm a little older than you," Ben says giving the manager a friendly pat on the back. "Of course we still have to use Ultracorps trains and Strong-Men to haul the stuff, 'no way around that yet, but we have humans do as much as they can."

"Nothing against those people of course," the manager says shaking his head as proof he really means it, "but we've noticed there's a large segment of consumers who desire food grown the old fashioned way. It's a niche we'd like to serve. Within the next year, we'll be the sole supermarket chain in the Los Angeles Metro Area that offers food one hundred percent grown by humans. We've only got three stores right now, but we've got plans for five more breaking ground in the next six months."

"I bet the owner moving on up to Governor helps cut through all that nasty paperwork."

"It doesn't hurt," the manager says with a smile.

"Sounds like you folks got some real schemes cooking. And thank you for the tour behind the curtains. I know it's a mite peculiar, but I like to know all I can about who I'm getting into business with. I always say, go ahead and show me the sausage being made, I'll still eat it," Ben says and slaps his thigh in delight at his own joke.

"It's my pleasure. Whatever it takes to get us into business together."

Ben spots dozens of large barrels in the corner, the large biohazard symbols on the containers warning him to stay away.

"Whoa, what in the Sam Hill is that stuff?" Ben points and asks.

"I think that's all Potassium Nitrate," the manager says, flubbing the pronunciation.

"Another preservative. It would very dangerous mixed mix with Sodium Benzoate," Ben says under his breath.

"Excuse me?" the manager asks.

"What's it for? Those symbols aren't very inviting," Ben stammers.

"I know it looks frightening, but I assure you it's all perfectly safe. As I said, we're trying to move away from Different labor, including Coolers. That chemical is a preservative they're trying out that can hopefully help us move away from using the refrigeration the Coolers provide. If you're worried I'm sure some egghead in the corporate office could explain it better. I could try to raise them on think.Net."

"No, no. That's not necessary, my boy," Ben says waving his hand dismissively. "I'm sure I wouldn't understand all that scientific gobble-de-gook anyway. I'm just shocked at how much of the stuff you've got. I don't know what from what, but that looks like enough for a hundred years."

"We are planning to be a fixture in the Los Angeles Metro Area for a long time," the manager says with a smile.

#

"Nurse, you've got to help me. My back has been killing me all week. If I miss another day at the docks, I'll lose my job," Ben pleads.

His latest disguise centers on grey overalls. This time, he splattered them with fish guts. Ben did not enjoy applying the stench, but it was necessary to sell his charade of being a dock worker. He's sitting on an exam table in a doctor's office. A young female nurse examines Ben while doing her best to hide her disgust at his offensive odor.

"The doctor will be in shortly," the nurse says while choking down her gag reflex.

"Tell him to come quick. I feel like I'm dying here."

"He'll be in as soon as he can," she says, then scurries out of the room, taking a deep breath as soon as she hits the hallway.

Ben waits a few beats, then pokes his head out of the exam room. He watches the nurse go back to the reception desk. He counts ten more exam rooms nearby, all full of patients. The doctor will not be coming to see him any time soon. Instead of succumbing to a fate of sitting bored and shirtless in the exam room waiting for the doctor for the next twenty minutes, Ben slinks out of the room, carefully pulling the door closed behind him.

He makes a beeline to a door marked "Dispensary." Ben is not here for back pain, he's here to assess the inventory behind that door. Some odd drug orders are linked to this location, and Governor Khan owns this clinic. A costumed caper to infiltrate the location was the only possible plan of action.

He tries the door, which is unsurprisingly locked. As usual, Ben came prepared. He pulls out a small tool from his pocket and turns a knob on the device, releasing a metal needle. He shoves it into the door lock and, after a few seconds of jingling, the door opens.

Ben rifles through the shelves, tossing aside boxes of penicillin, morphine, codeine, amoxicillin and many more drugs. There is nothing out of the ordinary. All Ben has accomplished is making an unfortunate mess for whoever cleans up this room. Despondent, he takes one last glance around the room and spots a small metal chest in the corner. It is secured with a heavy-duty lock. Ben spends several minutes alternating between jiggling his tool in the lock and cursing in frustration before the chest finally opens, revealing its booty.

Amphetamines, clonazepam, diazepam, and dozens of other drugs used to treat mental illness. These drugs do not belong in a clinic like this. They belong in a psychiatric ward. If these drugs are administered in the wrong dosage, or mixed, there could be disastrous results. The doctors who work in this clinic aren't qualified to dispense this type of medication. So what is it doing here?

As Ben's mind races through the possibilities, his ears miss the sound of the young female nurse stepping into the room behind him.

"What are you doing in here?" the nurse demands with a shout.

"I uh, was looking for something to help the pain," Ben stammers in response.

"I bet that's what you were doing. I know why you're really here," the nurse says, her face turning red with anger.

"You do?" Ben asks as panic overtakes him. He starts mentally preparing his escape plan.

"That's right. Now get the hell out of here, and if you ever show your drug-addicted face in this facility again, I'm calling the cops. You do need help, just not the kind we provide. Now move!" the nurse yells and points out the door.

"Okay, I'm going," Ben says, relieved he's been mistaken for a simple drug addict. He slinks out of the room while struggling to contain his smile. The nurse doesn't know it, but Ben found just what he was looking for, or what Gavin was looking for, to be precise.

20

I'm not going to argue that letting only Ultracorps employ Different labor is a fair economic practice. Of course it gives Ultracorps a productivity boost that no other corporation can compete with. Perhaps our government needs to do more to help companies that rely on human labor succeed. However, those calling for a repeal of the Different Acts of 1996 aren't thinking clearly. While confining the use of Different labor to Ultracorps creates a host of economic problems, it also ensures the safety of every citizen in the Metro Area. If every company was allowed to employ Different labor, there would be utter chaos. I for one will gladly take a hit to my paycheck if it means the proper precautions are taken to ensure another Danny Libdo explosion doesn't occur.

"Money Isn't Everything" by Forest Brown, think.Net News LA

I walk into the OEC office and hear voices talking. Voices belonging to Victor, Linda, and Captain Murphy. That is not good. What are they doing here so early? I feel thoughts trying to force their way into my head and I let them in. Linda must have heard me open the door.

>>>*I told Captain Murphy I gave you permission to get some breakfast with an old teacher. Go with it.*

<<<*Understood.*

That's a much better explanation than that I was illegally following a police detective. Especially considering that detective ended up dead. I walk into Captain Murphy's office as nonchalantly as I can. I wasn't doing anything wrong. I had permission to be outside. I was getting breakfast with my old teacher Larry Rosen. I make myself think it's true so I can be more convincing.

"Gavin, how nice of you to join us. Did you enjoy your breakfast?" Captain Murphy asks.

"It was good. I haven't been out to eat breakfast since I got arrested. Linda thought it would be okay. One of my teachers from Section 26 was in town, and he could only meet in the morning."

"I suppose you wouldn't mind if I called this teacher to corroborate your story?" Captain Murphy asks with a frown.

"Be my guest. His name is Larry Rosen. He's on assignment with the Federal Government so he might be hard to get a hold of, but if you hurry, you might be able to catch him before he gets out of the Metro Area," I reply.

I'm hoping that Captain Murphy doesn't call my bluff—it was a good one. If he does, there's still a decent chance Larry will cover for me anyway. He's good at thinking on his feet and lying to government men is old hat for him. On the other hand, he never returned my phone calls after I was arrested, so I'm not sure if I can count on him.

"Does that explain why I wasn't able to raise you on think.Net late last night when I called everyone else and told them to get in early?" Captain Murphy asks. His tone is indicating it doesn't matter what answer I give.

"There were some problems with think.Net last night. A few of the Librarians got the flu, and it messed the system up for anyone whose information was stored on those individuals," Linda chimes in. She's not much of a liar.

"God, you people think I'm stupid." Captain Murphy says and rubs his face. "I might not be a Different, but I did manage to graduate kindergarten. Do you really expect me to believe this B.S.? How about you, Victor? Do you have your own set of lies to add to the mix? What do you say Gavin was up to?"

"Gavin was out there risking his freedom, and based on that new wound in his side, maybe even his life. Why don't we both shut up and let Gavin tell us what he was doing? Go ahead and talk, Gavin. Captain Murphy is going to hear it one way or another," Victor says with the conviction only someone who wasn't in on my crime could have.

I'm caught red handed. It looks like the truth is my one possible defense. So I go ahead and talk. I tell them about following Rose, his attempts to burn down the house, him admitting that he was involved in the cover-up. Then I tell them the most unbelievable part, that William "Billy the Kid" Jefferson has been committing all the murders. I have to repeat that last part a half-dozen times.

"Gavin, there's no easy way to say this, but I think you might need to seek some sort of professional help. I don't know if there's anyone who specializes in treating Differents, but if there is, we'll find them. This OEC office will stand with you," Captain Murphy says. I'm both touched and offended.

"He's not lying," Linda says.

"I know he believed what he said. That's why I'm so concerned," Captain Murphy says. And he is.

"I went inside his head while he was talking, and he showed me the visuals. I'm no sports fan, but even I recognize William Jefferson. There's no doubt that's who it was," Linda says.

"This is nuts. You're telling me a basketball player who has been dead for seven years has returned as a serial killer? It's the craziest thing I've ever heard," Captain Murphy says, his eyes wide

"He went missing and was presumed dead. They never found a body, just a suicide note," Victor replies.

"Are you saying you believe this Victor? You're telling me Billy the Kid faked his own death, and now he's targeting Differents to what? Try to avenge his dead wife and baby? He's out of luck. Danny Libdo killed himself along with most of the Minneapolis Metro Area when he exploded," Captain Murphy says.

"That's how hate works. It's not rational," I chime in.

"How's he managing to kill all of these Differents? They couldn't all be Gammas, some of them must have been a threat. Hitting a three-point shot is a far cry from killing someone a hundred times stronger than you. How'd he get so good at killing?" Captain Murphy demands.

"Rose said he spent most of the last seven years in Eastern Europe training to be a killer," I tell them.

"I don't find it hard to believe at all. I met him a few times at charity events back in my playing days. He was the most intense and driven person I've ever met. William Jefferson was the kind of man who could do anything he set his mind to by sheer force of determination. I have no doubt he would make as good a killer as he was a basketball player," Victor says.

"Let's say I believe all this, a big assumption, what do we do next? The police aren't going to take Gavin's word for it, perfect memory or not. And the other person who could corroborate the story, Detective Rose, is lying dead somewhere in the slums. And if William really is the professional killer you say he is, that body is long gone," Captain Murphy says and throws his hands up.

"Might be for the best. The L.A.P.D. could try to pin it on me," I say.

Everyone nods in agreement. I was witnessed assaulting Rose, and interfering with his investigations. I'm a lock for the position of prime-suspect in his murder.

They keep talking, but I zone out. I'm getting a think.Net call from Maria. I wonder if she found the gun shop that's been supplying William.

>>>*Gavin, what side of the building are you on? I just got here.*

<<<*To the OEC offices?*

>>>*You don't know? Check the news. There was an explosion at an Ultracorps lab. I think it's the one you used to work at. It's bad.*

I end my conversation with Maria, and think about accessing breaking news. The alerts ring in my head: there was a massive explosion at my old lab. Hundreds are missing.

"Are we boring you, Gavin?" Captain Murphy asks.

"There's been an explosion at my old lab. Might be hundreds dead, lots of Differents," I say.

"That's terrible," Linda says, "I'm so sorry to hear that, Gavin. Should we finish this conversation later?"

"I've got friends there. I'm going to try and help," I say and start heading out the door.

"Like hell you are! That is not your job. We are not emergency services. I am ordering you to stay here!" Captain Murphy demands while stomping his foot.

"Order all you want. I'm going."

"And I'm going with him. You can either tell your superiors that both of your agents aren't listening to your orders, or you can say you decided to have compassion and send us to help. You can pick which way you want to go," Victor says.

We both head out of the office while Captain Murphy ponders his powerlessness.

#

My old lab looks like pictures of Germany after World War II, which is one large pile of rubble. If I close my eyes and try to connect the dots between what's left standing, there still isn't anything resembling a building. What could have caused such damage?

"The investigation is still ongoing, but based on where the blast came from they're thinking a Different lost control of his abilities. Peter Warsall, an Energy Producer, is the top suspect," Maria says. There's so much confusion and commotion, I guess she thinks it's safe to talk to us without being spotted by her judgmental cop coworkers.

"They think P-Dub did this? I knew him, and there is no freaking way. The explosions he could generate were barely big enough to kill a house cat," I say.

"That's the story until someone can come up with a better explanation," Maria says.

"Like a bomb placed by a psychopathic, serial killing, former NBA MVP?" Victor asks.

"It's safe to say the three of us are alone on working that angle. We can't get too carried away with that theory though. We don't know what happened here. It's important to keep an open mind," Maria says.

"Are there any survivors? I can't get through to any of my friends who worked here," I say.

"Not many. A few people walking on the street got away with relatively minor injuries. It was such a big explosion, there isn't much hope," Maria says, then she realizes she's talking about people

I know. "But it's still possible. Who knows what you Differents can do? And I'm sure think.Net is just jammed up by all the activity here. Emergency services gets first priority on bandwidth. That might be why you can't get through."

"Why aren't the crews searching through the wreckage yet? People could be trapped under there," Victor says.

"We're still waiting for the okay to move in. They've got some specialists checking to make sure there isn't going to be another explosion," Maria answers.

"I'm done waiting," I announce.

I start climbing through the rubble up towards the center of the pile, Victor following behind me. I'm not moving very quickly. My thigh injury is still slowing me down.

"What's the plan here?" he asks.

"I'm going to the center. It's the furthest I can get from all of these emergency workers and their racket. Then I'm going to turn my hearing up as high as I can and see if there's anyone making noise in the rubble. Then you can help me dig them out," I say with authority. I'm not sure when I became the one deciding on a plan, but it makes me proud that Victor is willing to listen.

"I can speed this up," Victor says, and then he grabs me by the waist of my pants.

In two leaps he jumps to center of the pile, carrying me like a bag of luggage. He is so freaking strong.

"Thanks, now don't say anything. I'm going to turn my hearing way up."

I drain all of the fluid from my tympanic cavity, which makes my eardrum much more sensitive. Then I push my brain's focus off all of the sounds I hear in the distance, and hone in on what's closer to me. I can hear the rubble settling into place and water dripping through the debris. I hear something else too, a rhythmic tapping.

I signal Victor to follow me, and I head towards the source of the tapping. The sound of the steps Victor and I take are deafening. I'm damaging my eardrums, but I can heal those later. If someone is trapped under the rubble, they might only have a few minutes before they succumb to their injuries or suffocate.

We arrive at the source of the tapping, and I point to where it's coming from. Victor starts tossing aside chunks of B-Crete that weigh hundreds of pounds. As he digs, another sound becomes clear. It's a voice. Sarah the Crash Test Dummy?

"Help! We're down here," Sarah yells.

"Hang tight! We're coming for you," I promise.

"Hurry! Gary isn't going to last much longer," she replies.

I turn down my hearing so my eardrums don't explode and join Victor digging. It takes a few minutes to reach them. The last bit of rubble is a Maceo Steel support beam. Victor and I get in position to lift the beam.

"On three. One, two…" Victor says.

Then the beam is thrown upwards from below. It is Gary. He has been holding the beam up to protect the people underneath it. He saved Sarah, Dr. Cole, and two other lab employees I don't recognize. Everyone besides Sarah is in bad shape. Gary looks like he got it the worst. There's a Maceo Steel pipe piercing straight through his chest.

"Gary, oh my God, hold on!" I yell.

Victor and I help the other four survivors out of the pit. Sarah helps lift Dr. Cole out. He's unconscious.

"We've got to get them some medical attention," Victor says as he throws Dr. Cole and one of the other employees over his shoulder.

"I'll help," Sarah says. She props up the healthiest employee. His leg is badly injured. He leans on Sarah as they start making their way out of the rubble.

"Bring back help for Gary!" I yell after them.

I climb down into the pit to join Gary. He's still breathing, but it is labored. I don't think he's going to make it.

"Hey Gavin, how's the celebrity life treating you?"

"You know the public. My fifteen minutes are about up. I might have to pay for that drink we had planned."

"That's okay, I probably shouldn't be drinking. It'll just flow out of the pipe," Gary says with a laugh that quickly turns to a horrific cough.

"Hang in there, Gary. Help is on the way."

"For someone with complete control of their body or whatever, you're not a convincing liar."

"The hell you say. It's all I've been doing lately. Besides, what do you know about lying?"

"More than you think, Gavin. I have to tell you something, and it isn't easy. I'm lucky I'm going to die afterwards."

"You can tell me later in the hospital."

"Gavin, listen to me!" Gary yells through his labored breaths. "You were right. You were right about everything. Nita did ask me to make friends with you. She wanted to know what you were up to. I'm pretty sure she knew Becky was alive when you went after The Beast. I'm sorry, man. If it helps, it started as a job but I kept hanging out with you because I liked you."

"That isn't possible. I already asked you about all that, and you told me I was crazy. You weren't lying. I can tell when someone's lying."

"Not as well as you think you can. If it helps your pride, Nita had to train me to hide my tells. Larry helped."

"Larry was in on it to? What about Sarah?"

"I don't think Sarah knew, but I can't be sure. I don't even know what the 'it' we were in on was. I just knew that having Nita on my side was good for me."

"I can't believe this."

"That's not the worst part... It's The Beast, Gavin. He's alive. That fall messed him up, but he was still breathing. I carried him to some Ultracorps facility and put him in a room made of Maceo Steel. Nita made me do it," Gary says and slumps his head forward.

"Where was it? Where did you bring him? You have to tell me," I demand.

Gary starts to speak, but then his eyes roll back into his head.

"Gary!" I say and give him a shake, but get no response.

Three medical workers jump down into the pit and join us. They go to work quickly, putting an oxygen mask on Gary and attempt to stick a needle in his arm but it breaks on his skin. I step back so they can do their job. I don't know what the treatment regime is for a large pipe impaled in the chest, but I'm guessing there's not much they can do. It's made of Maceo Steel, so cutting it isn't even an option. He starts to fade away, quickly. It took his last ounce of strength to summon the courage to tell me the truth.

I climb out of the hole, my mind struggling to comprehend the new information. Gary befriended me because Nita wanted him to, but why did Nita want to keep tabs on me? More importantly, what is she doing with The Beast, and where is he? He doesn't deserve to live after all the things he's done. God, do I wish I knew how to contact Nita. Although, maybe it's for the best that I'll get some time to think about what I'll say to her.

Victor sees me staring off. He walks up and puts his hand on my shoulder. We make our way out towards the police perimeter together.

"Do you know him well?" Victor asks.

"I'm not sure. We were friends, or I thought we were. I don't really know."

"We never know which deaths will hit us the hardest. Do you still think you'll be up to look for evidence? We'll have to wait until the police leave, but they seem happy to blame it on a Different. They aren't even considering the possibility of a bomb. We'll be on our own looking for fragments or some other clue. I've got some experience with explosives, but not much. Hopefully that cop friend of yours knows what she's doing. You going to be okay?"

"Yeah, I can push the emotions out of my mind. I'll be fine."

#

Gary's funeral has a quiet, somber tone befitting the situation. The crowd is made up of a few friends and loved ones, those that are still alive at least. I'm lucky Captain Murphy let me out to attend. He wasn't too happy about us running out on him. I spot people I assume are Gary's parents sobbing over the largest coffin I have ever seen. There are some fellow Strong-Men here to show their support, and it's a good thing, because they'll be needed to lower the casket into the ground. I spot Jason Jackson in the crowd. It brings back memories of going out with him, P-Dub, and Gary to the Cabotist bar. Now those last two are dead, and P-Dub is still being blamed for the explosion. I wasn't his biggest fan, but nobody deserves to die with blood on their hands that doesn't belong there.

The police still aren't taking the bomb theory seriously. Maria says they're doing their due diligence, but it seems like everyone would be happier if we could pin this all on P-Dub, call it an industrial accident, and move on. Maria sounded exhausted the last time I spoke to her. I think she's spending all her free time trying to find evidence to prove it was a bomb. I told her she should stop wasting her time; if it really was Billy the Kid, he's proven that he's a pro. He's not going to leave a trail of breadcrumbs back to his lair. We aren't going to get that lucky. I should stop thinking about this. I should be thinking about Gary. He deserves that much.

I spot Sarah in the crowd. She bears no sign of the bomb she survived a couple of days ago. She's standing with a middle-aged man I don't recognize, although there is something familiar about his red hair... Larry Rosen! My old teacher. I head over to stand with them.

"How's it going, Dummy? Larry?"

Larry gives me a nod.

"Hey, Gavin. I'm okay, I guess. How about you?" Sarah says.

I don't know if I've ever heard a non-smart-aleck comment come from her mouth. The look on her face betrays how she's feeling. She looks like she might rather be in the coffin. She was popular in the lab. I can only imagine how many funerals she's gone to the last few days. Only six people who were inside in the lab survived, and she's the only one who was able to walk away. She wasn't even taken to the hospital. It's because she's a Regenerator, but that doesn't seem to be alleviating her survivor's guilt. If only her body could heal from emotional trauma as well as it does from physical injuries.

Larry walks over to me, his chin hanging low. He steps close to me.

"Gavin, I'm so sorry about your coworkers," Larry whispers. "And I know I've owed you a phone call for awhile. Any chance I can take you to lunch? Pay off the debt with a free meal as interest."

"I don't know. I'm busy, and I don't think I'm allowed to go to lunch right now," I say back stone faced.

Larry opens his mouth to speak, but he suddenly goes silent. A priest stands in front of the massive casket. The crowd goes silent.

Think.Net alerts me that someone wants to talk to me, someone unidentified. Nita. Why does she bother hiding her identity? She's the only person I know who can do it, which pretty much defeats the purpose.

>>>*Hello Gavin, is the funeral nice?*

<<<*It's a great funeral, tons of fun. You're really missing out.*

>>>*I'm sorry, Gavin. I am not very familiar with death. I am still learning how to speak appropriately on the subject. I hope you can forgive me.*

<<<*I'll give you a free etiquette tip. If you know someone is at a funeral, you shouldn't call them to chat.*

>>>*This is not a social call, Gavin. As you know, Gary and I were friends. Unfortunately, my duties as Head Librarian make it impossible for me to attend in person. I was wondering if you might be willing to let me view the service through your eyes. That way I can still feel as though I paid my respects.*

<<<*Sure thing, friend.*

I open my mind to think.Net and let the Telepath see what my mind sees so she can send it to Nita. Because of my abilities, I've always had control of what I want to show Telepaths. I can feel them in my mind, but I direct what the feed shows.

I haven't really planned out how I'm going to confront Nita about Gary's confession, but maybe trying to plan is a mistake. She's smarter than me; catching her by surprise might be the best way to throw her off her game. I think I know just how to do that.

I let her see through my eyes for awhile, sending the direct nerve signals straight to the network. She sees the opening of the priest's speech. Some kind and true words about how well loved Gary was.

Then I change the channel.

Instead of showing Nita what my eyes are seeing and my ears are hearing, I show her my memories of Gary dying in that pit. She sees Gary using what little strength he had left to confess his crimes. I hope those memories burn in her brain like they scarred mine. I want her to know that Gary died with a heavy heart, weighed down by guilt over what she made him do. I want her to know that I understand exactly who she is.

>>>*Could you not have picked a more appropriate time for this revelation, Gavin?*

<<<*I don't let liars and criminals dictate to me what proper behavior is. The Beast is alive. You saved him. Why? Where is he?*

>>>*It is a complicated issue. I assure you he is being kept in a secure location. He can no longer harm anyone. He is a unique individual. His biology cannot go to waste.*

<<<*Oh, you already did all the killing you needed with your little toy so you put him away? I know he thought he was talking to God, and I know that was really you. Are you going to deny that?*

>>>*No, I am not going to deny that. I have no further reason to lie to you. The fact of the matter is The Beast is a killer, one I was not certain we had the power to stop. That left me to choose between two undesirable options. The Beast could go on a rampage killing hundreds maybe thousands indiscriminately before he was finally subdued, or I could give him a purpose. As God, I was able to drive him towards targeting the elderly and sick.*

<<<*Why couldn't you tell him not to kill at all?*

>>>*You met the man; he is a force of nature. I could steer him, not control him.*

<<<*What about Victor?*

>>>*Victor possesses similar speed and strength to The Beast, but Victor could not match the creature's ferocity or healing ability. I gave him less than a five percent chance of victory. The Beast also proved resistant to Telepathic attacks. He would have likely killed dozens of OEC agents before being defeated. The ensuing damage to the Los Angeles Metro Area would have taken more lives than The*

Beast did in his years of killings. By controlling him, I was able to limit the number of deaths. It is not a situation I am proud of, but it is my belief that the alternative was worse.

<<<And the Ultracorps opponents you bumped off were a bonus?

>>>As I said, I needed to give him purpose. He would not have been content to simply feed on the elderly indefinitely. Serving my needs and serving the greater good are not necessarily antithetical. The Beast saw himself as an agent of salvation. I had to present him with targets that fit with his skewed morality.

<<<You're one to talk about skewed morality.

>>>And you are? If I recall, you are ready and willing to put the law aside when it runs afoul of your own sense of ethics. What I do is not fundamentally different from what you did as the vigilante. You were willing to go against society's values to further your own vision of the world. I do the same. I am simply more capable than you are.

<<<Including blackmailing Governor Hayes.

>>>I assume you are speaking of his daughter, who is being kept safe in an Ultracorps facility. What you call blackmail I call giving a man who dedicated his life to public service the chance to recede out of the spotlight while maintaining his legacy. Releasing the news of Hayes' daughter would have had the same effect. He would have still resigned, but it would have been a more drawn out and painful process.

<<<And now you're bribing our current Governor?

>>>I am, or Ultracorps is, to be precise. If you believe Lewis Khan is the only bought politician in this country, then I have a bridge to sell you. The list of politicians who do not accept bribes is smaller than the list of ones who do.

<<<That doesn't explain why you put Gary up to befriending me. It doesn't explain why you told me Becky was dead so I'd go after The Beast, presumably so he'd kill me.

>>>The explanation for both of those incidents is the same. I believe you have the potential to be one of the most powerful

Differents on the planet.

<<<Flattery isn't going to get you out of this. Neither are lies, especially such unbelievable ones.

>>>Doubt me if you will, but that was why I had Gary befriend you. I already knew and trusted him. I desired a way to keep track of you outside of the official channels. And I am sorry I lied about Becky, but I did get conflicting reports from the police. At best I thought she was dying. I had lost control of The Beast and believed that you were our best, and perhaps only, hope of stopping him. I was right about that by the way.

<<<If I'm so powerful, why does Victor kick my ass in every training exercise?

>>>I said you had the potential to be one of the most powerful Differents, not that you were there already. By stopping The Beast, you proved that I was right about that potential. You simply need help reaching it.

<<<Is that why we've been so close since I got out of jail?

>>>If you were not ready for my help, I could not force it on you. I can only help you if you're willing to accept my aid. Would you have trusted me six months ago?

<<<I don't trust you now. You just told me that you lie to me whenever it suits you.

>>>I kept facts from you, an activity you yourself have engaged in. Or do you want to tell me the same thing you told the police about that Maceo Steel knife you used to defeat The Beast? Do you think I'll believe that you found it in an apartment in the Tower?

<<<No, I don't want to tell you where I got it.

>>>It is not necessary for you to tell me who gave it to you, because I already know. Doubtless, it is the same individual who told you about Hayes' daughter. The same individual who has committed several crimes against this nation while evading the authorities. The same individual who is obsessed with me because I knocked him from his perch as the smartest person alive. Benjamin Jacobs is one of the most wanted men in America. I imagine that if you are entertaining his theories, you are still not ready to accept my

assistance in helping you maximize your abilities.

<<<And how do you know about him?

>>>It does not matter how I came to possess that knowledge, but I also know that trying to convince you not to trust Ben would be pointless, considering your opinion of my own moral character. I will simply tell you this Gavin, the line between high levels of intelligence and madness is razor thin. Many of mankind's greatest minds have succumbed to that paradox. Imagine how difficult it would be to navigate that minefield with a brain a thousand times more powerful than any of those relatively normal human minds?

<<<I guess self-awareness isn't an element of your intellect. The exact same thing could be said about your mind. In fact, aren't you even smarter than Ben?

>>>I sense this conversation is becoming unproductive. Consider what I have told you. Do not let your emotions cloud your reason.

<<<And you consider the fact that I'm busy trying to track down Gary's murderer now, but as soon as I can I am going to find your safe house, kill The Beast, and expose you as a liar and a criminal.

21

That is why I spread my seeds of destruction. My Forgotten Sons are strong; they will not let go of the reigns easily. They must be forced out through disease, destruction, and death. Mankind's grip must be loosened before my Chosen Sons can knock them off the top of the ladder.

Chosen Sons: 29

The Beast pulls off the guard's Forte Silk breastplate. He has to fight the urge to eat the dead man inside the armor. He will not grant the man salvation by dining on his flesh. Someone who imprisons Chosen Sons does not deserve eternity in paradise. He attaches the breastplate to his crippled left arm. The arm is all but useless thanks to the bone-crushing sliding door and machine gun bullets, but by attaching three ForteSilk breastplates, The Beast now has a shield of sorts. He recalls an image of a Roman Gladiator he saw in a book when he was a child. He would like to think that is what he looks like.

The Beast tries on one of the guard's helmets, but his head is far too large. Instead, he wraps two ForteSilk arm guards around the sides of his head. The guards in this prison are likely prepared for The Beast. That means they have guns with enough power to punch through his skull. He may no longer look as imposing, but if it keeps a high caliber bullet out of his head, it will be a worthwhile trade. The Beast picks up one of the guard's machine guns. He has never fired one before. He has to tear off the metal trigger guard in order to put his massive finger on the trigger.

Armed and armored, The Beast heads up the stairs to engage the cavalry. As he approaches the second story, he can smell over a dozen men. They are sweating the cold perspiration of fear. That is just what The Beast is hoping for. He wants to exploit the guards' terror.

"Are y'all ready to die?" The Beast yells in a booming voice.

He approaches the doorway to the upper level, puts his shielded arm forward, and pulls the door open. He is greeted by the sight of overturned desks with armed guards cowering behind them. A mix of machine guns, rifles, and pistols are pointed right at him. Instead of charging forward like the guards would expect him to, The Beast plants his "shield" on the floor and fires the machine gun wildly towards the armed men.

All of his inexperienced shots miss, but he never intended to hit anyone. He achieves his desired effect and the panicked guards return fire. Hundreds of bullets fly towards The Beast. He hides behind his makeshift ForteSilk shield, which stops the bullets cold. A few ricochets make their way into The Beast's flesh, but none with enough force to do any substantial damage.

The Beast can hear the guards' commander screaming for them to "Hold their fire," but The Beast has been gifted with extraordinary senses. The normal humans cannot hear their leader's commands over the din of the gunfire. Only when several of the guards' guns click empty can they finally decipher the voice of their commander. Unfortunately for them it is too late.

The Beast lowers his shield and charges, leaping over the makeshift barricade with ease. Once he is behind the defensive perimeter of overturned desks, there is no stopping him. Most of the guards are not wearing any body armor. When The Beast slashes them with his one good claw, he shreds their pathetic human skin like tissue paper. He tears through four men before they even know what hit them. A few of the men with semi-automatic weapons still have bullets in their chambers, but a vision from a nightmare, moving with speed and grace that no creature should posses, is not an easy target. Panicked shots chase The Beast as he tears through the guards, but few of those shots hit their mark.

He tears out one man's throat and reflexively tastes the blood. Its flavor is sweet. It has been a long time since The Beast tasted fresh blood. He has to stop himself from filling his mouth with the man's flesh. These people made a career out of imprisoning Chosen Sons.

The Beast can think of few humans who deserve salvation less than this lot.

In under a minute, The Beast has killed everyone in the room, save one. The squad commander is struggling to put rounds into the chamber of a large caliber handgun. His shaking hands make it extremely difficult to manipulate the bullets. He finally manages to reload, but by the time he looks up to aim and fire, The Beast is standing right next to him. The Beast grabs the gun out of the commander's hand and crushes it. Then The Beast picks the man up by the throat. His massive fingers fit entirely around the man's neck.

"Where are my brothers?" The Beast demands.

The man answers with a gasp. The Beast loosens his grip so the man can speak.

"I don't know what you're talking about," the terrified man stammers.

"My brothers, other Chosen Sons… Differents. Where are all the other Differents being kept?"

"There isn't anyone else here."

"You're lying. Tell me where they're at?" The Beast growls.

"There's no one here. I swear it. You're the only one being held in this facility," the man pleads.

"What are you talking about? Ain't this Great Basin Prison?"

"Great Basin? This isn't Great Basin; it isn't a prison at all. It's a research lab."

"You're a scientist?"

"No, I'm a security guard. All of the scientists evacuated when the alarms went off."

"What were they all studying?"

"You. They were studying you."

The Beast was not expecting to hear that. He was expecting to hear that this was some high-security ring of Great Basin. Why would God send him to a research lab? Why would God save him after he fell from the tower, just to let humans poke and prod one of God's Chosen Sons? It makes no sense, mankind's worship of science was one of the reasons God had Cabot create the Plagues.

"Thank you. You helped a Chosen Son. You're going get your reward up in heaven. But to be sure, there's one more thing you can do for me." The Beast says and buries his teeth into the man's throat. The flavor is sweet and the feast is just beginning.

#

The Beast finishes the last bite of his meal. The guard was delicious. It has been too long since he has been able to eat the food the Lord meant for him. He knows he should have stopped and thanked God for the bounty before he ate, but his hunger led him astray. He knows the Lord will understand, but he should still stop and give thanks now. The Beast exhales deeply, closes his eyes, and drops to his knees.

"Lord, I know I was supposed to say this before I went and ate, but thank you for the meal. Thank you for everything you done for me. I don't know why you sent me to this lab run by the Forgotten Sons, but I know if you didn't I'd a died when I fell from that tower. I'm not sure why I still deserve the special treatment you givin' me, but I swear, whatever you need from me, I am ready to be your servant."

>>>*I sent you to the lab because that is where you belong.*

"Lord is that you? I thought you was done talking to me. But I don't understand, why do I belong in this lab? What do you want with me?"

>>>*You failed me, Thomas Calhoun, over and over again. You killed three of your own kind and almost died trying to kill a fourth. You failed in the mission I gave you at the Shimmering Tower. I meant for you to instill fear in the hearts of my Forgotten Sons. Instead you gave them hope.*

"I'm sorry I failed you. I did the best I could, I swear. I was going to kill all those people. I was going to show them the power that Chosen Sons got, but that boy Gavin, he wouldn't let me. I thought you wanted me to kill him, otherwise why would you keep putting him in my path? You said it yourself, I was made for death. I figured that's what you wanted done. I don't know how the boy beat me. He got lucky. He had help, somebody gave him that knife."

>>>*I do not want to hear your excuses. I gave you some of the greatest gifts I have bestowed on any of my Chosen Sons, and you have squandered them. You do not deserve the power I gave you. I am rescinding my blessing.*

"What do you mean? I'm sorry I'm such a failure. Just tell me what I can do to make it up to you, and I'll do it. I won't fail you again."

>>>*The only way left to serve me is through sacrifice. I will use you to empower a more deserving member of my Chosen Sons. If you want one final chance at redemption, go back into your cell and close the door. Prove your devotion to me through your own blood, and you'll get your reward in the hereafter."*

"I'll do it, Lord. I swear. You'll see. I have faith enough to move mountains. I'll do whatever it is you ask of me, even if it's rottin' in a cell."

The Beast pulls off his makeshift body armor piece by piece. Then he makes his way through the facility and back to his holding cell. There, he pulls one of the dead guards out of the cell's doorway, steps inside, and closes the door.

22

The Office of Exceptional Cases' express and sole purpose is to subdue and apprehend Different individuals. The organization is prohibited from engaging in any law enforcement efforts without actionable evidence that the suspect in question is a Different individual.

Article 4 Section 4 Different Acts of 1996

"So we're shut down?" Victor asks Captain Murphy.

"Essentially. They say they're still trying to figure out what to do with us, so you guys can make your COL Obligation payments for a while still, but we aren't allowed to go out on any calls," Captain Murphy answers.

"All because we responded to an emergency situation? We saved lives. They never would have found those buried lab workers if it weren't for us," I protest. And I never would have found out The Beast is still alive, but I don't think mentioning that will calm Captain Murphy down.

"Be that as it may, the powers that be were not happy that you two broke the rules. We are only empowered to track down Differents suspected of being criminals. The cops at the bomb site complained to their captains, who complained to their chief, who complained to the Governor, who called the head of the OEC Field Office Program in D.C., who then called me to ream me a new one. I had to say that I let you two knuckleheads go, so now I'm part of this too. We're all on the chopping block," Captain Murphy says, getting red in the face.

"Did you at least tell the OEC higher ups about Billy the Kid. We need allies to try and convince the police he's responsible for the bombing. Linda has my memories; she can corroborate my story," I say.

"Gavin, you seem to have forgotten how you got those memories. You illegally left the OEC office, violating your parole. Then you tracked down a police officer and beat a confession out of him. If Linda shares those memories, you are going to be the only criminal anyone goes after."

"I'll go to jail if that means they'll finally do something about William. I might have assaulted an officer, but I wasn't the one who blew his brains out. I saw who did it, and it's in my memories."

"You saw a black man who you thought looked like a famous basketball player. I'm sure there's a racially insensitive joke in there."

"My mind doesn't work that way. My memories don't get warped because I control my mind," I say flatly.

"I'm glad you think that, and maybe it's even true, but do you think anyone else will buy it? Let's say they somehow track William down and catch him. The only evidence they have is a confession that a criminal beat out of a crooked cop and one fleeting glance from that same criminal. You're the criminal Gavin. That isn't enough evidence to convict him. I'm not even sure if Billy faking his death is a crime. Best case scenario he gets indicted for failing to file tax returns or something like that. He'll end up paying a few thousand in penalties and interest. Maybe it'll be compounded, that will really stick it to him."

"I could go to the press," I argue.

"You think they want to implicate the L.A.P.D. in a cover-up with no evidence? You think they want to run a story about a dead NBA star who's really alive and a serial killer? No real news source will be interested, but I'm sure the think.Net tabloids would love that story. They can't make up a story that good," Captain Murphy says with sarcastic laugh. Victor and I don't crack a smile.

Before I can voice my next counter-point, my heads rings with an alert. Maria wants to talk. I take the call.

>>>*Gavin, I found something in the rubble. It's a large steel plate stamped with the name "Long Beach Foundry."*

<<<*There shouldn't be steel in the lab. It was made entirely out*

of post-Plague materials.

>>>That's what I thought. Which means it came from the bomb. The bomb must have been built there.

<<<Did you bring it to your captain? Is he sending officers?

>>>That isn't an option. My captain wasn't happy with all the time I've been spending at the site. I was ordered to stay away from the bombsite. I had to pretend I was a construction worker to get through to find the metal. They aren't going to want to see my evidence. The Governor already announced that it was an accident caused by a Different. I'm getting the impression that no one will want to make the new Governor look bad by admitting it was really a bomb, let alone one we don't have any more information on. If I bring the steel to my captain he'll tell me it's nothing, and I'll be suspended and maybe even locked in the Looney Bin if I mention Billy the Kid. That's why I'm telling you about it.

<<<Okay, thanks. I'm going to head down there, and hopefully Victor will tag along. You stay away; William is dangerous.

>>>And I guess you've got the monopoly on dangerous? I knew you'd say that, which is why I waited till I was most of the way to the foundry to call you. It's a long walk and out of think.Net range, so I'll see you when you get here.

She ends the call.

"You know Gavin, just because you do some sort of weird quasi-stare doesn't mean we can't tell you're on think.Net. People don't space out for twenty seconds in the middle of a conversation unless they're having a stroke," Captain Murphy says while rolling his eyes.

"It was my friend on the police force. She found something that links the bomb to a foundry in Long Beach. I have to go help her."

"Didn't you hear my whole spiel about how we aren't allowed out on missions and our charter only allows us to go after Differents?" Captain Murphy says with a huff.

"You said it yourself, Captain: we're done. The one chance we have of saving our jobs is proving Gavin's theory of a serial killer and a police cover-up," Victor counters.

Captain Murphy takes a moment and then says, "I can't allow you two to go out. What I can do is go to the bathroom for a good long while. Then maybe I'll head home for the day. Perhaps after a conversation with our resident Telepath. I hear she's great at covering tracks."

Captain Murphy walks out of the room. I wait until I hear the bathroom door close, then we run out of the building.

#

"She should already be waiting for us at the foundry," I say to Victor.

I'm struggling with my breathing. We've been running for twelve miles. The foundry is thirteen miles from the Slug line. Long Beach wasn't even technically part of old Los Angeles. We are way out, and far from help. I shouldn't focus on that fact. At least Victor is slowing himself down to keep up with me. He's even refrained from teasing me about my relative lead-footedness. He's starting to appreciate the skills I bring to the table.

"So she does whatever she wants without consulting the people she's working with. I know someone who does the same thing," Victor says.

"If you mean someone who does what's right and doesn't worry about the consequences, then yeah, we have that in common."

"They say shared values are the key to a successful relationship."

"I've got to focus on my breathing. All this chatting is slowing me down. If we're going to bother talking, it should be about our strategy, not gossip."

"If you couldn't stop yourself from blushing, you'd be beat red," Victor laughs, "What do you mean strategy? We're going to the foundry to look for clues. We'll do our due diligence, but here's no way he's living out here. There are literally thousands of abandoned buildings closer to the Metro Area. Nobody is so paranoid that they want to run a half-marathon every time they get hungry. He raided the foundry for materials. This is far enough out that the scavengers probably haven't even hit the place yet."

"Maybe not, but something about this doesn't seem right. It

seems too sloppy to leave such an easily traced piece of evidence," I say.

"You said he has friends in high places. He must be counting on them to keep the police away. That's why they keep insisting it was an industrial accident. And didn't you say your cop friend was told not to keep digging?"

"Yeah, she was, and we're about there. We should keep it down."

I managed to change Victor's opinion of me. He used to see me as some punk kid who got lucky with The Beast and ended up with a heap of accolades I didn't deserve. He still knows that's true, but he also knows I'm willing to risk my own well-being in order to do what's right, and he respects that. His attitude towards me has changed. He's still ribbing, but now it's actually in good fun as opposed to seething with animosity like it was before.

The foundry is surrounded by the husks of old apartment buildings ravaged by the Plagues and abandoned long ago. The foundry itself is a large complex of collapsed catwalks, half-collapsed smoke stacks, and a mostly-collapsed warehouse. The catwalks are unexpected. You don't usually see so much intact metal. It's surprising that it survived the Plagues and downright shocking that the metal hasn't been collected yet. I guess Victor was right that the scavengers haven't made their way out here yet. Thirteen miles to the Slug is a long way to carry metal.

"I guess there's no doubt where the metal came from," I say.

"After we make it back into think.Net range, I'm going to have to call my cousin. He's a scrapper, and this is the haul of a lifetime. We should make sure the place isn't wired with explosives first, but then again, he makes me go to karaoke every time we get together," Victor says.

We spot Maria waiting in front of the warehouse entrance.

"Aren't you guys supposed to be super fast or something like that?" Maria asks while tapping her foot.

"Talk to your pal Gavin. I could have been here an hour ago," Victor says and gives me a little jab in the ribs. It's a harder poke than it should be. I'm lucky I can't feel pain.

Maria smirks, "What's the plan? All three of us spread out and search? I'm assuming any materials used to make the bomb will be in the warehouse. There are some offices too."

"I'm worried the place might be booby trapped or something. Maybe you should let the two of us make sure it's safe before you come in," I say.

"I found out about this place, and now you want to steal all the glory," Maria says.

"We'll still need your help searching for evidence. Just let us make sure it's safe. Besides, isn't it police procedure to have someone on watch in case the perpetrator is here and makes a run for it?"

"Fine, I'll go around back in case he's inside and bolts. But don't you go searching around without me. Once you're sure you aren't going to explode, yell for me," Maria says and walks off in a huff.

"You like her," Victor says while Maria is still too close for comfort.

"Let's go check this place out. You can tease me later."

"I'll take the lead. If we're worried about booby traps, I've got some experience with them. We need to move slowly and carefully."

We walk up some concrete steps and approach the front door to the warehouse, stepping slowly and lightly. Victor takes the lead and begins to carefully push the decrepit front door open. There's an audible 'click' when the door gets about six inches open.

"I heard something!" I yell.

"I heard it too. The door is rigged."

"What do we do!?"

"We stay calm. We're still alive, aren't we? As long as I hold the door in this position, we're safe. What I need you to do is reach through the crack of the door and see if you can find the triggering mechanism. It's most likely on the floor."

I lay down flat on my stomach and reach through the crack. I grope around until I find something hard pressed up against the door.

"I think I found it."

"There should be a depressed trigger. As long as it stays

depressed we stay alive. Now, I need you to—"

Victor is interrupted by an incredibly loud boom. It's a sound I've heard before, a shot from a long range rifle. It only takes one look at Victor to know he's already dead. Half his face is gone. If I don't move now, I will be dead too. I pull my arm out of the doorway, turn, plant my feet, and dive.

The explosion behind me propels me ten feet through the air. I land with a thud as bits of shrapnel tear into my body. The chunks of metal and concrete become tiny knives that rip open my flesh but miraculously miss anything vital. There's another loud boom, and a bullet hits the pavement right next to my head. I scramble backwards towards the explosion, using the smoke and dust as cover.

I can't stay here long; the dive knocked the wind out of me. I don't have much oxygen in my lungs, and I don't want to breathe in the smoke. I replay the sound of the two gunshots in my head and try to echolocate the source. It came from the roof of the three-story half-collapsed apartment building across the street. If I run into the building, he won't have a shot.

I take off towards the doorway. A bullet whizzes by my head just before I duck inside. The building has been damaged by floods, the walls torn down to the bones. I take position and wait for Billy to come through the door but he could also come through any of a dozen windows or holes in the wall, more than I can watch.

Sure enough, he suddenly appears to my right, pointing a handgun. I dive behind a pile of rubble. He puts a bullet in my left shoulder before I get behind cover. Three more bullets land in the concrete pile I'm hiding behind. I pick up a small chunk of concrete and wait for him to show his face. I hope my fastball is working today. I should have brought my gun, even with Victor and his judgment around. I was taught this lesson last time when William killed Detective Rose, but I refused to learn.

"Drop the gun right now!" Maria yells. She heard the boom and came running. Now she's got the drop on William from behind. I start heading over to assist.

"Are you kidding me, lady?" William says to Maria.

A gunshot answers his disbelief. It was just a warning though. I hear the metal clank of his gun hitting the ground.

"That's officer to you. Kick the gun to my friend over there," Maria says.

William kicks the gun towards me. I drop my brick and pick up the handgun. There's an upgrade.

"Get on the ground and keep your hands where I can see them," Maria orders with an authoritative voice at a volume that shouldn't be possible considering her tiny frame.

William is getting onto his belly twenty feet away from me. As he goes down he drops a small, round metal object. What is that? The answer is a deafening blast that damages my eardrum and a blinding flash of light that destroys the photoreceptor cells in my eyes, leaving me blind. Did that lunatic set off a flash bang? I start reproducing photoreceptor cells as quickly as I can. My ears are ringing, but if I focus I can still make out other sounds.

What I hear sounds like a scuffle, and then William yells.

"Stay down! I don't want to hurt you!" I can't tell if he's yelling for effect or because his hearing is shot. Either way, I doubt Maria can hear him. I'm guessing William covered his eyes when the grenade went off, otherwise he'd be as blind as I am.

I can hear William shuffling around, trying to regain his balance after the flash bang. If I wait behind this rubble, he's going to come and kill me. It's going to take me at least another thirty seconds to regrow enough cells in my eyes to see. It occurs to me that he doesn't know I'm blind. I imagine the room in my mind's eye. He was about twenty feet away from me. I stand up from behind the rubble, aim my recently acquired gun at my best guess to where he's standing, and pull the trigger nine times. I hear William run and then hit the ground. That bought me some time.

I dive back behind the rubble just in time to avoid his return fire. He must have picked up Maria's gun. My vision is starting to return, but all I can see are shadows. I hear steps heading towards me. I pop up, aim at a shadowy figure, and fire a shot. I hear a scream, a female scream. I hit Maria! I drop back behind my cover and listen.

She's still breathing, thank God.

Then I hear another set of footsteps approaching me, William. I need to lead him away from Maria. I still only see shadows, but that's enough to get to my feet and start running. Bullets follow me, but I know I need to get him away from her. If I can buy myself a few more seconds, my vision should be back to normal. Then I can stop William and save Maria. I run towards a doorway I remembered to my left before the explosion.

My nose hits first. I feel the bone break while the rest of my face continues on into the solid object, and I collapse to the ground. I try to get back to my feet, but my nerve signals are all jumbled. My legs buckle under me. I think I damaged my brain.

"The Beast Slayer felled by a doorframe. Not exactly one for the storybooks. I'm sorry, kid. I respect you, I really do. You're a good man. You want to help people. But you can't help what you are and what you are-- is a threat to the human race," a voice in the darkness says.

I look up and see William pointing a gun at me. I get my power of sight back just in time to watch myself die.

"Wait! How many assists did you have in game four against the Lakers?" I ask. I'm desperate. For some reason I recall a distraction technique I read about once. Non-sequitur questions are supposed to be effective for throwing people off.

"I can barely hear you, but it doesn't matter what you say anyway. It's not personal, kid. It's about the survival of the human species. If your kind keeps reproducing, who knows how many more Danny Libdos they'll be? We have to go to war, deep down everybody knows it. The reason it hasn't started yet is because the human race doesn't think it has the firepower needed to win the fight. I'm going to show them that victory is within reach."

I try to lift up and aim my gun, but my arms and hands aren't working right. The gun drops from my hands.

William is about to squeeze his own trigger when a hundred and thirty pound wrecking ball barrels into him. I can't believe Maria still has any strength left. She has a bullet in her, can't possibly see anything but shadows, and I bet she's still deaf, but that doesn't seem to be slowing her down. Her blow knocks the gun out of William's hand. She starts trying to pin his arm behind his back. She knows what she's doing.

Unfortunately, William knows what he's doing as well, and he's got a hundred pounds on her. He throws himself backwards, slamming Maria into the wall. I hear one of her ribs crack. She lets go of William's wrist, and he swings around and gives her a full force upper-cut to the jaw. She goes down like a sack of potatoes.

I feel a surge of anger, which I let flow through me. I use the moment she bought me to find some strength in my weakened legs, and I stand and charge into William, tackling him to the ground. As I knock him down, he goes into a backwards summersault and is back on his feet in a flash. I stand up too.

We circle each other for a moment. My vision is about back to normal, so I'm guessing he can hear at least a little now.

"You aren't supposed to hit women!" I yell.

"Chivalry goes out the window when you're outnumbered, especially if one of your opponents is supposed to be the perfect human being. I didn't want to hurt her, but I have to stop you. The OEC is a farce. It lets the government pretend Differents can be controlled."

He assumes a stance with his hands open and separated and his feet a few inches apart. I recognize it as jujitsu—score one for all that time studying fighting videos on think.Net. Jujitsu is designed to use an opponent's own strength against him. A good choice for fighting me.

I take a boxing stance, hands close together and upright. I want him to think I don't really know what I'm doing. I throw a big clumsy right cross. As expected, he dodges it and moves in close to flip me on his hip, which is the right move if you're fighting an opponent who doesn't know what they're doing, but that's not me. I pull back my right cross and stick my elbow out. My elbow catches him in the back of the head, forcing him forward. I throw my own hip out and use my other hand to flip him over. He lands on his stomach with a thud. I try to drop down on his back with my knee, but he rolls out of the way before I can deliver the blow.

We both stand back up, although he's a bit slower than before. My elbow to the head rang his bell. We circle each other again, like two lions fighting for control of the pride. He assumes a stance similar to my boxer pose, but with his feet further forward than they should be. What is he doing?

He makes the first move this time. He throws a left that is an obvious feint. I prepare to catch the coming punch from his right hand, but instead he kicks me in the left shin, a good move if I felt pain. He follows that up with a roundhouse kick which I partially block, but it still bruises my kidney a bit. I shove him back. Now I know what style he's using, Muay Thai Fighting, kickboxing. That means all his punches will be for show; that stance is all about hitting with the kicks.

He throws a left cross, which is just to set up his kick. The punch hits my already broken nose. He doesn't realize that pain doesn't affect me. Then he throws the right legged roundhouse kick I was waiting for. I let it hit me in the side, then wrap my left arm around his leg, pinning his leg to me. I pummel him with a flurry of right hooks. He puts his right arm up, and I hit it like a martial arts master breaking a board. I feel the bone break under my fist. Another blow knocks out his tooth. Finally, he plants his left leg and pulls himself free, but he falls backwards. He hits the back of his head on the concrete.

I let him stand back up; I'm enjoying this. I like to imagine that each blow I land is a form of justice for all his victims. There are still a lot of dead bodies to atone for, including Victor. I take a stance and wave for him to come at me, like Bruce Lee in "Enter the Dragon".

To my surprise, he maintains his Muay Thai stance. He comes at me throwing a left hook towards my stomach. I get ready to absorb the punch again so I can react to his real blow, only something goes wrong. His left hook tears a hole in my side. As he pulls his hand back, he opens up a deep gash in my right thigh. I hit him with a straight right cross to the sternum, which pushes him back.

I slow down time and take a good look at his left hand. He's got a small knife that he's holding upside-down. It might have been small, but it still tore apart my insides. He managed to get deep enough to knick my kidney and large intestine. I have to cut off blood flow from the area. On top of that, he mutilated my thigh muscle. I route my blood around the wound, but that isn't going to make my leg any stronger.

I didn't anticipate how well armed he'd be. It occurs to me that he drew me into a martial arts fight because he knew I'd get caught up in my desire to show off my skills. Maybe he does know me better than I give him credit for. He charges at me, swinging his knife like a tornado. I slow down time to a crawl, but with my mangled thigh I'm moving like molasses and can't get out of the way. I just have enough time to see where the knife is going to cut me. I use my arms to deflect stabs headed towards something vital, but within a few seconds my arms have been torn to shreds. I try to throw a desperate punch, but he dodges it with ease and takes the opportunity to slice my patellar tendon in the knee of what was my good leg.

I drop to a kneel. This is how I'm going to die. I managed to defeat The Beast, one of the most powerful Differents who has ever lived, but I'm going to be killed by a regular man with a knife.

"I'm sorry, kid," William says as he prepares to deliver the *coups de grâce*.

This time, a loud boom stops him. It comes from the gun I had been shooting. William's gun, but it is Maria who put a bullet in his leg. William joins me in a forced kneel, just a few feet away.

"If you move a freaking muscle, I'm blowing you straight to hell," Maria says.

William whirls around and throws his knife at Maria. He misses. She pulls the trigger, but there aren't any bullets. William reaches into his pocket and pulls out a small object. I try to dive at him, but my mangled body moves too slowly.

"Watch out, he's got another flash bang!" I cry out.

William throws the grenade down to the ground, hard. Maria and I close our eyes, waiting for a flash that doesn't come. Instead I hear a loud hissing. William disappears into a cloud of smoke. This guy is carrying a whole battalion's worth of weaponry. I hear a thud and someone crumples to the ground.

"Maria, he's getting away, can you see him?" I ask.

I don't get an answer.

"Maria, are you okay?" Still no answer. I only hear William limping away as fast as he can. No one's chasing him.

I fumble around, trying to figure out what's going on, but I don't get my answer until the smoke starts to clear. Then I see a sight I wish I could erase from my vision. Maria is lying on the ground, out cold. She's in the fetal position with blood streaming out of bullet wound in her abdomen, a bullet I put there. I have to get her help.

23

It seems crass to write about sports at a time like this, but it is still my duty as a reporter. Just three months after the Danny Libdo Tragedy which decimated the Minneapolis Metro Area, we were once again reminded of the true depth and scope of the loss. Devastated by the death of his wife and child, William "Billy the Kid" Jefferson announced his retirement from the league while also thanking his fans for their support. Though the loss of a sports star does not compare to millions of lives lost in the accident, the announcement helps underscore the permanent scar left on our nation. When the National Basketball League restarts next season, it, like this country, will be far from whole.

"William Jefferson Announces Retirement from Professional Basketball" by Roger Burns, Minneapolis StarTribune

October 12th

Sit-ups: 0
Pushups: 0
Pull-ups: 0
Running: 0
Diet: 1,715 Calories, 129 grams protein, 193 gram carbohydrates, 47 grams fat.
Sleep: 6:11
Funds: $7,125.00
Ammo Count: 156 rounds 7N1, 265 rounds 9mm, 11 Stun Grenades, 11 Smoke Grenades, 12 Standard Grenades.
Activities: Eliminated Target 25, Injured target 26.

Target Notes: Eliminated Target 25, Victor, with a single shot from Dragunov Rifle. Engaged with Target 26, Gavin. Target suffered gunshot wound, shrapnel injuries, and severe lacerations from blade.

I was forced to retreat after intervention of a female L.A.P.D. officer. Personal Notes: Suffered gunshot wound to the thigh and broken right arm. Managed to get the bullet out of my thigh, but both injuries will slow me down for weeks. Also possibility that the injured L.A.P.D. officer will keep after me. Not clear if she survived the encounter. Need to beef up my defenses using the explosives provided by Money Man. Injuries push back timeline for implementing final plan, but delay will not cause major disruptions. Money Man still won't like it.

Mental State: Need to rest for weeks, which means no working out. Might go insane. Will attempt to take up meditation again.

24

There are many questions and few answers in the death of OEC agent and infamous former baseball player, Victor Campos. What we do know is that the agent was shot and killed far outside the bounds of the Los Angeles Metro Area. What we don't know is why he was out there, who killed him, or if the suspect has been apprehended. Thus far, the OEC office has been either unwilling or unable to shed any light on the subject. On the heels of the Beckett's Square tragedy, this death is another black mark on the OEC Field Office Program.

"Confusion Abounds in the Death of OEC Agent" by Roberta Clemens, Los Angeles Times

I collapse at the front entrance to the hospital. I've made it as far as I can go and lost as much blood as the human body can stand. I couldn't cut off the blood flow to my wounds because it would have slowed me down too much. I had to stop and drink a puddle on my way here so I could keep producing plasma, to mix with the white blood cells, red blood cells, and platelets I'm generating to create replacement blood. I'm still managing my immune system to have it kill off all the bacteria that was living in that tiny swamp.

"Help!" I scream at the top of my lungs.

I look over at Maria, who's lying a in a pile next to me. She looks deathly pale. She might have less blood in her body than I do. I feel for a pulse on her neck. It's faint, but it's there. She needs fluids and she needs them now.

"Somebody help! A police officer needs help!" I yell again.

#

This is the second funeral I've ever been to, and it's my second this week. I'm lucky I was allowed to attend. Captain Murphy had to call in what was probably the last favor he has left from the powers that be. I'm supposed to be locked in the OEC office twenty-four hours a day while I await my hearing, where they will no doubt send me back to prison. It's for the best. I proved I'm not hero material. I only beat The Beast because he didn't want to kill me; he wanted to convert me. Even still, I needed what was essentially a magic knife to stand a chance. Now I know that when push comes to shove, a normal human man can beat me.

There are plenty of police officers here to make sure I can't make a make a break for it, even if I was up for more adventures. Although, supposedly, they're here to show support for a fallen brother in arms. They might not have been huge fans of the OEC, but Victor was law enforcement, and that makes him a brother of sorts.

It's a good thing the police are here; otherwise it would just be Linda, Captain Murphy, and me. Victor didn't have any family and Maria is still recovering from the bullet I put in her gut. Another of my failures. There's a big crowd outside the cemetery, but they're all from the press. I'd love to believe they're all waiting to do a story on an accomplished government agent who died in service to the nation, but I'm guessing the reporters really want one more chance to rehash the story of Victor Campos: liar, cheater, and World Series tainter. Maybe the last paragraph will say something about how he turned his life around and served the OEC.

Victor deserves better than this. He deserved better than being shot in the back of the head by a serial killer I was chasing. I should be the one lying in a wooden box with half my face missing. I was the idiot who thought I was strong enough to fix the whole world. I was the moron who led us right into a trap. If I had listened to everyone who told me it wasn't my job to hunt Billy the Kid, Victor would still be alive.

This isn't the first time someone I know has been hurt because of my fantasies about being a hero. Becky's father died and she barely survived all because I was delusional enough to imagine I could take on The Beast. If I hadn't gone after him, he would have stayed in the shadows, feeding on the old and sick. Now, my insistence on going after Billy the Kid has left Maria lying in a hospital bed and Victor waiting to be put in the ground.

I deserve to be locked up. I'm the worst kind of dangerous, the dangerous who gets good people hurt and killed because of my stupidity. I should have stayed working in the lab as a fast food taste tester. There I might have actually saved some lives catching tainted food or cancerous additives. All I've ever accomplished by trying to be a hero is spreading misery.

I feel a mind trying to push itself into my head. It's Linda. Why is she talking to me telepathically when I'm five feet away from her? I let her in anyway.

>>>*Gavin, there's someone here who wants to speak with you.*

<<<*What do you mean someone here?*

>>>*Look at the line of officers in front of you.*

I look over the line of cops standing around the casket. One of them does look familiar, despite his moustache. He gives me a wink when he sees me staring.

<<<*Is that Ben? You know Ben?*

>>>*It is, and I do. Now why don't you two have a chat? Pretend I'm not here.*

>>>*Hey Gavin, I'm going to assume you put it all together and figured out Linda and I know each other from back in the day when we both worked on think.Net. I was her surrogate son before you. How about that Meat Sauce, huh? Haven't you wondered how I've been able to find you after we stopped our meetings? The problem with your total control of your brain or whatever you've got is that it keeps your mind from wondering. That question should have occurred to you.*

<<<*I should be more suspicious of you. I'll keep that in mind.*

>>>*You should be suspicious of everyone. Take our new Governor, Lewis Khan, for instance.*

<<<*You already told me about him. You're right by the way. Nita confirmed that Ultracorps is bribing him. Kudos to you on finding a unicorn; a corrupt politician.*

>>>*Okay mister smarty pants, then I suppose you also know what Governor Khan has been doing with all that bribe money. Fancy suits and ladies of the night? That's what typical corrupt*

politicians spend it on, and that's all he is, right?

<<<If I let you tell me what he's doing with the money, will you leave me alone and let me mourn in peace?

>>>It wasn't easy to figure it all out. Khan owns three grocery stores and a medical practice. All of these businesses have seen a sudden boom in sales, and for some reason, all those new sales are in cash. Really, none of this is surprising, your standard money laundering scheme. Where it gets interesting is when you try to figure out where the money went after it got laundered. See, each of these companies has started ordering some strange chemicals. The convenience stores have started ordering Sodium Benzoate and Potassium Nitrate. Those can be used as preservatives, but if mixed with a few other ingredients that could be picked up in any industrial supply warehouse, they—

<<<Enough, cut to the chase. I've had all the intrigue I can handle.

>>>You never let me have any fun. You know, it's perfectly natural for a person to want credit for all their hard work... Khan has been using his companies to buy chemicals to make bombs, lots of them. He was likely responsible for the bomb that blew up your old lab.

<<<Are you saying he's in league with William Jefferson?

>>>Well I doubt Khan was out there placing bombs himself. He's a little old and overweight to be a hands-on kind of bad guy.

<<<That's insane.

>>>Speaking of crazy, the medical center Khan owns has massive quantities of virtually every psychological drug on the planet, and the facility doesn't employ any psychiatrists. There was even a healthy supply of most every street drug in existence. Radical doctors at that facility. You know mixing those drugs incorrectly could result in psychotic behavior, like the behavior we saw from those demented Differents you stopped. And Linda tells me you couldn't figure out how anyone knew to target the Regenerator who had her family kidnapped. Stacey's status as a former OEC agent was classified. Guess who has access to complete files of every

Different in the Metro Area? It starts with a Governor.

<<<That doesn't make any sense. What would the Governor have to gain from killing Differents? Why would he want the public to be afraid of Differents? He's been taking those bribes in exchange for expanding Ultracorps power. A lot of the negative press towards Differents has also been directed at him for supporting Ultracorps. Why would any politician be part of a conspiracy that sends their poll numbers down? And if he's anti-Different, why would he be expanding their influence with one hand while killing them with the other? It doesn't add up. I don't care what weird activities his companies have been up to; there must be another explanation.

>>>Gavin, you're falling into the trap many highly rational people fall into, assuming everyone thinks like you. Some people do things that don't make rational sense. You're assuming Khan's primary goal in life is power. Usually a safe assumption for politicians, but maybe his motivation is to stop the Different "menace." Is it really crazier than a basketball star faking his death so he can return years later to start murdering Differents? Do you only believe in insane conspiracies that you figure out for yourself?

<<<What about Nita? Do you think she's part of it? Does she know where the money is going? Do you think she wants to kill Differents?

>>>Maybe, but my guess is she fell into the same trap as you did, assuming people are rational. You two share that weakness. Trying to figure out Nita is not a productive road to go down anyway. It's like a dog trying to figure out what humans do. I'm sure to them it looks like we waste a whole bunch of time on non-eating related activities.

<<<So you have no theories as to why she told me that I might be one of the most powerful Differents on the planet if I accepted her help?

>>>Oh, that one's easy. It's because it's the truth.

<<<What do you mean? I just got my ass kicked by a normal human being. I'm still healing.

>>>A normal human being who was a world class athlete and

renowned for having an incomparable work ethic and will to win. A normal man who killed dozens of other Differents over the last few months including your totally badass partner. In fact, you're the only Different who is still standing after crossing paths with that normal human. And that's considering that you aren't even close to getting the most out of your abilities.

<<<How can I get more out of my abilities?

>>>The human body is just a complicated machine. Instead of metal, it's built of cells. Differents are better versions of the same machine. It's the cells in their muscles that give Strong-Men their power, nerve and brain cells that make me so smart, even unique thermogenic cells that make Heaters hot. We're all machines made of cells Gavin, and as far as I know, you're the only person who has complete control of the machine. If you were a computer, I'd say you can program the operating system.

<<<But I can't grow cells from nothing. Cells are created by mitosis, one cell splits to make new cells. I can't wish my muscle cells into something different.

>>>Of course not, but if you already had some of those cells in your body, you could give them the resources they need to reproduce and spread all over. Your control over your immune system could keep your body from rejecting these "foreign" invaders like a normal person's body would.

<<<How am I supposed to get samples of these cells? Go up to a Strong-Man and ask if they'd be willing to donate their bicep to me?

>>>I imagine that Nita's offer of assistance has something to do with that. And we might have just figured out why she was saving a certain blast from your past. Linda told me that before he died, your friend Gary admitted The Beast was alive.

<<<You think Nita saved him to give me his cells? But why would Nita want to help me? Why would she want to make me so powerful? Won't that make me a threat to her?

>>> The Beast proved he was a little too unstable to be used as her muscle. But combine your brain and his body, that's quite the fearsome creation. It won't stop with The Beast's stronger muscles

and better healing. Eventually, Nita will give you Big Brain brain cells. She's counting on the fact that if and when you become like her, you'll think like her. She's of the opinion that the reason everyone doesn't agree with her is because they are not smart enough to see the truth she sees.

<<<Maybe she's right. Maybe I will agree with her.

>>>I have faith in you. If there's one thing you've got, Gavin, it's a clear moral compass. You believe with every fiber of your being that hurting people is wrong. I don't think Nita could ever take that away from you unless you let her. Call it a soul, call it an essence, call it your deep down, whatever it is Gavin, you've got the purest one I've ever seen. That's what truly makes you strong, and that's what makes you a hero.

<<<Thanks, but how am I supposed to get Nita to help me? I don't have any way to contact her. And even if I did, I'm on house, or rather, office arrest. This place is swarming with cops. I can't exactly run for it.

>>>You let me handle the cops. I had an inspiration from the bad guys we're after. I'm sure Victor won't mind his funeral being disrupted if it means avenging his death. Once you get clear from here, find a Walter. You figured out she can see through them during our first adventure, remember? I'm sure you can do something to get her attention. Meanwhile, I'll figure a way to blow the lid off the whole conspiracy with the Governor. Accept my knowledge request and run when you hear the boom.

I feel an alert ringing in my head from think.Net. A knowledge request from Rolland Bloom. How many fake accounts does Ben have?

Ben gives me a wink and then puts his hand in his pocket and fiddles with a something. The explosion creates a deafening boom and sends up a cloud of dust and dirt that descends onto the crowd. Everyone hits the deck, including me. Even though I can't see, I imagine the cemetery in my mind's eye, I point myself at the stone wall around the edge of the grounds and crawl. I flip myself over the top of the wall and listen to see if anyone is coming after me. I hear lots of screams, but nothing that sounds like "get him!" I stand up and break into a sprint. Thankfully, I'm mostly healed from my injuries and moving at close to top speed. I hear a voice in my head. Not think.Net, Linda.

>>>*Good luck, Gavin. I get the impression it might be a while until we speak again.*

<<<*Thanks, Linda. I could use the luck. Do me a favor, check in on Maria for me. Tell her I'm sorry for… everything. I'll fix it soon.*

>>>*I'll do it, and I'll be watching for news of your serial killer like a hawk. You promised me you'd get that son-of-a-bitch, and I plan to hold you to that.*

After I'm clear of the explosion area, I slow down to a brisk walk and continue away from the cemetery towards the Metro Center. Linda's final message rings in my mind. It goes along with the weakness that Ben pointed out, my inability to focus on more than one goal at a time. I can't forget about Billy the Kid because I have a chance to take down The Beast. The Beast, for all the harm he's done, has been contained. Billy the Kid is still out there. He's probably laying low considering his gunshot wound and broken arm. But as soon as he's capable, he's going to start killing again, and I have to stop him.

If I'm honest with myself, I will admit that Billy the Kid is better than I am. He's better at preparing and planning, and he's more experienced at killing than I am at fighting bad guys. His greatness on the basketball court, his work ethic, and his will to win translated perfectly into being a killer. He managed to take out Victor, who was stronger, faster, and more experienced than I am. If I go after William, he's going to be ready for me, and I don't think I can win.

I need an advantage. I have to become powerful enough to overcome the gap in experience. I have to do whatever it takes. If I really can take The Beast's abilities, then no amount of planning or preparation will be enough to stop me. It will be a deal with the Devil, but it's a deal I have to make. I need to find a Walter so I can strike my bargain.

It doesn't take me long to find a one; they're everywhere in the

Metro Center. The mindless clone is busy sweeping the sidewalk. Walter Reynolds produces these clones that are unable to speak or communicate. Telepaths can push simple instructions into their heads, which make them perfect for uncomplicated, repetitive tasks like street sweeping. Back when I was fighting The Beast, Ben and I realized that Nita was able to track The Beast and me. The explanation we came up with was that she's able to see through the eyes of the Walters. It makes sense. If Telepaths can push thoughts into Walters' heads, they can extract thoughts too. All I have to do is draw Nita's attention to this particular Walter.

I walk up to him and execute a shove. He doesn't even look at me. He keeps focused on his task. I do a little tap dance in front of him, kicking my feet and waving my hands, like Gene Kelly in "Singing in the Rain." I even nail a perfect split, but my dance routine elicits no response.

Maybe I need to add audio stimulation.

"From the halls of Montezuma, to the shores of Tripoli, We fight our country's battles in the air, on land…"

My reward for all my great showmanship and patriotism is the same normal blank stare the Walters always display. I should have known that wouldn't be enough. Plenty of teenagers do much worse to the Walters on a daily basis. I'm going to have to do something more outlandish.

I rip off the Walter's shirt and pants and place the pants on top of his head, making sure his eyes can still see me through the leg hole. He just keeps looking for trash to sweep up. It didn't work, and now I feel terrible for picking on a poor, defenseless creature. I don't know what else I can do to get Nita's attention. I don't have the heart to hurt a Walter. This was a stupid idea.

As soon as that thought passes through my mind, I feel a call come in on think.Net. It's from someone whose identity is blocked.

<<<*Hello, Nita.*

#

I've been sitting in the warehouse/hospital hybrid for twenty minutes before a doctor finally comes in the room. At least, he looks like a doctor. He's holding a chart, wearing a white lab coat, and has a stethoscope around his neck. Going against that theory is the fact that he looks like he's twelve years old. He's got a chubby face, smooth skin, and bright red hair. He's still a few years away from burning off all of his baby fat. He must be a Big Brain or something.

"Mr. Stillman, is it? Nice to see you, I'm Dr. Zaius. If you'll please remove your pants and bend over we can begin the examination," the doctor says, barely looking up from his chart.

"No offense, but are you a doctor?"

"Am I a doctor? What kind of a question is that? Don't you see the white coat and chest listening thingy? You can't get more doctor than that. Now please remove your pants and assume the position. I don't have all day. I have three other patients that are also having their butts removed," the doctor says deadpan.

He's clearly not a doctor but who is he? There's something familiar about his sense of humor and red hair. Larry Rosen, my teacher from Section 26. My mind flashes with anger. I left him more than a few messages on think.Net after the whole thing with The Beast and he never called me back. Now I know why, he's been lying to me for years.

"Larry, what are you doing here?"

"Who is Larry? I told you, I'm Dr. Zaius. I've been a doctor for many years and performed many butt removal surgeries. You have nothing to worry about," the doctor says with his hands on his hips.

"I suppose you performed those on chimpanzees since you came from the Planet of the Apes. I never understood what you liked so much about that movie. Those ape costumes were terrible."

"Because if 'Take your stinking paws off me, you damn dirty ape' doesn't send a chill down your spine, then you might not have a soul," Larry says with sincerity.

With the jig being up, Larry transforms himself into the short, fat little troll I always knew. It's not a pretty event to watch. His bones and muscles shift and contort under his skin. It looks like giant bugs are crawling around inside him. The human body isn't supposed to look like it's being beaten up by ocean waves from within. It takes him a few moments to complete the horrific process.

"Don't get too jealous. You can't have my abilities yet," Larry says.

"Enough! Why are you here?" I ask loudly and angrily. His attitude is infuriating. He doesn't talk to me for months and yet he still can't stop joking.

"Isn't it obvious? Emotional support. Don't you feel all supported now? I figured if you were ready to forgive Nita, you might be ready to forgive me too."

"Where was the emotional support when I was arrested after fighting The Beast? Where was it when my girlfriend left me because you told me she was dead? Where was it the last eight months? I left messages," I growl and rush blood to my face so I turn red with anger.

"I heard what you accused Gary of. I thought you'd lump me in with the rest of the conspirators."

"Shouldn't I?"

"I'm not just one of the conspirators, I'm the guy who started the whole conspiracy against you in the first place!" Larry proclaims. "It began innocently enough. Back in Section 26, I thought you were another Zeta who busted out in the crap-shoot that is being born a Different. But after a few weeks of working with you, I started to realize that you might be more powerful than anyone was giving you credit for. I remember telling Nita you were like a horse racing a human. A human can win that race over about a hundred feet because it's easier to get two legs and fewer muscles moving. But once that horse gets up to speed, it blows the human out of the water. You're the horse in that analogy, in case you were confused."

"Why didn't you tell me that in Section 26? Why didn't you try to maximize my abilities then?"

"Because you're unique, Gavin. If I had told everybody at Section 26 what I thought you might be capable of, you never would have gotten out of the building. That's how the government does things. You'd be there now, being treated as a human guinea pig, providing data to help them understand Differentiation as a whole. I didn't think that was right. I thought you deserved to be a person, not a science project. So I kept my mouth shut," Larry says. He's proud of the choice he made.

"You didn't seem to have a problem telling Nita."

"I needed to tell someone, and it had to be someone smarter than me. I got a C in biology in high school. I knew you had potential, but I had no idea how to maximize it. Nita and I had worked together to help out some kids with dangerous Differentiations. I wouldn't say that I trusted her completely, but I did trust that she was smart enough to figure out what to do with you. Plus, I figured she'd be a good ally to have if Section 26 started getting wind of how unique you are." He doesn't have any shame about lying to me for years. He truly believes he did what was best for me. I'm not sure if that should make me feel better or worse.

"And what about Nita buying off politicians? Are you part of that?"

"I don't know what you're talking about, and I promise you I had nothing to do with any of that. It sounds possible though. Nita is on the short list of people with true power in this world. In my job working for the government, I've met senators, congressmen, world leaders, and business magnates. Every single one of them is a lying, scheming S.O.B. It's how you get to the top of the ladder. I've never worried about climbing myself; I try to help where I can, which has mostly been helping poor Different kids who everyone else wanted to write off. I don't know what other activities Nita engages in, but I do know she's the only person in power who has shown the faintest glimmer of compassion for those poor kids. That's enough for me," Larry says with a shrug.

"So she sent you here to try to convince me she's not that bad."

"I'd say that's a third of the reason. Another third is that while there's nobody quite like you Gavin, I am an expert at teaching every kind of Different how to control their abilities. If this crazy experiment is successful, you'll still have to learn how to manage your new abilities. It'll be like old times, hopefully this time you won't lose control of your saliva glands again. That was a messy couple of days; you're lucky it's from when you can't remember."

"What's the final third of the reason?"

"Uhh, that's where it gets a little dicey. Did Nita tell you what the procedure was going to be?" Larry says while shifting his feet uncomfortably.

"She said she was going to implant tissue from another Different onto my body."

"But did she tell you who the Different was?"

"No, but I already know who it is. The Beast."

"And you're still willing to go through with this?" Larry asks even though being here shows I am already committed.

I recede into my own mind to ponder that question. I don't like the idea of having his muscles in my body, but that's an emotional reaction. My rational mind tells me that no other Different on earth has the unique combination of abilities that The Beast has. If I truly want to maximize my abilities, taking The Beast's power is the right choice. And if this works, I'll be strong enough to stop Billy the Kid, and I'll be strong enough to kill The Beast once and for all. I have to remember that those are my goals and not let Nita or Larry or anyone else stop me. My stubbornness is going to be an asset for once.

"Yes, I want to go through with it," I say.

"Phew. I was worried you'd freak out and punch me in the face when I told you it was The Beast. Honestly, I wouldn't have blamed you. Although I probably should have told you this before you said yes, but the procedure isn't going to be a simple muscle graft. The Beast isn't who he is from big muscles alone. He has extended nerve networks that let him move more quickly. He has dense bones that support his excess weight. He has unique marrow in those bones that produce red blood cells that carry more oxygen... At least, that's what they tell me."

"What're you saying? They're going to remove my brain and put it in his body?"

"No, no, nothing that crazy. They're just going to remove your hand and replace it with his. Just a simple hand transplant. Nita thinks you can grow the rest from there. The Doctor is a Speedster, so she can make sure all the little nerve networks get connected before the tissue starts dying. You'll be in good hands…," Larry says, continuing his trend of jokes at even the most inappropriate times.

"You're going to cut my hand off?"

"Well, not me, but yeah, the doctor will replace your right hand with The Beast's hand. They wanted to use his left, but that one is injured. Luckily, you're ambidextrous so it shouldn't matter which one they use. Hope you weren't too attached to your Mark of Differentiation. Old Beast boy never went through Section 26, no tattoo,"

"I'll find some way to get over it… I want to talk to him."

"Nita's not going to think that's a good idea."

"It's at least as good an idea as a hand transplant."

"Fair enough. I'll see what I can do," Larry says and pats me on the back. I want to turn around and break his arm. He's a liar and a manipulator and I don't trust him, but now is not the time for petty revenge. Good thing I can control my emotions. Besides, apparently all my "friends" are liars and manipulators.

25

Log of Notable Nita/Ultracorps Activity Week 221

Gavin had a call on his think.Net log without record of who was on the other side. Likely Nita. She has plans for the boy. Spoke to old friend who informed that Gavin learned The Beast is still alive and under Ultracorps control.

Theories: Nita has Gavin back on her radar. Might be able to use him to expose her. Need to keep him out of police hands so Nita still finds him valuable.

The explosion creates an airborne mixture of dirt and smoke that burns Ben's eyes. Despite the searing eye pain, he manages to spot Gavin escaping from the cemetery. The boy vaults the eight-foot stone wall like an Olympic hurdler, showing few effects from the myriad of injuries his body has endured in the last week. Ben takes off after him, using metal spikes on the tips of his shoes to scramble up the wall.

While atop the wall, Ben watches Gavin break into a sprint Ben cannot possibly keep pace with, at least under normal circumstances. Prepared as always, Ben pulls out a syringe from a pouch on his belt, burying the needle into his arm in time with his feet hitting the ground at the base of the wall. The cocktail within the needle contains adrenaline, Vitamin B12, and several other stimulants designed by Ben himself, so they must be highly effective. The chemicals will wreak havoc on Ben's insides, weakening his immune system and causing inflammation all over his body, but that's tomorrow's problem. Today's problem is keeping up with Gavin, who has the athletic ability of a world-class sprinter. The boost won't be enough for Ben to win the race, but it should make his silver medal more respectable.

"Where's The Beast Slayer?!" a police officer yells, still inside the cemetery and woefully behind in the race.

The question reminds Ben that he needs to take to the roofs while he follows Gavin. The boy will be wary of a police pursuit, and Ben looks like a potential pursuer in his police uniform disguise. He has to stay out of sight. He charges to the closest building, pulls out a length of ForteSilk with a hook, and tosses it to the roof where hook catches on the ledge. Using metal spikes on his shoes, and arms that probably need to lift more weights, Ben climbs up to the top of the building, looking like a kid struggling to hustle up the rope in gym class.

From his high vantage point, he can see Gavin slow from a sprint to a brisk walk, emphasis on the brisk. Ben has to spring from rooftop to rooftop to keep up with the boy. Fortunately for Ben, this is an upscale neighborhood where all the buildings were constructed from the same blueprints, so the roofs are relatively even in height as opposed to the architectural hodge-podge of new and old construction that makes up the rest of the Metro Area. Ben is slowed by a twelve-foot gap between streets, but with his grappling hook, spiked boots, and stimulated muscles, he manages to make it across while avoiding a fall down to the street and breaking a good number of bones.

Ben is pushing his body well past its limits in order to keep up with Gavin and remain unseen. Even with the stimulant, Ben can't exert himself for much longer. Mercifully, it only takes a few minutes for Gavin to reach his goal, a Walter mindlessly sweeping up bits of trash from the street.

As Ben suggested, Gavin taunts and humiliates the poor creature, all so Nita will take notice and make contact. Gavin performs a series of acts that debase himself more than the mindless creature, before finally, in one final depraved act; he de-pants the Walter and puts the garment onto the clone's head.

Gavin stands still and silent for a moment. Presumably, Nita has made contact. Gavin breaks into a jog, headed north. Ben takes several deep breaths then resumes his roof-bound pursuit. Much to his chagrin, Gavin turns into Grand Park, and Ben has no choice but to repel down from his rooftop perch using his ForteSilk rope.

He follows Gavin into the verdant space, trying his best to keep a safe distance while keeping pace with the speeding young man. Ben's nose is infected with the offensive odors of plant life. He can feel the living molecules invading his body through his lungs. Ben has never understood the appeal of being in nature. Why would someone want to surround themselves with such foreign and potentially dangerous organisms? The saving grace is that the foliage provides cover to keep Ben hidden from Gavin's frequent over-the-shoulder glances.

The greenery keeps Ben out of Gavin's view, but it does not stop a heavy-set police officer from breaking into stride right alongside him. It takes Ben a few seconds to realize the cop isn't chasing him. The officer is trying to assist Ben, whose blue uniform gives him the appearance of a fellow officer in pursuit of suspect.

"You need backup, buddy?" the heavyset officer says between huffs and puffs.

"Umm, no, I'm good. Just getting in some exercise," Ben stammers.

"You're chasing The Beast Slayer, aren't you? They said he might be heading this way. You didn't call it in yet? You trying to steal all the glory?"

"I'm not sure it's him."

"So what? Call it in, or I'm going to," the cops says.

Ben has to make a decision. He wants to follow Gavin, it might be the only way to stop Nita. All Ben's detective work may have exposed some of her plans, but even if he could prove it all, political corruption isn't enough ammunition to take her and Ultracorps down, Gavin even said so himself. Now, if Ben could prove that Ultracorps lied about The Beast to everyone, including the government and that Nita is keeping that serial killer alive for her own ends, that would provide the catalysts needed to force change. The public outrage would be too large; there would have to be a response. Nita would be fired for sure and probably put on trial, even if it was just juvenile court. If Ben can keep following Gavin, the boy will lead Ben right to The Beast.

The problem is that if Gavin is arrested, he's not going to be leading anyone anywhere. Nita will batten down the hatches, and Ben may never find where The Beast is being held. He who fights and runs away lives to fight another day, and Ben would like more days. He sprints ahead of the officer and watches Gavin take a sharp right turn heading east across the park. Ben breaks off the pursuit and addresses the heavy-set officer bringing up the rear.

"I can't keep going," Ben says, which is partially true. "Go ahead and call it in. He's moving west across the park," he adds, lying through his teeth.

The officer disappears into the think.Net stare, and Ben takes the opportunity to disappear into the park.

#

>>>*Where are you Gavin?*

<<<*What do you mean where am I? I'm in the middle of doing exactly what we talked about, Ben.*

>>>*You got away, the cops didn't catch you?*

<<<*Not yet. I'm on a Slug headed towards the facility. I'm sure Nita will use her control of the trains to keep me safe.*

>>>*Good, that was a close one. I was worried for a minute. So where is this facility?*

<<<*How do you know it was a close one...? It was you. You were the cop who was chasing me. I never saw your face. Why were you chasing me?*

>>>*I wanted to know where you were going. If something went wrong, I figured you could use the backup.*

<<<*Concern for my well-being doesn't sound like you. This wouldn't be about finding The Beast and exposing Nita now would it?*

>>>*Is that so bad? You said yourself that exposing some bribes won't exactly shock the world, it's small potatoes. Now secretly keeping a serial killer alive? That's a blue-ribbon Yukon Gold potato right there.*

<<<*I'll call you after the procedure. Once I'm strong enough to stop Billy the Kid, you can expose your little girl nemesis to your heart's content. I'll even help.*

>>>*But what if The Beast doesn't survive the procedure or they kill him afterwards? A dead body won't have the same effect on the public psyche. We have to shove it in Nita's face now, while she least expects it.*

>>>*This was your plan all along, wasn't it? You don't care about me living up to my potential, or getting powerful enough to stop Billy the Kid, or all that crap about how I was a true hero. I'm bait to get the fish you're after: the little girl who stole your job.*

<<<*I meant what I said about you being a hero, but while you getting big muscles sounds great and all, it's not exactly world-changing stuff. Stopping whatever Nita has planned is the priority.*

>>>*Stopping whatever Nita has planned does sound super important, or it might be, if we knew what the "it" was. You're obsessed with Nita, Ben. I recommend you do some soul searching on that fact while I'm living up to my potential. Thanks for helping me even if you didn't really mean to. Goodbye.*

The call ends and Ben shakes his head. He wonders why nothing can ever be easy. Looks like he's got some more sleuthing to do. He's not going to let Gavin stand in the way of taking Nita down.

26

Of course we need more human industry. Just like we need to call our grandmothers more, eat more vegetables, and be kinder to our fellow man, but this vitriol directed at Ultracorps comes off as the complaints of petulant children. This company entertains us, shelters us, feeds us and has done so since the Plagues, often at its own expense. Accidents happen, just like mom burned dinner on occasion, but accidents don't negate all the things she or Ultracorps did for you.

"It's Supposed to be the Home of the Brave" by Forest Brown, think.Net News LA

The Beast is strapped to an operating table. Maceo Steel bands hold him to the Maceo Steel table top. ForteSilk Strands are wrapped around his neck like a chain, the last line of defense in case he somehow breaks the unbreakable Maceo Steel bonds. I could understand the facility workers' fear if The Beast looked like he once did. The Beast that terrorized the Los Angeles Metro Area was a creature straight out of a child's nightmare, a giant pile of muscle covered in hair and leathery skin and armed with claws and teeth that screamed death.

But now he looks like a dog you might rescue from the pound. His body is frail and weak, at least by comparison. His hair has fallen out in patches and his leathery skin is peeling off in sheets. He no longer has canines or claws; they were either removed or fell out due to the same reason the rest of him looks so emaciated. His left arm looks like it was broken and shot a while ago, it's completely mangled. Despite his pathetic look, I still have to stifle my mind's natural progression to anger. If I let my emotions flow freely, I'd run over to the table and try to strangle the life out of him. His neck might actually be skinny enough for me to do that now. The rational part of me knows that I can't kill him, yet. I need to take his strength first. I need to be as powerful as The Beast to defeat my enemies.

He's a force of nature, even if he doesn't look like one right now.

Larry seems to read my thoughts.

"They keep him pretty well sedated on Tranq at all times. It's hard to blame them; there were some... complications a couple months ago so they decided sedating him was the safest thing to do. That much Tranq has some major effects on his metabolism, which explains why he's looking so skinny and disheveled. It doesn't matter though. You're after his genetics, not his actual body. You might have to regrow some muscle on your new hand, but that'll be a drop in the bucket," Larry explains.

"Is there some way to wake him up?"

"He's awake, or as awake as he gets at least. You just need to get his attention."

I clap my hands and yell, "Thomas Calhoun!"

Using his real name worked. The Beast's glazed-over eyes shift into focus, or something like it anyway. He can't lift his neck enough to look at me squarely, but I can see his eyes move to me.

"Gavin, 'zat you? Great to see ya. I was worried you might have died after our little tiff on the roof. I'm glad I can't count killing you in my list of sins," The Beast says, sounding as demented as ever.

"You've still got plenty of sins left on that list, don't sleep too soundly."

"The Lord is givin' me a chance to atone," The Beast says with a grin.

"You don't deserve atonement. You're a monster. I came here to tell you that not only did I beat you, I'm going to take your strength. I'm going to take every 'blessing' God bestowed on you and make it my own."

"I knew it was you. When the Lord told me I'd get one more chance to help one of my brothers by giving him my power, I knew He was talking about you. I knew we was kindred spirits, Gavin. Remember when I told you? Now, I get to prove it to you, and I get to be redeemed."

"Redeemed? Don't you get what's going to happen? They are going to cut your hand from your body and attach it to me. I'm going to use the stem cells I harvest from your hand to make myself as powerful as you are. I promise you that whatever I do with that power, Cabot would not approve."

"The God's own son had to endure much worse than getting his hand cut off. I'm happy doing my part to serve the Lord. As for you, everybody's gotta walk their own path. You'll find your way out the darkness, eventually," The Beast says. The excitement of our conversation is bringing him back to consciousness.

"No, I won't. Don't you remember trying to convert me? I would have rather died, and that's still true."

"You think that now Gavin, but one day that'll change. The Lord's light shines down upon you. How else do you think you beat me, a servant of God, using them puny muscles you got now? The Lord ain't going to let you die until you serve His purpose. That's why He kept me alive when I fell from that tower. It was so I could help you. We're all a part of God's plan, Gavin."

"You're a fool. You were never talking to God. You were talking to a thirteen-year-old girl who runs think.Net. She used your ignorance and desperation to play you like a fiddle. She sent you to that Tower to kill one of her enemies, and when I beat you, she's the one who saved your life. She only did that because she had more uses for you, including mangling your body to make me stronger. Nothing you did was part of God's plan. It was all the schemes of a megalomaniacal child." I'm getting a little carried away, trying too hard to twist the knife.

"God works through many vessels," The Beast says without even skipping a beat. He's not giving me my satisfaction.

I rack my brain to come up with a response, but then I remember what Ben told me. One of my flaws is thinking that everyone sees the world the same way I do. The Beast is a lunatic. I'm not going to convince him of the error of his ways through logic and reason. Nothing can change his mind.

All I can do is push the disturbing things The Beast said out of my head and focus on the task at hand. Arguing with a religious fundamentalist is not what I am here to do. Twisting the knife into

The Beast's side is not what I am here to do. I am here to become powerful enough to stop William Jefferson and Governor Khan. As a bonus, maybe The Beast will die from the procedure. If not, I will find him and finish the job.

#

I ignore the sounds being sent to my brain from my ears. I can't stomach the thought of hearing my own bone get severed with a saw. It takes less than thirty seconds for the doctor to lop off my right hand, just above the wrist. In that time, the nerve signals in my hand transition from screaming bloody murder to saying nothing at all. It is a truly bizarre experience. Almost like I lost someone important to me. The nerve signals in my right hand were part of the cacophony of information that rang constantly in my head. A percentage of that "noise" is now gone. As a replacement, all of the nerves around my severed hand are sounding alerts like crazy. Telling me, in case I didn't know, that my right hand was chopped off.

It took the doctor longer to get through The Beast's skin and bones because his tissue is tougher than my tissue. They sedated him so heavily he wasn't even conscious. I'm a little ashamed to admit how disappointed I was about that. I was hoping he would have to endure the agony. He can't ignore pain signals like I can.

The Speedster doctor moves like a blur over to the bucket of ice where The Beast's hand is being kept, ready to be attached. At first I was worried about the fact that she didn't have any nurses or assistants to help with the procedure, but watching her in action is a sight to behold. She could replace a whole emergency room on her own. Three of her could staff an entire hospital. I wonder how many Speedsters are smart enough to pass medical school. I guess we'll never know; Differents aren't allowed to work for anyone but Ultracorps, and Ultracorps hasn't gotten into the hospital business yet.

The doctor goes to work on The Beast's hand, separating the various tendons, nerves, arteries, and veins that will need to be attached my corresponding tissue. She works at hyper speed, which is good because it would a take normal human way too long to do that same thing; the cells in the hand would start dying. The doctor finishes with The Beast's hand and repeats the process on my arm, identifying the various areas that need to be reconnected.

"Here goes nothing," she says. Those are the fourth, fifth, and six words she's spoken to me. She begins attaching The Beast's hand to me. She matches up the center of the palm to my forearm then uses a fancy-looking screwdriver to drill screws into my bone. Those screws are attached to a stainless steel plate, which is in turn screwed into The Beast's hand, holding it in place. She puts in a second and third plate to stabilize the attachment. It's necessary: The Beast's bones are much thicker than mine, and the hand is barely attached. The plate will only be necessary until I can grow new, thicker bone tissue.

After the bone is in place, she pulls out a microscope from under the table and works on attaching the other tissue. She sews in tiny sutures to attach the various tendons to one another, then the veins and arteries, and finally the nerves. The whole procedure is finished in less than six minutes. I have to imagine that it would take the best human surgeon in the world somewhere around eight hours.

She puts some final stitches into the skin connecting the new me to the old me, wipes some sweat from her brow, and speaks to me through her medical mask.

"I hope you really are capable of all those crazy things Nita seems to think you can do. If not, this is going to get ugly. It's a mess in there. All of The Beast's tissues are much larger and thicker than your corresponding tissue. I felt like I was attaching an adult hand to a five-year old. We've got a Cooler, I'm going to keep your old hand on ice in case this whole thing goes south. There's a chance we could reattach it, but the longer you wait, the less likely it will work. I hope you can figure out how to make this all function in short order. Good luck," the doctor says. If I survive this, I'm going to be sure to tell Nita that this doctor needs some training on the psychological aspects of practicing medicine. She chopped my hand off and never told me her name.

The doctor checks my massive I.V. bag to make sure it is flowing into my arm. Then she wheels the table with The Beast out of the room. I hear her head into another room down the hall. I want to wonder about if they're trying to save him, and if so, what for, but I have more pressing matters to attend to.

I increase my heart rate back to normal. I had it as low as possible so I didn't bleed out on the table, but if I want my new hand to survive, the cells are going to need blood. The problem is that my new arteries are much bigger than the old ones. I feel blood spilling out from the poor connections like water pipes that haven't been properly fit together. Still, some blood is making it into my new tissue. I'm just going to have to keep making new blood to replace what I'm losing.

That's why I've got the largest I.V. bag in history leading into my arm. It is full of water, electrolytes, every vitamin and mineral the human body needs, and even carbohydrates, fats, and proteins. It is primordial soup of the human body. If everybody had a glass of it every morning, vitamin deficiencies and malnutrition would disappear. I can only imagine how expensive it is. It's nice to know Nita cares about me so much. Or at least cares that much about making me her weapon.

Now that I've got the blood flowing, I have to repress my immune system to keep it from attacking The Beast's foreign cells. I hope there aren't exotic, fast-acting viruses or bacteria in this makeshift hospital, or I might not survive.

The next step will be getting my new nerves to function. The doctor used miniature sutures to attach the nerves, but I still need to connect over a microscopic gap. I signal the nerves in my right arm to grow new axons, which attach to the corresponding nerves in The Beast's hand. The connection seems to work, which is something. Feeling the hand attach to my neural network is an odd experience. A new voice joins the jumble of nerve signals in my head, but it's speaking a different language, a much faster language. I can't make sense of many of the impulses, but I can identify pain. The Beast's hand didn't like being cut off.

I lift up my arm and look at the hand. My instinct is to rip it off.

Not just because it's foreign to my body, but because of what it represents. Who knows how many people this hand killed? How many wives did it make widows? How many children did it make orphans? My hand tore Becky in half and murdered her father.

The rational side of my mind knows that the hand didn't do anything; it's a tool made of skin, muscle, and bone. The emotional side of my mind is horrified to think that The Beast is now a part of me. It wonders, irrationally, if somehow this hand will turn me into a monster. It's afraid that somehow the hand will control me, not the other way around.

If I were a normal person, I'm not sure I could get over my emotional reaction to the hand. At the very least, it would take me weeks and maybe some therapy to accept it. Luckily, I'm a freak who doesn't have to deal with the emotions I should be feeling. I simply turn off the emotional centers in my brain and the fear, anxiety, and anger disappears. The rational voice is all I hear, and it knows I control the hand, or at least I will.

My new hand doesn't have a Mark of Differentiation. That's something new to like about it. The Beast never went through Section 26, which means he never got the pleasure of being tested and permanently marked with the results. Not having a tattoo is against the law. Another of my many infractions.

I try to make my new hand into a fist. It works, but I closed my fingers with such force that what was left of The Beast's claws dig into my palm. These new nerves require a much less powerful electrical charge in order to activate, which explains how The Beast can move and react so quickly. I need to learn to use this hand, and once I do, spread the new nerve cells all over my body and relearn how to use all of my limbs. I'm going to be in this bed a while.

#

"Are you sure about this? This might count as breaking the Hippocratic Oath," the Speedster doctor says, her face full of concern.

"I'm sure. If I want bones like The Beast, I need to replace my old human ones. That will be much easier to do if it's part of the healing process. Healthy bone is difficult to alter," I answer.

"Don't you want to start slow? Maybe a leg or something," Larry advises, relying on his non-existent expertise.

"I can't start growing my new muscles until I have a frame to support them. Plus, it'll be easier to grow and spread The Beast's periosteum cells all at once, which will in turn grow the chondroblasts and osteoblasts I'll need to form new, stronger bone," I say.

"Oh, of course. Did that make any sense to you, Doc?" Larry asks.

"He knows what he's talking about, and I'm inclined to defer to his expertise. My medical training didn't prepare me for treating individuals with control over their body's tissue growth," the doctor says.

"Damn. I was hoping you'd say he was full of it," Larry says with a comedic frown.

"Sorry to disappoint you, Larry. Let's get started, Doc," I say.

The doctor picks up a small mallet. I don't think that's a normal part of her medical kit. She winds up and brings the mallet down on my shin. The bone cracks in dozens of places. My new nerves scream signals of pain that ring in my head. I shut down the alerts; there's a lot of pain coming in my near future.

After her first strike, the doctor hesitates for a moment and looks to me. I give her the nod to go ahead. She turns into a blur, bringing down strikes all over my body with speed and grace. How can she move so quickly, yet also be so precise? She is truly impressive.

Larry doesn't see the beauty in watching her work. He looks like he's going to be sick.

"I can't watch this. It's like a scene out of a horror movie. I'll come back when you're more than a sack of broken bones."

#

"Okay, how about five more reps?" Larry tells me.

I'm sitting in a wheelchair with a weight designed to exercise my new hand on my lap.

"I know how many more reps I should do, and it's more than five.

If I don't get more satellite cells into my blood stream, I'll never be able to grow new muscles," I answer.

"Sorry, just trying to feel useful. We're way outside my area of expertise here. I still can't believe you made us break all the bones in your body; it looked like that doctor was breaking up old bathroom tile. I hope whatever you do to grow some muscles works. You're pretty creepy-looking right now. You basically look like a seven foot skeleton. You need some meat on those bones."

I still don't know how to feel about Larry. It's easy to fall into previous habits, joking with him like we're old friends. It's even easy to listen to him tell me what to do, just like when he was my teacher in Section 26. Now I know he was scheming with Nita about me the whole time. He says it was all for my own good, and I believe he thinks that, but I'm worried what else he's willing to do for my own good. No matter what, I can't let our banter wipe away the memory of his lies. I may forgive but I will not forget.

"I'll fill out if someone lets me exercise. Muscles grow through injury. I'd like to get out of this wheelchair," I say to Larry the conspirator.

"Hey, don't let me get in your way. I'm ready for this whole process to be over. I'm sick of having to scrub every nook and cranny of my body before I come in here."

"I'm sorry, regrowing ninety-five percent of the tissue in my body is a bit of a complicated process. I've been focused on enlarging my organs to support my new, bigger body. I need larger lungs to pull in more oxygen, a bigger heart to pump my oxygenated blood, a bigger liver and kidneys to clean the toxins and waste out of my bloodstream, and a bigger digestive track so I might be able to eat one day and get off this I.V. bag," I say as a squeeze the metal prongs that exercise my hand. "That's just for starters. If I had to fight infection too, it would make it all take longer. If my immune system was active, it would be trying to destroy all the new cells as foreign invaders. Once most of my body contains the new genetic material, my immune cells will know the new cells aren't invaders. Otherwise, I might have to fight crime in an Astronaut space suit."

"Speaking of your look, I don't really know the delicate way to ask this so I'm going to blurt it out," Larry says while shifting uncomfortably in his chair. "Are you going to look like The Beast when this is all said and done?"

"There isn't an easy answer to that. I'm going to be as tall and heavy as him, but I'm not going to grow the hair. There isn't really any point in that. The issue is what to do about his leathery flesh. It serves as an armor of sorts, and should help protect me from guns and knives. The same is true for the claws. They serve a purpose, but..."

"They'll make you look like a monster?" Larry says.

"Bingo. I'm leaning towards not stimulating any of those cells."

"Sounds like the right way to go. I'll leave you alone so you can concentrate. I want Nita to think I'm useful though, so I'm going to stay here and watch some shows on think.Net."

"How helpful."

Larry goes into the think.Net stare and zones out. I do twenty more reps with hand resistance weight. I have to concentrate to keep my movements coordinated. I am still trying to fine-tune the integration of my old and new nervous system. I've spread the improved nerve cells all over my body, but there have been some side effects. I find it takes more of my focus to move my body, a byproduct of the fact that the new cells require less of an electrical charge to operate than my old ones. I'm still having a bit of trouble controlling my new hand, but at least I can move it.

The repetitions with the weight damage my new muscles, which causes them to release satellite cells. Those satellite cells are supposed to be used to make the damaged muscle stronger. Instead, I direct my vasculature to funnel those cells away from their parent muscles and into the muscles in my other arm. Soon I have a culture of cells in my right arm's bicep. I stimulate those cells to start dividing. It works, and the cells start growing at a rapid pace. I'm in business.

#

"It's alive! It's alive!" Larry says, hamming it up.

I'm taking my first steps on my new legs. I'm walking between a set of parallel bars so I can stabilize myself. Considering I don't really have any better control of my arms than I do my legs, it's a blind leading the blind situation. I stumble on my fourth step and crush the bar when I try to catch myself. I end up on my back.

"That's okay, Frankenstein was a little stiff too," Larry says with a chuckle.

"Actually, Frankenstein was the doctor. The monster didn't have a name," I say back.

"I see losing the ability to walk did nothing to contain your smugness."

"This is a temporary setback. No one else has ever grown a whole new body. For all you know, I'm doing great."

"Is your lack of hair a temporary setback too? I'm having a hard time believing you're making progress when you're still smoother than a newborn baby. And thank God we had some giant clothes made for you," Larry says while shuddering in mock disgust.

"I told you, I'm having trouble getting my hair to grow back because my follicle cells got all mixed up, and I don't want a layer of fur. I'll fix it after I've got everything important working," I reply.

I flip onto my belly and try to do a push-up to get to my feet. I push so hard I throw myself up high enough to hit my head on the ceiling. Despite that, I manage to recover and land on my feet. These new muscles are incredibly powerful, and I'm loving my new, super fast reflexes. I'm not particularly enjoying having to relearn how to use my body again, but I did it before back when I first Differentiated, and I can do it again.

"You stuck the landing, but we have to deduct some points for the concussion. You hit that ceiling pretty hard, you okay?" Larry asks.

"I'll pretend I was testing my new and improved thick skull. It worked well. I barely felt a thing."

"You never feel pain."

"Okay, I barely registered any damage at all."

I start walking again. If I concentrate and move slowly, I can take somewhat controlled steps. Between my new powerful muscles and much more sensitive nervous system, what would have been a slight twitch of a limb in my old body now leads to a wild swing. It feels like I'm handling an egg with everything I do. But I always had to concentrate to control my body, now I just need to concentrate harder.

I finally get a few steps going in succession. I end up stumbling out of the rehab room and into the hallway.

"Whoa there, Gavin. Don't go too far!" Larry yells after me, his voice trembling with concern.

"What're you so worried about? Where am I going to go? Is there even anyone else in the facility?" I ask.

The answer hits me like a ton of bricks, The Beast! I've been so focused on creating my new body, I forgot that the monster who made it all possible was still here. As soon as I think of him, all the emotions associated with him come along too: anger, fear, hatred. My mind wants to experience them all. I need to know where he is.

I start walking more quickly. I stumble a bit, but I don't care. I go through the hallway, looking in rooms that are all empty. I finally get to a closed door and try to twist the locked doorknob. I crush the Pho-plastic handle. That isn't going to stop me. A slight push with my new, improved muscles sends the door flying off its hinges, revealing… another empty room.

"What are you doing, Gavin?" Larry asks, catching up with me.

"You know what I'm doing. Where is he?"

"Two seconds ago you could barely walk, and we were joking around. Now you're out for blood. Where did this all come from?"

"I couldn't do anything about The Beast when I was an invalid. Now I'm not anymore."

"What, you're going to kill him? Arrest him? Thank him for your new body?" Larry asks and throws his hands up.

"I don't know what I'm going to do, but whatever I do starts with knowing where he is."

"Well, I'm sorry I can't help you with that. All I know is he's not here."

I turn around and head towards Larry. I stand up straight, making good use of my new imposing frame. I get right in his face.

"Tell me where he is!" I say while staring him down.

"I told you, I don't know. You used to say you could always spot a liar."

"It has recently come to my attention that I might not be as good at that as I'd like to think."

"Wow, finally a hint of self-doubt. I didn't know you experienced that. I guess you're going to have to trust me. They took him away a few hours after your surgery. I have no idea where they took him. Frankly, I don't care. I wasn't here for him. I'm here for you. Because I care about you."

"You're just helping Nita pull my strings," I say.

"Ohh, is that why I stood up my girlfriend? Is that why I've been ignoring angry think.Net calls from my boss? Is that why I've left other kids who need my help out to dry? I'm sure Nita has her schemes, but that has nothing to do with why I'm here. I'm here because you can barely walk, and you're wanted by the police again. I'm here because I have the rather naïve notion that you might listen to me. I'm here because I thought I might be able to stop you from doing something incredibly stupid."

"And I thought I could trust you. I guess we were both wrong," I say.

"You always were stubborn. One of these days you're going to figure out that there are people who care about you and want what's best for you, and those are the people you should listen to. It might happen sooner than you think. Until then, go ahead and do whatever stupid bullheaded thing it is you're going to do. I'll see you soon," Larry says with a dismissive wave of his arms. Then he walks away down the hallway.

I go on think.Net, and call Rolland Bloom.

<<<*Ben, we need to find The Beast.*

27

Log of Notable Nita/Ultracorps Activity Week 223

Discrepancies between Eat-N-Go order records and Ultracorps delivery logs.

Theories: Expect to see discrepancy on Eat-N-Go records explained by Khan laundering bribe money. Discrepancy on Ultracorps logs more puzzling. Possibly food being redirected to feed The Beast and/or other hidden Differents. Need more info.

"I'll say it one more time. I need access to your shipping records for the last year. The paper copies, not the easily manipulated files on think.Net. And don't try telling me those were all lost in the explosion at the lab, because I know you have backups, and I know Ultracorps just opened this facility to manage those files. I don't want excuses," Ben says to a terrified young man sitting at the reception desk of the Ultracorps records office.

Ben is wearing an expensive-looking blue pinstriped suit, outfitted with shoulder pads that make him look larger and more intimidating. He has his head shaved to a buzz cut and used his chin putty to give himself one of the squarest jaws on the planet. The costume is half G.I. Joe and half Atticus Finch. Ben once again nailed the look, and makes the perfect faux FBI officer.

"I'm very sorry sir, but like I told you, I can't let anyone in without authorization and nobody else is in yet. I heard on the radio that there's some sort of delay on the Slug, and for some reason, I can't get on think.Net to make a call. It's like you said this place just opened up. It's my first week. I don't know what I'm supposed to do," the receptionist says back with nervous panic. This is clearly the most terrifying thing that has ever happened to this young man.

Ben reaches into his pocket and pulls out a leather wallet. He opens it, revealing a shiny gold badge and an I.D. with the large letters FBI. These are movie-quality props that Ben spent hours fashioning in his basement.

"I'll tell you what you are supposed to do; you're supposed to look at this badge. You're supposed to realize that saying no to me means you're saying no to the United States government," Ben says, his face turning red. "Have you ever heard of obstruction of justice? If you don't tell me where the records are and let me through, I'll arrest you. The judge isn't going to care that the trains were delayed or that think.Net was down, he's only going to care that you stood in the way of a federal agent attempting to perform the duties of his office. Now, are you going to let me through, or are we going to do this the hard way?" Ben moves his hand towards his waistband, threatening to pull out a gun that isn't there.

"Please don't arrest me," the receptionist pleads. He bought Ben's Oscar-worthy performance. "I'm trying to do my job. I don't want to break any laws. The records room is down that hall, third door on the right. I don't know where anything is kept. I'm just here to greet people."

"Thank you, young man. You did the right thing, trust me. We're after some bad eggs here, and those records might hold the key to tracking them down. Don't tell anyone I told you, but we think they might be hiding Tranq in the food deliveries coming to the Metro Area. These are real bad guys, the kind that sell to kids, and we might catch them thanks to your help," Ben whispers that last part so the receptionist feels like he's in on the made-up secret.

"Really? Wow," the receptionist says, his terror melting into a puddle of pride.

Ben gives the kid a nod, and then walks past the desk. Halfway down the hall, his head starts spinning, and he puts his hand on the wall to regain his balance. It's an unfortunate side effect of Ben's efforts to clog up the think.Net system. Ben has been and continues to make hundreds of think.Net calls a minute using his collection of fake accounts. His inner monologue is split into hundreds of different voices, each making a talk request to another of his accounts. His brain has barely enough power left to keep him walking in a straight line. It doesn't help that he's physically exhausted from climbing all over the Slug tracks this morning and disabling junction boxes.

Ben doesn't have any better options, even considering the near-crippling fatigue. If he didn't jam up the local think.Net node then the kid at reception would have insisted on calling his superiors, superiors who would likely have a firmer grasp on the legal precedents requiring officers to have warrants to force their way onto the premises. It would have worked its way up the Ultracorps chain of command; maybe even Nita herself would get involved.

Ben straightens himself out and continues on into the record keeping room, a little more slowly now. Once he's inside the office, his excitement gives him a second wind. Ben starts tearing through filing cabinets and folders with surprising speed for a man whose attention is divided in a hundred different directions. This records room has more information than Ben could have hoped for.

He finds delivery receipts then cross references them with accounts receivable, and for a little added excitement, the quarterly earnings reports. He starts with the last three months but soon expands that to six months, and then the whole year. Somewhere along the way he adds accounts payable into the mix, to really get the party going.

Ultracorps recently reprinted all of these records after they were destroyed in the lab bombing. This office was only opened in the last few weeks. That might mean Nita didn't have a chance to go back over everything with a fine tooth comb. Long shots are the only targets Ben has left.

It's unlikely Nita made a mistake, being sloppy is not really part of her DNA, but there's always a chance. She might not have planned on the second most powerful mind on earth auditing her records. If The Beast is being held in the Metro Area, then he will need to be fed, and that takes an enormous number of calories. Nita's not going to advertise the whereabouts of her secret prison/lab, but any facility that saw a large uptick in food deliveries is a possible location. Food has to be delivered into the Metro Area before it's dispersed to the various Ultracorps offices. That could be the weak point in any record keeping shenanigans.

Ben is so deeply engrossed in his forensic accounting, he doesn't hear the commotion in the hallway, a commotion that is headed his way.

"What the hell do you mean there's an FBI agent in our records room? Who told you to let him in there? Did he have a warrant? I'm late to work one time and this whole place falls apart!" a gruff voice yells.

The owner of the voice, a stone-faced sixty-year-old Ultracorps executive, charges into the office. He's greeted by the sight of Ben sitting on the floor in a messy sea of papers. To the uninformed eye, Ben looks like a toddler who made a mess in daddy's office, not a genius putting together the intricate pieces of a financial puzzle.

"What in God's name is going on here?" the executive demands.

"Hello, sir. Please excuse the mess, it's part of a Federal investigation," Ben says without looking up from the paper in his hands.

"Are you kidding me? It looks like a bomb went off in here. I'm going to see a warrant this instant or there will be hell to pay." Unlike the receptionist, this man is too self-important to be intimidated by a possible FBI agent.

"Of course, sir. I have it right here."

Ben gets to his feet and approaches the executive while reaching into his suit pocket. Once he's right next to the executive, Ben pulls out a length of ForteSilk rope. He uses his other hand to strike like a cobra, right at the man's neck, hitting a nerve cluster which drops the older man to his knees. Ben flips the executive onto his belly and hogties him with the grace of a rodeo champion. The entire assault and restraint take less than five seconds.

"What do you think you're doing? My lawyer is going to have a field day with this. When it's all over you won't be able to get a job guarding—" the executive's voice is muffled by a wad of blue pinstriped fabric Ben tears off his suit and uses to gag the older man.

Ben returns to work at his unique style of accounting. A few minutes later, the previously terrified receptionist from the front works up the courage to go see what happened to his superior in the back room. He spots his boss hogtied and gagged in the corner and yells out "Mr. Peabody!" Five seconds later he lays bound and gagged next to the executive.

Three hours and several paper cuts later, the receptionist and executive have been joined by a dismayed security guard, who will probably lose his job, and two nice older ladies who work in the accounting office. Ben used the utmost care while tying those two up and made sure the ForteSilk wasn't too tight. All of the homemade gags torn off of his suit have reduced the once fine attire to tattered rags.

Ben finally finds what he is looking for, a discrepancy in the accounting records, and it is on a much larger scale than he expected. Ultracorps has records of large food deliveries to Governor Khan's grocery store chains Eat-N-Go. Manna products, but also rice, flour, beans and so forth. Most people would look at these records and shrug, but most people didn't also see Khan's grocery store records, or have Ben's photographic memory. He notices that the Ultracorps records are for double what Khan's records say they ordered. That means half of these food orders are going somewhere else. There are delivery logs in a separate file which show mysterious shipments being unloaded at a storage depot near the train yards. Presumably, this is where all the chow is going.

It's too much food for The Beast alone, it's enough to feed hundreds maybe thousands. Nita is going to be in so much trouble. Ben heads out of the office, his mouth salivating at the prospect of all the Nita schemes he's going to thwart.

28

The tragedy at Ultracorps Labs serves as a reminder of the pitfalls of relying on Different labor. While Ultracorps has been a boon in helping this nation recover from the Plagues, it was a band-aid for an emergency situation. For those of us old enough to remember automobiles, I liken the situation to using a "donut." For my younger readers, a "donut" was used to replace a flat tire on your car. These wheels were designed to be used temporarily, long enough for you to drive to the mechanic and get a new full-size tire. If you drove too far, the "donut" would blow. The explosion at Ultracorps proves that it's time to stop relying on stop-gap solutions and turn back to traditional human industry.

"Time for Solutions" by Roberta Clemens, Los Angeles Times

The gap between roofs is about thirty feet. I should be able to jump over it with ease. I take a running start and leap into the air. I end up jumping at least fifty feet, taking me clear over the roof. I smash into the side of the building next to my target and land in the alley with a thud.

I'd say I misjudged my jump a tad. On the plus side, that fall would have broken more than a few bones in my old body. My new body merely suffers some minor bruising, and considering my new cells regenerate so much faster, the bruises will be gone in a few minutes. I'm trying to focus on the bright side.

Instead of jumping between the roofs I decide I'll walk the last few blocks to the warehouse. Walking is still its own form of adventure, though I'm slowly getting the hang of it. As long as I stay focused, I can keep from tripping over my own two feet. I have to move slowly so I can walk and keep my eyes peeled for Walters. I don't want Nita to know we're on to her. There shouldn't be any out here near the Slug yards, but she might be using them as an alarm system of sorts.

This would be a good place to keep The Beast. There's easy access to the Slug in case Nita decides to move him, and no one lives out here because of all the noise from the trains.

I get to the block where I'm supposed to meet Ben. For once, he isn't wearing one of his ridiculous disguises, just normal jeans and a T-Shirt. No chin putty or makeup at all. He sees me coming, and his eyes light up as he runs to meet me.

"Look at you! You're magnificent," Ben says as he pokes me in the arm like I'm a science project. "Was it difficult? I can only imagine what it's like to grow a whole new body. On second thought, I can't even imagine."

"It took a while. I've still got a few kinks I'm working out. It's not an easy process to describe," I answer.

"You passed on growing The Beast's fur, claws, and teeth. Can't say I blame you. It should keep children from running away at the sight of you. You could pass as a garden-variety Strong-Man, albeit a completely hairless one…"

Ben could go on talking forever, but then he looks up and sees my face. I'm making sure to furrow my brow and squint my eyes to show my annoyance. I hope I'm doing it right.

"I'll address the eight-hundred-pound gorilla in the room," Ben says when he sees my look. "I was surprised by the call. You weren't too happy with me the last time we spoke, what with the whole secretly following you thing."

"I want to find The Beast, and I knew I could count on you not to let the issue go. It's too juicy a chance to expose Nita. Enemy of my enemy and all that."

"What did Nita say when you left the hospital?" Ben asks, turning the conversation to his obsession as quickly as possible.

"She didn't say anything. I spoke to her once the whole time I was recovering. She asked me a few questions about how things were going and ended the call as soon as I asked where The Beast was. Larry was the only one there when I left. He wanted me to stay and recover and said something cryptic about seeing me soon, but he wasn't exactly in a position to keep me from leaving."

"Who would be? You're quite the specimen," Ben says and raps his fingers on my chest.

"Which warehouse is it? Where is The Beast?" I ask.

"That one," Ben says and points. "You see, I was able to infiltrate the new Ultracorps records office using one of my characteristically brilliant disguises. I impersonated an FBI officer and was able to… You don't care. The gist is that Ultracorps has been over-reporting orders to grocery stores all over the Metro Area. Those stores have been getting half the deliveries, yet no one's complaining. By digging around transport logs and the like, I was able to determine that the food deliveries were getting rerouted here. It should be more than enough to feed The Beast a hundred times over, even if he's regrowing a hand. Can he do that?"

"I don't know."

"If we can prove that Nita's been hiding The Beast, she'll be finished. There's no wiggling out of keeping a mass murderer alive and hidden. Hell, with all the food that's being sent here, she might be keeping a hundred secret prisoners. We might find Jimmy Hoffa down there. It's good you called me when you did. I was going in soon no matter what, but backup won't hurt. Let's go take her down."

"You mean make sure a dangerous sociopath can't be released to wreak havoc again?" I ask.

"Sure, that too. Let's keep it quiet until we find him. I'm sure Nita has a plan B in case of being discovered, and I'd rather not find out what it is," Ben says in a whisper.

"We need to be careful, Nita knows we're working together, this could be a setup."

"When I'm dealing with Nita, I assume everything could be a setup. Just stay on your toes. It's the best you can do," Ben says under his breath. He's got some serious ego issues, which isn't very surprising considering his job was stolen by a little girl.

We start to tiptoe, but that's not really something I've mastered yet. My massive feet pound the pavement like a large herd animal. That's basically what I am now that I weigh eight hundred pounds.

"Seriously? It sounds like there's an elephant behind me. Couldn't The Beast stalk his prey without making a sound?" Ben asks.

"I told you, I'm still working out the kinks," I reply.

"I'm guessing you're not willing to wait out here while I reconnoiter, so that rules out the stealth plan. We'll have to go with our own plan B, shock and awe. Why don't you make us a surprise entrance through one of the walls? You can handle that right?"

"Even if I don't mean to."

I step up to the wall of the warehouse, wind up and swing. My massive fist cuts through the B-Crete wall like it's paper. Filled with confidence from my punch, I lower my shoulder and charge. I bust through the wall like a football player breaking through a banner on game day. I'm a freaking powerhouse. It feels good to experience the upside of my new abilities.

Ben follows through the hole. The warehouse is gigantic. I didn't realize how large it was from the outside. There are endless rows of shelves that stretch up to the top of twenty-foot ceiling. Each shelf is full of massive shipping containers that came straight off of trans-continental delivery trains.

"What is all this?" I ask.

"Beats me. It certainly doesn't look like a secret prison. There must be a basement or something where they're holding The Beast," Ben says, his eyes already beginning his search.

"I want to know what's in these containers."

I go up to the closest shelf and start prying open one of the large Pho-Plastic containers. I'm stopped by a series of loud booms coming from deep in the warehouse. It sounds like I do when I walk, only more deafening. The sound is getting louder. Whoever—or whatever—it is, it's getting closer.

"Do you hear that?" I ask and turn to Ben, but he's not there. He seems to have disappeared entirely.

The booming footsteps keep getting louder until their source comes into view, a massive Strong-Woman. She might be the largest person I've ever seen. She looks like she's got about a thousand pounds on me, which puts her close to a ton. She stops about fifty feet away from me, and I hone in on her tattoo. Lisa Bryant: Beta: Physically Enhanced. I put my hands up to show I don't want a fight.

"Who are you!? What are you doing here!?" the massive woman demands.

"Relax, Lisa. I'm not here to hurt anyone or steal anything. I'm looking for someone, someone dangerous."

"How do you know my name?" Lisa asks with a hint of panic.

"I read it off your tattoo. I have excellent vision."

"You don't look like someone with Enhanced Senses. You look like a Strong-Man to me, a small one maybe, but definitely a Strong-Man."

"I'm both, well, kind of. It's complicated."

"I'd ask you to show me your tattoo, but even my eyes can see you don't have one. Care to explain?" she demands.

"I lost my tattoo as a result of a recent medical procedure. It's the same reason my Differentiation is difficult to describe right now."

"Is that so?" Lisa says switching to the calm tone one would use when talking to a crazy person. "Maybe it'd be a good idea for you to go back and see the doctor who performed your 'procedure.' In any case, whoever you are, you need to leave here right now."

I slow down time to consider my options. I'm sure Ben would tell me not to give her my name or any other information because then Nita will know we were here. But honestly, the cat is already out of the bag on that. If this woman files an incident report, you wouldn't have to be the smartest person alive like Nita to figure out that the giant hairless man seen in your warehouse is the same one that just left your medical facility.

"My name is Gavin Stillman. I'm with the Office of Exceptional Cases. I have reason to believe that The Beast may be held in this building. I'm here to find him," I say with all the authority I can muster.

"Oh, you're The Beast Slayer you say? I thought I recognized you from the papers. You know, usually they say the camera adds ten pounds, but I guess in your case it took off about six hundred instead," Lisa mocks.

"I know how crazy it sounds, but I am Gavin Stillman. I underwent a procedure to give me some of The Beast's abilities, which is why I look like this. The Beast was involved, which is how I know he's alive and might be here. Are there any secure rooms? Maybe a basement?"

"That doesn't sound crazy at all. You're totally right, this is a combination storage warehouse and monster prison. Great work, Sherlock."

"It's possible that you don't know about the holding facility. The person who is keeping The Beast alive does not want him found for obvious reasons."

"Of course."

"If you could let me look around, I might be able to find it."

"Listen crazy, you aren't doing anything like that. Now I don't want to hurt you, but I will if you don't turn around and walk out of here in the next three seconds," Lisa says and her eyes go cold.

"Please, you have to believe me. The Beast is going to kill again. It's a matter of time."

"One… Two… Three," Lisa says.

We stare at each other for a second. Then Lisa breaks into a run, barreling towards me like a bat out of hell.

I slow down time again so I can make a plan. Even if I had forever, I don't think I could come up with a better option than getting the hell out of the way. I bend my legs and jump. Surprise, surprise, I misjudge my leap and end up crashing into a row of shelves. I hit hard, which stuns me for a moment, but the blow from my leap is nothing compared to the Strong-Woman's punch. She hits me with an uppercut that sends me hurtling two hundred feet deeper into the warehouse. I land, bounce, and skid into another row of shelves.

My new bones are truly impressive. Somehow, none of them broke from the punch or the ensuing flight and crash landing. I've got some bad bruises and a small hemorrhage in one of my recently enlarged kidneys, but considering that punch would have liquefied the old me, I can't complain. Getting some distance between me and the Strong-Woman is also a boon. I've got some time to think strategy.

Obviously, she's stronger than I am, but she's also slower and clumsier, at least theoretically. They gave me access to The Beast's file when I started working as an OEC agent. He managed to take down one of my fellow agents who was one of the strongest Differents that ever lived. They believe The Beast did it by using his superior speed and agility. That's what I have to rely on. I suddenly wish I had allowed myself a few more days in rehab to work on my coordination, but here I am.

Lisa comes around the corner and hurtles towards me. I stand my ground like a bullfighter staring down his prey. At the last second I juke to the left, leaving my foot out. She trips and smashes face first into one of the shelves, knocking it down and causing a domino effect which topples a few more rows.

"Great, now I'm going to have to clean all that up," Lisa says as she stands back up.

"I'm not looking for a fight. Just give me a few minutes to search the warehouse. I don't want to hurt you," I plead.

"Ha, ha. Good one, little man."

Lisa charges at me and throws a sloppy haymaker I duck under with ease. She left her whole right side exposed, and I pepper it with a dozen quick jabs and hooks. It feels like I'm hitting a brick wall, but she lets out a few grunts that let me know I'm hurting her, at least a little.

She keeps throwing clumsy punches, and I keep dodging them and unleashing a flurry of counters. For every swing she takes, I answer with ten. I float and sting like Ali in his prime. I'm a butterfly mixed with a bee, mixed with a demon out of hell. I can tell she's starting to tire.

My victory starts to seem like an inevitability as I continue to wear her down. But then my inexperience with my new body comes back to bite me. I trip over my own two feet like a toddler who just learned to walk and still hasn't mastered the process. Lisa doesn't hesitate to exploit my folly. She lets loose with a hellacious kick, which punts me through the air like a football. I land at the base of one of the shelves.

The force topples the shelf and a few containers crash down on top of me, shattering as they land. I end up buried under a mountain of rice. Why is there so much rice here?

She really let me have it with that kick; she cracked one of my ribs. I guess my bones can break. I start directing my body to heal the bone. Now I need to dig myself out of this pile of rice.

I start swimming upwards through the grains. It takes a few second of breast stroke to dig my top half out. As I'm trying to extricate my lower half, Lisa finds me. I can't dodge her with my legs buried. She reaches down and grabs me, wrapping her arms around me in a vice grip. I flex my arms to get free, but it feels like I'm wrapped in Maceo Steel. I kick back with my legs, but without any leverage the blows have no force behind them.

"That's enough! I'm going to hold you here till I figure out what to do with you. Stop squirming or I'll crush you like a bug," Lisa yells in my ear.

"Gavin, can you still turn your ears off!?" Ben yells from behind some shelves.

"Who is that?" Lisa demands.

"Yes, I can!" I yell back and start filling the tympanic cavity in my ear with fluid.

"Good, do it!"

"What is he talking about!?" Lisa demands.

She keeps talking, but I can't hear what she's saying. A few seconds later, she lets me go. She drops to her knees, covering her ears with her hands. Ben has some sort of noise weapon and it worked.

I don't let the opportunity pass me by. I raise both my hands up over my head and bring them down as hard as I can right on the base of Lisa's skull. The blow smashes her face into the floor, forcing her chin a few inches deep into the B-Crete. I roll her over. She's still conscious, albeit barely. She looks like she isn't going to be causing any more trouble. I drain the fluid out of my tympanic cavity and hear Ben walk up to us.

"Thanks for the save, although I'm not sure what took you so long to get involved," I say to him.

"I'm the brains of this operation. You're supposed to be the muscle. I didn't want to step on your toes. I was saving that trick for an emergency, you'll never guess where I got the idea," Ben says.

"Okay then Brains, any brilliant theories as to what this warehouse is? It sure doesn't look like a prison."

"While you were engaged in your boxing match, I looked through some of the containers. There's a whole lot of Slug fuel, WormLights, raw Manna, dried fruits and vegetables, B-Crete, and Maceo Steel beams and pipes of various sizes," Ben says as he tries to catch his breath.

"Did you find any sign of The Beast while you were searching?"

Ben shakes his head no.

"Great, so there's basically what you'd expect to find in an Ultracorps warehouse. Congratulations. Brilliant detective work," I say sarcastically.

"Something doesn't smell right. It doesn't make sense to keep construction materials and food stored in the same place. Basic supply chain logistics teaches that it's much more efficient to have specialized warehouses to distribute your goods, especially if your supplies come in bulk shipments like these do. If there's anything Ultracorps loves, it's efficiency. They own hundreds of warehouses around the Metro Area. Why store all this in one building? There are enough supplies to build and feed a village."

"I don't know, and I don't care. We didn't break in here to solve the mystery of how Ultracorps supply chain logistics work. We need to get out of here, now. She might have called Nita or the police before we got into our brawl."

"Not yet. I need to know what this place is," Ben says. He walks over to the dazed Strong-Woman and gets right in her face. "Tell me, what is this place? Why are there so many different supplies stored here? Did you see The Beast?"

The dazed woman stares at him.

"She's probably deaf from your little sound weapon. Between that and the concussion I gave her, I don't think she's going to be giving any information."

Ben isn't satisfied. He snaps his finger next to her ear and keeps repeating his questions.

I get a think.Net alert. Linda is calling.

>>>*Gavin, how's your recovery going?*

<<<*Um, fine I guess. What's up?*

>>>*I don't want to rush you, but you might be running out of time. It looks like Billy the Kid is off the disabled list, and he's making up for lost time. Three Differents were found dead outside of Ultracorps employee housing. I can't imagine anyone else did that. Do you think you can get yourself out of the hospital soon?*

<<<*Yeah... that shouldn't be a problem. I'm already out.*

>>>*You are? Why didn't you tell me? What are you doing? Are you on Billy the Kid's trail?*

<<<*Not exactly. I'm working on something else.*

>>>*Something else? What could be more important than tracking down the man who killed your partner and my son? Wait, don't tell me. I already know the answer. You're going after The Beast.*

<<<*Ben thought he found where they were keeping him.*

>>>*Let me ask you Gavin, how many people has The Beast killed lately? I'm pretty sure the answer is zero. Meanwhile, Billy the Kid assassinated dozens of people and set off a bomb that killed hundreds. I thought the whole point of your little deal with the Devil that is Nita was so you could become strong enough to stop him. I should have known it was really part of your obsession with The Beast and Ben's obsession with Nita. You two deserve each other. If you come to your senses, you can talk to me at my apartment.*

She ends the call to emphasize her point.

"I don't know what it's for. They never told me. I stack the containers when they come in and guard the place. That's it," Lisa pleads.

"You're lying!" Ben screams.

"Ben, that's enough! She doesn't know anything because there's nothing to know. It's a warehouse. I can't believe I let you drag me here while there's a serial killer on the loose who has access to explosives. I don't suppose you did any more investigations into what's happening with the bomb-making materials that Khan purchased?"

Ben shakes his head no.

"Of course not. Who cares how many people Billy the Kid kills if Nita isn't involved, right? I'd be madder at you if I wasn't guilty of the same crime myself with The Beast."

"Nita's schemes are bigger than one killer. It's going to affect the whole nation, maybe the world," Ben says with complete conviction.

"Maybe you're right, but we aren't stopping her tonight. Now maybe, just maybe, we can stop a serial killer and save the lives of some of our fellow Differents. Come on. We're going to Linda's place. If you don't come I'm going to tell her you were too selfish to help me," I say appealing to the quasi-mother son relationship he seems to have with her.

"We can't leave yet, I'm telling you, she knows something," Ben says and looks right into the dazed Strong-Woman's eyes.

"And I'm telling you we're leaving now. Do I need to carry you out?" I say and stand up to my full, extremely imposing height.

29

I give that to you my Chosen Sons: a blank slate. I give you a world that is waiting to be rebuilt in my glory.

Chosen Sons: 58

The Beast's hand hurts. It is a funny thing. How can something hurt that no longer exists? There are all sorts of tubes going into his body. They are making him strong again. The Lord did not let him die. The Beast knew He would not. This was a test of The Beast's faith. The Lord needed to know that The Beast would truly do anything the Lord asked of him, even give his own life. The Beast has proven he is the most loyal servant God could hope for. Whatever the Lord needs, he is happy to provide. Considering The Beast is still alive, there must be more to do. He prays to God and hopes He shares His vision for the future.

>>>*You are right my child, I am not finished with you.*

"Lord, I knew you wouldn't let me die. I knew it was just test. I'm ready to keep servin' you Lord. Just tell me what to do."

>>>*I need you to heal and be patient, my child. The time for freedom will soon be at hand. My Chosen Sons will ascend to their proper place at the head of my table. I need you strong to enact my will on earth. To that end, some Forgotten Son servants are going to help you. Let the humans earn their salvation by aiding a Chosen Son.*

The door to The Beast's room opens and humans in white lab coats come in. One of them is carrying a tray with a blade on it. The blade shimmers in the light, it is a Maceo Steel knife attached to a stump. A new divine hand for a Chosen Son. The Beast smiles.

30

Perhaps an entire editorial dedicated to me saying "I told you so" is poor form, but I'm indulging myself nevertheless. While the entire Metro Area celebrated "The Beast Slayer" and his heroic feats, I stood alone on an island. I maintained that laws are passed with good reason, and they should not be thrown aside when we decide we like a particular criminal. I warned that the OEC Field Office Program was a bad idea, and letting a criminal serve as law enforcement agent was an even worse idea, but my position was dismissed as mere fear mongering. Now, the Field Office Program is in shambles and being questioned nationwide. One agent is dead under mysterious circumstances, and the other has disappeared, escaping police custody in the process.

"Some People Don't Change" by Roberta Clemens, Los Angeles Times

I fold my arms together as I step out of the stairwell, as it's the only way I can fit through the doorway, and walk down the hall to Linda's apartment. I pass by a large mirror and catch a glimpse of myself. Instead of myself, I see some sort of giant, hairless man with a stretched out version of my face. I've looked in the mirror and seen a different face before, back when I did my old man vigilante disguise and my fat-face thing, but this is a whole other level. It's not just my face that's foreign; it's my entire body. I'm a living Kafka novel.

"That must be a weird experience," Ben says when he sees me staring at the mirror.

"You're telling me. My brain isn't really accepting the visual information it's receiving. I don't feel like I'm looking at myself. I feel like the mirror is a window, and I'm really seeing a different person."

"I'd love to give you some advice, but I've got nothing. I've memorized several books on psychology, and none of them offer any insight on how to cope with growing into an entirely new person. You're breaking new ground here. On the up side, if things ever die down you'd make a hell of a thesis project for some kid getting his psych doctorate."

"At least there's that. Let's keep moving," I say.

I shut down the various confused emotional centers of my brain and keep walking. I get to Linda's door and knock. I hear her come to the door, but she doesn't open it. She's spying on me through the peephole. She's got a view of my chest.

"Can I help you?" she asks.

I lean down so she can see my face through her peephole.

"Hi, Linda."

"Gavin?! Is that you? Come in, come in," she says and opens up her door so I can step inside. "My God, what happened to you?" It's nice to know I still look enough like myself for her to recognize my face.

"You don't like the look?" I ask.

"It's impressive, no doubt about that, but I've never been one for muscles."

"Oh shucks, the whole reason I did it was to impress women. What a waste."

"Let's not stand here in the hallway, come in you two. Can I get you guys anything?" Linda asks.

"I'm starving pretty much all the time now. If you have any Manna Bars that would be great," I say.

"I can do better than that. I've got a whole pot of Meat Sauce in the cooler, but it'll take a while to heat up," Linda says with a satisfied smile. It makes her happy that I want her food.

"Cold is fine," I blurt out.

"I'll go get it. Have a seat in the living room. And it isn't just the three of us. A friend is here," Linda warns.

"Captain Murphy?"

"No, he hasn't left his apartment since the office got shut down. Having one of his agents killed and the other go missing sent him into a bit of a tailspin. It's someone you'll be happier to see," Linda says and winks.

Linda has an unbelievable apartment. It's huge. I can only imagine what the rent is, and when you add in the insurance Differents have to pay, it must cost a small fortune. I guess she made good money back when she was working for Ultracorps. It doesn't hurt that she's old enough not to have to pay any Section 26 debt. Her only COL Obligations are for the tiny bit of extra food she requires and the Different upkeep tax we all have to pay.

I walk into the living room and see Maria standing there. My heart almost jumps out of my chest. I haven't seen her since I shot her by accident. I knew she was alive, but there's something different about seeing her with my own eyes.

I run over and wrap my arms around her. She winces and pushes me off.

"Easy, I'm still recovering," she says.

"Sorry, it's great to see you… And sorry for the shooting you," I say and look down to show my shame.

"At least I don't have to hear you brag about how good a shot you are anymore. It's nice to see you Gavin. Although I'm not sure I'm seeing you."

"I underwent a procedure. It's hard to explain."

"Don't bother, I'm sure I wouldn't understand the details. Linda told me enough. It sounds like I wasn't the only one who spent the last few weeks in the hospital. Who's your friend?" Maria asks, looking at Ben.

"This is Ben. He's been helping me with the investigation. He's the one who figured out the link between Governor Khan and the bomb."

"M'lady," Ben says with an awkward bow.

Linda comes into the room with a big pot and a ladle.

"Do you need a bowl?" she asks.

I take the pot from her hands. "I'm good." Linda shakes her head at my boorishness.

All four of us sit down on chairs in the living room. I shovel ladlefuls of Meat Sauce into my mouth as we talk. It's full of sugars, fats, and proteins; it's just what I need.

"So kids, what's the plan?" Linda asks.

I turn to Maria, "Did you get a chance to check out the most recent killings?"

"Three Differents were shot outside of Ultracorps employee housing. Two were killed with small arms, and a Strong-Woman was killed with large caliber bullet. No witnesses," Maria says.

"Three at once, and at Ultracorps housing? It's a big departure from the slow, methodical approach he was taking before. I'm worried that we're running out of time before he does something big," I say.

"Okay, so what do we do? We don't have any leads on his whereabouts," Maria says.

"That's not true, there's Governor Khan," I say.

"I'll just bring him in for questioning," Maria says with a laugh. "I'm sure I won't have any trouble getting that warrant." Maria waits for the rest of us to join in on the joke, but we're all stone-faced.

"I'm not suggesting we see a judge," I reply.

"You're serious? What, we're supposed to kidnap him? Haven't you broken enough laws already? Have you lost your mind?" Maria asks.

"I have to admit, I agree with Maria—not because I care about the law, of course," Ben interrupts. "Let's say you can make it into the Governor's mansion, probably a safe assumption considering your new-found abilities. You bust through the guards and kidnap Khan. That doesn't mean he will talk. I'm guessing he's more of the die-rather-than-talk type. If he's willing to throw his whole life away to fund these attacks, he's got the resolve to withstand whatever pain you can inflict on him, even with your anatomical expertise and new imposing form," Ben says.

"We don't have any better ideas. And time is wasting," I argue.

"True enough," Ben agrees with a nod.

"This counts as a good idea? You're talking about attacking a Governor! Even if you pull it off, every cop in the Metro Area is going to be after you, even more than they already are. The National Guard won't be too far behind. Do you even have any evidence to link Governor Khan and William Jefferson? The cold, hard, present before a judge kind? Not just the word of a single Big Brain Different," Maria says.

"I looked through his records. Trust me. It's true," Ben says.

"I don't trust you; I just met you. And even if Gavin does, that doesn't change the fact that you're talking about a capital offense. I want to help, but there has to be a better way than committing borderline treason. Even if you get Khan to talk, you won't even be able to do anything with the information because you'll be too busy running for your lives," Maria says, her face growing red with anger.

"There isn't any other way, Maria. We can't wait around and hope for more clues. Who knows how many more people will die before William leaves a trail?" I say.

"No. I'm an officer of the law. I can't be a part of this," Maria says and stands up from her chair.

"Since when do you care about rules? You've been defying orders ever since I met you," I plead.

"Ignoring my commander is different. It's an infraction. I didn't swear an oath to be obedient. I *did* swear to uphold the law. If we beat a confession out of Khan, we won't be able to use it in court. He won't ever pay for his crimes."

"Who cares about the law? We're talking about saving lives. Billy is going to kill again, he has explosives and Governor Khan is the only one who knows how to find him," I implore. I stand up to keep the conversation going. Linda and Ben have realized they aren't really involved anymore.

"I wasn't tracking Billy down to kill him, I was tracking him to arrest him. Is that what you're doing? You don't get to dole out justice. That's for the courts. You're losing perspective here Gavin, and frankly I'm a little afraid. How did you get your new abilities? Linda told me you took The Beast's hand? You mangled and tortured another human being because you wanted his abilities?"

"He's a monster," I reply without hesitation.

"So what? There are plenty of monsters in every prison in the country. Maybe we should start doing experiments on them. After all, who cares? They don't matter. Linda also told me you were trying to find The Beast before you came here. It wasn't enough to mutilate him, you needed to be his executioner too?" Maria takes a breath and her accusations continue. "You're so strong now you can execute all the criminals, and we can be safe and sound living under your iron fist."

"I'm not talking about taking over the whole city. I'm talking about stopping a killer and a terrorist," I reply. I don't understand why she's being so obstinate. This isn't any different from what we've already been doing. We broke the law the entire time we were hunting Billy the Kid.

"You're talking about assaulting the Governor. You and Big Brain might be convinced that you're infallible, but I'm not. You want a police officer's help, then you do it the police officer way. I was investigating the killings long before you showed up Gavin, and I'm going to keep doing it my way without resorting to committing my own crimes," Maria says.

"She's not going to be convinced, Gavin," Ben says to me, reaching up from his seat to put his hand on my shoulder.

Maria waits for me to say something, but I have nothing else to say.

"I thought you were a good man. Enjoy your prison cell, Vigilante," Maria says with vitriol and heads to the door.

We sit in silence until we hear Maria slam the door shut.

"She isn't wrong. It's going to be hard to act on whatever information Khan gives us with the entire police force in pursuit," I say.

"I can help you get in without causing a commotion," Linda says.

"Do you really want to get involved, Linda? When it's over, you'll have to go on the run with us," I say.

"I know the danger. I'm willing to do whatever it takes to catch Martin's killer."

"I can help too," Ben offers. "I can jam up think.Net so if things go wrong, it'll at least take a long time for the police to respond. You see, I'm capable of maintaining multiple streams of consciousness, that's what all the Librarians do. If I have each of these streams make a call, which I can because I have tons of dummy accounts, it'll overload the area Telepath, making it impossible for anyone in Khan's compound to make a call... Thanks for letting me explain."

"Sounds like a plan, Ben. Let's go break some laws."

#

"Ben took the think.Net node down. We should make our move," Linda says.

"If we climb up to that roof over there, I should be able to jump across onto the top of the mansion, even with you on my back," I tell her and point to the roof a nearby building.

"You *should* be able to make an eighty foot jump? That's great for you, since you'll survive the fall if you should miss. Maybe not me though. I can get us in without risking any breaks to these old bones," Linda smiles slyly. "Follow me."

"You're going to use a cool Telepath mind trick aren't you?"

"Yes, I am, but I need to concentrate. Pushing thoughts into an unreceptive mind is a lot more complicated than having a mental conversation with someone. And remember, if this goes south, the guards are just doing their jobs. They didn't have anything to do with killing Victor, or your friends at the lab, or Martin. They don't deserve to die."

"I'm an expert in human anatomy. If anybody knows how to take someone out without doing any permanent damage, it's me."

"Let's try to avoid putting your arrogance to the test," she says dryly.

We approach the stately mansion. The building is the size of forty normal apartments, and the grounds are covered by trees and bushes, which cost a fortune to maintain. The entire compound is surrounded by a stone wall with a massive wrought iron gate. I've always wondered why we Americans give our leaders such ornate houses like this mansion or the White House. I thought we fought for independence to end the era of kings, and there's something downright royal about giving them "castles" to live in.

We approach the front gate. The hunched-over officer perks himself up when he sees us coming. He shakes the cobwebs out of his head and steps out of the small guard shack. I can't blame him for zoning out. It's late.

"Can I help you?" the bald guard asks.

"We have an appointment to see the Governor," Linda says.

"I don't think so. The Governor doesn't have guests at 4AM, especially not middle-aged women and their giant, hairless pets."

"Would you check the schedule, please?" Linda asks politely.

The guard goes into the shack and comes out with a clipboard.

"What do you know, here you are! And might I add that you look radiant ma'am, and not a day over thirty. Let me escort you to the Governor," the guard says and leads us into the courtyard.

"Why are you having him lead us?" I whisper.

"People will see him with us and assume everything is okay," Linda replies.

As we walk through the courtyard, a bunch of young men in suits rush by us. One of them stares, then he sees our officer escort, shrugs and moves on. Linda knows what she's talking about. I'm getting the impression that she had an exciting life in her younger days.

We head into the entrance of the mansion. There we see Roger, the assistant to the Governor. The young men in suits surround him and everyone looks upset.

"I have no idea what's going on. I don't have any control over think.Net. I have no idea why it's down,'' Roger pleads.

"The Governor has that speech at the Frobash Society tomorrow, and I had all my notes stored there. What am I supposed to do now?" one of the panicked young men asks.

Roger ignores further pleas from the suited men and turns his attention to us.

"Hey George, what's up?" he asks our escort.

"I've got the Governor's four o'clock here. I'm taking them up."

"Go ahead," Roger says, waving his hand towards a giant marble staircase behind him.

We make it halfway up the stairs before Roger finally thought about what was happening.

"George, wait!" he says and charges up the stairs towards us. "Did you say you were taking these two to see the Governor? It's four o'clock in the morning!"

Linda waves her hand in front of her face and says, "These are not the droids you're looking for."

"These are not the droids I'm looking for," Roger repeats and heads back down the stairs.

"That was awesome! Extra points for sneaking in the Star Wars reference," I say.

"I couldn't resist. I'm a big fan. I made a damn fine Princess Leia Halloween 1981. You know, they were supposed to make a third one before the Plagues screwed everything up."

"Yeah, I've heard that."

We follow our original guard up the rest of the stairs and down a long hallway. We're lucky it's so late. Linda would have had to Jedi mind trick many more individuals if it were during the day. We finally arrive at the door that I presume leads to a sleeping Governor Khan.

"Here we are. I'm sure Governor Khan is waiting inside for your meeting. I'll go back downstairs," the guard says.

"Thank you," I call after him.

"You should be thanking me," Linda says.

"Thank you. Are you ready for this?"

"Remember that if you kill the Governor, no matter how much he deserves it, you aren't going to be able to track down Billy the Kid because you'll be too busy running from the army."

"Understood."

We push open the door and step into Governor Khan's bedroom. It is adorned with antique wood dressers and wardrobes that survived the Plagues. The walls are covered in expensive-looking paintings of grassy landscapes. There is a giant old wooden bed against the wall. I can hear Governor Khan snoring. It sounds like he suffers from sleep apnea.

I turn the dial on a WormLight hanging from the wall, which releases Manna into the Pho-Plastic tube, which in turn activates the bioluminescent bacteria within.

The sudden influx of light wakes Governor Khan from his slumber. He sits up in his bed and looks us over. I watch his brain struggle to process what's happening.

"What's going on? Who are you people?" he demands.

"We are your reckoning, Governor Khan," I tell him.

His eyes hone in on my face but it still is takes him a moment to recognize me. "The Beast Slayer?"

"That's right. I'm here to ask you some questions, and if you tell the truth, you might live," I say.

"I'm in your head. I can tell you want to scream for the guards, but you don't want to do that anymore, do you?" Linda asks. I can see sweat forming on her brow. It's probably been a long time since she used her abilities so heavily in one night.

"No, I don't. I can handle you two on my own," Governor Khan says.

"That's better," Linda turns to me, "but speaking of guards, it's a matter of time until the thoughts I put the guard's head get replaced by new thoughts about how crazy it is for the Governor to have a meeting at four in the morning. We need to do this quickly so we can get out before this place goes on high alert. And to be safe, you should barricade the door, Gavin."

I do as she says and push one of the giant wooden dressers in front of the bedroom door. The dresser must weigh close to five hundred pounds, but I move it like it's made of cardboard. I'm loving these new muscles. I pile another wardrobe and a dresser in front of the door for good measure.

"Good job, Gavin. Now ask the Governor your questions. I'll make sure he tells the truth," Linda says.

"Okay, Governor Khan. To start, have you been taking bribes from Ultracorps?" I ask.

"Yes, I have," Khan answers without hesitation. Linda is good.

"In exchange for what?"

"I approved the water contract, which former Governor Hayes had voided, and promised continued support for Ultracorps projects."

"What did you do with the money?"

"Several things. I bought my niece a Mighty Rover. I bought a necklace for a young woman I was seeing. I bought—"

"Did you give some of the money to William Jefferson?" I interrupt.

"Yes, I gave him $35,000 of the money I received from Ultracorps."

"Is that all the money you've given him?"

"No, I've been funding his efforts for the last seven months. All told, I have given him $48,600."

"Why did you give him that money?"

"To buy food and other necessities and to purchase equipment so he can kill Differents."

"Well at least now we know we aren't committing felonies for no reason. That's a relief, huh, Linda?"

"Keep asking him questions. People are starting to congregate downstairs. I can feel more minds. The guards might be realizing what's happened," Linda says, her face now dripping with sweat. She doesn't want to tell me, but I can see that the strain is wearing on her.

"Okay Governor, did you have anything to do with the bomb that blew up the Ultracorps lab?"

"Yes, I purchased the material used in the bomb, and plotted with William, who placed the bomb."

"I knew it wasn't P-Dub. What about Arnold Chapman, Stephen Grange, Robert White, and Stacey Rothschild? Did you have anything to do with their violent outbursts?"

"I don't know who those people are."

"Those are the names of the Speedster, Acid-Flinger, Heater, and Regenerator who committed 'terrorist' acts recently and who mostly wound up dead."

"Yes, I was heavily involved. I provided the narcotics that made the Speedster, Acid-Flinger, and Heater violent. I also used my access to classified documents to identify and target the Regenerator. I ordered William, who in turn ordered Detective Rose, to kidnap her family."

"You're making this too easy, Linda. The cops should use Telepaths all the time. You could solve every murder in the Metro Area," I say.

There's a loud banging on the door.

"Governor Khan, are you okay? Do you need assistance?" Roger asks through the door.

Linda signals for me to be quiet and then stares at Governor Khan.

"Everything is fine, Roger. Please leave me alone," Governor Khan says.

I hear the doorknob twist back and forth.

"Governor Khan. I'm sorry, but will you please open the door? I have to confirm you are unharmed. I am concerned that there was a security breach," Roger calls.

"I told you. I'm fine. Now unless you want to be demoted to taking care of my dog, I recommended you leave me alone and let me get some sleep," Khan replies, but his voice doesn't carry the anger it should. Linda can only do so much.

"I'm sorry sir, I can't do that. Okay boys, move in," Roger orders.

There's a loud smash on the door. It sounds like they're trying to force it open. Unless someone out there is as strong as Hercules, it shouldn't be a problem.

"Linda, can't you make them all think they're chickens or something?" I ask.

"There are five people out there, and that's more minds than I can influence. You need to hurry up and get the information out of Khan before they break that door down."

On cue, bodies start flying at the door in rapid pace. It doesn't matter how many guards there are though. That door isn't going to budge.

"Do you know where we can find William, Governor?"

"He has a compound on Washington and National. He spends his time there preparing when he is not out hunting down Differents."

"Okay Gavin, we got what we came for. Let's get out of here," Linda urges.

"Not yet. Tell me, why you did all of this, Governor?"

"It's simple. Differents were sent here by the Devil to test mankind's faith. Satan made you as false Gods for us to worship in order to steer us away from the one true Lord. It is the duty of every person to fight Differents, as it is the duty of every righteous man to fight the Devil. It is a struggle as old as time. I am simply trying to do my part."

"Great, he's a Sapienist. I'm fighting religious nut jobs again," I say.

"William is no true believer," Khan adds. "He simply arrived at the same conclusion as me even without having faith. He understands that it is only a matter of time until a Different is born who threatens the entire—"

I don't hear Khan say "world" because a loud explosion drowns out his words. A hole is blown in the wall next to the door, and men rush in with their guns drawn.

"Don't move a muscle!" George the guard yells as he points his handgun at Linda.

Linda reacts on instinct and dives for the floor. This spooks George, who squeezes his trigger. I move like the wind, leaping between Linda and the gun. The bullet hits me in the chest. I feel it tear into my skin, but my muscles are so thick it doesn't go very deep. It feels like I got stabbed with a sewing needle.

The other officers join in the shooting. I dive on top of Linda and feel bullets riddle my back like pins in a pin cushion. Soon, I hear their guns click empty. I pick up Linda and charge towards the bedroom wall which leads to the outside. I turn around and leap backwards, blasting through the drywall and bricks like a finish line. I land on my back in the middle of the courtyard, Linda is laying on top of my chest, unharmed.

"That was fun, huh?" I say.

"Oh, yeah. I'm going to start getting shot at every Friday night."

We hurry over to the wall of the courtyard. I wrap one of my arms around Linda's waist and hurdle the ten-foot tall wall like an Olympian. I land, let go of Linda, and we break into a light jog.

"Can you link me up with Ben?" I ask Linda.

I feel my mind connect with another, like my own direct think.Net.

<<<*Hey Ben, we got a location on William Jefferson. We're coming back to you now.*

>>>*You might want to do that on the double.*

<<<*Was there a problem jamming up think.Net?*

>>>*No, that went fine. What we didn't count on was that the guards have radio transmitters they use in case think.Net goes down. The police have them too, so they can all talk. I've got a scanner that lets me listen to their chatter, and let's say you're going to want to get a move on.*

I end the call and look up the street. Sure enough, there's a wave of men in blue uniforms headed right for us. They're going to be able to see us soon with their normal human eyes.

"Linda, we've got to run."

She nods, and I pick her up with my left arm and break into a sprint. I haven't really run with my new body. I keep pumping my legs and moving faster and faster. Soon I become a blur, covering ten blocks in twenty seconds, and I still don't think I'm running as quickly as my body is capable of moving. Unfortunately, this is another task I have no practice with. I try to round a corner and end up skidding out and slamming into a building. I try to position my body so I take the brunt of the blast, but Linda still screams out in pain.

"I heard something over there!" a voice yells in the distance. It's followed by a host of footsteps heading in our direction.

"We've got to keep moving," I say and extend my hand to help Linda up.

She takes my hand and tries to stand, but collapses back to the ground with a whimper.

"I can't. My neck, it hurts too much. Leave me here. Go stop William," Linda pleads.

"Not going to happen. I can't let you get arrested for my stupid plan," I argue. "I won't be able to handle the guilt."

"I don't have to be a Telepath to know what you're thinking. Don't do it, Gavin. The police are just doing their jobs."

She's right. I don't have enough control of my strength to be sure I won't accidentally crush a cop's skull if I try to fight them. I need another exit strategy. I look all around me before I finally look up. The building I slammed into is about four stories tall. I bend down and lift Linda up, carefully cradling her neck to keep it stable. Then I leap into the air, and land on the roof like a cat. Four stories straight up is not a bad standing broad jump.

We sit silently on the roof waiting to see how well the police officers tracked us. The footsteps arrive at the base of our building.

"Look at the B-Crete here. It's all cracked, looks like something slammed into it. The Strong-Man might still be around here. We should search this building," one of the police officers says.

That isn't good. At least they don't know they're hunting Gavin Stillman yet. Plenty of them are still chomping at the bit to get some revenge on the Vigilante who assaulted officers and got away with it. I don't know how I'm going to get out of this, and I might kill Linda if I keep running with her.

"I saw him go this way! Come on!" a female voice yells. It's a voice I know, Maria.

I hear the group of cops run off. She came through for us.

#

>>>*There's still some confusion about whether we're hunting down a Strong-Man or Gavin "The Beast Slayer" Stillman. You've got a little while till we sort it all out.*

<<<*Thanks for the update. And thanks for saving us, Maria. I know you didn't want to get involved, but I'm grateful you did.*

>>>*I didn't think Linda deserved to rot in a cell. She was nice enough to check in on me while you were getting your procedure or whatever done. How is she?*

<<<She's got some whiplash, but she'll be okay. She'll have to find some place to hide out where the cops won't find her.

>>>She's safe. The only description they've got is that she was a middle-aged woman. Everyone at the Governor's mansion was a little more focused on the hairless giant.

<<<That's a relief. I'd hate to think I ruined her life.

>>>Nope, just your own. You aren't going to tell me what you found out about William, are you?

<<<I'm going after him alone this time. I can't bear the thought of getting anyone else killed like Victor.

>>>Good luck then. Do me a favor and ask Linda to scrub this call from my record. Talking to a wanted criminal isn't going to be great for my career. Take care of yourself, Beast Slayer.

<<<You too, Officer Vasquez.

We end the call. She's not happy about how things went, but considering she risked her career to protect me I think I'll be able to repair the relationship, eventually. I turn to Linda and Ben.

"Do they have any leads on us?" Linda asks.

"No, and the good news is they're on the hunt for me. You're safe to go home. She did want you to scrub our call from the think.Net records."

"I'll do that," Linda pauses. "I don't think you should go, Gavin. We should try to find a way to get the police involved."

"You too? Isn't it a little late for protests? You two wait at Linda's apartment. I can handle him by myself," I say to Linda and Ben.

"It isn't worth the risk to go after Billy the Kid. It's the Governor who's to blame for all this anyway. We should be focusing on exposing his link to Ultracorps and Nita," Ben says.

"I don't care if William's a pawn. He killed my partner Victor, my friend Gary, and Linda's son. He has to be stopped. We can figure out how to take down the Governor later. If I don't stop William now, more Differents are going to die," I reply.

"I'm telling you Gavin, it's a mistake. I was making sure the Governor told the truth, but it wasn't necessary. He was giddy to tell you everything, especially about where William is," Linda says.

"But he wasn't lying, right? So William is in that building he told us about. The Governor was probably excited because William has a trap waiting for me. I'm sure his plan is well-designed and would have no problem taking out the old Gavin. The new Gavin? There's no way he's ready for me. Did you see my back? The gunshot wounds from the Governor's guards have all but healed already. Let William scheme all he wants. I'm unstoppable."

"He managed to kill Victor, so don't be so sure of yourself. Anyway, I don't think it is a trap. Khan wants you to go after William because he wants William dead and Khan figured you're unstoppable now," Linda says. "You make a good weapon."

"Why would Khan want William dead? They're working together," I reply.

"I don't know. We had to get out of there before you could ask him about it. I don't get to look through all of the contents of his mind, Gavin. I only get to see things people are thinking about. I know he wasn't afraid that we were there—he was happy, and pretty satisfied with himself," Linda says.

"He's a religious lunatic. There's no point in trying to figure out what a maniac's motivations are. He isn't logical. Maybe he thinks William will be a martyr for Sapienism or something like that. Let William enter the Sainthood for that wacko religion, what do we care?"

"I don't know Gavin, but I do know that killing him is playing right into Khan's hands. If you're so unstoppable, you should be able to beat Billy the Kid without killing him. If I can suppress my desire for revenge on my son's murderer, you and your controllable emotions should be able to do the same," Linda scolds. She's using my pity for the loss of her son as a weapon against me.

"I'll try," I say and I make myself mean it.

"I'm coming with you," Ben adds. "I'll gum up think.Net so no concerned citizens can get the police involved. No need to thank me. It's only the second time I'll have done it in the last few hours."

"Okay, Ben. And thank you."

31

William Jefferson receded from the national spotlight four months ago when he announced his retirement from the NBA. Though rarely seen in the following months, Jefferson kept in contact with a few close friends. Those friends recently reported concerns about Jefferson's well being to the police, who in turn went to the former sport star's apartment and found a letter. Though police representatives would not go into the specifics of the letter, sources did confirm the letter indicated that William Jefferson has taken his own life. Those same sources reported that Jefferson left his estate to several worthy causes. A spokesperson for the Minnesota Timberwolves reported that team officials were "devastated.... William Jefferson was able to overcome every challenge that presented itself on the basketball court. Unfortunately, overcoming the death of his wife and child was one battle he could not win. It is a sobering reminder of the humanity of every player in our league." Jefferson is credited with restoring the nation's faith in the legitimacy of professional sports in the years following the Victor Campos scandal.

"William Jefferson Missing, Suicide Likely" by Roger Burns,
Minneapolis StarTribune

November 5th

Sit-ups: 125
Pushups: 300
Pull-ups: 50
Running: 6 miles, 36:00 Minutes total, 6 minute mile average. Ouch.
Diet: 2,020 Calories, 152 grams protein, 227 gram carbohydrates, 56 grams fat.
Sleep: 8:18
Funds: $26,727.50
Ammo Count: 150 rounds 7N1, 240 rounds 9mm, 11 Stun Grenades,

11 Smoke Grenades, 12 Standard Grenades.

Activities: Eliminated Target 27: Male Gamma Energy Producer, Target 28: Female Gamma Enhanced Senses, and Target 29: Female Beta Physically Enhanced.

Target Notes: Targets came upon me while setting the final explosive at Ultracorps Employee housing complex. Target 28 heard me. Could not chance them reporting my activities. Drew the trio out into the main courtyard. Eliminated Targets 27 and 28 with my 9mm handgun. Target 29, Strong-Woman, proved resistant to small arms fire. Dragunov effective. Eliminated Target 29 with single head shot.

Personal Notes: The Money Man not at designated meeting. Note explaining he could not attend. Said to contact him if any major disruptions to plan. Left an additional $10,000 to throw me off. He's making move sooner than expected. Wonder who he will send. More bought cops? Time to make preparations to evacuate Metro Area after execution of plan.

Mental State: Concerned about lack of response to my only "friend" betraying me. This was always the likely outcome. Thought he'd be smarter about it. Still, Money Man represented only regular human contact. Worried social isolation will lead to mental instability. Must address in the Seattle Metro Area.

32

This just in, Governor Lewis Khan has been attacked in the Governor's mansion. The Governor is unharmed, but the suspect is still at large. He is described as seven feet tall, 800 pounds, and hairless. Suspect is likely a Strong-Man Different and may be dangerous. He does not have a Mark of Differentiation. Individuals who spot the suspect are urged to keep their distance and contact authorities.

Think.Net Breaking News Alert

William's "compound" is an abandoned warehouse. The windows are missing and the roof is partially collapsed, but for a Pre-Plague building it's in pretty good shape. If it was closer to the Metro Center someone would have patched it up with B-Crete and made it into condos. Instead it's left to rot, or in this case, become the secret lair of a serial killer.

It's a good time to pick a fight, 6:45AM. The sky is just starting to lighten. Twilight is the most difficult time for the human eye to see clearly. The combination of shadows and well-lit areas make it so the eyes can't choose whether they should adapt for day or night. I have the same problem, but my ability to rapidly change the number of rods and cones in my eyes and direct my pupil dilation, lets me adapt more quickly. It also helps that I'm going to use my bare hands while William will rely on his guns. Fists are easier to aim.

My best chance at taking William alive, like I promised Linda, is going to be getting the drop on him. Once he starts shooting, things are going to get dicey. I'm not bulletproof, more bullet resistant. I'm not willing to die to keep my word. If it comes to it, I won't hesitate to kill him. I'll pretend I don't like the sound of that.

I make my way around the old warehouse and approach a door in the back. I have a sudden bit of déjà-vu. This is an eerily similar situation to the foundry where Victor was shot. I take a quick scan of the buildings facing the door. There isn't a good vantage for a sniper. I put my hand on the door and try to open it slowly in case it's wired. My concerns are correct, but my new muscles betray me. I end up pushing too hard and throwing the door wide open, right through the click of the booby trap.

The explosion comes from somewhere behind me and propels me forward into the large, mostly empty warehouse. Shrapnel riddles my body. The old me's flesh would have been torn open. The new me is just covered in small cuts. The flash from the explosion distorts my vision, and one of my eardrums bursts. I try to stand up, but my damaged ear affects my balance. I rush blood to the area and signal the cells to begin replicating.

"Who are you?" I hear William yell from up above.

He's standing in an old office above the warehouse floor. He's looking down on me through an empty window frame. He has a look of recognition mixed with bewilderment when he sees my face, but his confusion doesn't stop him for long. He lifts up an assault rifle and pulls the trigger, the gun spits out a stream of bullets.

I scramble to my feet, falling over as a bullet hits me in the back. I use my arms to throw myself behind a pile of debris. I take bullets to the thigh and shoulder in the process. These assault rifle rounds penetrate deeper into my muscle than the handgun slugs, but they still don't do all that much damage. My priority is getting my ear fixed so I can stand. I'm already having enough problems keeping balance in my new body. I need to buy some time.

"Who was the most difficult defender you ever faced!?" I call up to him.

"Now I know you're not a real basketball fan. It was Leroy Hubbard. Everyone knows that!" he yells back. Then he throws something down which lands behind me. Grenade! I scramble towards it, taking another bullet in the back in the process. I grab the grenade and toss it up towards the office. It explodes in mid-air but forces William to hit the deck. I need twenty to thirty more seconds to heal my ear. I hide behind a concrete column.

"You're new and improved, aren't you?" William yells as he

picks himself back up and takes aim with his rifle.

"My general manager made some upgrades to the roster since I lost to you in the playoffs," I yell back.

When he opens fire on the column, I realize how stupid I was with that cheesy line. He wanted me to talk so he could figure out where I was. The concrete column absorbs the bullets, but now I'm pinned down. There's no other cover around me. I need to distract him.

"You must have figured out how I found you. Governor Khan sold you out without a moment's hesitation. He wants me to kill you," I yell to him.

It takes him a few seconds to respond, which is perfect because I need seconds. "Maybe he's confident that I'm going to kill you. I did take out your partner, remember?"

My eardrum has mostly recovered, but I need a way out from behind this column without taking ten more bullets. I start looking around for something I can throw at him and realize I'm still thinking like the old me. I grab the column I'm hiding behind. My fingers sink into the concrete like it's a loaf of bread. Then I pull, yanking off a hundred-pound chunk, which I promptly hurl up at the office. The chunk smashes through the office walls like a wrecking ball.

I take a running start and leap to follow the path of the concrete I hurled, but I misjudge my jump and end up smashing through the old drywall below the window frames. I have to catch myself on the floor to keep from falling back down to the ground level. I do a pull-up to throw myself the rest of the way into the office and cover my head as soon as I get to my feet, preparing for an onslaught of bullets that doesn't come.

I scan the office looking for William. There's a map of the Metro Area up on the wall with "X"s all over it. I recognize two of the locations: the Ultracorps main office and the employee housing complex. There are over a dozen more "X" markings. Are those the locations of his next targets? I have to find him to make him explain.

I spot a back staircase he must have escaped down, run over, and lean down to look. I don't want to walk into a hail of bullets. He's below, fiddling with a small object in his hand. He pushes a button on the device. I'm about to be hit by another explosion. I rush fluid to my tympanic cavity to protect my eardrums.

A series of explosions go off. I cover my face to protect myself, but the blasts come from underneath the office. I turn and dive towards the window, but before I can make it, the supports holding up the room give out. The office collapses down to the warehouse floor. Chunks of ceiling and wall crash on top of me, but they only cause a few more bumps and scratches.

I dig myself out of the pile of debris, look around to locate William, and hear the all too familiar boom of a sniper rifle. The bullet tears into my chest, ripping through the fibers of my new, tougher muscles, coming to rest in the middle of one of my ribs. It would have gone straight through the old me, puncturing my lung and severing my spine. William prepares to fire another shot.

I do my best impression of Victor's acrobatic dodging moves from when we fought the Regenerator. I'm much faster and more agile than I was when I tried this the first time and quickly become a blur of somersaults, back flips, and jumps. I start moving my dance routine towards William, who fires five shots that whiz by me. Then he holds his fire, keeping his gun trained on me. I crouch and prepare to cover the rest of the ground between us in a single leap.

As I am about to jump, William fires. The bullet tears through my right knee, shattering my kneecap and severing my ACL, PCL, MCL, and causing massive muscle damage. My jump turns into an awkward, off-kilter dive that sends me to the floor. I land and immediately start rolling horizontally. A bullet lands right next to where my head was.

I keep rolling, taking refuge behind a wooden desk, but William doesn't shoot again. Why is he holding his fire? I remember that the Dragunov sniper rifle has a ten-round clip from when I looked it up on think.Net. I quickly count the shots. There's the one in my chest, then five more that missed me during my dance, the bullet that tore through my knee, and then the one that just missed my head. He's got two shots left. No wonder he's being judicious. I need to get him to use those last two shots.

My chance comes when one of his flash bangs lands a few feet away. My ears are still protected from the fluid in my tympanic cavity, and I close my eyes to withstand the flash. He doesn't know these things though. I stumble out from behind the desk. The stumble is only half-acted. My right leg is in rough shape. I contort my face so I look confused and make my eyes look unfocused, but I see William clearly. As soon as his finger squeezes the trigger, I hit the deck, and the bullet flies over me. As I get up, I pick up a small piece of concrete off the floor. William squeezes the trigger again. He has a clear shot at my head. I hold up the concrete to stop the bullet. It hits with enough force to smash the concrete chunk into my face, but that just hurts my pride.

William releases the clip from the gun and reaches for another in his belt. I have to end this now. I try to run, but my right leg is too damaged. I drop to all fours, which takes the weight off my leg, and then I charge. I look like a lion closing in on his prey.

William manages to get the clip into the gun, but before he can cock it, I rip the rifle from his hands. I snap the gun in half like a twig and toss the parts aside. William responds by pulling out a six-inch long combat knife from his belt.

"Really?" I ask.

I stand there and let him plunge the knife into my side. I regret my arrogance as soon as the blade goes in. William knows what he's doing, and the blade cuts deep enough to nick my left kidney. He twists the knife as he pulls it, which wreaks further havoc on my insides.

He tries to stab again, only this time I grab his arm by the wrist. This is the arm I broke in our first fight. I can feel a brace under his shirt. I squeeze, re-breaking his radius and ulna bones, causing him to drop the knife.

"It's over. I win. Don't make me hurt you more," I growl.

William doesn't listen. He winds up for a roundhouse kick to my injured kidney. I punch down on his leg as it travels through the air, shattering his shin. He drops to the floor, crying out in pain, and then finally starts talking. I have to drain the fluid out of my ears so I can hear what he's saying.

"You're winning, but I've still got a comeback in me," he says.

"What do you mean?" I demand. "What were the "X"s on the map?"

"Do you know why Khan wants me dead? It's because I'm the only one who can link him to what's about to happen. Call it the opening shot."

William puts his hand on his belt and pushes a button. I try to leap away, but the massive explosion brings the entire warehouse down on top of us.

33

Log of notable Nita/Ultracorps Activity Week 224

No chance to investigate Ultracorps activity. Busy aiding Gavin Stillman with Governor Khan and Different serial killer. Hoping he will return favor by helping me investigate Nita.

A cacophony turns to stillness as all of Ben's many think.Net calls come to a rapid end. Hundreds of voices are snuffed silent in an instant. He had been lost in a mental world, using his fake accounts to place calls to his other phony accounts, thereby exceeding the capacity of the Telepaths working the local think.Net node and making it impossible for anyone else in the area to use the system. But now the many voices in his head have turned back to one as he is cut off from think.Net. It is a jarring experience. As soon as his brain processes that it once again inhabits actual reality, Ben takes stock of his surroundings. He sees the warehouse that Gavin entered to deliver some vigilante justice. The building has been redecorated in a somewhat radical fashion, as it is now collapsed and on fire.

Ben is hit by an acute twinge of concern for Gavin's well being. It's been a while since he felt something like that. Ben climbs down from his rooftop overlook wondering what he could possibly do to find Gavin in the rubble, and also wondering what he could do to dig the massive boy out if he does locate him. He's spared from confronting his own impotence when Gavin pulls himself up out of the rubble. The boy is bleeding in several places and one of his legs is mangled, but he's alive and Ben is relieved.

"I guess you won. Congratulations?" Ben yells quasi-sarcastically to Gavin, covering up his flirtation with human emotion.

"We've got to go, now!" Gavin screams in response.

"Go where? Can you even walk on that leg?"

Gavin's answer is bolting next to Ben in the blink of an eye.

Gavin gets down on all fours and throws Ben on his back like a rag doll. Ben has never ridden a horse before, but from what he has seen in movies, all he's missing is a saddle. The newly gigantic-sized Gavin probably weighs as much as a small equine, though the proportions are a bit off. Gavin breaks into a clumsy gallop; he's only using three of his limbs as his mutilated leg is all but useless.

"Hi ho, Silver away!" Ben yells. "I've wanted to say that ever since I was a kid. We couldn't afford any think.Net time growing up, but one of the radio stations played the old recordings. So mighty steed, where are we going?"

"I saw a map covered in "X"s in William's compound. At first I thought they might be his next assassination targets, but now I think they are bombs that are about to go off. One of the spots wasn't far from here," Gavin says, struggling to engage in conversation while doing his best speeding herd animal impression.

"Running towards a bomb that's about to go off does seem like a good idea. I can see why you're in such a hurry. Maybe you can leave me at the next stop?"

"I have to know if I'm right. I memorized the map; if they really are bombs we need to evacuate those locations. I'm trying to call Maria or Linda, but it keeps telling me my account is invalid. I guess the cops got me suspended. Can you get through?"

"Nope. All my fake accounts are getting the same message as you. I don't know what's going on, but I have some theories and none of them are good for us."

Gavin comes to a screeching halt which causes Ben to tumble off his back, hitting the side of a building with a thud. The building is a hangar-sized, grey B-Crete construction that's about as plain as a building can be.

"We're here. It's a Walters Storage facility," Gavin says while lifting himself back into limping bipedalism.

"Who would want to bomb Walters?" Ben asks as he picks himself up off the ground. "I'm fine by the way. Thanks for asking."

"Khan is a religious nut. Maybe he sees the Walters as demon imps or something like that. It doesn't matter, we have to figure out if Billy the Kid really planted a bomb here," Gavin says. He grabs the handle of the front door, rips the door off the hinges, and tosses it aside. Gavin limps inside and Ben follows, muttering about lower back pain.

There's an older security guard sitting with his feet up on the desk. He's startled out of his think.Net stare and greeted by the sight of a giant, hairless, bleeding man. He doesn't even notice Ben.

"How can I help you?" the guard asks in a trembling voice, the terror forcing his brain into the instinctual act of posing that exact question to whoever walks into the building.

Ben steps in front of Gavin, indicating that as the less terror-inducing member of the partnership, he will handle the speaking role.

"Hello, sir. I need to ask you if there has been an unusual activity in this facility. Any unexpected maintenance or repairs?" Ben asks in a friendly voice.

"There was a guy here yesterday, said somebody called about a busted latrine. I didn't have a work order, but I figured nobody would go in there on a volunteer basis. There isn't any reason to keep it clean. The Walters don't care how disgusting it is as long as it works, and I've got my own bathroom up here."

"Sir, we're going to need you to exit the premises and get as far away as you can," Gavin commands. "Where is the latrine?"

"You don't have to tell me twice," the guard says as he stands up from his desk. "Latrine is in the corner of the storage floor behind me. You can't miss it." He hustles out of the building as fast as his legs can carry him.

"Did you notice he was on think.Net when we came in?" Gavin asks. "That means the problem is with our accounts, not the whole system. If we can use the Walters to get Nita's attention, I can tell her to evacuate the buildings."

"Are you completely insane?" Ben asks while doing the swirly index finger signal for crazy. "If you do that she'll know where we are."

"Most of the "X"s were Ultracorps properties. She's the only one who could possibly contact all of the buildings quickly enough to order the evacuations and the only one with the authority to get it done. This is not a debate," Gavin says and puts his foot down literally and figuratively.

"Fine," Ben says with a frown when he sees the look of determination on Gavin's face, "but after you talk to her we need to skedaddle on the hop."

The pair hustles onto the storage floor. They're hit by a wave of body odor that out-stinks any high school locker room. The entire space is chock-full of what must be hundreds of beds, many of them occupied by Walters silently slumbering away. They come here to sleep and eat between shifts. They have no reaction to the motley duo running through their dormitory.

Ben spots a doorway marked "Latrine" and points. They head inside and are greeted by a wall of odor that must rank in the top ten worst all time smells. It puts the previous body odor concoction to shame. Ben swallows down his natural reaction to the funk.

"You'd think it would be clean considering they're basically all janitors," Gavin says, waving his hands in a futile effort to ward off the odor molecules.

"Don't complain to me. You're the one who can turn off his sense of smell," Ben replies holding his nostrils closed.

The two begin their search of the house of horrors. Gavin rips open a closest, revealing a complicated-looking device about the size of a briefcase. There are all sorts of wires and a blinking red light.

"Ben, I found it. Please tell me you know how to disarm bombs," Gavin says waving his partner over.

"I read a field manual once," Ben says as he takes stock of the device.

"That means you know more than me. You handle this, I'm going to go get Nita's attention." Gavin heads back to the clone storage area.

He grabs the closest Walter, rousing the poor creature from a well-deserved rest. He rips off the Walter's pants and puts them on his head, the same tactic that garnered Nita's attention before. It has no effect this time. Gavin lifts the Walter up and throws it high in the air, over and over again. The Walter's eyes go wide, but it takes no action to keep itself from receiving the same treatment a toddler might endure. Despondent, Gavin grabs another Walter and adds it to the mix, essentially juggling the two hapless creatures. Then he waits, confident that if this doesn't get Nita's attention then nothing will. After a few more moments without a response, he comes to the conclusion Nita isn't going to call. He heads back into the latrine.

"Nothing from Nita, and I went a lot further this time. Any luck with the bomb?" Gavin asks.

Ben pulls a wire out of the device, then puts his hands over his head and cowers. His instinct to shield himself was unnecessary, as the blinking red light on the device ceases its terrifying illumination.

"Was there ever any doubt? It was a simple design; Billy boy wasn't worried about his bombs being found. But Gavin, if you want to evacuate those buildings you better figure out a way to do so right now. That thing was going to go off in the next hour."

Before Gavin can ask any follow-up questions, they are interrupted by a booming voice that echoes off the buildings like a siren. It belongs to Nicholas Werden, Gavin's old roommate and Los Angeles' Town Crier. He's responsible for waking up the entire Metro Area.

"The time is 7AM. The time is 7AM. Get your morning off to a jumpstart with an Oasis Burger Manna and Egg sandwich. The egg came before the chicken when it comes to breakfast at Oasis Burger," Nick yells so the whole Metro Area can hear.

Shortly after Nick finishes speaking, there's a loud boom in the distance. Then another and another. Ben counts sixteen booms before they come to a terrifying stop.

"I guess I was wrong about that hour," Ben says to Gavin, whose face is frozen in horror.

34

Whereas Ultracorps and its subsidiaries have been largely responsible for the construction of the Metro Areas. Whereas Ultracorps and its subsidiaries are providing food and other essential services to the citizens of the United States of America. Whereas Ultracorps provided many services free of charge in the years following its founding. We hereby Commemorate May 3, 1995, as The Unified Logistics Technology and Research Applications Corporation Appreciation Day.

The Unified Logistics Technology and Research Applications Corporation Appreciation Day Act of 1995.

"Hold still, I've almost got it," Linda says as she digs into me with a pair of pliers.

It's not exactly the proper implement to remove the bullet from my rib, but beggars can't be choosers. I'm pretty sure it's not sterile either. Nothing is in this place. Ben's secret hideout looks like it hasn't been cleaned in months. It's absolutely covered in Oasis Burger wrappers. It's a basement for some reason, even though there are countless abandoned buildings above ground that we could be inside. He's really personifying the filthy nerd stereotype.

"There," Linda says and drops the bullet on the floor.

I could have pushed the bullet out as I healed my muscle tissue, but Linda was so insistent. She wanted to do something to feel useful. I can't blame her. We're all feeling pretty useless right now.

A hatch opens and a ladder is lowered in the corner of the room. Ben climbs down.

"I finally got a good signal on the radio. It is chaos out there. At least sixteen bombs went off all over the Metro Area. The police are estimating that a minimum of six hundred people were killed and about four hundred of those were Differents. Most of the Differents were killed by bombs at the Ultracorps employee housing complex. The bombs were well placed," Ben continues. "William planted them so that they made the earth underneath the buildings give way and topple like dominos. The walls might be made of Maceo Steel, but that didn't do anything to protect the people inside. The force of the impact killed a lot of people. The other bombs went off in a few Ultracorps-owned warehouses and laboratories and the Construct furniture factory. He also hit a couple of think.Net nodes, killing the Big Brains and Telepaths inside. Think.Net is down all over the Metro Area. That last one's a little surprising though; it seems to be down in places that weren't hit. Maybe Ultracorps is redeploying their personnel or something."

"We should go try to help any survivors," I say.

"You? The cops will show their appreciation for your help by arresting you. Linda and I can't go help because for some reason the Slug is down, even though I didn't hear anything about bombs hitting near the tracks or fuel depots."

"How are they explaining the bombs?"

"They're just calling them explosions, and this time I don't think it's a conspiracy. Without think.Net or the Slug, communication is almost impossible. The radio station I was listening to was literally sending runners out to gather information. It was pretty funny hearing the out-of-breath reporters try to deliver the news. One of them sounded like he was puking in the background."

"Yeah, sounds hilarious," Linda says, deadpan.

"I guess you had to be there. The radio wasn't my sole source of information. The L.A.P.D. is using walkie-talkies that I can hear through my scanner. I get the impression the Governor's office implied you might be involved in these bombings. The police have other priorities at the moment, but once all the bodies are collected and the fires die down, they're going to be coming for you. It's safe to say your days as a celebrity are over."

"I liked being a vigilante better anyway. So what's our next..."

I trail off because I'm getting a call on think.Net, from Nita.

"Nita is calling me," I say to Ben and Linda.

"How? Think.Net is down. You should take it, and ask her how she's calling. Oh, and ask her about the Slug too and ask...," Ben says.

I hold my hand up to silence Ben and accept the call.

>>>*Gavin, are you well? Were you able to stop William?*

<<<*Yes, I stopped him. Then he killed himself. How do you know I was fighting him, and how are you calling me? Think.Net is down all over the Metro Area.*

>>>*Ultracorps is in the process of reallocating resources. We had to cease normal access to the network.*

<<<*Reallocating resources. What the hell does that mean? And why is the Slug shut down? It doesn't seem like any of the bombs should have affected the trains.*

>>>*Ultracorps leadership has made the decision that we can no longer supply services to the Los Angeles Metro Area until the safety of our employees can be guaranteed.*

<<<*What are you talking about? Are you crazy? The Metro Area was devastated by those bombs. People are injured and they need help. People need to make sure their loved ones are okay. People need to be able to get around the Metro Area. People are going to need food.*

>>>*We have come to the conclusion that despite whatever damage may be caused, Ultracorps cannot in good conscience ask its employees to risk their lives. All Differents in the Metro Area are advised to make their way to the Slug Yards. Trains will be waiting to move those individuals out of the Metro Area.*

<<<*You mean right next to the warehouse where you're storing all sorts of supplies to keep the Differents fed and housed? And didn't you see me trying to get your attention through the Walters?*

>>>*Think.Net was down.*

<<<*This was before the bombs. Ben and I both got cut off from think.Net right after William blew himself up. You knew this was going to happen, didn't you? You let them bomb the Metro Area.*

>>>*That is not important. What is important is how we as Differents decide to handle this situation.*

<<<*By taking a whole bunch of food and fuel and fleeing the Metro Area? That's how you want to handle this? You say it's for*

the safety of Differents, but you know William is dead and the threat is over. People are going to die—people are dying right now. We're needed now more than ever, and you want to run? Why are you doing this? What are you trying to accomplish?

>>>*I am freeing our people.*

She ends the call.

Love my story? Hate it? Share your opinion and help support me at the same time. Write me a review on Amazon or GoodReads. Your feedback will help prove to the world that someone read this novel and maybe other people should too. Thank you!

Want more of me? Visit my website at natkozinn.com

And now the first section from my novel Different Paths, the third and final book in the Chosen Different series. Available now.

Excerpt

My capillaries pull fluid out of my eyes, bending my cornea to focus my vision at a target a thousand yards away. An aid comes onto the stage and taps a microphone, sending out a loud boom from speakers on either end of the stage. The Governor is sparing no expense for this press conference and that includes electricity.

The aid recedes, and I take a quick scan of the gathered crowd. Well, the back of their heads anyway. Luckily, I have perfect memories of the back of every head I've ever seen. I spot an odd-shaped brown skull belonging to Ben, who's about fifteen feet behind Linda. My eyes move up to the two dozen police officers gathered in front of the stage. I'm sure they have some plainclothes friends in the crowd. There are also National Guard soldiers with rifles standing on the buildings closer to the podium. This is a normal security deployment; the Governor is simply being cautious. I make myself believe that.

Governor Khan finally walks out onto the stage, his bald head covered in beads of sweat. Despite his disheveled look, he walks with a spring in his step.

"Thank you all for coming. I have an important announcement," the Governor says without looking up from his notes. His oratory skills don't compare to those of our old Governor. "I am proud to announce a partnership with Sagamore Industries to complete the first fishing vessel constructed entirely by human hands in Los Angeles in over thirty years. This ship is merely the first step towards increasing food supplies—" the Governor stops mid-sentence and hangs, like someone activated pause on a think.Net show. Linda is doing her thing!

"Okay, pay attention now; I'm going to say something important. It concerns the bombs that devastated this Metro Area a few short months ago," Linda says through Khan's mouth. The crowd quiets its murmurs.

"I have used this office to repeatedly accuse Gavin Stillman of causing the explosions, and many of you did not believe me. It turns out your doubt was well-placed. Not just because it never made sense, but because I am responsible for the bombs that devastated the Metro Area. I am a terrorist."

The crowd erupts in a wide range of noises, but Governor Khan gets louder, and they all grow quiet.

"I used money from illegal bribes and laundered it through my supermarket chain and Medical center to purchase the ingredients for the bombs, as well as the cocktail of drugs that I used to induce the Different attacks that we all forgot about after the bombs. Later, I will deny these accusations and say a Telepath made me say all this, which is true, but it's also true that I'm guilty. If you look through my financial records or search my properties, you will find incontrovertible proof of my crimes. If the police refuse to look into this matter, you the public should demand justice, and reporters, you should do your part to help unravel the web. You're in for a real surprise when you find out just who my accomplice was. Now, I may stay here and try to dig myself out of the hole I just fell into, or I may run off the stage in disgrace. Let's find out."

The Governor shakes his head like he just woke up. Then his face turns a deep crimson, and he rushes off the stage, chased off by a slew of screaming reporters in the crowd. Looks like he went with option two.

As soon as the Governor leaves the stage, there's a deafening boom followed by a whistle. I can tell from the pitch that it's from a bullet headed right towards me. Bullets on a trajectory towards me have a particular tone, and I've been shot at enough to identify the sound. I slow down my perception of time so I can think this through, but even my recently improved muscles and nerve fibers can't help me dodge this shot. I try to dive to the right, but that just puts the hole in my left shoulder instead of my right one. The rifle was high-caliber; it cuts through my hardened bone like a hot knife though Manna. It knocks me from the edge of the roof and onto my back.

"Target hit. Repeat, target hit," a mechanical voice says… a radio. There's someone else on this roof.

I was too focused on the Governor. I let someone sneak up on me, a spotter who helped the sniper put the bullet in me. I access my just-formed memory of the sound and replay it in my head. It came from my left. I get to my feet, using only my right arm. I turn towards a post, where the radio holder must be hiding.

As I stalk over, a fresh-faced young man in camouflage gear pops out of the hiding spot. He has a jittery finger resting on the trigger of his army rifle. I don't think he has the wherewithal to pull the trigger, not that I can blame him he is facing a seven foot tall, five hundred pound hairless monster of a man. Becoming terrifying was the price I paid for stealing The Beast's strength.

"St-Stay where you are!" the National Guardsman stammers.

"No thanks," I say and take a step forward.

That jittery finger turns steel and holds down the trigger, I underestimated him. Hot metal tears into my flesh, my dense muscles stopping six slugs before they can penetrate into my organs. I rip the gun from the young man's hands and toss the weapon off the side of the roof. I grab the man by the throat, my massive fingers wrapping entirely around his neck. I should make him pay for thinking he could hurt me. All I'd have to do is squeeze…

Why did I think that? I drop the soldier, who gasps for air as soon as he hits the ground.

I hear footsteps reverberating in the building below me. National Guardsmen, and lots of them. I'm on a ten story building though, so I've got some time. Their heavy guns will slow them down… which really isn't that comforting. I've got to get moving before that sniper gets another shot at me. I take a few steps to get a running start and leap twenty feet down onto the building next door. As soon as I land there's another boom that tears into the flesh of my back, putting a hole in my lung. That boom is joined by another, but I leap before that hits, making it on to another roof. More booms chase me, but I scramble away, leaping like a frog on lily pads until I'm finally out of range of the shooters.

Want more? Buy Different Paths (Chosen Different Book 3) on Amazon.